the mexicans

William George Rasmussen

William George Rasmussen

Angel on the Border

Copyright © 2007 William George Rasmussen
All rights reserved.

ISBN: 1-4196-7367-X
ISBN-13: 978-1419673672

Visit www.booksurge.com to order additional copies.

PREFACE

This book is a fictional work employing entirely fictional characters. Readers who have enjoyed its predecessor, The Genesis Riders, will find much the same set of characters with a number of interesting additions. But the venue is new and more widespread adding a greater international mystique, with crisper flavor and varied color. In this work we get to listen in a little more on the conversation of the bad guys, who seem to come off as real persons while they go about doing their bad things.

It's a little difficult to specify a single standard genre. What could we say? Intrigue? Yes, that word would help to describe terrorists at work in America, motivated by mysterious, dangerous minds, joined together in an underground web of interactive cells cloaked in subterfuge, using devious devices to inflict death and destruction on a grand scale. Mystery? Of course there is mystery at every turn for those seeking out the terrorists; those working to interrupt uncivilized acts so destructive that civilized minds fail to comprehend the mysterious minds of the perpetrators. Suspense? Outcomes are rarely evident, where events turn on the compulsive behavior of devils with a twisted death wish to join their spiritual master and hordes of virgins for their reward. Action? When the defenders of the nation are at work against evil foes, excitement abounds in fast moving action where trouble is always waiting at the next turn, or even the next step. Action in spades, yes. Political? Everything is called political these days.

And what about Romance? Our characters are fleshed out as mature men and women with a healthy vigor, intelligent and humorous at times. Most are either married or close to it and most of them are Romantics in the classical sense; they find their soul-mate, they speak of a yearning heart, they fall in love and they stay that way. We don't

The Mexicans

talk about the details of their loving relationships but we do eavesdrop in on their personal conversations and we feel elated when we do.

Much of the language is conversational, in the vernacular. A few of the words might offend, but nothing we weren't familiar with as preteens. Our characters, even the bad guys, don't use lewd or lascivious language or innuendo but we give the men sway for an occasional scatological term used among themselves. We see all of our agents and their wives (most of them have one), as clean-living and responsible people, loving the good and hating the evil. Maybe that's old fashioned in the modern world, but we'd like to believe not.

The Mexicans, second in a series, portrays realistic terrorist targets in the United States threatened by realistic terrorists employing realistic tactics planned to accomplish their destructive purposes. Both the targets and the tactics are we think responsibly thought out and have real potential which is why we write about these ideas. If we can imagine it, who else can imagine it? Events in this book are not intended to be inflammatory or to defame any particular group of people except as that group may have left its footprint already in the pathway of events leading toward the demise of the American way of life. <u>Message?</u> The message is of Hope. In a world flush with the mindset of murderers, there are yet the truly heroic; thank God for them.

We hope you enjoy the book. There are a few slow parts; the boring scenes and conversation serve mostly to clarify details but also to show that politics and protocol of modern civilization are often bureaucratic. If you do like the book, watch for the next series of NSA agents at large, 'Caldera'; there's nothing boring when this guy take his swing.

William George Rasmussen, author

CHAPTER 1
The Pacific Connection

The ocean going freighter slipped into the Port of Seattle just before dawn and headed for its berth at the wharf, ready to start unloading its cargo of shipping containers from points across the Pacific. This cargo was from friendly nations; favored nations that had good commercial ties through the major banks of the world. It was an excellent example, typical of the Commerce Department's successful policy of mutually beneficial trade between favored trading partners. The goods in these containers were exports from those friendly nations of Asia, New Zealand and Australia.

There at the wharf, miles of trains were standing by on spur tracks with their flatbed cars eagerly awaiting the offload call for their turn at the dock. Most of the cargo shipped across the continent would be carried by these trains and hundreds of others like them, loading at the major ports on the west coast and the east coast and some on the Gulf coast. From the wharf the trains would carry their cargo hundreds of miles across country and down, over mountains and plains, through tunnels, over trestles and across bridge spans into the heart of the nation to the waiting champions of commerce; the manufacturers, the distributors, the wholesalers and the retailers. The economy of the nation and indeed the world thrived on the efficiency of this distribution system.

At their destinations, the railroad yards, sidetracks and spurs lead off the last few miles to the manufacturing plants and warehouses. The trains uncouple the cars, depositing them for final delivery by shuttle engines down the spurs and to the receiving warehouses. There the containers are unloaded and broken down into smaller quantities; their merchandise repacked and then shipped according to individual order, by smaller half-size and quarter-size containers and even smaller size crates and cartons. The crates and cartons are stacked on pallets

The Mexicans

and wrapped with self sealing plastic-wrap for their safe and dry transport. All orders, large and small will be delivered by truck to the customer. That's how the system works; that's the drill.

On this day in Seattle, two particular containers were off loaded onto a train headed for the Midwest; one to a warehouse near Wichita, Kansas, the other to a warehouse at Iowa City, Iowa. Two others in particular were offloaded onto a train headed for warehouses at Pecos, Texas and McAlester, Oklahoma. There, at those distribution warehouses, smaller shipments would be made to specific farms and workplaces in remote parts of the mid-south and mid-central states where the goods may be further broken down and shipped by truck to destinations in cities where the orders originated.

It was all very efficient, an excellent example of the Commerce Department's successful policy of mutually beneficial trade between favored nation trading partners. And it was all based on trust; rarely did anyone inspect the cargo.

With the Port of New Orleans shut down to all shipping on the Mississippi River, much of the river traffic was now diverted to ports to the west, over as far as Galveston Bay through the Intracoastal Waterway, to rail heads at the port cities. Rail transport had taken up much of the flow of diverted shipping north to the great cities of the Midwest.

As larger ships passed through the channel at the north of Lake Calcasieu, and ocean going deepwater barges plowed the water ahead of them and as they made their way, great undercurrents pulled water from the connecting inland water basins and bayous out into the shipping channel. Undertows, they were called, often lasting for hours as the slow barges pushed the water ahead and sucked the inland waters to their undersides and rear beneath them to fill the void. Black Bayou was one of the affected water basins, its shoreline often drained right down to the muddy bottom by the strong outflow of current.

NSA Officer Jon (Swede) Olafsen and his team of agents regularly patrolled these shorelines below the Lake Charles metropolitan area as he performed his job of surveillance, keeping watch for signs of attempted incursions by smugglers, drug runners and even terrorists trying to sneak into the United States to do damage. His responsibility included Louisiana's Calcasieu, Cameron, Jefferson Davis and Vermillion Parishes. For Swede it wasn't just a job to be seen on patrol and deter the bad guys from their bad plans; Swede was serious about his work. He and his agents had developed one of the best band of informers in the state. Swede was a natural hunter from his youth and he hunted the woods and bayous like a bloodhound, knowing full well that the bad guys were there; that's what spurred him to the trail. He brought in more than his share of suspicious characters and his rate of convictions was at the top of the list.

Colonel Phil Bragg knew Jon from his first day as a new NSA officer recruit; it was Bragg who recruited him. There he was in Southern Louisiana, an engineer supervising site preparation of a new industrial project, when Bragg and a team of agents encountered him as they searched for some bad guys known to have been dropped off by boat into the bayou country. Bragg asked Jon about some Middle-east looking guys sneaking around the woody swamps nearby. He had asked the right guy; Jon had spotted them twice over the past two days and he quickly tracked them to the place where they were holed up, a fishing shed used by some of the locals. Jon knew of the shed and figured it out right quick. They arrested the illegals and Bragg hired Olafsen on the spot, offering him the grade of Second Lieutenant. He was good at recruiting in the field and Olafsen fit his model of a good Operations Officer.

Jon (Swede) Olafsen was a graduate of Auburn University's Engineering school and a natural for the outdoors projects; single, age 26 at the time, born and raised in Shelby County, Alabama. During the next five years, promotions came swiftly as his performance dictated; he was a natural for the work and loved it. He became so well known in the organization for his friendly ways, most of the agents affectionately called him Swede, even though he wasn't Swedish; he was a Dane. After displaying excellence in the recently completed Mississippi River terrorist operation and taking a couple of wounds, Captain Olafsen was promoted to Major, his present grade.

The Mexicans

That terrorist network had brought about the widespread disruption of the waterways of lower Louisiana and it served as the warning that kept Swede on top of his game. There were certain places that he watched regularly; the fishing camps on Black Bayou where he had encountered those terrorists that had purchased land and stashed hidden explosives in a failed attempt to block shipping at the Port of Lake Charles.

On his pass through this area this morning the undertow coming from the Intracoastal Waterway had drained the shoreline to a low point, so Swede saw it as an opportune time to get a look at the bottom land. When he did he found a skiff that had been sunken and was standing there flooded full with water.

"That's strange," he thought, "the water has been low for hours and the skiff is still full to the oarlocks. What's keeping it flooded, or better yet, what caused it to sink to the bottom if these floodwaters fail to escape?"

He dug out his hip boots from behind the seat of his 4WD pick-up and pulled them on over his sneakers, then waded the soft mud of the bayou bottom to where the skiff was resting. Pulling on the skiff he was able to rock it loose from the muck, which would allow the floodwater to escape faster through any hole that might be there; then he waited a few minutes and watched the flood line to see if it began to drop. But it didn't change at all. He did it again, this time loosening the skiff completely from the mud.

"Nope, this sucker was sunk on purpose by someone wanting to hide it. So what's going on? If they didn't need the boat any longer they would have scuttled it and been done with it. Someone planned to return and leave the same way they got in; all secret and unnoticed."

Now, it's no crime to want to float the Bayou, but to Swede It looked darned suspicious.

"I wonder what I'll find at the fishing shack."

He pulled off the boots and drove the quarter mile to the entrance of the fenced compound; but his key wouldn't open the padlock. The compound property was still under control of the NSA terrorist investigation. He tried a few more times, but no.

"No kidding? This is not my padlock!"

So, he got out his bolt cutters, cut the chain and opened the gate. The storage shack was about two hundred yards inside. He checked his weapon for bullets and walked toward the shack. As he neared the front, he saw that the door was open a crack; nearing further, he could hear movement inside.

He backed off a safe distance and called the Lake Charles Police.

"Rich, this is Swede Olafsen .... yeah, it's me. I need a back-up team at the Black Bayou fishing compound; the place where we knocked off the terrorists last summer; you were there, you know where it is. There's something going on here and I may have to get involved in the next few minutes, so hurry it up, would you?"

"I'll get the cars over that way to you in about five minutes, maybe less. Hold on a minute ... OK , ... yeah, ...OK, they're on their way, Swede, they know the place. Stay on the line with me, Swede, until they get there."

"OK, but I can't keep talking, I'll just keep the line open so's you can hear in case something happens."

He made his way back to his pick-up and watched from behind it.

Nothing happened. In a few minutes two cruisers pulled up.

"Swede, what's going on?" the Sergeant asked.

"Jim, is that you? Yeah, it's you; well, we got people moving around in there and a skiff hid down at the shoreline, or unhid, rather, with the water level down to nothing. Something's not right; this property is off-limits to anyone but the Feds and the lock's been changed. You got your bull horn?"

"Got it right here." He retrieved it.

The Mexicans

"OK, now we got you four guys and me. Let's surround the shack and give 'em the invitation. Quiet, till we call 'em out, hear?"

Jim Fourcher, the Sergeant, gave orders to the others and they moved quietly to position. Just as they got ready, shots started coming at them, a barrage. Two of the cops were hit.

"Damn!" The Sergeant cussed as he called in for help.

"The SWATs, Rich, we need the SWATs; these guys are hammering us with automatics."

They kept their positions and took care of the bleeding men. They would be alright with the bleeding stopped. Fourcher, called for an ambulance.

"Better make it a big one; we may be taking more casualties."

In five minutes a SWAT team arrived. They took position, made ready, and sprayed the shack with a couple hundred rounds of steel penetrating shots and then stormed the place before the guys inside could get ready for them, if they were still alive. As it happened, they weren't.

"No matter," the Lieutenant said, "it could have been bad if we'd tried to fight it out with these guys; just look at the arsenal they have stowed away in here!"

Two of the men had moved the cutting table and removed the loosely packed dirt from the floor, uncovering the underground storage hold.

"Damn! That hold is stuffed full! They could've held off an army and picked 'em off one by one, or by the dozens. From here I can see missile launchers, Kalashnikovs, grenades, and those are mortars. Let's be sure to get a good count on all of these munitions and weapons, Frank."

"Yes Sir. Darn sure, they weren't here for duck hunting. We'll need a six-by to carry all this stuff, Lieutenant; I'll get one on the way."

He made the call to the station.

"We did the right thing, Gerry. You can't give sway with these guys; they just take it for weakness." Jon was glad to have this one behind him. "Man, I really appreciate ya'll busting this up for me. I could've been floating in the channel by now. Jim and his guys got the worst of it, but he say's they'll be OK. The ambulance should be here pretty quick; we'd better adjust these tourniquets while we wait for them."

The police took charge of the crime scene and got statements from all the officers. They would sort it all out and Jon would be in the middle of it for a few days. He called Colonel Bragg and gave him the report.

"Get what you can on those guys; find out who they were and where they came from. If you need me to support you, let me talk to the officer in charge. They're not going to want you walking through the crime scene, but get what you can and bring it in. We'll have to get started on our own investigation. OK?"

"OK, Colonel; here, talk to Lieutenant Dupre, Gerald Dupre. I'll see you back there when I can get what information I can and get loose from the questioning. That'll probably be a couple hours. I'll let you know how it goes." He gave the phone to Gerry.

After they talked for a while, Lieutenant Dupre assured the Colonel that Swede would be free to take all the information he needed, photos, too. So he did and after ninety minutes of statements and questions at the police station, he headed to New Orleans. By then he was getting hungry and he called Misti.

"Let's eat at Maubie's, Honey. I just worked up one heck of an appetite. I'll walk you around to a Cajun Two-step."

"Jon; you know I'm always ready for dinner with you at Maubie's."

CHAPTER 2
The Venezuelan Connection

It seemed like there was a visitor to the Mexican Embassy from the Iranian Embassy nearly every day wanting something. Today Ahmed al Hamdi was the visitor bowing and being greeted in the pleasant diplomatic fashion common to the current political climate; the two nations were friendly, but most of their international dealings took place in Venezuela, these days. Al Hamdi was a sort of Iranian Ambassador at large for President Alhaminijah.

"Please come in Mr. Ambassador; come in and make yourself at home; it is good to see you again. How can we help you? I am at your service."

Hugo Felix Diego, the Mexican Minister of Foreign Affairs greeted him. It was his business to keep good relations with all countries, at least on the surface. Actually, Mexican President Vicente Calderon was very suspicious of the Iranians and he didn't trust their dealings with Julio Jimenez. The Venezuelans were busy these days in Mexico inciting the peasants to discontent with his regime; not openly, of course, but Venezuelan money was used very effectively to hire agents to do the work for Jimenez.

"Hugo, my friend, you are looking well, very well. Tell me, is Francisca feeling well? We have all been very worried for her since the accident."

"Francisca is doing much better since her leg has knitted well enough to limit the pain medication. The surgery on her face turned out quite well. I expect we will be making a public appearance soon; thank you for asking."

There had never been an arrest in the case of the speeder who ran the red light and struck his wife outside the Embassy. While Diego

The Mexicans

was away the days after the accident, many Venezuelan requests that had been pending at the Embassy for long months were approved by his staff much to his displeasure; but they had been told it was by his order to do so. He sent his assistant back to Mexico City to stamp and file internal documents at a reduced pay grade, but the damage was done.

"Oh, that is good news, indeed. I am so pleased to hear it."

"So, al Hamdi, what can I help you with today?"

"A very small request has come to us from one of our business interests In Tehran, Hugo. As you are aware there has always been a great interest in my country for hunting and fishing and particularly with the businessmen who often take vacations in various parts of the world to engage their sport. I have invited several of them to join me on my sport charters into northern Canada. When I spoke to them of the wonderland that is there, available to those who like to charter guided flights into the wilderness areas, well, I didn't expect the response. Truly, it was overwhelming."

"Yes, I can understand; the Canadian wilderness is amazing; I have been there on occasion, myself"

"A friend has asked to set up a travel venture based in Caracas just for that purpose, so that his hunting and fishing clientele may spend a week or two here with their families enjoying the beaches and other facilities while they embark on sporting adventures into Canada. The demand is great at the moment, but of course that may not last if he cannot get his business underway soon. That is what I come to you about today. My friend would request clearance to fly into Mexican airspace using his fleet of small planes and tour guides. He has given me a list of six aircraft that he would use. Our needs are quite simple; registration of the planes in your country allowing for the flyover at normal altitudes, flight control protocol, et cetera."

"I see no reason to withhold approval of such a simple matter. Leave your papers with me and I will have my assistant make the arrangements – one week and you will have your registrations, no more. Is that satisfactory?"

"Yes, my friend that will be very satisfactory, indeed. Thank you."

"You are most welcome. Goodbye, then, and give my regards to your lovely wife."

"Goodbye, Hugo."

After al Hamdi left the embassy, Diego instructed his assistant to take care of the matter.

"Also, you will inform our friends at the American Embassy."

By the end of the day news of the air space accommodation had reached Felix Echevarria in Monterrey. Echevarria alerted his friends in various communities to watch for the aircraft and inform him of their actions; he suspected something fishy about the fishing charter planes. Echevarria had been in this business long enough to have developed good instincts.

Three weeks later, the first report came back to Echevarria.

"Felix, one of those aircraft from Venezuela just flew over, but he didn't go north of the U.S. border; he dropped down to land outside the town of Tepehuanes in the countryside. My informer told me six men got out and walked toward the village. Two hours later another plane landed at the same place and dropped off another six men. They seem to have some business in Tepehuanes."

"Do you know what they are doing there?"

"No, they just seemed to disappear. No one has seen them."

The next day and the day after similar reports came from Echevarria's friends, but in different locations. Two drops occurred at Cuauhtemoc and two outside Ciudad Jimenez at a farm field. The men all were on foot and walked toward the nearby villages. Again, the men seemed to fade away after entering the villages.

Within the week, Echevarria had received several more reports and they all appeared to be duplicates of the first. To date he had not been able to find out where the men went after entering the towns. His friends had not been able to learn of anything unusual. It appeared likely they had a prearranged place to stay and remain out of sight. By this time, Echevarria could wait no longer to report the arrivals to his superior; he didn't like having to do that for fear of jeopardizing his position. He was never certain of transmission security.

The following week, Echevarria made another report involving several more villages. That got some attention in Washington D.C. and prompted Air Traffic Control officers to conduct a review of flights into the U.S. by those six registered aircraft. They turned up records showing regular over-flights entering U.S. airspace from Mexico and exiting into Canada, just as would be expected by charter sports flights.

"It appears that these aircraft are serving as a shuttle service into Mexico and Canada as well. Does Mexico attract flights for sport fishing or hunting?" FBI agents were now involved in the investigation.

"I don't think so; not flights, mostly flies."

"Very funny. Send a copy of the report to the CIA officer in charge and put a hold on the investigation. There's nothing here for us; they've apparently never touched ground in this country. We'll look at it again in thirty days."

It started out as a public demonstration, there in Oaxaca, down in the south of Mexico, near the Bay of Tehuantepec. The Socialists were stirring up the poor people, telling them that the power belonged to the people, not the corrupt government; it was led by politicians who had stolen the election. Soon the demonstration became a disruption; mobs of people had gathered in large crowds, moved to uprising by the ranting of the Socialists. It was the Jimenez political movement. The name of Julio Jimenez was heard everywhere.

Within a few days, the mobs had stopped traffic flowing through the city by flooding the streets with demonstrators. Local police were ordered by the federal government to quell the disruptions which had grown into a controlled riot. But the mobs of demonstrators held their own against the police; the action of the police served to fuel the shouting rhetoric and the rioting masses grew into ever larger mobs.

Soon the city was entirely in the control of the Socialists; government offices were ransacked, the employees driven out. With mobs threatening to take control of all private property, terror began to reign among the well to do families in the affluent residential neighborhoods. That forced the federal government to send in the Army to put down the uprising with brute force. Heads were cracked and some of the most violent rioters were shot. Tear gas attacks only slowed them down at first, but as they increased the potency level and the intensity of the gas attacks, the mobs finally dispersed back into their barrios. It had taken more than a week to stop the uprising, but no one expected it to remain quiet for long. The Socialists were getting as much funding as they could use from Venezuela; they had the means and they had found ways to smuggle in weapons. Soon they began to warehouse automatic rifles, grenades and explosives.

News of the uprisings spread across the globe with front-page pictures and extensive reporting on the internet. Jimenez's reputation among the Socialists gained increasing stature throughout Latin America; his star was on the rise. Student demonstrations were breaking out on all the campuses, demanding more voice in the administration of the University. It would only be a short time before the demonstrations turned dangerous. To some there appeared here to be the seeds of another French Revolution; people desperate for better living conditions, better health care, and jobs with a steady income. Disease and death were increasing in the poor barrios while the governing elite siphoned off the capital for their own purposes, using earnings from the nation's oil fields to build huge personal accounts in foreign banks waiting the day of their choice to take flight into grand retirement.

The Mexican population was literally controlled by the military and the local police, all of them taking payoff from political office holders friendly to the drug and smuggling trade moving through the country to the northern border. Conditions like these could only be sustained by terror and force of arms under a fascistic form of oppression. Newspapers tried to tell the plight of the people to the world in editorials

The Mexicans

and heroic reporting, but soon enough, the newspaper publishers were forced out of business or out on the street. The country badly needed a political and economic hero, indeed a savior, in these turbulent times. Instead, they had President Vicente Calderon.

CHAPTER 3
The Canadian Connection

Kali bin Shalah finished prepping the small airplane; he was ready to take off and the passengers were nowhere to be seen. Bin Shalah had a really short fuse and everyone knew it so it was a little unusual for him to be left standing by the airplane, propellers turning and no one ready to climb aboard. He pulled out his cell phone and clicked the talk button; he had just finished telling Turushpa they would leave in five minutes; plenty of warning, he thought.

"Where the hell are the passengers, Turushpa? My gas is burning and we have to make it to Tegucigalpa before noon."

"I am sorry, Kali, they all decided they needed to take another leak and there is only one toilet. These guys aren't used to being pushed around; don't forget Turi; he bled out in two minutes."

"Turi didn't take them where they wanted to go, he just fed them. Too bad he was such a lousy cook. Anyway, my nine-millimeter trumps his pocket knife"

"Yes, except that he's in the seat behind you. They won't come out until they are all together, so give it another minute, Kali; maybe a pint of gas."

"Try making a landing without the last pint of gas."

A minute or two later the six Hezbollah managers appeared, looked disgustingly at bin Shalah and began to climb in the plane; a full load without travel bags, just a few sticks of deodorant.

"Gentlemen, we are to refuel at Tegucigalpa at noon and again at Durango where you will spend the night. Tomorrow we will leave at 6

The Mexicans

am, refuel at Ciudad Juarez, again at Casper and again at Moose Jaw where we will spend the night. The next day we will leave at 6 am, refuel at Prince Albert and make water at Shed Lake. Your return flight will be waiting there. If there are any other aircraft on the lake we will continue past Shed Lake and make water at Weyakwin Lake where you will await the return aircraft; but that is unlikely. You should be landing at Petosky by the end of the week. There your people will meet you with ground transportation to Detroit. Do you have any questions?"

"Go."

The men were very quiet during the flight. They drank water and ate Snickers candy bars, occasionally pointing out something on the ground below. Most of them napped for an hour after the first hour or so. As they approached the landing field at Tegucigalpa, bin Shalah made contact with the controller and asked to speak to Carlos Fuentes.

"Carlos, is everything in order?"

"Yes, Kali. Your fuel bill has been paid in advance. We will have you back in the air within fifteen minutes. I have two Port-o-potties waiting, twelve bottles of water and a box of Snickers, just as usual."

"Very well, we will begin our descent."

Hours later, they landed at Durango where a team of Mexican police were there to meet them.

"Remain in the aircraft. Let me see your papers."

Bin Shalah handed down a large envelope containing fifteen thousand U.S. dollars.

"What is this? There are papers here for only three of you. Where are the other papers?"

The Chief was clearly upset; he placed his hand on his sidearm as he spoke and the other officers moved forward to the airplane.

"I'm sorry, sir; you are correct, there is another envelope here."

The Canadian Connection

He handed it down to the Chief, another fifteen thousand. The Chief emptied the two envelopes and passed them back to bin Shalah.

"The papers are all in order. You may proceed to the hanger."

"Thank you, sir."

The passengers didn't like police and they had no respect these.

"Swine, pigs, dogs; let me put a bullet in their dog brains."

"Another time, Uruk."

They were to spend the night here at the airfield with accommodations that could best be described as austere, and that would be generous. One large room in the hanger with six single beds made of iron and a set of wires with springs. The mattresses were a full two inches thick and one wool blanket was rolled up for a pillow or a cover according to one's preference. There were two Port-o-potties and a roll of tissue in each.

"Excellent, but we are hungry now."

"The food will be brought by a local service provider. It should be here in fifteen minutes."

"Tell him to be on time. There are no more candy bars; is he bringing more?"

"Yes, yes. And more bottles of water. There will be water and candy bars at every stop."

"Very well."

Soon the dinner was delivered; the men were pleased with the food.

"This is very good chicken and the rice, too. What is this thing?"

"Oh, that is an avocado, a vegetable and that one is a guava, a fruit."

"There is no taste to this thing."

"Put salt on it, Nauri; it has a very light flavor." Elam liked the avocado.

The Mexicans

While they ate their dinner, another man delivered the Snickers and water.

After dinner and a candy bar, they were ready for bed.

Another vehicle drove up to the hanger and let out six party girls to help the warriors through the night. There were giggles and roars of laughter for awhile and then the girls left.

The next morning they were served breakfast burritos from McDonald's. Breakfast burritos were very popular in Mexico and the Hezbollah all enjoyed them.

"We have something in common with the western infidels, now. We will allow a few of them to live and cook breakfast burritos, eh? Ha, ha."

"Also a good many party girls will live and entertain the warriors, eh? Ha, ha."

At nine am they landed at Ciudad Juarez for fuel, water and Snickers, then went on to Casper for another stop and refreshments. Here, they found a rodeo underway just outside the air field which captured their attention; they insisted on staying for more than an hour, putting them late for their arrival at Moose Jaw. The sun was below the horizon when they made their approach, providing barely enough light for a safe landing. But for them, it was well worth the time. They talked about the rodeo events all the way to Moose Jaw and again on the flight the next morning.

"I'm going to learn to ride like that, Nauri. They have horse riding schools in the U.S.; that's one thing I'm going to do."

"You're going to do your duty, Diyala. But, maybe we can do the horse school, too."

"Yes, we can do both, Nauri, that's good."

The morning flight was shorter than the others, but it was necessary to have a full tank of fuel before heading north into the wilderness to be sure the plane would make it back to refuel. There wasn't much to see at Prince Albert.

"Do you know what that girl asked me last night while we were messing around?"

"What did she say to you, Belah?"

He giggled as he remembered the girl and the joke she told him.

"She said, "A man asked the vendor at the store if he had Prince Albert in the can. When he said "yes", the man said, "Well, why don't you let him out?" That's what she said."

Belah giggled as he finished the tale.

"Don't you see? Prince Albert is a pipe tobacco, you know that; why aren't you laughing?"

"Belah, you ass! You told that girl where we were going? You told her we were going to Prince Albert, Canada? You pig! What if she tells someone that? And then someone else tells it and pretty soon the CIA hears it? Do you not think the CIA gets information from prostitutes who service men like us? That was really stupid, Belah. I ought to slit your throat and leave you up here in the lake. When are you going to learn? You're supposed to manage a workplace but you're not fit to handle the responsibility because you talk too much."

"Hey, Nauri, it was a funny joke; don't be so uptight."

"But, Nauri, I didn't tell her we were going to Prince Albert. Didn't you see her? She was rolling her own cigarettes and she used that tobacco. Didn't you guys see her?"

"I did, Nauri; I saw her smoking that strong stuff. I didn't know what it was, but it was really strong, like pipe tobacco."

"You all better not be lying; you'd better be telling the truth. If I find out you lied, I'll fire you all."

"Honest, Nauri; that's the way it was. She was kidding about it because she said she always told that joke when she laid up with a man."

"Alright, that's the end of that. But don't let me hear your telling that story again; do you hear?"

"OK, Nauri; I hear you. That's the end of it."

The airplane was quiet after that until it settled onto the water at Shed Lake. As they dropped down they could see the other plane waiting for them to take them to Michigan.

"There it is, men. One more trip and we'll be in the U.S."

"In the United States."

"I can't wait to get started at the workplace I get, wherever it is."

"I just know that what we do will be the beginning of the end for the infidels."

"Yes, when we finish this great work we have to do."

"Allah is great! Allah is great!"

CHAPTER 4

The Mexican Connection

The new visitors were well accepted into the small Mexican communities where they took up lodging. They seemed to have unlimited pesos which they gave freely to the families they interviewed; that got the attention of everyone rather quickly. They hired local carros, taxis, for their transportation needs, paying generously to have one or two on hand at all times. One of their first contacts was with the local constable after which they asked to meet with the local judge.

They explained to the officials that their purpose was to distribute welfare payments to the families of immigrant workers in the United States and that the purpose of the payments was to prepare the economy for a new program whereby the illegals in the U.S. would have the opportunity to be accepted as legal workers. The program had not been given widespread notice, and would not be, until certain legal and political adjustments had been completed. The officials fully understood the need for discretion and accepted their own payments gracefully.

Since their arrival, walking into town and making arrangements with the officials, the twelve men worked diligently to fulfill their purpose: they asked to meet and talk with every family that had a family member working somewhere in the United States. They did not explain what their interest was, usually saying simply that "we are not allowed to divulge that information", but everyone assumed that they were somehow involved in arranging for permanent resident status in the U.S. through the government, maybe even amnesty and citizenship for the workers there now, and for their families, later.

Often a briefcase would be opened revealing small packets of green cards among the other papers, but they were never referred to or brought forth out of the briefcase. And when speaking between themselves in English, occasionally they would exchange words like "congress", "civil rights", "Senator Fulbright", etc. It raised some concern that the men all looked swarthy, but they were clean shaven wearing short haircuts. While in their offices they dressed in summer weight khaki suits with white shirts and red ties, though not always the same shade or pattern. When out of the office, they usually dressed casually with open collar but always very neatly. Their use of the Spanish language was typical of someone who had learned it in school. All of this went to give the impression that they might have been sent from the U.S., though they never did say so.

They were taking a census of those families having relatives working in the U.S.; only those families were interviewed. The information included names, relationships, addresses and telephone numbers of the ones who were north of the border, also the names of the local family and the amount of money they had been receiving from the relatives each month. After providing the information, they were given a like amount of money as they had been receiving from the relative, with the assurance that they would receive the same money payments regularly each month as long as the relative remained in the U.S. It was more than anyone could have hoped for, a welfare payment, guaranteed by the visitors who called themselves the Council for Unification.

Who would turn that down? Life in the villages was often just hand to mouth existence; few families had a regular income, rather they made their living by planting gardens and raising small farm animals, goats, pigs and chickens, for food. When they had extra they sold it at little stands along the roads into and out from the village, mostly to bus riders going home from jobs in the city. The small sums earned from produce and other occasional work in the city supplemented what they raised at their homes and what they received from relatives working in the U.S. House repairs, clothing and medicines took most of what they received. But they always held back enough for their church donation as best they could. This offer of extra income was indeed a Godsend, they thought.

They were told to write or call their relative to inform them of the new arrangement. They should also tell their relatives that they should expect to be contacted soon by a member of the Council. They should not be afraid when they are contacted; there would be an offer for a new, better job in the same location and the welfare payments being given to their families would continue as a part of that new job. It all sounded too good to be true, but there was no reason to doubt the sincerity of these men, and the Padre said they should expect gifts from God; he said they should not question the gifts when they came. The Padre also had been given a monthly stipend to assure his continued faithfulness.

After the second month as the payments were given out, the family representatives were asked if they had told their relatives of their new benefits and the message they had been instructed to tell them. If they had not done so, they were encouraged to do so within the next few days. Then, the Council prepared a list of the relatives in the U.S. and their addresses and telephone numbers, but only those relatives who had been informed of the arrangement.

The others who had not been told of the arrangement would have to wait to be included in a follow-up list. It was clear that they intended to contact only the relatives who had been briefed by their family. This current list then was sent by mail to a Post Office Box in the city of Detroit, Michigan. From there, the names on the list were added to other lists, regional lists, made up from names that had come in from this and other communities in Mexico.

Those regional lists were then mailed to Post Office Boxes in a number of cities, including Los Angeles, Seattle, Denver, Phoenix, Dallas, San Antonio, Memphis, Atlanta, St. Louis, Omaha, Chicago, Cleveland, Pittsburgh, Philadelphia and Boston. There, the regional lists were organized into smaller lists according to smaller cities within the region and distributed by mail to Post Office boxes in each of those cities and a few rural towns.

It was there, in the local cities and towns, that the names on the lists were divided up to the cell members who would be responsible for

The Mexicans

contacting the Mexicans to explain the plan and the jobs they would be given, should they decide to accept the positions. The pay for the new job was greater than the pay they had been earning at the other jobs; the family welfare payment would continue as before, in addition to their new pay. It was an offer few could refuse and most of those that did soon returned to accept when they found out that their friends had all accepted.

The new jobs were housed in warehouses in the low ends of the cities usually near the railroad tracks. In the rural communities, the jobs were in the barns where the agricultural products were stored, sorted and packaged for shipping, the fertilizer, chemicals and insecticides. In the city warehouses they packaged materials that were not identified; some they mixed by weight, some they counted by item or by measure. The items all were individually wrapped with tarpaulin and packed in containers, the heavy items in wooden crates, the lighter items in cardboard boxes, and labeled.

After packing, the boxes and crates were stacked on pallets and moved to the storage area by forklift where the pallets were stacked high nearly to the ceiling on shelving and steel frames. It was all very similar to packaging operations in any of hundreds of warehouse across the country. At regular times, the packaged goods were loaded onto trucks and delivered to the end users.

The work was clean, not heavy, and lunch was provided for the workers in a kitchen lunchroom in the back of the warehouse where they took their breaks. Who could ask for a better deal? There was just one requirement; no one outside the organization was to be told of the work or the location, under penalty of extradition back to Mexico and loss of all pay and benefits. They didn't want any unions to know about their jobs.

"No problem, there, boss," they'd say.

CHAPTER 5

The Iranian Connection

Harry Foster relaxed on the beach, thinking about the afternoon of fishing on the ocean he had arranged. Life was really slow at Zihuatanejo; really, it was more like dreamy, nearly like sleepy, following their late breakfast at the hotel. He always favored that quiet little place whenever they came down, which was not often. That, incidentally, was the subject he was mulling over as he sipped the weak Margarita – Harry liked the drink but he hated the effects of alcohol on his presence of mind, so the weak mix was his drink, never more than three in one day. Harry Foster never, not ever, allowed himself to lose acumen, a virtue he was famous for among the White House staff.

"How long has it been since our last vacation?" he asked his wife, Lydia.

"Oh, come on Harry, you know it's been five years at least; I've given up trying to keep up with our vacation calendar – it simply is ghostly, not to say ghastly. Of course, you know I'm not complaining, Dear ; it's just that we are a rare breed, you and I; always planning or doing or controlling something important – something we think is important, and not taking time out for a long breath. I really like it down here, don't you, Harry?"

"We think? Did you say, "something we think is important"? Is that what you just said? Have you considered whether the President thinks what we do is important? Hmm. Maybe you're right; maybe his business isn't really so important. After all, he hasn't called me for nearly two hours today. Do you suppose he might not call again until after lunch? Yes, I like it down here."

"OK, Harry, I get it. I didn't mean to get you upset; your heart rate must be approaching sixty. I was only kidding. Wherever you are that's where I want my vacation to be, even if it's the White House or Camp David or Timbuktu; that's where I'm happy, when I'm with you. After nearly thirty years, I can hardly go to the bathroom without you being nearby."

"Hey, come on now, that's almost tacky. You know, in all those twenty-eight years the only times we've been in the bathroom together is when we shared a bathtub after you'd had the second glass of champagne. Say, what about joining me in a bath tonight; does that sound spicy? By the way, where is Timbuktu?"

"In Alaska, Dear; everybody knows Timbuktu is way up there in Alaska, or maybe it's in the Northwest Territories, I'm not absolutely certain. Anyway, it doesn't matter; the idea is that it's a long ways away and that's all that counts. No one wants to go to Timbuktu; no one in their right mind, at least. The bathtub sounds exciting, Harry."

"What about the guy whose family is living there with him in that igloo? Do you suppose he don't want to go there, maybe 'cause he's already there?"

"Don't get cute. Not to change the subject, but if we don't get a call back from Karyl today I'm going to call the president of Auburn University and find out what they've done with her body."

"Forget it, dear; she's busy with her studies. OK, maybe she's busy with her friends, I don't know. But I do know that Karyl has her own life now and you might as well get used to it; she's a grown woman, ready to graduate, maybe, in another year. No kidding, now, give her a little more space and she'll respond a lot better to your inquiring mind."

"No, you don't, Harry; you're not getting me off her case with that stuff about being grown up. You know we have always had an understanding with her that she keep us informed on what's going on down there; that loose University lifestyle may be acceptable for some parents, but I'm a lot more protective of my daughter and you should be, too. Who knows what goes on around that college campus? Sure, Auburn's got a good reputation, moral standards and all that, but what are good morals for one student may be debauchery for another one; don't you see? Heck, you don't even care."

"Alright, we'll call her after dinner, that'll be about nine-thirty, her time. What about that fishing trip? Are you still going with me?"

"Thank you, Harry. Of course I'm going fishing with you; I'm still after that marlin you keep promising me. Whenever you say, Lover, I'm ready to go."

Lydia could be real accommodating when Harry came around to her way of thinking on an important subject. Besides, Harry deserved some relaxation after all that mess on the Mississippi River and the inquiries afterward. She was so proud of him, the way he stood up to those investigators and defended the NSA agents. When it all came out, every one of them turned out looking like heroes; Harry was right all along. No one at the White House worked as hard or as long as Harry and everyone envied him for the way Lydia was there for him at home and at the office, too, whenever she could be of help and sometimes when she couldn't, but thought she could. No one could accuse Lydia of not supporting her man. They were a perfectly matched pair and still very much in love.

The water was peaceful, the fishing was the best ever and Lydia got her marlin; a hundred and thirty-six pounds of fish. Lydia was so proud of her catch;

"Rembrandt goes to the dining room; my marlin goes over the fireplace; that's final."

But, no one was arguing as they sent it over for mounting.

That evening the dinner was really special and after dinner there was the champagne – two glasses for Lydia. Before they went up to the room she called Karyl's number and got an answer right away. She was so excited about the marlin she never said a word about her not calling them. Karyl had a new boy friend, Pre-Law. That was good enough for Lydia who wished her a great future as a lawyer's wife; that's when Karyl knew she'd had the second glass of champagne already.

"Mother, you know I'm going to Law School when I finish here this year; maybe we'll be partners. I'll bet you've had a second glass of champagne. You know you can't hold it."

The Mexicans

"Dad's already drawing the bath water", her mother told her as she winked at Harry.

Harry signed the check and said a few words of love and goodbye to Karyl and they went upstairs to take a bath.

The next morning Harry Foster was just beginning his day at 6:30; even at Zihuatanejo it was hard to break old habits. He rubbed his eyes as he turned on the television to get the morning news. Then the telephone rang; the secure cell connection that had its own encryption.

"Hello."

"Good morning, Mr. Foster, this is Bill George, I hope I didn't wake you; I hoped to catch you early before you got out on the fishing boat. We have some unusual activity out of Venezuela and into Mexico. It's come to us from the CIA operatives down there. I have a meeting very soon with the President; you might want to be ready for a quick return. Just a little heads up; sorry to be the harbinger of bad news at this time. You must've just got there."

"Really, it's a big bore, Bill. What kind of activity?"

"What we have been able to learn from Caracas and Tehran is they are ferrying specially trained Hezbollah and other terrorist groups into the rural countryside of Mexico, using small charter aircraft, six men in a drop. They have been very secretive, attracting little notice by the local magistrates or the federal government. There are presently more than a hundred in that country in the smaller villages, and their numbers are increasing each week. This is all under the auspices of Alhaminijah with the cooperation of Jimenez. Our contacts in Tehran tell us that they plan to increase their presence there by double or triple before the year's end.

"What's it all pointing to?"

"Sometime during the year-end holidays they plan to unleash a series of organized disruptions on U. S. soil with much destruction. They have unlimited funds with which to operate and purchase weapons from North Korea by way of friendly nations. There is suggestion that

The Iranian Connection

they may also collaborate with Jimenez to disrupt the political stability of Mexico from within."

"Thanks for calling Bill. I'll call the President. See you later."

"You're welcome, Harry."

The President would be available at 7 am EST; that gave Harry a few hours time to think this through. The President will want a meeting of his principle Cabinet, Advisors and staff; he could be sure of that. He reviewed the calendar of each one likely to be called in. Most were available the next two days until 10am. He pushed the Presidents button and got the reply;

"I'm here, Harry."

"Mr. President, I have just received a call from Bill George. I got it on my recorder. You will want to hear this; it is only a three minute recording."

"Ok, Harry, send it up, I'll be in the bathroom for a couple minutes. The recorder is on, go ahead and send it up."

Harry sent it up; the President came in.

"Got it, Harry; hang on while I listen to it."

When it was over, the President asked Harry to gather his National Security council for a 9 am meeting the next day in the Executive Conference Room. That included all those Harry had considered earlier; Forrest Taylor Hughes, the Vice-President; Phyllis Morales, Secretary of State, William George, Secretary of Homeland Security, Reginald Dwyer, FBI, and himself, National Security Advisor to the President, his closest aide. CIA never attended these meetings; the President spoke with CIA privately.

"Mr. Hughes may not be in town. As you know, Sir, he is at Camp David briefing the House Intelligence Committee on the substance of the U.N. leaks."

"Well, get him back here for the meeting."

"Of course; if you'll excuse me, Sir, I'll get it together."

"Thank you."

"I'll be back in time for the meeting. Goodbye, Sir."

Harry was an hour making calls to get the meeting scheduled. Then he called for his military jet to pick up him and Lydia that afternoon for the flight back.

"I'm afraid it's as you said yesterday, Lidi, we just don't have a lot of control over our personal time. I'm really very sorry; but we'll try real hard to get back down here before the season ends, believe me."

Lydia could always tell when Harry felt incompetent to control matters in their personal life; he used that short nickname, which she found kind of refreshing. But she had never been able to assure him that she didn't mind those times; whatever she would say didn't sway him, he always felt that he needed to apologize just as though it were his fault when something he had promised didn't work out for her. Lydia knew his sorrow and she loved him for his confliction.

"Oh, Harry, don't worry about it; I'm anxious to get Marly hung over the fireplace, anyway. We'll get away again soon and maybe share another bath. I love you."

"We don't have to be on vacation for the bath deal, do we?" Harry perked up. "I mean, we have a better bathtub at home and better champagne too, for that matter."

"Hmm. I guess you're right. Harry, I just love it when you talk romantic. Just one more thing you need to do for me to make up for this, Harry; you need to join me at Church this Sunday and start taking your spiritual life seriously. No kidding, Harry, I love you and I don't want to end up when this is all over and not have you there with me."

"I will, Lidi, I really will. You know, I've been thinking very seriously about that recently. Angel Suarez has a way of settling certain things in my mind; he seems to simplify things for me and it's hard to resist his reasoning. You've got a date this Sunday, Lidi."

CHAPTER 6

The Korean Connection

The huge transport vessel had been at the dock in the Pusan harbor in South Korea for nearly two weeks, the cranes busily unloading raw materials and textiles for use in the booming Korean economy. Automotive plants, apparel factories, computer assemblers, farm machinery and many other industrial plants stood waiting with jaws open, ready to chew up the raw goods and spit them out as highly desirable finished goods, day in and day out. Except for necessary down time for maintenance, the plants operated at near capacity, roughly 23/6.5, year around.

Then, after relieving itself of that burden, offloaded onto rail flatcars, and after the engines moved the emptied string forward off the loading dock, the swivel-hipped loaders began their next act; loading the ship for its return voyage. One by one the loaders clamped the waiting steel-skinned giants in their steel grip and hauled them aboard the ship from off their flatcars, the engines lurching their two-mile long string of cars and merchandise forward another fifty or so feet, positioning each next car to the loading position for its turn at the plate.

When the last container was slipped into the last remaining position, the crew set about securing the load with titanium cables, tying down the stacked containers firmly into place so that the load held as one, assuring the Captain of no slippage on the rough seas.

"She's good to go, Captain, Sir, tight as a rump drawn up inside a pretty's girdle. Nothin' gets in and nothin' gets out."

The first mate is a rounder, but he knows his business and the cargo is ready for the high seas. Tugs then begin to move the ship from the dock out to the channel and beyond the port waters. From there, it's

The Mexicans

the Captain's tough love that keeps her safe and slips her into the port waters of Sydney, eight days later.

Here again the stage is set for a repeat performance of the smooth off and on burlesque routine, masterfully officiated by the ship's cast of stevedores. You'd think the monotony of seeing the boxes come and go, most of them resembling the ones that went before, would cloud the deckhands' eyes of any minor differences from one to the next. There are few things as common as a shipping container, yet here was Scurvy Jim Potter making an unusual observation:

"Mr. Ridley, we just off-loaded that one there on our last visit a month ago and it hain't been cracked, and I see four or five more just like it."

What're you hallucinating about Jim? We're loading shipping containers, not whores."

I ain't hallucinatin' Mr. Ridley, someth'n here ain't just right; see them marks there on the end corners? Those are my off-loading marks, so's I'll know the count. I'd know them marks anywhere, those're my marks. If they'd been opened, the seal on the edge would have been replaced and the marks would be gone. These hain't been done that way; they're just like they were when I off-loaded them."

"Yeah, OK, Jim; you got good eyes and a good memory, but it ain't our business when someone dispatches a container to the wrong place. The poor guy probably got fired, so's now you need to say a prayer for his starvin' family."

"I know it ain't my business, but look here, now, we've had something to talk about for a change, something unusual; what's wrong with that?"

"Nothin's wrong with that, Jim, nothin' at all."

"Where're they headed to now, Boss? You got the manifest there in your hand, ain't ya?"

"Headed to Seattle, Jim; see, Sydney, Seattle, that guy just got them out of order by their destination, probably from one sheet to the

The Korean Connection

next. It all can be figured out when you put your mind to it, now, see what I mean?"

"Yeah, Boss, you got the education. You're a smart guy, Boss."

Three weeks later, the container cargo from Sydney, Australia, including a few from Pyong Yang, North Korea, was unloaded at the Port of Seattle. Two of the reshipped containers were unloaded onto a deepwater barge headed over the Straights of Juan De Fuca to Vancouver, Canada, for subsequent delivery by train across Canada. The other four were delivered by train to Star Crescent Imports warehouses, two at Chehalis, Washington, and two at Tulare, California. The Sydney shipments went elsewhere.

The Korean shipments were well transported, well received and well handled by the Star Crescent warehouse employees. Using a fork-lift the crates of Uzis and crates of Kalashnikovs and crates of machine guns, and the crates of hand held rockets and the crates of grenades and the crates of mortar launchers and all the boxes of ammunition were carefully unloaded and stacked in the sub-basement. Soon they would be trucked to their destination sites down and across the Pacific Coast states to cities where the Hezbollah managers were recruiting and training their future team leaders. Private property was the one thing the Hezbollah liked the most about the United States, next to probable cause in the Ninth Circuit.

As for the Canadian shipment, both containers went to Sudbury, Ontario. There, the shipment would be broken down and delivered by truck transport to Rodham, Ontario for redelivery through Detroit and Buffalo. The warehouse locations were all remote agricultural areas, this being farm equipment, clearly stated on the shipping documents and the crates. There was always a good deal of farm equipment arriving during the off season, replacements for prior years' worn out equipment and implements; this kind of equipment had a depreciable life of twelve years at today's rate of productivity gains, some even less with competition for produce, hogs and cattle getting very keen on the world market. No one wants to fall behind using obsolete equipment; it's just too hard to catch up. The Departments of Agriculture knows all this and they stand behind the

33

farmer with subsidies and low interest financing. It's what makes us strong.

Those shipments would be shipped by truck ostensibly to small family farms in the northern United States as their orders are received. Canada is known to be a major supplier of agricultural equipment on both sides of the Canadian border. Who would ever suspect that it would end up in unlikely places for farm equipment, or that the Pacific Coast farm equipment would end up that way, too? And why would anyone suspect terrorist ordnance to be exported from Australia? After all, if one can inspect only one or two percent of cargo, one should concentrate on the usual suspects, not on our favored nation trading partners; that just makes good sense.

But commercial contracts are carefully crafted by lawyers, just as are shipping contracts. No worries, mate.

CHAPTER 7
The Nexus Connection

The return from Zihuatanejo was swift and uneventful thanks to the skill of some of the Air Force's best pilots assigned to Foster's itinerary. Pilots loved assignments like this one; it meant a trophy for each of them in the form of a letter of commendation from Mr. Harry Foster who was arguably, the second most important man in the White House.

The next morning while Harry Foster was checking out the audio-visual equipment and calling offices to be sure that everyone showed up on time for the meeting, Lydia was calling her interior designer to arrange for help with the hanging of the marlin over the fireplace and relegating the Rembrandt to the Dining Room. She didn't mind cutting the vacation short since she had such a prize to show off to all of her friends, which is why she was hurrying the designer to hang Marly, but not without the greatest of care.

By calling the experts to do the job Lydia felt assured that equal care would be given to both Marly and the Rembrandt. After all, it cost Harry an extra five hundred to get the taxidermist to work all day and night getting the thing ready for them in time for the flight back - not counting the tip, and Harry tipped big for special treatment. She just wished that Harry could be there to supervise the hanging, too. He had such a good eye for leveling and centering all the things that get hung.

President Cooper asked Secretary George to give the briefing that he gave Harry about the Mexican-Iranian connection out of Venezuela and their plot against the U.S. When George had detailed everything that was known, the President continued:

The Mexicans

"Mr. Foster has prepared a confidential memo containing the pertinent facts that we know. Study this well and we will meet again in one week after we all have had time to consider the situation and our response to it; obviously there are international implications. In the meantime, we will inform the Cabinet and seek their input, as well. We need cool heads to study on this, lots of them. Secretary George, please see if you can get John Smoltz here this afternoon, if possible. We'll need to get his NSA people on this quickly and quietly; no media, no leaks, please. We've got to formulate a plan to interrupt the terrorists at the border before they can get into the country and do damage."

With the meeting over, President Cooper turned to Harry Foster for advice.

"Harry, do you think Brother Angel Suarez might be willing to help us investigate the activity in the Mexican villages? He and his wife have done some remarkable things working with the NSA people. We really need someone to read the signs in Mexico and he has consistently shown himself to be both reliable and discrete. Whether or not he would balk at matters of espionage we would have to determine and then set limits accordingly. What about it?"

"Well, Sir, our officers in the NSA say he has good instincts for reliable information. They should know, after all that time they worked with him to rescue those two airmen down there in Louisiana. Together, he and his lovely wife would not likely be suspected of intelligence gathering. They are well known as missionaries working with their Association in New Mexico"

"Yes, being Latinos and seniors as well should defray suspicions about their presence below the border; after all, there are thousands of Latino-Americans going in and out of Mexico every day. They could be most effective at seeking out information on these would-be intruders, where they've settled and maybe who they're talking to. We need to invite Br. Angel and Miranda to meet with us soon. Can you arrange that?"

"I'm certain of it, Mr. President."

"Good. Let me hear back from you as you make these arrangements. Thank you, Harry."

"Yes Sir." He exited to do his work. It was just before noon.

The Homeland Security meeting was set for 3:30 that afternoon. John Smoltz, Director of NSA would be present. The second call was to Angel Suarez and his wife, Miranda. As he placed that call he was reminded of how well those two had managed the incident on the Korean freighter out on the Pacific Ocean.

"The ideal pair for this work," he thought.

The call to Br. Angel's home in Socorro came as a complete surprise to them, but a very pleasant surprise. Since their involvement in the Louisiana incidents, their lives had settled back to a more normal pace; boring by comparison.

"Brother Suarez, I hope I haven't intruded in your work by such a late call this afternoon."

"Harry; Harry Foster, this is such a surprise! It's good to hear from you. My, no; your call is always welcome at anytime."

He motioned Miranda to come and listen as he talked.

"How are Miranda and yourself? I have very fond memories of your last visit to the White House."

"We are very well, thank you. Well rested, too, having just recently finished a very relaxing and interesting two-week voyage across the Pacific, but you know about all of that. And, yes, Miranda and I often recall that auspicious visit to the White House and the hospitality we were shown. We had never dreamed of being graced with such dignities, meeting the President and so many other important people. Yes, it's good to hear your voice again, Harry."

"Br. Angel, I'm calling for the President; he asked me to offer his personal greeting and to ask for your confidence, once again. Could

The Mexicans

you arrange time to come up here and meet with the President and some of his advisors? There is a matter that he believes you can help him with, a matter that just got on his agenda today. We can send a plane for you and Miranda if it's convenient and you could be back home in two days, I'm sure, unless you wished to stay on for a longer visit."

"Of course, yes, we are at the President's call at any time. Would you hold on just a minute, Harry?"

"Miranda, dear, can you be ready to fly to the White House in the morning?"

"I most certainly can, Angel." He eyes were sparkling with excitement.

"We can be ready anytime in the morning, if that is soon enough; this evening if need be, Harry; whatever is best for the President."

"Shall we say 9am at Albuquerque airport? Is that too early?"

"Not at all, we are usually up before six. We'll be there at the airport and through security before nine."

"Excellent. I'll send a military plane for you and I'll meet you on your arrival here, and thank you both; please pardon me; I'm in a bit of a hurry, and give my regards to Miranda. I'm leaving now to inform the President. Have a pleasant flight, both of you. Goodbye."

"Thank you, Harry; we'll see you there. Goodbye."

"Oh, Angel, what could possibly cause the President to want to meet with you now? It must be terribly important; Oh, I can't wait to visit the White House again! This is so wonderful!"

"We will know very soon, my dear. These things tend to move along very quickly, as we have seen. We'll know soon; let's get packed and have dinner out tonight."

"Yes, let's do that, dear." Miranda never turned down dinner out; she loved her dates with Angel.

The next morning at 8:55 the Colonel escorted Br. Angel and Miranda to the large jet airplane that Harry Foster had sent to pick them up for the flight to Andrews Air Force Base in Virginia. There, they were escorted to an awaiting helicopter and flown to the helipad at the White House grounds. They were beginning to get used to this VPI treatment and often winked at each other with just the hint of a smile as they politely accepted the repeated dignities the Air Force officers showed them. They had enjoyed the flight and the luncheon and now the reception on this beautiful but chilly October afternoon.

It was just after 4 pm that the President was free to sit down with Br. Angel and Miranda and welcome them to the White House. In fifteen minutes the President's called meeting would begin and he wanted to personally invite both Br. Angel and his wife to participate. Of course they were honored to be able to accept.

"Thank you both. I feel quite personally, that you two have an important role to play in certain of our affairs south of the border. That's the reason I asked you to come. And I believe, rather I should say, your country believes, that when you hear all the facts, you will see your way clear to help us out in this situation. If you'll excuse me, now, I'll prepare for the meeting and see the both of you there in about fifteen minutes. Mr. Foster will escort you to the meeting room."

"Of course, yes; we will see you there, Mr. President."

"Oh, my, Angel, he wants me to be in the meeting along with you. The President himself has asked me to attend. Goodness, what is next?"

"My Dear, if I had to write a book about what is next, I think I'd title the book 'God's Not Finished With Us Yet'; what would you say, would you read it?"

"You know I would, Angel."

@@

The President's meeting with Br. Angel and Miranda began right on schedule and included most of his National Security team as well as the Secretary of State and the Assistant Secretaries for National Security

The Mexicans

and for Mexican Affairs. After the President opened the meeting, he briefed the attendees with a description of the Mexican incursion that had been discovered.

"That is the situation we are faced with; that is the problem we are gathered here to address."

Many at the table had little or no prior knowledge of the President's two guests. President Cooper asked Harry Foster to give a background briefing on Br. Angel and Miranda and he asked for a brainstorming period where ideas put forth could include all options, except war.

Foster recounted the history of Br. Angel and Miranda in the NSA investigation of the downed aircraft incident in Louisiana and the rescue on the Pacific Ocean. Most had heard of the Korean freighter event through media reports but had no knowledge of American involvement until now.

Next, they held a period for ideas on how best to respond to this Iranian terrorist invasion that apparently was being prepared south of the border. The question of Mexican involvement in any investigation was discounted because of doubts as to the Mexican government's effectiveness and its political ability to control its countryside. Secretary of State Phyllis Morales summed up her position.

"We simply don't have enough information to begin serious discussions with that government; the police and border control officers are notorious for using their positions for personal gain and their involvement could make matters worse, even dangerous for U.S. agents, either official or unofficial. The initial efforts should be made completely undercover, with no official knowledge whatsoever by any U.S agency or Mexican authorities"

"Well, what about that, Harry?"

Although the President asked Foster for his thoughts; they would be the same ones that he and Foster had arrived at earlier..

"That's where the Suarez team could come in, Mr. President; to gather information by personal observation and contact with local citizens. With their native backgrounds and appearance Br. Angel and Miranda could blend in anywhere as native Mexicans, so long as they had appropriate identification papers. Also, when using their true identity as U.S. citizens, they would appear as innocuous as any other Latino-American couple visiting the country."

When the attendees agreed on the Suarez team as the initial best option, the President turned to the two of them.

"Brother Angel, Miranda, you should know that any undercover operation holds a high degree of risk. I'd like for you to think very hard about this; talk it over very carefully. Just give Harry a call when you have decided what you will do. Please don't feel obligated to accept this proposal. If you should decide to join in this, I can assure you that our NSA agents will be available to you at all times, of course."

"The opportunity seems inviting," Br. Angel responded, "sitting here in the safety of the White House, Mr. President, but I think we will take the time as you suggest and call Mr. Foster in the morning. Miranda would be happy to accept this very minute, I can see it in her eyes, but I fear I am more concerned for her safety than she is. We will respond in the morning, certainly; and thank you all, we are humbled by your confidence."

Later, in their comfortable White House guest room, Br. Angel and Miranda spoke very seriously of the proposal, but it was clear Miranda had taken an immediate liking to it.

"My dear Angel, let us take the bitter pill if that proves to be the outcome of this calling; we have had such a wonderful life here, you and I. I think we can offer ourselves up to this need of our homeland, taking whatever risks it may bring to us, just so long as we do it together. I don't feel it merely as an exciting attraction, Angel; really, it is more a feeling of duty but with an eagerness to forsake the boredom of our late years. So, let's do it."

CHAPTER 8

Marching Orders

"I'll offer Colonel Bragg as your witness at this point." John Smoltz had just finished his testimony before the Congressional inquiry looking into the Mississippi River disaster and the disruption at the Detroit NSA office that resulted in three employees being killed and another wounded.

"Thank you General Smoltz. And may I say for the record that your testimony is a stunning tribute to the dedicated efforts of your heroic force of agents. I'm sure I speak for each member of this Committee in commending with the highest level of appreciation, the fine men and women of the NSA, in particular those of the Louisiana District. We'll break for lunch now, without objection."

The chairman was clearly impressed by Smoltz' testimony and personally touched by his calm presentation, especially coming on the heels of his recent period of depression over the shooting death of his close friend and Adjutant, Tommy Fitzhugh. Everyone on the Committee knew of the Detroit incident.

When the Congressional inquiry resumed, Colonel Phil Bragg was the first witness called. He testified to the reports he had filed with his superior, John Smoltz, all pertaining to the Mississippi River operations, and all documentation that had been developed under his supervision throughout the Louisiana District. In addition, he responded to questioning about the activities of his agents investigating the radio transmissions in the Thibodaux and Houma areas, and about his suspicions of information leaks that may have led to the Mexican incident on the border, when the airman was being returned to his people.

The Mexicans

The next witness called was Major Bob Crumpton who testified as to the specific actions taken on the ground by NSA agents assigned to the Mississippi River investigations. He gave testimony on behalf of all the agents because of his personal involvement and first hand observations of all significant events.

In the end, operations conducted by the Louisiana District of the NSA were adjudged to have been fully justified and no fault was found in their actions, either of commission or omission. It was found that the Louisiana District investigation of the steamboat operation had been unjustly interfered with by collaboration of certain of the Detroit staff with terrorist operatives intended to delay the NSA investigation and allow time for the terrorists to move the Miss Ohio Riverboat downriver and execute their plan of blowing up the river abutments.

They found the actions of Dan McAllister, the NSA managing agent in Detroit and his office assistant to be traitorous, resulting in extensive infrastructure damage, property damage and more than one hundred lives lost in the Mississippi Delta. The deaths of Fitzhugh and the traitors themselves were attributed to the actions of agent McAllister, who was also responsible for disclosing the identity and thereby causing the murder of NSA officer Reggie Halbrook, targeted by the terrorists in a murderous firestorm during the NSA incursion at the River farms.

A week later when the final Congressional Inquiry report was issued, NSA Director John Smoltz had his secretary retrieve the copies of his orders promoting and reassigning Phil Bragg and Bob Crumpton to his staff in D.C. He had her change the effective dates to October 1, 2006 for the promotions and November 1, 2006 for reassignment. As he signed the orders, he asked,

"Would you let me have two copies for each of the men, please? And get me on a plane to New Orleans in the morning."

That afternoon, following his meeting at the White House, Smoltz had been informed by Harry Foster of the President's directive that he should make plans for a Special District operation to be based in one of the southern states of Smoltz' choosing to facilitate investigations along the southern border. There would be a meeting within a few

Marching Orders

days to flesh out activities of the new operation. He called Phil Bragg in New Orleans.

"Phil, I'm making plans and they include you and Crumpton. I'm coming down there to talk to you tomorrow so be there in the office by noon, Crumpton too. I'll be there then. Top Secret, Phil, this involves the White House."

"We'll be here, John."

Next morning John Smoltz called Phil Bragg just as he arrived by taxi at the office building.

"Phil, I'm entering at the front door, buzz me in please and hide the buckets and mops, I'm not here to play those games today, and tell Misti to order in the Cajun crawfish, same as she did last time." He pushed the buzzer at the door with the sign 'Janitorial Supplies' and the door opened.

"Come in, John; how about some iced tea while we wait for the crawfish lunches. No heads, right? That's what I told her."

"Very funny, you know damn well I don't talk to crawfish, I just eat them, no heads. Hello, Bob, how're you today?"

"Just fine, John, it's good to see you again."

No one ever mentioned how John looked; it was too near a reminder of that week-long period of depression that knocked him out of commission after Tommy Fitzhugh was gunned down. Smoltz sat down and opened his briefcase. He was ready to get right to the promotions; that'd get things started off well.

"For your information, Phil, the President has asked Angel and Miranda Suarez to take on a special assignment by Presidential Order to work on and below the border gathering information on the terrorists I told you about and where they might be holing up. Notice that I said "below the border". That means we have to give them a lot of support and keep closely in touch. Now here are your Orders. I brought two

45

The Mexicans

copies for you, Phil, and two copies for you Bob, just so you'd be fully informed before we start bickering here." He handed them the Orders of promotion and transfer, watching to see their reactions.

"Dang, General, a promotion to Lt. Colonel; this is fantastic!" Bob was elated. "What a great break; really, John, I honestly didn't think I'd be in order for this for another couple of years, or more. I don't know what else to say but thanks, you get my vote for Mr. Goodguy - oops, I mean, General Goodguy, sorry."

Phil was equally pleased;

"John, I know darn well Beatrice isn't going to want to call me General, it was hard enough getting her used to 'Colonel', but I'll try real hard to get her used to it and to make you proud of me and this decision."

He gave John a handshake and he'd known him long enough for the hug. But he wasn't sold just yet on the transfer part of the deal.

"So, tell me, John, what will you do if we should refuse the DC assignment?"

"Well, Phil, I don't think you will because I have other plans and places for you to spend your time; DC will just be your official workplace address. You see, the President wants you to start up a new operations detachment; he called it a Special District to encompass the southern border end to end and wherever the work takes you. You will be selecting the city where you want to have the District office; you can even select the new janitor uniforms.

"Crumpton will be your District Manager and you can flesh out your team of agents from wherever you like. If you should prefer to live in D.C. and direct operations in the Border District from there, as my Adjutant that will be up to you; even better for me as I will make use of your spare time by letting you keep an eye on all our other Districts. You'll have some of those duties in any event."

"When do we get the briefing on this new area of operation, John? It sounds strangely like Mexico is part of the new territory, since you've made it clear that the Suarez team will be pecking around below the border. Truthfully, that aspect makes the offer a little more attractive; that's a smart pair and very effective."

"Phil, you are asking a question that I can't answer; this is the beginning of a new District given by presidential directive. We'll just do what it takes to be able to provide them support and do the work that needs to be done to protect this side of the border. It's all on us to make it happen. What do you think about the new territory, Bob?"

"I like it. Come June I'll be getting married and anywhere with Rebecca will suit me just fine. Really, I do like it, I do. That's why I haven't asked a bunch of questions, like the Colonel, now to be General. He has to explain it to Beatrice, so I think he needs all the ammo he can get; no offense, Boss."

Bob Crumpton was without doubt Phil Bragg's ideal Operations Officer which is the reason he was selected by Smoltz to be Operations Manager for the new Border District. A cowboy by background, horse breeder from Wyoming, Crumpton had graduated from the University of Wyoming and from West Point where he was a scholar-athlete. He was an Army Captain when he was recruited into the NSA as an Intelligence Officer.

Still single, but engaged, Crumpton was a devout Baptist believer and often led others to a saving knowledge of the Lord, especially when he found himself with injured and dying men. And it didn't make any difference if they were good guys or bad guys, Crumpton knew the Lord would accept all of them by "heartfelt repentance, confessing sins and believing in the Lord's ability to save you from Hell, through His act of grace, taking your sins to himself on the cross." Crumpton had a way of explaining God's love.

"You really have a great attitude, Bob. What if I decide not to go and you have to suck up to Fuzzy Longmeier or Jim Franklin instead of me? They might give you a homestead assignment at La Cucaracha Ranchero or patrolling the Mud Flats along the Rio Grande. Will you still feel suited to it?"

"You won't turn it down; I know that for a fact. It's just what you've been wanting, a new beginning, and you know you've been bored to death with the usual old NSA stuff. On the border you'll be free like a Mustang. Besides, I'll be there to keep your butt safe and Beatrice will appreciate that. Yahoo! Let's go TexMex! Let's go join Angel on the border, Brother Angel, that is."

CHAPTER 9

By Order of the President

The Presidential Order was brief and it was classified 'Presidential Privilege', that meant it was not going to be divulged.

"By this Order, the President of The United States does commission Angel Suarez-Rivera and Miranda Davida de Suarez to take actions consistent with the President's desire to obtain information about terrorist movements and/or illegal incursions into the United States across its Border with Mexico."

You could call it carte blanche because it contained no restrictions between the commission establishment paragraph and the President's signature; that section was all blank white space, and below the signature, the Presidential Seal. There were hundreds, maybe thousands of people who would kill for a carte blanche order from the President of The United States. Some would even call it a license to kill. Harry Foster called it "a level of confidence rarely shown by any President," as he spoke and delivered the document to Angel and Miranda Suarez; he had invited them to stop by his office to see the Order.

"Of course, you understand that the document cannot leave this office due to the classification phrase embodied in it. However, I can assure you both that it will be honored by the full faith of the government of the United States of America. I will see to that because seeing to it is my responsibility, given me by the President."

"Yes, of course, Mr. Foster, we understand." Brother Angel responded

"Now, Brother Angel, here are documents I have prepared for you to take with you. You will see they contain transcriptions of the conversations we had some days ago about the influx of Iranian terrorists into these various areas in Mexico. Each area has been clearly identified where the teams seem to have settled for the time being. To the best knowledge of our CIA people, that is where they remain to this day, at each town specified.

"From what they have been told by their informers in Iran the terrorists' plan is to prepare for coordinated acts of terrorism across the border, but there is no certainty how or where they plan to cross the border; you will note that most of these villages are quite remote. These we think are just staging areas where they can make plans and not be noticed. So, it's not readily apparent where the entry points will be at this point. Sooner or later they will have to be moving northward into the border towns. You can see how they are scattered across the country. I'll leave it to your best judgment as to how you will approach the problem. The one thing for certain is that there are no significant identifiable targets showing up yet.

"I have also obtained the most detailed maps we now have of the physical characteristics of the Mexican terrain, the elevation and the waterways, the roads and pathways, the fencing and railroads and the location of farms, small communities and industries. The other set, here, are detailed maps of the cities, the streets, the buildings, city dwellings and adjacent suburban homes and communities. As you can see, the types of shops and businesses are indexed and listed in the tables given and even some of the business names. By these maps, you should be able to know exactly where you are going before you get there; you can become knowledgeable of these places, able to speak confidently about almost any of the locations.

"You probably know that the American Dollar is the currency of preference in these border towns and if you are posing as tourists, it would be well to use dollars; that would normally be expected of tourists. In the briefcase you will find a supply of dollars in differing denominations, but mostly the smaller ones, singles, tens and twenties, that you will need to use as travelers in the border towns and the cities. But, in the lesser traveled areas you will be more likely to use pesos, old bills, typically the predominant currency, except for smugglers, government officials and drug dealers; they always use dollars. So, we have prepared a supply of old pesos in the briefcase as well, a larger quantity of course, due to the lesser value of the peso. You needn't be concerned about accounting for either the dollars or the pesos; they have already been accounted for. You may request additional currency supplies as needed by use of the debit card we have included."

"Hmm; I see the debit cards have our correct names on them. We won't be using an assumed name, then. That will allow anyone to check us out freely. Good. We will use our Missionary Association as the ostensible reason for our visiting those small villages where the terrorists are staying. There are many poor people in the rural villages, many uneducated. In truth, our Association has often talked about the need to make a survey of the conditions there with the idea of establishing foreign missions. It will work out well, we'll do both. Anyone checking on us will learn of out Association connection. I will inform the Association of our vacation trip so they won't be caught off guard by any calls."

"That should work out well; really, we couldn't have planned a better cover story. Excellent; tell me again, what is the name of the Association?"

"It is the Free Will Missionary Association of New Mexico; our offices are in Socorro."

"Very well," Foster continued, "Now, here is a package of other items," and he opened a small briefcase. "There are several sets of body wires and recorders, very small in size for convenience and in forms that should not be noticeable. Here, take a look, you see there are lapel pins, broaches, boutonnieres, key holders and other common items; each contains a tiny microphone. They transmit over a distance of about two hundred yards, so you will want to keep the recorder within that range. You may find these useful for recording your observations or for conversations with others."

"Oh, Angel, I haven't seen you wear a boutonniere since Pablo and Teresa's marriage. How long has it been? Twenty years, I think. Here, let me clip it on your lapel."

"Miranda, my dear, we don't have time for that sort of thing; now come on, we are wasting Mr. Foster's time."

The Mexicans

"There it is; it looks real. It really does! Now, Mr. Foster, let's slip the recorder into my purse; this one looks like a checkbook, let's use it. OK, did I turn it on correctly, Mr. Foster?"

"Yes, it's on and ready. It will be idle until a sound activates it; then it will record whatever the microphone picks up."

Miranda moved to her Angel and embraced him in a dance position. Then she snuggled up and whispered into the boutonniere, "I'm ready, my darling Angel; tell me something that I should know in secret."

"You are amazing, my love, simply amazing. Yo te amo, mi amor."

"Oh, Angel, I just love it when you speak romantic. Let's dance around the floor one time."

They danced a hesitation waltz, Br. Angel guiding, twirling them around the room, twice. Harry Foster couldn't help himself; he clapped at the demonstration.

"Oh, I wish I could dance Lydia around like that, so gracefully, so lovely."

"Thank you, Mr. Foster. Now, let's see what the recorder picked up. How do I play it back?"

"It's very simple, Miranda; just press the red button and say "playback"."

Miranda pressed the red button and spoke softly, "Playback."

The recording was clear and picked up even the breathing of Miranda as she whispered and as she danced. When it was over, Harry Foster asked her:

"Miranda, what did you say about speaking romantic?"

"I said, "Oh Angel, I just love it when you speak romantic.""

"Yes, that's it; that's what I thought you said. It reminded me of Lydia, for some reason." But he didn't go into that. "OK, you two dandy dancers; let's put the recorder up and continue with the rest of this.

"Now, here are poison pens, should you wish to render someone temporarily unconscious. Oft repeated injections will cause termination, so, while they might save your life, be careful handling them. Now, I know that you are a man of God, Br. Angel, a missionary, and I know that you are mostly responsible for bringing the Bible to Indian reservations and as a result, most of them have now accepted Christ. You were responsible for rescuing the downed airmen during Katrina. Now, there is hope that continued talks between our leaders might bring an agreement for the illegal immigration problem and this operation may have a great deal to do with that. Surely you would want to live to see that. Therefore, the pens."

"Yes, Harry, we would very much like to see that. You know much of their story; we have taken it as our calling to minister to lost people, providing a friendly voice to the unsaved and it truly has been our great blessing over the years. Now, this generation is very troubled; daily we see the growing influence of the Anti-Christ spoken of in the Revelation of John. We know that the coming of the Lord is described by these events. Of course, we want to be His witnesses in the world as these things unfold. This is our calling. Therefore, yes, the pens."

"Good, I understand full well your motivations and I'm almost persuaded it will be as you say, but I must constrain myself to matters I can reason with. This information that you and Miranda will gather will be of the utmost importance to the President and others working to protect the nation from these invaders and their plans to destroy. You understand the urgency of these worldly events."

"Of course, my friend; this world is where we must live and we must apply reason, as you say, to our worldly purposes. And God does not object to reasoning; He invites us through Isaiah, saying "Come and let us reason together." He wants us to use the intellect He has given us, and He follows by giving us a parable that requires reasoning; "Though your sins be as scarlet, they shall be white as snow; though they be red like crimson, they shall be like wool." The answer to the parable is clear to believers: Sin separates us from God and can only be washed clean by the spiritual blood of Jesus Christ, the sacrificial

Lamb of God; it is the crimson red blood that purifies the soul, making it pure as the Lamb Himself. There is reason to God's purpose, Mr. Foster, the reasoning that brings redemption. But a keen mind can be a stumbling block for those who must have intellectual probity to understand the mystery of God."

"Thank you for that, Br. Angel. You've been an inspiration in times past, as well. But now let me continue; it's very likely that many of your friends of the National Security Agency will be working on this same project on our side of the border. Your work, the gathering of intelligence, will aid their work day by day. I think John Smoltz has in mind to assign Phil Bragg and Bob Crumpton to lead the border operations. I'm told Smoltz is using your border assignment as incentive for them to accept their assignment on this side; it shows their esteem for your investigative talents, Brother Angel."

"Colonel Bragg and Major Crumpton are good men; that is comforting to know. We will look forward to working with them."

"Let me leave you for now while you get familiar with this material. When you feel prepared to begin the assignment we will arrange your return and you can make your plans. The time is upon us to begin. I'll be available to you at my office. Just call me when you are ready or if you have questions. And let me say it's a pleasure to have you on board, Mrs. Suarez."

"Thank you, Mr. Foster. Though I have remained quietly attentive, I am truly excited to be working with my husband again."

"And you will be his primary asset, I'm sure of that."

CHAPTER 10
The Suarez Connection

When Br. Angel and Miranda sat down alone together, they each took a deep breath and Miranda let out a slight sigh;

"My goodness, Angel, all this cash, we might as well wear 'CIA' on our jackets. If we are to be tourists shouldn't we be using traveler checks and credit cards?"

"Just what I was thinking, Miranda; as usual you are ahead of me. Yes; traveler's checks and credit cards and we buy our pesos from the local banks. And we wear tan shorts, white socks and sneakers from Wal-Mart, just like our neighbors do on vacation."

"Now, don't be putting down Patsy and Fred. They know how to go."

"That's what I meant, dear. We will do just what Patsy and Fred do and we'll be the perfect pair of tourists, taking bus rides all over the countryside. And the camera can't be an expensive one, either, remember that. Also, ball caps and beach hats and bright shirts with big flowers all over will do just right."

"That's the picture, Fred ... oops, sorry ... Angel. And don't forget to keep your little mike clipped inside your boxer shorts and turned on at the right times."

"What?? My 'little mike' turned on? He laughed and gave Miranda a big hug. You have a responsibility there, too, my dear. You'll have to operate the receiver."

"Oh, phoo, let's get serious, we can't stay here forever, though I must say it's been lots of fun being here with you. Give me some of those maps of the countryside, Angel; I want to pick out some interesting places to start. Let's not go too far down on the first swing through. You know, this is going to take us a while to make the rounds to all these places and do some sniffing and peeking while we're there; and there are more of them coming every week, he said.

"Now, Angel, I think we should get your travel agent to arrange a few local travel agents for us in Chihuahua and Durango and Culiacan and Hermosillo, those are all state capitols. There should be a hotel and restaurant in those towns. Then we schedule a week at each of those towns and take local bus trips around to the small towns where the Iranians have holed up, whatever the agent can arrange for a pair of old tourists. You can see there are at least a dozen of those locations they have spotted for us in those states, here on the map. One whole month in this western part and then we will plan to move into the east. What do you say, Angel? Is that a good plan for a starter?"

"After that I guess we'll do Saltillo and Monterrey and up to Nuevo Laredo and the border towns over that way. Yes, that's a good plan to begin with. Let's think it through for a couple of days and talk about it before we call the travel agent and set it in concrete. That'll give us time to shop for boxer shorts and pack a couple of bags; that is, if you've definitely settled on the boxer shorts."

"Oh, go on. Buy the jockeys if it means that much to you. By the way, Angel, are you going to bring this up to the Association? I wonder if there might be some contacts in Mexico we could use if we needed them."

"I've thought about that, Miranda. We can't reveal any of this even to our associates. I'll just have to take a vacation leave of absence while we do this work. They will know we are in Mexico observing conditions in the villages, but not what our business it. But, you are right about the contacts. Al Maldonado comes from down around Chihuahua. I'll tell him we're going to take a vacation down there and maybe he can give me some names and numbers; I'd like to have local contacts everywhere we go. You know, with a few to start with, we might be able to keep expanding the names and numbers as we go. As long as we know what sort of people they are and that will follow mostly from the first ones; Al is a Missionary and a good Christian man, you know his wife, Elena, don't you? She's been to some of the meetings."

"I know Elena and I know Al Maldonado. Are you losing your memory, Angel? You've been away from the Association for so long, you can't remember the old days anymore. I know we can't talk to them about this work we're doing, but we ought to keep up with our friends. Why don't we have them over for dinner as soon as we get back? Patsy and Fred, too. We'll have to ask them to watch the house while we're gone on vacation."

"Well, we can't just have Al and Elena over and not invite Ray and Martha Coronado and maybe Ben Figueroa and Josephine; they're back from Venezuela, aren't they?"

"Angel, I can't cook for all those people, I'll be a nervous wreck. We'll have to do it over two evenings, Friday and Saturday; you cook steaks and I'll get some of the sides from the deli. That way I can make the salad and the onion rings and bake sweet potatoes for two pies. No? Oh, OK, we'll have them all over Friday and we can sleep late Saturday."

"Good. I'd like to know what that guy, Jimenez is trying to do down there in Venezuela, and we'll get some names from Al. Nobody needs to know what we're going down there for; just a winter vacation. I'm going to call Harry Foster and tell him we'll go back tomorrow about 9 in the morning. He can arrange that and you and I will go out to a really nice restaurant tonight, after I get a shower."

"I'm ready to go, that sounds fine to me."

He called Harry Foster;

"Harry, Miranda and I have looked over the material and we have made a preliminary plan to begin. We are ready to return and prepare for our first incursion as tourists; that will take us through the weekend. Perhaps we can be on our way by early next week."

"Very good, Brother Angel; I'm sure the President will be pleased at that."

The Mexicans

"Can you arrange for our departure about mid-morning tomorrow and, if you can, let me know what Phil Bragg has decided, if he has made up his mind to take the assignment on the border. I'd like to call him, but I don't want to be premature. Also, we'll be going out in town for dinner at the hotel down the street; they have a dinner dance at the ballroom, I have noticed."

"That sound really nice; I wish I could dance well enough to go to one of those. I'll find out if Bragg has decided and let you know in the morning. Have a good time."

Miranda took the phone.

"Thank you, Harry. Come and visit us some time and we'll get you on the dance floor in a matter of a few hours. I don't mean to be impertinent, but you should learn to have a little fun now and then before you get too old to enjoy it; and bring Lydia. We'd love to have you down to Socorro, Harry. That is, anytime when we're not sneaking around below the border. See you in the morning."

"I'll keep that in mind, Miranda, and thank you. Enjoy your dinner and goodnight."

Dinner was exceptional: Lobster bisque, Greek salad, braised lamb chops in wine sauce, potato casserole with sharp cheddar, skewers of asparagus tips, stir-fried sugar peas and bean sprouts, apple pie ala mode and coffee. The wine was one of the best on the menu. The band began to play during dinner and the early dance couples took to the floor along with Br. Angel and Miranda. They always danced during dinner; it was good for the appetite and the fast two-step was good for the waistband. Miranda most loved the waltzes and Br. Angel often led her to the hesitation Waltz, her favorite. She loved to pose at each hesitation and look into the eyes of her Angel; he loved it too; Miranda was so beautiful and danced so gracefully. Afterward, they walked by moonlight, slowly back to the White House.

"Oh, Angel, what a lovely evening this has been! The dinner was so good and you danced like a twenty-eight year old; the band played all of my favorites, it was so romantic. Let's just walk awhile, I hate for it to end."

"I'm glad you enjoyed it, Miranda; I did too, but don't fret, it's not over yet, my dear."

"Angel, was I fretting?"

The White House guard recognized them and saluted.

Next morning, they were up to receive breakfast at 7 o'clock. At 8 o'clock, Harry Foster called to tell them their schedule for departure; they should be at the heliport at 9:15 for the flight to Andrews Air Force Base and from there on to Albuquerque. They were expected to arrive at Albuquerque at 5:10 pm with no scheduled stops.

"I talked to Phil Bragg this morning," Foster informed them as he escorted them to the heliport. "He is accepting the new assignment and Major Crumpton will be joining him as well. You may be interested to know, they each have been promoted as a result of their actions in the Mississippi River events; well deserved, I'm sure. Colonel Bragg now has the grade of Brigadier General; Major Crumpton has the grade of Lieutenant Colonel. They will begin setting up the new District operation right away; new offices early in December. Bragg hasn't selected a location as yet."

"Well, that is good news. Thank you, Mr. Foster."

As they turned to enter the helicopter, Foster called out;

"Come back anytime; the President and all of us enjoy your company."

"Give him our regards and you come to visit when you can find the time. Goodbye, Harry."

The flight to Andrews took less than ten minutes. The flight from there to Albuquerque had taken on an additional passenger to be dropped at Colorado Springs; they arrived at Albuquerque at 6pm, had dinner at a good restaurant, near the airport, and then drove the 75 miles to the stucco ranch house at Socorro. They were both tired out from the flight and settled down to rest before unpacking.

"Angel, have I been dreaming? I have this crazy idea that we, you and I, have taken on a job as a pair of spies and we're going on an endless set of bus trips sneaking peeks and taking pictures and recording conversations with hidden mikes in your shorts and my bra and we're doing it just for the fun of it. Shouldn't you call the psychiatrist or drive me straight to the nut house? Where in the world would I have gotten such a wild idea?"

"Yes, my dear, I promise to call a psychiatrist just as soon as we arrive at Chihuahua; and there we might both enjoy an exciting mental breakdown. Their facilities I am told are some of the best in Mexico. But, before we arrive there, I am hoping that it all gets sorted out and we are back to normal; two very healthy people, married, much in love, dancing our way through life, with plenty of hidden mikes and poison pens to ward off evil spirits. We need a really good night's sleep, my dear. It'll all look very natural in the morning, I promise."

"Well, I hope so, Angel. Would you pour me a small glass of Chablis, dear? I feel like I need a little help to relax."

He poured the wine and a glass for himself. "Well, I'll just fill yours to the brim, my dear, to set the stage for relaxing," and he winked the sly look that amused Miranda.

"Whatever you say, Angel."

CHAPTER 11
Movements

"Colonel Bragg, this is Angel Suarez, how are you?"

"Brother Angel, I'm fine, where are you?"

"We are at home in Socorro, getting organized for a long missionary trip. I am told that you will be attending to business in a new location and with a new grade level; that is good news, congratulations!"

"Thank you, Brother Angel. It's good to hear your voice. Yes, I have had a bit of good fortune. After the way things ended at the Mississippi the future looked a little uncertain, but Bob Crumpton saw that the evidence indicated a mole in our NSA house somewhere. Turns out it was a mole, an agent in the Detroit office. The conspirators were exposed and killed by their own hands. After they cleaned up that mess, we made it through the Congressional inquiry with high marks and that lead to the promotions. Crumpton was raised to Lt. Colonel and I got a star."

"That is good news; so let me call you General Bragg; now, that's much better."

"I know you didn't call to hear about all that, but I just wanted you to know how things turned out since you were such a big help to our operations down there. John Smoltz tells me that you and Miranda came through with your own high marks and a Presidential Order to play on his team under Harry Foster. John gave me a rundown on the kind of work you'll be doing and from what he said it looks like we'll be working in tandem again. I'm all for that."

"I am too, Phil. Harry Foster told me you'd be in the loop on this missionary work. That's good; we want to keep in close touch with you

The Mexicans

while we're there, that's one reason I called. We're going to do our best to be seen just as missionaries, down there to document the needs of the poor in the remote villages, but I think we should have a more secure means of communication back to you."

"The problem of communications did occur to me; I'll have the Comm guys include your cell phones into our security system; it uses the best of our encryption code systems."

"Yes, that's exactly what I had in mind; that would be ideal. We can begin right away using that linkup, can we?"

"Yes. I'll call and get it arranged right now."

"Fine; we've planned our first missionary trip sometime early next week as soon as I can arrange our travel connections, so you can expect to hear from me when we get on the bus. It's been good talking to you and please pass along my congratulations and best wishes to Bob Crumpton."

"I will and give my regards to Miranda. Good bye."

☙❧

General Bragg had been watching the news coming in from Oaxaca in lower Mexico; he was concerned enough to fire off a memo to John Smoltz.

"John, I'm real uneasy about sending Br. Angel and Miranda down into Mexico without any protection; these reports of uprisings in the south are disturbing, it may be only weeks before they move up to the north. I'd like to arrange for some undercover surveillance of the Suarez team; someone we could trust to keep them out of trouble. I'd recommend we run this idea by Foster, if you agree."

Smoltz was well aware of the political demonstrations in Mexico and had his own concerns. Bragg's memo was what he needed to get the ball rolling. He called Bragg right away.

"Phil, I agree with you and I'm sure you'll get the go ahead on this to get a man down there for that purpose, at least one. I'll pass your recommendation up to Foster; if I could make the decision right now,

I would. If I was closer to the action, like you are, I'd start the ball rolling and be ready for the go ahead. This is going out of here today, priority, with my comments to support you."

"I'll do it; I've got a man in mind. Thanks, John."

It was not long before Smoltz got the call back from the White House; Phil Bragg's request to send an undercover agent into Mexico was under consideration.

After speaking with General Bragg, Br. Angel called his travel agent.

"Yes, you heard right, Felix. We plan to travel by public bus transport from Socorro to Chihuahua and stopover for seven days. Then, we'll bus to Torreon and stopover seven days. Then, we'll bus to Durango, stopover six days. Then, we'll bus to Hidalgo del Parral and stopover six days. Then, we'll bus back to Socorro. We'll need two tickets, for Miranda and me. Also, make the reservations at the best accommodations available in each of those four cities. We will leave mid-week, next Tuesday, Wednesday or Thursday, whichever will make the best connections. And I will need the name and address of a reliable travel agent in each of those cities who can arrange local transport to the surrounding communities during those seven days at each location. Do you understand?"

"Let me see if I can read my notes." Felix repeated the itinerary and the local travel contacts. "I will need a day or so to put this all together, Br. Angel. It may be Monday before I can call you back, but, yes, I understand and I'm sure I can arrange this, at least within a day's leeway at each of the cities. But you must realize, Angel that the quality of the bus and taxi service in these remote areas down there will not be the best and I can't guarantee the quality of the hotels and restaurants, either."

"That will be alright. Let me know as soon as you have something. Thank you, Felix."

"One more thing, Br. Angel, dress very modestly, like missionaries; whatever you do, try not to appear as tourists in these remote villages,

The Mexicans

there are people there who lie in wait for tourists. And stay in groups whenever possible. Also, take pesos, small bills, no dollars, no traveler's checks, and make sure that your pesos are old bills, so that it will become known that your pesos are not marked. You are elderly and Latino, that is good if you appear not to have much money.

"Wear old shoes, they won't assail you for old shoes and small peso bills. Wear the hat of a padre, carry your Bible and don't smile much. You will gain their respect when they think you are a missionary, as of course you are. Give to the poor, loose change only, and shower your pastoral blessings liberally. If I'm not too presumptuous for asking, is your Association starting on a mission of mercy down there?"

"We go where we are needed, Felix. And thank you for the advice; we will do as you say and will be very cautious and pious. I appreciate your good wishes, Felix, my friend."

"I'll call you as soon as I have some of this scheduled. Goodbye."

"Miranda, my dear, do you remember how we planned our tourist persona back in the White House? How we would look like Wal-Mart manikins? Well, I just got the straight scoop on that; it's modest, worn clothes, old shoes, Padre hat, small pesos, old bills, the real missionary mantra. According to Felix we wouldn't last long with new shoes and travelers checks. I guess those federal agents know a thing or two after all."

"No lipstick, no eye shadow and mascara, no blond hairdo, no leather pants, no five inch heels? Oh, Angel, I'm afraid I just couldn't stand the change, really!"

"Make the sacrifice, dear. I'll still love you."

"Of course, dear; but what about my public image, the paparazzi, my self-esteem? Oh, dear, it's just too, too much!"

"The sacrifice, dear. The sacrifice is beautiful. And your natural beauty always shines through, you know that."

"You are right, of course. Peel those onions for me, would you, dear?"

CHAPTER 12
Resettlement Movements

As the first of the month approached, General Bragg had received congratulations from his many friends in the NSA and other government agencies, including Harry Foster, who sent a personal letter from the President, along with the normal Presidential letter of congratulations.

"I realize", said the letter, "that as a National Security Agency officer, the rank emblem of your Grade is not worn on your shoulder as a military man's rank is worn, but I am enclosing these General stars as my gift to you in appreciation of your very creditable martial works in protecting the security of our nation. I have asked that they be mounted within an appropriate frame along with this letter, which I have signed with great satisfaction and with my thanks and my highest regards. James Madison Cooper, President of the United States."

General Bragg was very proud that the President would select him for such an honor. On that day early in October, 2006, he took down his framed NSA Commission letter on the wall behind his desk and replaced it with the framed Presidential Letter with the mounted stars. It hung there, just over his right shoulder, opposite the photograph of Beatrice over his left shoulder. Unlike many of his counterparts, none of his degrees or letters of appointment or any other photographs graced his walls. A proud, capable man of discipline and action, he was not by nature an ostentatious man. He loved his wife dearly and he loved his work and lately, with the examples given him by certain of his associates, he had begun to love the Lord.

Now, with his new assignment officially begun, he turned his attention to his first need, an office location and the transition from the New Orleans office of the Louisiana District to the Border District office, newly created by order this day. He studied the maps he had been looking at for the past few weeks and made his decision as to the geographic locale. He wanted it in a central city, not too large, but with good living conditions and transportation. He decided to make a personal visit to Phoenix, Albuquerque and Amarillo Far enough from the border to be unobtrusive but close enough for quick access. The centrality of the office was not essential since his officers would be dispatched to various locales where they would operate in singles or in teams, as the situations demanded. He called Beatrice.

"Honey, can you be ready to go with me on a trip to select our new city site, say, by in the morning or early afternoon? I'd like to get underway on this and I know you're getting antsy, too. Let me know so I can arrange a flight out, can you?"

"Phil, dear, you know me well enough and that's why you already have selected the date and time. Yes, dear, I'm ready to get out of here; you know I'm pretty fed up with the smell of that river, what's left of it; it's getting to be oppressive. Morning will be fine, just call me when you know – I'm with you, babe."

"Gotcha. I'll get it done right away and let you know. Thanks, Hon."

Next he called Fuzzy Longmeier in Alexandria.

"Fuzzy, I'm going to get out of here for a few days and get a town lined up. Can you handle things for me?"

"You bet, Phil, I got you covered. When are you leaving?"

"I'll try for a morning flight, early afternoon if there's nothing out in the morning. Do you want to have Misti transfer calls or are you going to come here?"

"Guess I'll come there, Phil. Tell Misti I'll be there before noon, I'll leave here pretty early with Penny. By the way, I've heard the smell from that riverbed is getting pretty testy. D'you think it'll be too much for Penny? She's got a real squeamish stomach; bad tastes and smells sometimes make her nauseous."

"Well, I can tell you it's kind of overpowering when you're out in the street, but it's not as bad indoors. They're thinking it'll be about six months before they get the concrete laid through the city bed and that'll help a lot. You'll just have to take her to dinner in the Quarter pretty regular and she'll be OK, I think; they all like that treatment and John has been approving some extra expenses just for that. Besides, if I'm reading John right, he's going to offer you the District job; don't hold me to that, though."

"You're right, Phil, Penny's coming with me for sure. If I don't see you in the morning, have a good trip and don't worry about a thing; I'll call you if I need you."

"I'm not expecting you will. Thanks, Fuzzy; I'll see you when I get back."

"Misti, see if you can get me two seats out of here about mid-morning going to Phoenix. I'll be gone a few days; Longmeier will be coming in to relieve me late in the morning, so hold any calls for him unless it's bad important."

"Yes sir, General, I'll call you right back."

Misti liked the new title, "General"; she liked working for a General. "It's as high as you can go." She was hoping that Jon Olafsen would get the call from Bragg to join his operations on the border. That'd mean they would get married and she could maybe keep her job as Bragg's Assistant, or even something better. Everyone in the District wanted to go with Bragg to the new frontier.

General Bragg packed his briefcase with a few essentials, extra telephone, a few maps; most of what he needed was on the laptop. He wasn't going to carry any business with him on this time out except for the new assignment and he was glad Longmeier had decided to come to New Orleans to take charge in his absence. For sure, he would be the pick for Bragg's replacement, mostly because Bragg had recommended him. John Smoltz knew there were some bad feeling from the past between those two, but he also knew that Bragg had a high regard for Longmeier's ability and his morals, two things that Smoltz had to have outstanding in his District leaders.

"Colonel, oops, I mean, General, you're on flight 812 leaving at 9:15 in the morning, direct to Phoenix with, ahem, only two stops, arriving at 3:18; you know me, I get the best for you. Is that OK?"

The Mexicans

"Direct with only two stops. Yeah, that's OK; we don't get much direct service out of here anymore. Now, see if you can get us a car at the airport, full size Buick. I don't know how long we'll want to stay at each of these places, so I may make our other reservations myself, but I'll call you and let you know what we'll be doing. We'll be in each town for two or three days, then return and we'll need cars at the other airports, too. I'll let you know more when I call in. The tickets will be at the airport?"

"Yes, at the check in counter."

"Thanks, Misti. How's Jon doing? You talk to him more than I do."

"Oh, General, you know Jon's doing fine. He's just lonely."

"Reckon he'd like a border assignment?"

"He'd – we'd love it."

Bragg's phone interrupted them; it was Bob Crumpton.

"General, I just got off the phone to a buddy of mine in Wyoming, Carl Burkett. Carl operates a charter fishing business; he takes groups of fly fishermen to remote places in the Rockies, Wyoming and Montana, and he does a lot of week-long trips into the Canadian Rockies and the wilderness areas of Canada. He had some news that got my ears itching. You listening?"

"Yeah, yeah; go ahead."

"Well, turn on your recorder; this may be serious."

"You're on."

"Well, Carl was flying a group into a clearing up in northern Saskatchewan, near a cabin he uses and he sees a small plane taking off; so in a few minutes they get to their touchdown strip in the clearing and there was small prop plane on the lake getting ready to take off and about six guys waiting to get in. This thing took off really steep; it had to, to get that bunch of guys out of that little clearing, so it had plenty of power. What was strange; it was more guys than usual for a normal fishing bunch – they normally take four - and none of them had fishing equipment; no backpacks, no obvious gear, no fishing hats, not even a ball cap. They didn't seem to have any luggage unless it was already loaded."

"Big fishing party, so what?"

"Well, Carl's been in the business for a long time but he says he's never taken that big a group in a small plane and they all looked like Ali Baba, know what I mean? If they'd had luggage it could have been overloaded, but it didn't act like it was carrying an extra load. So, I'm thinking, drop offs into Mexico; why not drop offs into Canada?"

"I get it, Bob. Where would that plane go to unload the six guys?"

"Carl says they could go nearly anywhere, Canada or the States; fishing parties are so common they get flagged through just by their registration number and visual appearance, along with the pilot's call-in. They figure their fishing and hunting traffic is routine so they just pass them through without inspection; good neighbor policy on the border. They could be headed anywhere and not draw suspicion, 'cause it's a big tourist business and they spend a lot of money on license and fees every trip."

"We've got to get a handle on that operation. How about looking into it a little more and get back to me? I'm headed out for a few days. Did your friend get the aircraft number? See what you can find out, would you, Bob?"

"I'll check with Carl; I think he may have seen the registration; anyway he can ask around and see if anyone else has seen that kind of thing going on. I'll pursue it with Air Traffic Control. Have a good trip, Phil."

CHAPTER 13
The Mexican Direction

Miranda's dinner was keeping her busy and she loved it; it had been some time since she'd had six guests for dinner, but it was always easy when Angel did the steaks on the barbecue. It was fun picking things up at the deli and fun making just a few things, biscuits and desserts. The real cooking was left to Angel and his magic grill; he could turn out some delights on that grill as long it started out as a cow, or a pig, or a chicken. And he always knew just the right mix of barbecue sauce or steak sauce; moderate to suit the tastes of everyone. So Miranda was at ease, now, with the rest of it in his hands. She poured the wine, seeing that Angel gave her the nod.

"Now, Al, I'm counting on you for some names of contacts down there; that's your home town and you have lots of friends, is that right?"

"Yes, Angel, my roots go all around down there, especially in the north. Give me a day or so to dig out the addresses and telephone numbers; some of those friends I haven't talked to in years, but we always send Christmas cards and we get notices of births and marriages all through the year. Everyone likes to get a present from the U.S. and we like to keep up appearances, too. We usually go down there on vacation to visit family a couple of times during the year and then we get calls for visits by the Association, now and then, as well. By the way, what's got you interested in a long vacation, if you don't mind my asking?"

"Oh; well, you know Miranda and I haven't been through Mexico before, except for a business visit, now and then. This is the first time we've really got the bug to see the old country. I'm kind of interested in the arts and crafts. I have thought about the possibilities of opening up a distributorship in Albuquerque; it might be good for retirement income; you know, importing unusual things."

The Mexicans

"Maybe so, Angel, but could you sell enough of it around here to make it pay?"

"People go crazy in some of those cities up north for really good art and unusual jewelry and deco items. I noticed that while we were on that last mission. If nothing else, it could give me something to do that might keep me active, but I'm not so sure I could make it pay for itself. By the time I get through this first swing, though, I expect to know more about that and where to go for the better quality works. Those places are down in Mazatlan and Oaxaca, those ancient places."

"Hey, Angel, I'd be careful. You might want to think twice about going down into the south of the country. Have you been watching the news? They've had some really big uprisings in those cities by the Socialists – it's the Julio Jimenez people gaining political influence. In fact it turned into lawless rioting in Oaxaca; you don't want any of that. But the import business sounds like a good idea for a retirement. I'm still a little young, but you're in position to be doing things you want to do, not things you have to do. Besides, you'll still be in the Association, right?"

"Oh, yes, we'd never want to give that up. You're right about Oaxaca; I just hope it doesn't spread north while we're down there. I'm hoping this may be a way to direct some Association work down that way among the poor villages; the government doesn't seem able to help them. Say, you won't forget to write down those contacts for me, will you? I'd feel a lot better going places where I know someone and can get some idea of areas to avoid."

"I won't forget. Hey, those steaks look like they're about done, don't they? I'll have one kind of medium rare if you can do one that way. Elena likes hers well done."

"I'm holding yours over here on the edge of the burner keeping it warm, it's just about the way you like it, no blood, just a little red streak in the center."

Ben Figueroa walked up with the red wine.

"You guys ready for a glass?"

"Sure, Ben, but put just a touch of wine in it for me, would you? It goes well with the glass." Al kidded a lot.

"Ben, while we're on the subject, what's going on down there in Venezuela? I saw where Jimenez was getting friendly with the Iranians. Is Jimenez just a Marxist like Fidel or does he have greater designs on the entire continent?"

"Yeah, I saw that, too. Jimenez is like a fox; I think he's a Castro want-to-be. It looks like he's building a military-political party like the Sandinistas had in Guatemala. Only he's got the oil money to do it fast and he passes it around to dissidents in some of the other countries. I think he's trying to get his hands on the whole continent, maybe Mexico, too. I heard he was pumping lots of money up there to get a political party established that he can control. We need to keep our eyes on him."

"I hope the CIA is doing that. There's a lot of feeling building up in Mexico against the U.S and we don't seem to know how to control the border. I hate to say it but we're experiencing an invasion and it can't be good for those of us who have our history up here. It can't be good for anyone if it gets out of control and it looks like it might get that way." Al had some real misgivings about the politics of immigration in the U.S.

"Invasion is a military term, Al, these people are generally peaceful." Figueroa wasn't afraid of the Mexican workers.

"Yes, you're right, Ben," Br. Angel interjected, "but if Jimenez can turn Mexico into a Socialist country, like he seems to be doing in Venezuela, he might make it a military problem. At any rate, we have to recognize that things are changing in this hemisphere. The U.S. doesn't seem to have the influence that we did twenty or thirty years ago and that may not be a good thing. We'd do well, I think, to outfox Jimenez in Mexico before things get really out of control. The people need jobs; that would help a lot."

"Food for thought, Angel," Miranda stepped in to suggest dinner. "Right now, we need food for the body. Are those steaks ready?"

The Mexicans

"All ready, dear. Do you want to bring the plates or will these paper towels be alright?"

"Smarty."

The steaks were just right; at least everyone said so. The evening social all went well; Br. Angel picked up the information he was looking for; Al Maldonado had prepared the list he had promised for contacts, and the guests talked of Miranda's dinner for a week.

By Monday morning Br. Angel and Miranda were ready to go, only waiting to hear from Felix as to their arrangements for transportation and hotels; at 11:30 Felix called with the itinerary arranged.

"You will leave tomorrow morning at 10:20 from Socorro and travel by Greyhound to El Paso arriving at 4:30pm where you will spend the night at the Melody Inn. Wednesday morning you will leave the City Bus Station at 9:00 am on Lineas Mexico for Chihuahua, arriving there at 3:35pm. Your reservations are at the Chihuahua Mejor hotel for the seven night stay you wished. You will leave Chihuahua on Lineas Mexico at 8:40 am for Torreon arriving at 4:18pm and you will stay at the Casa Hermosa for seven nights.

"You will leave Torreon at 7:55am on Lineas Mexico for Durango arriving at 12:50, staying at Hotel Durango for six nights. You will leave Durango on Lineas Mexico at 7:30am for Hidalgo del Parral where you will stay at the Villa Hidalgo for six nights. You will leave Hidalgo at 6:50am for Ciudad Jimenez where you will change buses leaving at 8:10 for El Paso, arriving at 6:05pm, where I have you staying at the Melody Inn leaving the next morning at 9:25 on Greyhound to arrive in Socorro at 3:30pm.

"I think you will find the accommodations satisfactory, but I'm not sure of the Hidalgo hotel. You may wish to change your itinerary if you find the place unsuitable. The hotel there will assist you in arranging auto transportation to the local towns. I have the names and addresses of reliable travel agents for you in the other cities. If you can stop by today, I'll go over the ticketing with you or, if you prefer, I can run by your place and deliver them to you later this afternoon when I close up here."

The Mexican Direction

"Yes, Felix, I'd appreciate that, if it's not too much trouble for you. We will expect you around 5pm or so?"

"That will be good. I'll see you then."

"Miranda, we are leaving in the morning at 10:20 from the Greyhound bus station. We'll be spending the night at the Melody Inn at El Paso. Felix will deliver our tickets and the hotel reservations this afternoon after he closes. We can finish packing this evening and be ready to leave after breakfast. I'll see if Patsy will mind driving us to the bus station."

"Wait a minute, Angel, I'll walk over to her house and talk for a few minutes. I just saw her in the yard so I know she's at home. I'll be right back. We'll leave at 9:30, is that OK?"

"That might be soon enough. Or we can leave at 9 and have coffee at the Breakfast Nook after we check our bags; it's just a block or two from the station; we can walk."

"I'll let you know about that; let's see what Patsy says. Oh, and don't forget to call and stop the paper. I'll be right back, dear."

Next morning at 9:15 they checked their bags at the bus depot; their bus was running on time from Albuquerque. Patsy let them off at the Breakfast Nook and said goodbye, hoping to hear from them now and then. She had the house keys and would take up their mail, visit and feed the dogs everyday and clean the dog mess from their back yard, and check on the appliances once in a while. She was glad to be of help.

"Just call us now and then, so we don't worry so much."

Alone now, Br. Angel looked into Miranda's loving eyes.

"Have I told you lately that I love you?" and he gave her that sheepish smile. "Well, Darlin' I'm telling you now."

"Why don't you sing it to me like you used to, Angel? No one will mind, they're all busy with their breakfasts. The waitress looks kind of romantic, too."

75

The Mexicans

She liked to kid him at times like this.

"You know how coffee affects me in the morning, dear."

"Yes, I know, and don't think I don't appreciate it, Angel, but this isn't the place for your coffee romance. Did you see my new nighty I bought for the trip?"

"No, let's see it, are you wearing it underneath?"

"Silly. We'd better be getting back to the bus depot; we wouldn't want to miss the bus and the Melody Inn."

As he chuckled, they left the Breakfast Nook, walking hand in hand down the street.

The ride was comfortable and scenic; much better than they had imagined.

"Leave the driving to us", Miranda read the sign over the driver's seat. "This is fun, Angel."

They played the 'guess what I see' game for awhile and then moved on to the license tag game and then made faces back at the kids in the cars passing them on the road, ignoring the birdies. A glance at the sports page and then they were stopping for lunch in Truth Or Consequences at the popular restaurant there.

"Baked chicken and rice, that's nice."

Br. Angel loved baked chicken. A short nap and a half hour stopover at Las Cruces waiting for the connecting passengers on the bus from Deming and then they were on their last leg. Br. Angel had time to review their Mexican itinerary several times before they reached El Paso, just a minute late. The taxi driver was a Middle Eastern man who said very little.

"Taking a job from an illegal immigrant", Br. Angel thought, "or maybe not."

They settled into the room at the Melody Inn with the king size bed, washed up and changed for dinner downstairs.

The Mexican Direction

"Miranda, we'd better soak up all the comforts we can tonight, after this night it's not going to be the same for a few weeks."

"Don't think a thing about it, Angel; think of all those who are hungry tonight."

"Amen, my dear. You are so right and I'm so forgetful sometimes, I'm ashamed."

"Don't you say that Angel. You've given the best years of your life to help those who suffer. It's just that sometimes we fail to count our blessings. God knows you are doing what He put you here to do; everyone who knows you knows that, even the President knows that. Let's go down early for dinner."

"That's fine, dear, I'm hungry, too. I'll take just a minute to call Phil Bragg and see if we are using his NSA special telephone service now."

He dialed the special number and received the automatic voice response.

"Who do you wish to speak with, please?"

"General Bragg, please."

"One moment, please."

"Phil Bragg, here."

"Well General Bragg, this is Angel Suarez. I'm in El Paso, calling from the Melody Inn, just testing your NSA service; it seems to work. Miranda and I will leave at 9 in the morning for Chihuahua. I'll call you soon after arriving there tomorrow evening, to test my cell connection. I'm not sure how well that operates down in Mexico."

"OK, Br. Angel; it looks like we have a good relay system. How'd it work for you?"

"I just dialed and the automatic voice asked me who I wanted to speak to and I answered "General Bragg". The voice said, "One moment, please" and then you answered. Just like clockwork."

"They've improved it a lot; that's really nice. Well, you and Miranda have a good journey and call me real often so we'll know your safe. Take care, now."

"We will, Phil. Goodbye."

"Give me a minute to wash up, dear; then I'll be ready to go."

Next morning, they got up a little later than usual, went down to breakfast at 7 and were ready for the taxicab at 8:15 for the short ride to the bus station. Lineas Mexico was the largest passenger bus service in the Country, serving all the cities and towns on the main highways with regular service. The bus was comfortable but not quite the same as the Greyhound. The odor of Mexican food was pungent, the restrooms were less than spic and span and there was litter on the floors and some of the seats. This particular bus had traveled overnight from Monterrey, had been serviced and was now headed back with a fresh driver.

The bus crossed the river bridge and stopped at the bus station in Ciudad Juarez, the border city just across the Rio Grande. They were scheduled for a thirty minute stop there taking on passengers and the bus was fully loaded when they departed, with a dozen or more passengers standing. The next stop was at El Sueco about two and one-half hours away. After the first twenty minutes the passengers who had been standing, by then were sitting on the floor and in the stairwell, several of them asleep. After stopping at El Sueco, they would have another two hours to go before arriving at Chihuahua.

Miranda leaned her head over on Br. Angel's shoulder and closed her eyes.

"Angel, if I should go to sleep, please don't wake me until we arrive."

They didn't talk much with the bus being so crowded and the chatter was constant. Now and then Miranda would ask "How much longer, dear?"

When they made the El Sueco stop, the aisles cleared and the atmosphere wasn't as oppressive.

"Just another two hours from here, then we'll be there. Hold on, dear."

Miranda sat up and began reading her book. She didn't bring the picture books that they liked to spend time looking through as they traveled; she didn't want to open any unnecessary conversations and have to explain away all of the snapshots, deciding it was best to be cautious on this assignment. They both missed that pleasant distraction, but they'd find other things to keep their minds occupied; the countryside was enough to keep them from being bored. Finally;

"Chihuahua! Oh, I'm so glad we've arrived. I really need to stand and stretch, Angel. Gee, this looks like a big place."

CHAPTER 14
Scouting the Territory

"Miranda, I want you to stay close by me while I get our luggage and a taxicab, I don't know much about this city except what I have learned from the map. Our hotel is not far from here, but we may have time to drive by the office of our travel guide as we go. Let's get off, now."

They got their rolling bags and exited the bus station where there were two taxicabs, unoccupied.

"A quando es la oficina del Senor Gutierrez, Agente de Viajar? Is it nearby?" he asked the first taxi driver.

"Si, la oficina del Senor Gutierrez es centro, cerca, es muy cerca de aqui. Just a few blocks, Senor."

"Good, you speak English. If you will take our bags, we will check into El Chihuahua Mejor, and then you may drive us to the office of Senor Gutierrez."

"Yes, sir; please get in," and he put the bags in the trunk.

In just a few minutes they were checked into the hotel. Br. Angel decided to call one of Al Maldonado's references who lived in Chihuahua. His mother answered.

"I'm very sorry," she told him, "Luis is in Monterrey for the week. But he will be back on Sunday. Could you call back then?"

"Yes, of course, but is he usually in Monterrey during the week?"

"He is there this fall going to the University, but he is able to come home on Saturday and he returns on Monday, if those political Socialist groups will leave him alone."

"Well, I'll try to call him then; thank you very much."

"Well, dear, we'll just wait a few days to begin looking over this city; Luis Gonzales is in Monterrey. Al gave me other names, but let's see what we can arrange in some of the nearby towns."

He instructed the desk clerk to have their bags taken to their room, and then they left in the taxi for the office of the travel agent. Felix had telephoned ahead to advise Juan Gutierrez of their arrival and that they would be in need of local transportation. He was pleased to see them at his office. Although it was just about closing time, he stayed open while they talked.

Br. Angel had five towns to investigate from there, besides Chihuahua. They were Ojinaga to the northeast at the border, Cuauhtemoc and Guerrero, mountain towns to the west, El Sueco to the north and Buenaventura, west from El Sueco.

"We may want to stay the night if there are facilities for us in these towns, otherwise we will have to return here on the same day. What can you suggest?"

"Well, Brother Suarez, I can arrange fairly good accommodations for you, but they may not be as excellent as you might be used to; some will be at haciendas that will take visitors overnight, some at small hotels or rooming houses. Let me take a little time and I'll have arrangements for you in the morning by ten o'clock. There will be a bus leaving for the mountain towns at noon, if you wish to begin there. We often have calls for visitors, mostly sightseers. Felix advised me that you were missionaries on assignment to assess the needs of the rural poor."

"Yes, I am making a needs survey, hoping to open up opportunities to do field work. We will gauge the economic conditions of our Mexican brothers in rural areas. This is our first effort; we hope to make good contacts and get a fair appraisal of the most urgent needs, to begin with. Tomorrow morning will be just fine. We will see you at ten o'clock. Thank you very much, Mr. Gutierrez."

The hotel they were staying in was bright and clean; the room was satisfactory, though not up to U.S. standards. There was enough hot water for showers before dinner. And the bed, though sagging in the middle, was alright.

"Oh, we've had much worse in some places we've been, Angel, I can't complain over anything here. It's clean and so am I, now, after that terrible bus ride."

"Let's see how well they can cook, dear."

"Arroz con pollo, my favorite. I think this is the standard dinner fare south of the border, along with the plantains and other local vegetables, which are really quite good."

"I like anything you like, Angel. Let's enjoy our time together. This can be an exciting experience if we let it. Best of all, the people are friendly and they respect us for our missionary work; that is a definite plus. You don't find that all the time in the States, at least not up north."

"You're right, Miranda, as usual. I'm looking forward to the rural conditions even more than this city environment. I believe we have a learning experience ahead of us in those mountain villages. Let's keep a good diary of this trip; it will be useful for the Association in planning its foreign missions. I think we have ignored these people too often in the past."

Breakfast was cereal and fruit, different fruits they had not tasted, not until now and they enjoyed the strong coffee.

"These people really like that strong Cuban style coffee. I may have to start using cream with mine while we're here; it tastes really good with cream, Angel, you should try it."

Miranda liked to start every day on a positive note.

"It was all very good, dear, but I did add a bit of sugar to the coffee while you weren't watching me. Next time, I'll use the cream instead."

They took their time at breakfast and walked the downtown streets for half an hour before returning to the hotel to get ready for their day, which they expected would take them to the mountain village of

Cuauhtemoc. They packed their bags before going to meet with Juan Gutierrez at his office.

"Here is my plan for your itinerary, Brother Suarez. You will go first to Cuauhtemoc, leaving here at noon and arriving there an hour later. The road is very good to this town and you will find the tourist house where you will stay to be very nice and the food is also good. I have you there until tomorrow at 2:30 when there is a bus going to Guerrero. It may be that you will want to spend longer that one day at Cuauhtemoc and if so, you can delay the Guerrero visit for the next day and take a morning bus to Guerrero at 7:30. Now, Guerrero is about an hour's ride. You'll have an hour before the bus returns from Guerrero, so you can decide if you want to stay over or return the same day.

"For your next visit, you will want to take the morning bus from Cuauhtemoc to Buenaventura, leaving at 6:30, arriving at 9:20. The accommodations are quite comfortable in this pleasant little town and the same bus leaves from there ten minutes later, at 9:30 going to El Sueco, where you will also have good accommodations. When you decide to return to Chihuahua from El Sueco, you will take the same bus that you were on when you came here from El Paso, it is a daily bus on the same schedule and it will stop at El Sueco at about 1:30. You should be there a few minutes before that or you might miss the bus.

"There is a bus leaving for Ojinaga each morning at 6:30 arriving there at 9. Ojinaga is a border town and there is a fairly nice hotel there, with restaurant. The returning bus leaves at 4:30pm and again at 6:30 the next morning, except on Sunday. Departures from Chihuahua are daily including Sundays.

"Should you need to leave sooner from any of these towns, you might find a publico that can take you, but I can't give you a reliable schedule for any of those. A publico is a private car with a licensed driver and they run whenever there is enough demand to make it pay, so you can hire one just for yourselves if you need but it will cost at least three times as much because they often carry six or more passengers, when they can. It is not unusual for a publico to leave on a regular schedule if there are workers who make the trip each day, but we can't rely on that. Does this schedule look satisfactory for your needs?"

"One question; is it usually necessary to make a reservation for any of these bus routes?"

"No, Br. Angel, they don't take reservations, it is always the first come basis. But, it is rare when the seats are all full, except sometimes at stops along the way for local residents going short distances."

"I think this will be satisfactory. We will be back here in about 5 days, unless we decide to stay longer at one of the towns. If we do, we will decide on Ojinaga then. We will want to stay a day longer here before leaving again. If necessary, we will adjust our plans for the remainder of our trip. I will pay you now and again if we need your services later on."

They paid Mr. Gutierrez a reasonable fee and ordered a taxi to take them to the bus station. It was nearly noon, time for their departure. The prospect of being on their own now was exciting, but there was a little apprehension, as well. To assuage the possibility of attracting robbers, they had dressed in very common, older clothing and shoes. Both wore the headdress typical of missionary workers, black hat for Angel and dark scarf for Miranda. Their bags were obviously worn and they rarely laughed out loud.

Before the bus departed they held hands and prayed for a safe journey. Others bowed in prayer with them when they saw what they were doing. Nearly everyone in these rural cities and towns were devout Christians, mostly Catholic. The prayer gave them comfort and they felt at ease as the bus pulled out on its way to Cuauhtemoc.

CHAPTER 15
Location is Everything

Phil Bragg made a few calls before he and Beatrice left for the airport. His three-city selection tour to choose the new District office location was important to him but the selection of his staff for the new Border District was really more important and he wanted to let his choices be known as soon as possible, now that the plan had been divulged. His most important choice, Bob Crumpton, had been settled weeks ago; he was to be the lead agent and control all District operation assignments. Eventually, he would take over as Director.

Bragg had dropped the word to Swede Olafsen obliquely by mentioning it to Misti, and now that there had been enough time for Misti to call Swede, he wanted to get that one settled, so he called him first.

"Jon, I need you with me in the new Border District. It's your choice to make but I want you to know I made my choice some time ago. You don't have to give me a definite answer now, but now's a good time to be thinking of it. Do you have any thoughts yet, yes or no?"

"Sure, Colonel, oops, I mean, General; sure I have thoughts on it. I'm with you all the way; I wondered when you'd call, if you'd call. Of course you know that Misti and I are planning to get married, so she'll be coming with me. That'll leave the New Orleans office without a secretary and I think she's thinking about maybe having an opportunity with you in the new District, maybe the same job as now or maybe not. When you get back from your trip maybe you can let her know what you have in mind. But as for me, I'm in and thanks for asking me."

"Misti goes with you, I know that. That's why I had to get your situation settled first. I think I might have mentioned, I guess around the time she worked the undercover decoy with you and Solomon and the wire, that she might have a future as an agent in training. That little sting operation went off without a hitch, thanks to all three of you, but Misti was the key and she was the one putting her life on the line, so, yeah, I've got plans for her and it's not as my secretary. She's a natural like Mandy, with good potential and plenty of guts. She could be my newest agent on the street and I hope that doesn't make you nervous."

"I agree with you, totally. She'd be great on the team in more ways than one. Do you mind if I sort of drop the word to her, not officially, but maybe unofficially?"

"Go ahead, I wouldn't want to see her tear up, it might cause me to change my mind about her. I'll see you when we get back, Swede. I guess you know that Crumpton's on board. Take care, now."

"I'll do it, General; and thanks."

Next he called Ron Jensen.

"Ron, I know you must like it over there in that Baton Rouge assignment, but I'm going to offer you an opportunity to get away from the smell of that river bed if you want to join my new District on the border. How far along are you with romancing that little girl Amy? Reckon that'll be a problem?"

"Hello, General, I appreciate you calling. Amy and I are getting married next Sunday at her Church in Natchez; everyone in town is going to be there. She's been treated like a local hero since she helped us clean out that farm full of terrorists. I came a long ways to find the girl who could hogtie me and make me like it and she did that. Randy and I have been thinking about going if and when we would get the call. Have you talked to Randy?"

"Not yet, but I'm about to. You don't have to make up your mind now; I'm leaving for a week or so to visit a few cities over west of here to decide on an office location. Just let me know when I get back; I'll call you."

"No need for that, General, I've already decided I'd go with you if you asked me. I've about got to the point of asking Amy to come, but I didn't want to until I got your call; I know she'd love to go with me as soon as we get married, if not sooner. By the way, thanks for the promotion to First Lieutenant. Maybe I'll be ready for those Captain bars in a couple years."

"Well, tell Amy I admire what she did for us back at that farm in Natchez, with her inside reporting and the testimonies she got for us. That was some important eyewitness evidence that helped cinch the warrants we needed to go in. She's a brave little girl and smart; if she comes with you, maybe she can be of help again. Anyway, give her my regards, and I'm glad to know you'll be on the team. I'll be talking to you in a week or so. Take care."

"OK, General; I'll tell Amy what you said. That'll make her day, maybe her year; she loves this work."

They arrived at the airport with time to spare, so he made a few more calls. Randy was pretty well settled in at Lafayette with Mandy and wasn't sure that she'd be too anxious to make the change.

"I'll see how she takes it, General, and I'll call you back, if you don't mind."

When he told Mandy that Bragg had called with the offer, she jumped up, excited.

"Oh, Randy, that is so great! When will we be leaving? I've got to tell Mama, I know she'll be excited, I can't wait to go. You should have told him we'd be going, call him back, Randy, call him back right now."

So, that was that; Randy called Bragg and signed on, so to speak. Phil Bragg was pleased at that; he knew them for a really good team. He often spoke of that special investigative work they did when they made those cold turkey visits and convinced those truck drivers to work with them and to drop off the drums and other evidence Bragg needed to obtain the warrants. He would have hated to lose either of them. Randy was promoted to 1st Lieutenant after just six months as an Officer. Bragg had plans for Mandy as a recruit.

Before the plane left, Bragg had talked to Shepherd Turner, who had recently gotten engaged to Bobbie Beauchamps. They were ready to go, just hoping for the call. Their wedding had been planned for

The Mexicans

weeks and the big day was nearly here, next Sunday afternoon at the Blessed Savior Catholic Church in Baton Rouge. With his new rank of Major, Bobbie was so proud of him she couldn't believe he would really be hers until he handed that ring to the priest. And then she couldn't keep her hands off of him. Shep was a really handsome guy and he loved Bobbie with all his heart and soul.

Simon Pederson was single and loved to travel; Bragg was pleased with Simon's investigation at the Winnfield mine, especially his fearless fighting during the takedown of the terrorists. He took his wounds in stride and was back on the street in little more than a week. No one ever hated a hospital bed like Simon Pederson. Simon received decorations for valor and had been promoted to Captain.

And last but not least, he asked David Solomon, the third member of the Misti team that exposed and brought to justice the terrorist collaborators that had infiltrated Bragg's own office in New Orleans. Solomon loved being a part of Bragg's command. He was promoted to Captain for that undercover job. Bragg saw Solomon as a rising star.

By that time, they were ready to board the flight to Phoenix.

"Well, Phil, now that I've got you back, how'd it all turn out? Did you get the ones you wanted?"

"It all worked out just fine, Hon, we're going to be just fine, and it's a relief off of my mind to get those decisions settled. One thing you'll like, though, is the weddings that will be taking place over the next couple weeks. Ron Jensen has finally asked Amy Neville to marry him. I guess he had to face it; it was true love between them and he didn't want to have to leave her. She's really a sweet girl and crazy out of her mind for Ron. He's her fairy prince come to take her out of Natchez and she nearly swoons whenever she get close to him. They'll have a really nice wedding; her family is very traditional."

"Well, bless his soul; he finally took the plunge. Lucky guy; she's a real prize."

"And then, Jon Olafsen, you know, 'Swede', and Misti Fontaine will be getting married before long and that should be a big church wedding

Location is Everything

in New Orleans just before they leave for the border. We've all known how that would turn out; big romance, two swell people."

"Jon reminds me so much of you when you were his age; just about when I snagged you, too. When I think of Jon, I think of an action hero, like in the comic books. I know you think a lot of him, and Misti, too."

"I guess I'd put him up there right next to Bob Crumpton. It was a real pleasure to promote him to Major; he earned it and I expect before long he'll force me to promote him again; he's worth every penny. Here's another one, a super agent; Shepherd Turner and Bobbie Beauchamps are engaged and will be marrying in about a week at Baton Rouge. That'll be a beautiful Cajun wedding, just like Mandy's. We won't want to miss that one. Her folks are down home, traditional, really nice, good people."

"Oh, yes, I love it; those Cajun weddings are so festive. They aren't just about getting married; they're about eating and dancing and toasting the couple all day long; the whole day's planned around it and I do, I just love it."

"Of course, you know about Bob Crumpton and Rebecca Delocher. Well, they'll be getting married but I'm not sure when; she still has to finish the school year at LSU. She may want to transfer to another school and just go ahead and leave with Bob, but I don't know. Bob hasn't said much about changing their original plans. That will be a terrific wedding there at Slipsom. He's a member of her church and they all love him like one of their own, around there. So, we'll wait and see about that one. But that's four weddings, Bea; you'll have to buy a few more dozen handkerchiefs to get ready."

"I know it, Phil; I've gotten to know and love every one of them, especially since that awful war on the river. Things like that draw us very close to each other. I feel such a close kinship with them all, now, knowing that any one of them may have saved your life, and you, theirs. Such closeness I couldn't have imagined until you went through that whole night of shooting and killing. They're all like family and I still can't get over Reggie being all shot up like that and dying."

The Mexicans

Phil Bragg started to tear up a little, just thinking of Reggie Halbrook and the closeness he felt to each of his agents.

"You know, Bea, I'm not sure I should stay with them on the border; maybe we should just go ahead and take the D.C. post. When you get so personally close to your people it can make a difference in how you handle things, you know, discipline and the like. I've thought a lot about it and I've worried some."

"Oh, Phil, I know how it must be, they're like your own. But, don't forget, you have Bob Crumpton who'll be directing things on the ground and he's the perfect one for it. You'll have to be in D.C. a lot, too; you know what John Smoltz told you. As his Adjutant, he's expecting you to take a hand in other Districts as well. I don't think you need worry about being too close to everybody and the operations on the border, except to review and plan. That's really your job there, isn't it? Planning and control?"

"Yes, that's what the Order reads, Bea. Of course, you're right; it's just a matter of keeping it in perspective. I guess I'm tough enough for that and the river things will fade as time goes on. Honestly, Hon, I don't know what I'd do without you. Now, let me look back over this map of Phoenix and try to figure out the logistics. Tomorrow could be a lot of fun; I mean we're free as birds out there for the first time in a while. We need to find a nice place for dinner and dance; they say that's getting real popular with the retired folks who get loose like this after all their years of work. I'm feeling that kind of free, here with you on the plane, headed to the golden west; you know?"

"I know, Phil, and I know you; this will pass about the time we set down in Phoenix. Go ahead and study the map; you'll need all the help you can get. I'll be here."

CHAPTER 16
Things Begin to Look Sort of Risky

As the bus entered the centro, the downtown center, of Cuauhtemoc, Br. Angel knew that it was time to get serious, the time had come for him to begin his investigation; he wondered if he was ready for it and, if so, where he would start. They collected their bags and found a local carro, a private car for hire, to take them to the tourist house where Gutierrez had directed him, not far from the market square. They were shown to a large room with a double bed and a small table, two chairs and a chiffonnier with a mirror. Then, given directions from the lady of the house, they walked the two blocks to the Estacion de Policia.

Br. Angel had decided it best to first check in with the local police official to explain their purpose for the visit. He showed his credentials as a member of the Missionary Association of New Mexico and asked for directions to the poorest section of the town where they could begin to take their survey of need. The local constable was receptive to their purpose, since their town had for many years been one of the poorest in the state.

"Yes, Brother Angel, we have many poor families who have sent their sons to work in the U.S. to earn money to send back. But, because of the Border Police and the trouble they can expect as aliens, most of the families will be reluctant to speak even to a missionary. Besides, didn't you know of the Council coming to help out? Many of our poor have already been given money assistance from the Council."

"No, Sir, I wasn't aware of a government assistance program; we will need to learn of this program before we begin our survey of the poor. Where is this Council from? Is it an agency of the state or the federal government?"

"Oh, I'm not sure of that. Just a moment, I can ask Maria, the clerk." He disappeared into the rear office. Soon he reappeared with a woman. "Here is Maria, our clerk. She can tell you about the Council and the help they are giving."

"Maria, my name is Brother Angel Suarez Rivera and this is my wife Miranda Davida de Suarez. We are here as missionaries from New Mexico to witness the situation of the poor in this state and to make a survey of our findings."

"Yes, Sir, Brother Angel, I am happy to meet you."

"Can you tell me about the Council that is here helping out the poor families? It is good news, but I have not heard of them until now. Perhaps our help will not be needed. Do you know who sent them here, which Agency of the government they work for or which Agency is their sponsor?"

"Oh, I don't know for sure, but you can ask them when they come back; they are called the "Council for Unification." I think they have gone to another town, Guerrero, I think. Do you know Guerrero?"

"Yes, I know it is a town up in the mountains. But, do you know of someone they are helping? I could ask them and save a trip to Guerrero?"

"Yes, there are many families that are being helped. If a father or a son is working in the U.S. they give them assistance. I think maybe it is an agency of the U.S. getting names to begin to issue the 'green cards' for the workers that aren't U.S. citizens, but that is only my guess, they don't tell them, they just get the names and give them the money. I have friends and neighbors who are getting money every month because they have the relative working in the U.S. It is a very good thing they are doing."

"Yes, it sounds wonderful. Is that all they need, just a name? Don't they want to be able to verify the names? Don't they need to have an address or a way to contact the relative to be sure they are working in the U.S.?"

"I think they have to know where they are living and the telephone, but the family is told to call or write to the relative and tell them about the Council. We can go to talk to my cousin; she will be able to tell you."

She asked the constable if he would answer her phone while she took Br. Angel and Mirada to speak with her cousin. He agreed, so they left to walk over to her cousin's house, not far away. They walked through the town center and a quarter mile down a dirt road to her cousin's house; it was a small, yellow stucco house with a vegetable garden. She called in from the doorway:

"Honoria, it's me, Maria. I have someone to see you."

Honoria appeared at the doorway.

"Maria, come inside, are these your friends? Please, come in."

They entered and she offered them a chair at the table in the kitchen.

"Please, sit down. I have some guava juice or tea if you like."

Maria told her they were missionaries surveying the needs of the poor and she showed her Br. Angel's business card.

"It seems like the whole world is trying to help the poor people of Mexico all at once; isn't that strange, Honoria? But, they can't offer to help if the Council is doing it, so maybe you can tell them about the Council. They haven't heard of it."

"Yes, I can tell you, but please don't make trouble for my husband. I think the Council is going to help him get a green card. As long as he is working in the U.S. they will give me money every month, as much as Julio sends, so he will be able to live better and get a car."

"That sounds very good, indeed, and we are happy for you, Honoria. But, how do they know if what the people tell them about their relative is true? Do they talk to your husband about it?"

"No, I don't think so. They just want to know where he is and we are told to contact him and tell him that they will want him to come to see

The Mexicans

them for the green card job. I think he will have to go to see them, but I'm not sure, I think we will have to tell them where to go. If they don't want to, it's OK, but then we will not get our money, either. They are not trying to scare us; it is all up to us if we want their help."

"My goodness, that sounds like a wonderful program. Do you know where they are sent from? Surely, some government Agency, I suspect. Did they leave a paper, a leaflet to say what they are doing and who has sent them? And are they a large group, moving with their own transportation?"

"No, I don't know for sure; as I told you, it seems like it must be from the U.S., a green card program of the government, I think. They don't leave any papers, they just talk and take information like the missionaries do. They were a dozen or so at one time, but some of them left before the others and they travel in carrier vans. You can find out, though, your Missionary Association will know. This is very new, it is just about two months now since they first came to see us, so you haven't been told of it yet, don't you think so?"

"You are probably right, Honoria. I will call my office and ask. They may be able to find out. I am very grateful for your help. Miranda and I will stay the night at the guest house and return tomorrow. Thank you for the tea and we will go now. Goodbye."

They made their way outside and waited for Maria; then they walked back. It was a warm day and very pleasant in the foothills of the mountains. At the guest house, they relaxed on the porch in the shade, drinking tea and talking over what they had encountered that morning.

"Miranda, this must be the work of the Iranian invaders. The benefactors obviously are not sent from a government agency, nor are they an agency of the U.S., neither government nor a private aid group. They seem to have purposely been vague about their origins, leaving no printed leaflets and not clearly identifying themselves as government workers."

"Yes, Angel, but they have become an important source of the poor people's income. And when people come to give you money and to keep giving you more, you wouldn't want to look a gift horse in the mouth, would you? No, you'd just take the money and say "Thank you", or "God bless you", or some other words of appreciation. I mean, you wouldn't ask questions for fear of bursting the dream bubble."

"Yes, that's exactly right. They have some purpose in what they are doing, but it is not clear. I think we will leave here and continue on to our next town tomorrow. We will not speak of this group, but simply ask for the status of the poor and make notes of what is said. I'm hopeful that if these people are in the other villages, they will want to remain apart from us and we shall not act aggressively in any way; we will try not to seem inquisitive."

"Angel, are you concerned for our safety? Surely two missionary workers should not be of concern to those people, so long as their work is not impeded by what we do. I think that we should make it our practice to speak with the local constable at each village at the very beginning, just as we did here. Your business card is our best asset; they know who sent us, or they think they know. As you say, we will be as shadows, merely observing the poor, praying publicly and giving to those that ask. And we will be just fine."

The dinner was rice and pollo, stringy chicken but it had a good taste, very Mexican. The asada was fresh lettuce, green and red peppers and guacamole, very Mexican. They drank coffee with egg custard for desert and they were very full.

"A very fine dinner, Senora Guzman, very good indeed; thank you."

It was a very quiet night except for the dogs barking occasionally off in the distance. Neither of them slept soundly, being in a strange environment and even a little worried at what they had learned that day. Uncertainty isn't a problem in a familiar setting, but it proved to be worrisome to them as complete foreigners. In the morning they woke early and held each other very closely for a long time. Their bus was to leave at 6:30, so they would have to ask the householder to order them a carro to pick them up shortly after 6am.

"My dear, these are days of uncertainty, I know, but our security is in our faith in the Lord and our reliance upon His good care. Now let's pray a little longer this morning before we begin this day."

And they spent a long time on their knees, holding hands, each praying in turn, softly, for the safety and comfort of the other and for the serenity of their mission.

Their breakfast was waiting for them at 5:45, a sort of rice pudding with milk and sugar, fruit juice and coffee. The cab was there and took them to the bus stop by 6:20, in plenty of time for the bus to Buenaventura, about 160 miles away, but it was a very mountainous terrain and the road would require great care and that meant slow progress.

"My goodness, with a road like this one, I don't see how we can make the trip in only four hours."

Br. Angel hadn't expected such a poor road. It was soon apparent that slow was not a notion the driver embraced. Even when the road seemed to disappear from view altogether on the worst of the curves, the driver seemed totally unaware of the brake pedal. When the car seemed to be going headlong over a cliff, miraculously solid ground was still there, somewhere, for the tires to dig into, like mustangs running the ridge of a mesa.

The experience was nerve-wracking for Miranda. She held on to Br. Angel so tightly that he had to catch his breath.

"My dear," he whispered softly, "this is just the way they drive here; try to relax and trust in God for our safety. I don't know if the driver is trustworthy but I know who is."

"I'm sorry, Angel, I know whatever happens we will be alright, but what about the driver? Let's pray the driver will be in the arms of God, at least until we get to Buenaventura. No, I'll take back that last part; that sounded very selfish."

They tried to relax and enjoy the scenic drive. Between all of the ups and downs and curves, occasionally they drove through a small settlement, usually identified by a few small vendadores selling various sorts of comidas in tiendas, some no more than little stalls alongside the road; fresh vegetables and fruits grown locally. Now and again the driver would stop and ask his riders if anyone wanted to buy anything. The vendors liked the drivers who gave them that bit of consideration and usually repaid them with a piece of fruit or some vegetables when their riders bought from them. Several of the riders selected some of the offerings, after settling on a fair price, usually a little more fair for the vendor, but the produce was always excellent and the aroma helped to offset the body odor of some of the riders.

As they passed a point where the view was especially panoramic, the driver pointed out a double set of mountain peaks in the distance.

"Over there, you see what is called 'Las Tetas' by the local people."

It was readily apparent why they would give that scene such a name. Miranda blushed a little, but it was all in good fun and she wasn't offended by the driver's notice. Most of the riders chuckled. The mountain scenery was truly delightful and the feeling of danger was long forgotten as their attention was taken up by the natural splendor of the countryside.

CHAPTER 17
Mountain Villages can be Captivating

Sure enough, in just four hours the bus dropped down into Buenaventura, a placid little town with its centro, its town square, and its local constable's office. The business community was typical; vendors of comidas, fresh vegetables, chickens ready for the kill, farm raised catfish, fruits del pais; the paneria for tortillas, the zapateria for shoes and leather repairs, the farmacia for medicines, mostly over the counter mixtures, the medico to get you back to work, the abogado to help you with the difficulties of the law and filings of forms.

There was a banco, a branch of the state bank to hold your savings and offer liens on your property when your crop fails, and a small restaurant that opened from 10 to 2 on weekdays and 10 to 8 on Saturdays. If you wanted your cerveza or cola at any other times, you had to drink it warm at the farmacia or the gas station; ice was not common at any place other than the restaurant and refrigeration was very expensive. The cock fights were the Saturday afternoon sporting events and a touring rodeo came around about twice a year.

There was no bookstore and no theatre, but two churches sitting just a block off the centro where the people flocked on Sundays with their Bibles; Catolica and Baptista, where marriages were solemnized and celebrated, babies were baptized and last rites were conferred on any day of the week. It was pretty much the standard offerings of a small, but comfortable rural town.

Br, Angel and Miranda got directions to the best guesthouse from the bus driver and he pointed them to the constable's office where they made their first stop and spoke to Vicente Fuentes, the constable. Br. Angel introduced he and Miranda, offered Constable Fuentes his Missionary Association business card and explained that they were on an expedition through rural communities of northern Mexico to assess the situation with the poor and to determine the extent of need. They expected to be here for a day or two while they made their survey speaking to typical families in the poorer sections of the community.

"You could be of great help to us if you would direct us to the areas of severest poverty as well as any local aide services working with the poor people. You see, here, I have a map of the community that was prepared by engineers some time ago. Perhaps you could mark the areas we are interested in."

Br. Angel showed him the map.

"Oh, well, this is a very good map and up to date; things don't change much in this little town. Yes, I can show you, here, see, these are two barrios of greatest poverty; one is very much a slum of homemade shelters. You must be careful when you move about here."

"We are prepared to assist the people during our visit with offers to help; I have pesos to distribute to the needy. With God's help we believe the people will treat us kindly since we are here only to help."

"I will go with you, if it will not hinder your work, at least for the first hour or so. The people will see that they have nothing to fear and they will trust you. When do you wish to begin?"

"That is very good of you, Constable Fuentes, very helpful. We will go to the guest house and set our things down; then we will have lunch at the restaurant and be ready to walk at about 2 pm. Will that suit your schedule?"

"Very well, I shall expect you about 2 this afternoon. We shall get you started right away."

"But, if you can join us for lunch we shall be there at the restaurant at about 1 o'clock and I would consider it my pleasure to have you as our guest; we have funds for that purpose."

"Very well, then, I shall join you at the restaurant at 1 o'clock. Thank you, sir."

"Good. Until then," and they shook hands.

They walked the two blocks to the Casa Linda Blanca, the guest house the bus driver had recommended. It was a pretty, white two-story cottage-style house that had been converted to a Bed and Breakfast several years ago when the new owners arrived. It was immaculate inside and out, a gem of a guesthouse for this part of the world. The couple who owned and ran it were retired school teachers from Monterrey, Carlos and Merced Pacheco, very friendly and hospitable by nature. Miranda was delighted.

"Oh, my, how lovely, it is very lovely!"

She spoke with obvious relief, never expecting such a nice place.

"My goodness, I could learn to love this; and the setting here in the mountains, it's just dreamy. Angel, we must spend more time here, two or three nights if the work will extend that long."

Merced Pacheco was equally delighted to have an expression of appreciation from one who was so obviously refined, a cultured person of good taste.

"I am indeed flattered, Mrs. Suarez, you are most gracious. Thank you for your kind words and welcome to our home; we will do our best to make your stay here a pleasant one. Let me show you to your room."

She led the way upstairs to a bright, cheerful room, carpeted, with flood lamps and pillowed rockers for the evenings, and reading lamps at each of the nightstands.

"We ask that you not smoke in the house, but we have a screen enclosed porch should you wish to smoke. The bathroom is just to the right in the hallway; normally there is plenty of hot water for the bath. I hope you will be comfortable here; there are extra pillows under the bed. Breakfast will be at 6:30 until 8 o'clock. Should you wish to take lunch or supper here, please let us know in the morning when we will announce our menu of the day."

The Mexicans

"I'm sure we will want to take all of our meals here, Mrs. Pacheco, and we are not fussy eaters; whatever is the daily menu I'm sure will suit us very well. Believe me, it is a relief to find such a fine place as yours."

While Miranda was taking the upstairs tour, Br. Angel was talking to Carlos Pacheco on the back porch, taking in an expansive view of the residential areas beyond. When he told him of their meeting with Vicente Fuentes, Carlos seemed a bit unsettled.

"Brother Suarez, I would suggest that you be careful how you conduct your business in Vicente's presence. He has a way of turning information to his advantage. When you offer to distribute to the poor, he may wish to be an intercessor in the matter. There are many poor people here who have bad feelings about the constable."

"Oh? I'm surprised to hear that; Fuentes seemed so officious. We agreed to meet him for lunch at one o'clock; he is to guide us to the poor areas of the town."

"Perhaps you will want to excuse yourself from your walk with him today seeing that Mrs. Suarez is feeling tired and needs a rest. There are certain things you should be aware of in the community. We will be pleased to arrange your visitations and escort you after we have had time today to talk over the local situation, and it will be our pleasure to escort you free of charge. Please, this is only my suggestion. I don't wish to intrude, believe me. I wish only for your own good and the good of your efforts here."

Br. Angel studied the demeanor of Mr. Pacheco while he talked, trying to discern his motive for offering advice to them. He seemed sincere in his concern for their welfare and their work with the poor. And Br. Angel was well aware of the tendency in this country for local police and politicians to line their own pockets when there was money available. Certainly, he knew nothing at all about Fuentes. He decided that Pacheco was the more likely to be sincere in his willingness to help.

"I see. Yes, thank you, Mr. Pacheco; we will take your advice in these local matters and also your offer of help. I'll disengage from Constable Fuentes' offer of help and return shortly."

He told Miranda of his conversation with Carlos Pacheco and his suggestion.

"I believe it's best to rely on these good people for advice in these local matters, but we can't just dismiss Fuentes; he may take offense to that. I thought we would beg off the visit this afternoon, offering as an excuse your need for rest. What do you think?"

"I do feel comfortable with these people and we know nothing about Fuentes, so, yes, I think you are completely right to do that, dear. Don't be long, will you?"

"I'll just tell him and leave him money for the lunch we had promised him. Don't worry; I'll be back in ten minutes or less."

He walked across the centro, the town square, to Fuentes office and explained the need for rest after the long trip from New Mexico.

"But, let me show my appreciation for your kind offer of help. Even though we will have to postpone our lunch, today, I should be pleased if you would still accept our offer for your lunch, until we have the opportunity to join you another time." He placed a twenty-peso bill in Fuentes hand as he thanked him and shook his hand. "We will rely on your kind assistance while we are in your town. Thank you, sir."

"Of course, Brother Suarez, of course; please come to my office at any time it pleases you."

"Very well, then, goodbye for now."

And with that, Br. Angel retraced his steps to the Casa Linda Blanca.

That afternoon, Mrs. Pacheco served a light lunch for them on the screened porch, well shaded and with a pleasant breeze. When they had finished their lunch, Mr. Pacheco joined them and began a conversation that would be very informative.

"I feel compelled to advise you of a matter that has given me much concern these past several weeks; a matter taking place right here in Buenaventura, but also, I am told by friends, taking place in other villages in this state, perhaps elsewhere. We retain very close connections to our friends at the University in Monterrey; oftentimes we have visitors who bring information of things taking place in other areas. We have noticed a pattern of influence settling into many of the rural communities and it is this influence that I should like to make you aware of, for the benefit of your work."

"Believe me, Mr. Pacheco, we are very interested in whatever situation exists that would interrupt or impede the work that we have undertaken in this community and others. Please continue; what you say is very interesting; it is very welcome."

"You see, Br. Suarez, villages like ours in Mexico provide little opportunity for the local people to earn a living that will allow for them to raise their families and grow the town so that future generations can remain here. There simply is no industry or commerce to sustain a healthy and educated population. But you are aware of this problem because it has in a way become the problem of the U.S. by fostering illegal immigration to gain employment and in some cases illegal activity that pays high stakes for the criminal in the U.S. We see many of our employable people leaving to take work across the border so they can send help to their families here at home."

"Yes, that is a very unfortunate situation; but we hope a way can be worked out to allow more people to come as guest workers. Being separated from their families, not being here to protect them is another problem, I'm sure."

"That in itself is not the problem that causes worry; there actually is very little illegal activity in the community, no drugs, no smuggling. The problem we see is an invasion of our own country by foreign agents who would hide their activities and use our soil to make war on the U.S., and yet we cannot simply expose these people. You see the difficulty is that the invaders are insidiously buying their way into the hearts and minds of our people here and those who have entered the U.S. illegally by freely distributing money to them in return for their cooperation."

"We were told of such a program at Cuauhtemoc, but very little seemed to be known about the people and who they represented."

"They are not obviously subversive; they cloak themselves in disguise as a government benevolent program. They don't make it clear as to what government they represent and many people have been given to believe it is a U.S. agency quietly preparing a "Green Card" program for illegal workers in the U.S. to be hired away from their illegal jobs and employed in legal jobs. But there is no evidence whatever that such a government program exists, either U.S. or Mexican."

"Yes, we have heard nothing of any green card program being offered and if it were, I'm sure it would not be done in secret."

"That's right; but these people are giving money to the families here; a monthly income equal to what they have been receiving from their relative in the U.S., in return for informing the illegal relative about the program. And the people are giving those men all of the information on their relative, the name, the address and the telephone. The workers are told that if they decide to accept the new job when it is offered the monthly payments to the family will continue and the new job will pay even more. The families encourage them to cooperate or they will be cut off from their new monthly incomes. Naturally, they cooperate, thinking that they are doing nothing wrong since no one tells them it is wrong. And if they were told, who would they want to believe?"

"Of course, it would be hard for the workers to turn down the offer; it means better income there and also here, for the family."

"But, don't you see? It is an evil foreign agency paying money to amass an army of employees to do their evil work in the U.S., whatever that might be, whenever their time comes. If I were to guess, I'd say they are agents of Iran; they look like Iranians but dress as Americans, in suits and ties."

"And do you suppose that Fuentes is being paid also, to turn his eyes away at what goes on?"

"Yes, of course. Nothing could go on without Fuentes either being paid off or eliminated one way or another. He must surely be complicit for them to operate unrestricted as they do. I'm certain there must be a payment for him to look away, perhaps even to be seen as encouraging their program. That man is not to be trusted in any of this."

The Mexicans

"Have you and your friends determined if there is a higher involvement of state or federal officials, payoffs perhaps?"

"We simply don't know. This is a rather new situation. We are watching it closely to see what will be the next stage. Some of the recipients of the payments have explained to us how the program works, but they don't care where it comes from and they don't want to interfere with an important benefit to themselves, obviously. They guess it to be some sort of green card program in the offing. At this point I really don't believe there would be information passing up to the higher government officials. The villages are all rather small with only a constable and perhaps a judge to influence. They would not have reason to want a higher level of official to be involved, neither the local peasants nor the politicos."

"But what of your friends at the University; do they not wish to bring the matter to a higher level?"

"You must realize that this is a different culture than your own. It is one thing to be aware of things that are happening and quite another to try to influence their outcome. I am telling this to you to make you aware of what you will be finding as you visit the countryside speaking to the poor. Many of the poor are already in much better straits with the monthly payments and would likely not want to participate in your census as long as things are as they are now. The Council has informers and we must realize that they may want to eliminate outsiders who seem to be too well educated or too curious. So far, that has not happened, but you and I should not want to test these people. Perhaps you may wish to delay your survey for another time or perhaps visit another area of the country where these foreigners may not be active as yet."

"Do you suppose it would be wise to leave here soon and perhaps meet with your friends in Monterrey to better learn the extent of the foreign incursion? I mean, if it is confined to the villages, perhaps it would be easier and less risky to discuss the problem in the large city, even at the University."

"Well, I suppose I could meet with you there in a day or two and we could meet with my friends. What did you have in mind to do with what you find out?"

"I think that you would like to see things return to normal in your town so that your plan for a tourism industry could be realized one day. Obviously, the current environment would not allow for a greater influx of outsiders; that is most likely why they have chosen the villages. When we encountered the same situation in Cuauhtemoc we left there for fear of our safety. Nothing can be done without evidence of illegal activity. Perhaps there will be a valid explanation, but we should not turn away from evil, if that is what it is. Would you be willing to participate in documenting the information that is known?"

"You are right about my interest in the tourism industry; that is my plan for our future and so I have reason to wish for this to be investigated, Brother Suarez, but how is it you would be interested in doing all of this? I mean, you are only here as a missionary, aren't you?"

"If you would be interested in arranging the gathering in Monterrey, I would be interested in participating and in taking the lead. All of what we have to offer will wait for the meeting, if you will allow me to be discrete for the time being. But we are not here without credentials."

While this discussion was going on, Merced Pacheco and Miranda had quietly slipped in and sat down, listening intently. Miranda felt compelled to speak.

"Dear friends, Angel and I are as we presented ourselves, missionaries with the Free Will Missionary Association of New Mexico, and have been for many years. It is our calling to be of service to those to whom God has called us. On this occasion we have other business as well, but you shouldn't feel that we have misrepresented ourselves. Follow your good instincts, now, and do what seems right for you. We wish only to help our friends."

Mr. Pacheco appeared relieved.

"If you two will proceed on to Monterrey tomorrow, I will call my friends and arrange to meet you the next day, Merced and I. That will be Sunday. Call me when you have taken your hotel and I will contact you there. Will that be agreeable, Br. Angel?"

"Yes, of course, very much so, Mr. Pacheco, Carlos. This has been a fortunate turn of events; God is in our work here, you may be sure of it, and I believe He has selected you good people to help in the work and we will thank Him for bringing us to you."

When they retired to their room, Miranda talked of her visit with Merced and how she felt drawn to her almost as though they were sisters.

"She talked of her life, her work and her marriage and it was as if she were relieving herself of a great tension, as though she had needed someone to confide in and had found that person in me, a perfect stranger; and I felt that I was to be that friend she needed, a real friend. I can't tell you how much empathy I felt for her."

"You are always very compassionate, my dear; that's your nature and one of the many reasons that I have loved you all these years. Go on, don't let me interrupt you."

"Thank you, my Angel. Well, as she went on over times past and the years of working as a University instructor, she seemed to be describing a life that was unfulfilled - and then it became clear. I know she loves Carlos and they have had a good life together, but they hadn't taken the time to have children, it's just the two of them. Isn't that sad, Angel? I just know Merced would have been a marvelous mother, but the time is past, it's lost forever, she'll never know the one great fulfillment she now longs for."

"Oh, my, I didn't ask about their family; that is sad. But, you know, Dear, I've seen that before with University professors; caught up in research and writing and sending the students on their way to a full life, but not seeming to realize the limitation they have placed on themselves. It's all so surreal, so lofty, but leads to an empty ending. Well, perhaps this will be an opportunity for these good people to reclaim that sense of loss by taking on a new sense of purpose with this investigation. Perhaps we have found a pair of friends that will become a pair of collaborators."

"Angel; I believe this is an opportunity to share our faith with these people."

"It could be a good opportunity, a good beginning, indeed. I'm glad she felt that compassionate nature of yours, my dear. Tomorrow will be a new day for us; there is a great promise in this group of intelligent people we are about to become associated with. Let us remember our first love and our first calling. I have the feeling there are lost souls to reach here. Exciting times are on the horizon, I feel it. Now you lead us in prayer, please."

Miranda asked for those blessings that would provide the fruit of God's good will in the lives of these they are about to minister to and she asked God's blessings on Angel and herself in their love and in their work.

"Goodnight, Angel. I love you."

"And I love you, Miranda. Goodnight, my love."

The next morning they finished with their bathroom chores and walked downstairs to the breakfast nook overlooking the brook rambling down through the cut of the ridge. Br. Angel loved the mountains.

"Such a pleasant scene to begin the day; I believe this will be a good day for us."

Carlos was already making telephone calls and Merced was moving through the house with a song on her lips and a lilt in her walk.

"Good morning Brother Angel, good morning Miranda, just sit right down here and I'll pour your coffee for you. The pancakes and eggs are just now on the griddle. You can begin with the fruit bowl and cereal if you like. The bacon is in the broiler. We'll be ready in a jiffy. Did you sleep well? I thought I heard a wolf howling about midnight."

"We slept very soundly, Merced, thank you. The wolves were taking care of their own business at midnight; that would never stir either of us. My goodness, that bacon smells good. How do you make your pancakes so perfect? They look like they came from a cookie cutter."

Miranda was ready and eager after stepping outside for a breath of fresh morning mountain air.

The Mexicans

"I used a cookie cutter. I learned that from my mother. You pour the batter onto the griddle and when they start to firm up on the bottom, you use the cookie cutter to get the round shape and flip off the excess when it browns. Sometimes I use other shapes if there are children at the table. I'm glad you like them."

In a few minutes they were all seated and Br. Angel asked the blessing. The fruit bowl was delightful, every kind you might want. A small bowl of All Bran with fruit got it off to a good start.

Carlos made his morning contacts and told them about their visitors. They were all excited about having a serious meeting on the situation with some folks who they hoped could have some influence.

"Pancakes with eggs and bacon are just the thing to hold a person for the whole day if all they did was ride the bus. I guess it'll be an all day ride, arriving there about 10:30pm. I'll make reservations at the hotel before leaving this morning, if you can direct me to a good place to stay, Carlos."

Carlos suggested the University Inn where most of the visiting guests stayed. It was clean and modern with a good restaurant. After breakfast, Br. Angel made the reservations. They had coffee and talked over their plan and Carlos described the others they would be meeting in Monterrey. Each of the friends should be asked to invite a member of a family receiving the monthly payments to tell them about their experience. Only those people who were known to be reliable would be invited. One from each village that had been invaded would be sufficient, and that one should be able to prepare a list of families that had been signed up and what cities the relatives were working in. That work should continue until all affected communities had been included in the survey.

"Clearly, Br. Angel, we cannot assume to have direct contacts within every community affected, that simply is not possible with such a small group as ours. We will need to recruit those friends who will be able to make contacts in those other communities where we have no contact. Some planning will be needed to complete the inquiries through contact persons. Once we have prepared an agenda of villages, the methods to be used will become evident. I am sure that we will be able to complete the survey to a high degree of accuracy."

Mountain Villages can be Captivating

"Yes, that is a good plan. But I would not wait for the completion of the entire survey before we begin sending off the names and addresses. As the information comes in it must be acted upon or we may never find out what the invaders have planned for the workers in the U.S. Earlier in our discussion you correctly assessed that this appears to be an effort to amass an army of invaders already inside the U.S., possibly to do some destructive work. That is exactly the purpose of this survey; to stop them from carrying out their plans. That is the commission Miranda and I have been given. I cannot be more specific for we are bound to secrecy. We will control the transmission of information as it comes to us, and we will do so without delay. Do you agree?"

"Yes, of course. My group can do nothing more than gather the information; the use of it is beyond our means. Your participation in all of this is truly a Godsend for us."

"My friend, God has been sending us around the world for a lifetime and to places you could not imagine. We rely on Him for support in everything that He directs. You and Merced are a perfect example of the ways in which God brings His people to a task, to accomplish His will. We can be thankful for every task we are given; it will reap a reward, unmatched in this world. Now we must get ready to take our leave, the bus will arrive in thirty minutes."

They got their bags ready, visited the restroom, then stopped at the large window in their pretty room and spent a few minutes absorbing the breathtaking view.

"We'll come back here soon, my Dear; this is too lovely to leave for long. While we're here in this country we will visit this room as often as time will allow."

"Of course, Angel, I love the serenity of this place, too. A weekend now and then will fit well with our lifestyle; as we both know, Dear, you can be such a romantic."

The taxi driver took their bags as they made their goodbyes; sorrowful at the leaving, after having made such a close mutual commitment, but looking forward to working their plan in Monterrey. The taxi waited the few minutes they needed, then drove them to the bus stop.

The Mexicans

As they waited, Vicente Fuentes, passing by, stopped.

"Are you leaving so soon? But you just arrived."

"Yes, I'm afraid so; we will have to return another time. Just now, we have business at another calling. But, thank you for the hospitality of your beautiful village; we will look forward to returning soon."

"Well, goodbye, then and come back when you can stay longer."

The bus turned into the centro and stopped nearby. In five minutes they pulled away heading for El Sueco and the connecting bus for Monterrey.

CHAPTER 18
Gatherings of Eagles

Settling into their seats on the bus, Br. Angel and Miranda tried to relax while looking forward to a long and bumpy ride, eighty miles of it, to El Sueco.

"Miranda, are you satisfied with the arrangement we have made with the group of instructors at the University in Monterrey? I mean, do you think that there is enough dedication in the people here to be able to work on this plan we have designed with Carlos and Merced? I wonder if it's possible with such a group to keep them operating in secret for the duration of the work; what do you think?"

"You know, Angel, I have had some trepidation about that. Obviously, there is some risk in a plan that includes people whom we have never even met and know little about except that they are friends of our new friends. But, as I thought about it, I can see how these people would be very worried; after all, they must realize that their way of life is in jeopardy by invaders from a Middle Eastern country, and a Muslim country, at that. Remember, they have already come to the point of expressing their concerns about these invaders to us, strangers; it's brought them together as a group to speak their minds.

"So, it's really not much of a step, now, for them to support intervention by the U.S.; after all, they rely on the U.S. economy for their own welfare. Yes, if they are as Pacheco describes, I think they will work with us, not against us. They know a friend from an enemy; surely they must see us as friends. There is a risk in exposing our investigation here, but I believe there would be greater risk without them."

"Very well; I agree with your reasoning. But, I wonder what guideposts we can watch for as we work with them, not so much as a group, but by individual actions and what they say individually. Should the guideposts merely be our intuition, our feelings, or should we test by some other standard? Informers can be well established in such a group, reporting to intelligence agents, Mexican or foreign or revolutionary. We don't want any information about our work to get beyond these few people. How can we verify their fidelity?"

"I would trust my intuition to raise the red flags. After the first flag, I would observe very carefully and verify my feelings by the second flag. We should draw a position on each one; what are they actually contributing? As John gave us, we must judge them by their fruits. If any appear to be there merely to take note of what others are doing and what is decided, I would call together those we think to be reliable and settle the matter. If at any time things seem not to be operating well, we should withdraw from the group."

"Again, my Dear, you show valuable insight. I agree. But if there is risk, then their infidelity would favor the invaders; and that seems unlikely."

"I feel better now that we have decided that; I was a little concerned, but not now."

"The bus we board at El Sueco may be very crowded and noisome; now will be the best time to call General Bragg. We must inform him of this situation we've found and our next steps. He can relay that to the others."

He dialed the special number that would transfer his call to the secure automated voice system.

"To whom do you wish to speak?" the voice asked.

"General Bragg, please."

In a moment Phil Bragg answered, "Hello, Br. Angel, where are you?"

"Hello, General Bragg; we are on a bus about an hour from Buenaventura traveling to Monterrey. We should arrive there by 10:30 this evening and will stay at the University Inn. Let me tell you what we have found these past two days. We have visited two remote villages and inquired of another; the first was Cuauhtemoc where we also inquired of Guerrero before going on to Buenaventura. What we found was the same at all three villages; it is an extraordinary story. I assume you are recording this?"

"Yes, you can go ahead."

"At each village the invaders have established contact with all families that have a relative working in the U.S."

He went on to explain the program the invaders have offered the families; the money, the identity and address information, the instructions for the relative and the new jobs.

"They call themselves the Council for Unification but they claim no official status or authority for what they do; they appear to be Iranians. The people have assumed it is the start of a Green Card program for eventual citizenship in the U.S. We decided it best that we not remain in the villages, drawing attention."

And he recounted their experiences with the constables at each town and the meetings with Carlos and Merced Pacheco.

Bragg was amazed at what he had heard.

"I could never have imagined such a brazen scheme. It looks like your friend is correct; they appear to be amassing an army of invaders that are already positioned within the population, to accomplish their purposes. The extent of what they have in mind is only limited by one's imagination. It's an amazingly inventive plot."

"Yes, and that is why I have good reason to believe in the sincerity of these people and their group at the University. We will meet with them on Sunday at the University Inn. At that time we expect to arrange for the collection of the names and addresses from those villages where Pacheco's friends have existing contacts and then expand from those contacts to contacts in other villages. I'll transmit the data to you as we accumulate it. When the collection effort is well underway perhaps we will return to Socorro for a few days, but we cannot leave the work undone; we will not leave Monterrey until we have a sufficient survey for you to track their operations. You will have to decide that time."

"That sounds like just what we need, names and addresses of the relatives in the U.S. so we can send our people to investigate their operations. What about money Br. Angel? Surely you will have to buy your way into the hearts and minds of those willing to gather information."

"I don't expect to need large sums. We will offer expense money and rewards as an incentive. In these poor villages fifty or a hundred dollars for a list of names and addresses may be enough. We shall see. In any event it will not exceed our ability to access funds at the bank in Monterrey. I expect my ATM card will work as well down here as at home."

"The ATM card works worldwide. Be generous with that reward and make them understand that we will check out the information before they get all of their money. Recruiting friends from friends is a good plan. And when you find reliable people, get their attention, don't let them have to decide – money can turn cowards into heroes, and good information is worth a great deal; it's all we have to go on. I'll send this report on to Harry Foster right away."

"I'll call you when we are settled in Monterrey to get the CIA update on recent arrivals. These invaders seem to remain in the general area where they arrive and visit only other villages nearby their original village. Their workings are very low key; they seem to wish to remain out of sight and to do their work only in the remote areas. There is no indication that they themselves will move toward the border to cross into the U.S. We will do our work from outside the villages to avoid any contact with them; thus far our cover as missionaries has served us well."

"Well, good. I'll let you go now and get busy with plans for dealing with this. Send me the names and addresses when they start coming in and we will begin tracking on our end. Take care, my friend, and give Miranda my best regards, too. Goodbye."

"Goodbye, Phil."

"Miranda, dear, we are connected now to our friends. I'd rather wait until we are in our hotel before making any more calls, unless something unexpected happens. How about, if I turn toward the window, you rub my back for a few minutes, right in the middle? This seat is really swayback."

"Oh, Angel, of course. But are you sure it's the swayback seat? I'm not so sure about that." and she massaged his back with her strong hands. "Does that help your back now, my sweet romantic husband? My, that is a very swayback seat."

But by that time her Angel was sound asleep.

In about an hour, she woke him.

"Angel, dear, wake up. We have to change buses now; we're coming into El Sueco."

The next bus was newer, heavier and more comfortable. Angel and Miranda dozed away the early afternoon. As they approached Chihuahua, Br. Angel called Juan Gutierrez to advise him of their changed itinerary.

"If you would, please telephone the hotel there in Chihuahua and let them know we will not be returning as we had expected. They may be holding a room for us. I'll call you when we will be coming back to Chihuahua. Goodbye for now, Mr. Gutierrez."

The trip was very boring for the rest of the afternoon with occasional stops, passenger changes and pit stops; the toilet on the bus was out of service. About 6pm they had a thirty minute stop at Torreon for dinner at a very modest restaurant; the fare was the national staple, arroz con pollo, tortillas, guacamole salad, sour cream, and tea, or beer with lime juice.

The last leg of the trip was four hours with a brief stop at Saltillo. Finally, they arrived in Monterrey, a busy city about two and a half hours from the U.S. border. They were very tired but before long the taxi delivered them to the University Inn where they breathed a great sigh of relief and visited the grill for a late dish of ice cream before going up to their suite.

The suite was pleasant, but they hardly noticed; they brushed their teeth and fell into the bed to a sound sleep.

The Mexicans

Miranda was on the top of a high mesa riding a swing, reaching high up in the air, while Angel stood below guiding the swing. The air up at the top on the arc was so clean and fresh she kept urging him; "Angel, this is so much fun; higher, Angel, higher." And Angel never seemed to tire of making her happy; but he cautioned her, "Hold on tight, my love, hold on tight to the ropes; don't fall. But if you should fall, I'll catch you, so don't worry." She felt so safe.

Br. Angel was riding a mule up a mountain pass, slowly wending his way up to a mesa. Up there, standing at the crown of the mesa he could see hundreds of people waiting for him, needing him. Miranda was there at the front of the crowd, her arms extended, waiting to hold him when he reached the top. But the mule was very tired so he got off and let the mule rest a while. From there he walked, leading the mule the last quarter mile. As he approached the top, the view was magnificent, unlike anything he had ever imagined. And Miranda held him tight and whispered into his ear, "I knew you would come, my love; I just knew you would be here. I waited for you; they all have waited for you." And, with that, he felt his strength returning.

In the morning they slept late, showered and dressed for breakfast at the Inn Restaurant, bright and clean, serving very good food. They were pleased and decided this would be the right place to stay.

CHAPTER 19
Things Change in a Hurry

Phil and Beatrice Bragg thoroughly enjoyed their time together searching out the cities that he had marked as potentials for the new Border District office. Phoenix was sensational for personal reasons, in particular the Scottsdale area. Beatrice easily had decided this would be the place for her. As their plane rose from the runway heading for Albuquerque, Beatrice couldn't help but say one more time:

"Phil, if we have our choice of locations, this should be it, hands down. I would love to go house hunting in Scottsdale; just driving through those beautiful residential streets gave me goose bumps. Don't you just love it here?"

"Yes, I love it here, too; but we have to remember that it is the Agency's business that we are about; the best location for travel is important, though, and Phoenix is a hub for Southwest Airlines, so your selection could be the best after all. Let's check out these other two before we get too serious about Phoenix. "

"Of course, Phil; I knew all that, Smarty."

For the next two days they looked over Albuquerque, without prejudice. And without prejudice, they pretty well discounted Albuquerque as a serious location.

"One of the most important aspects of a good location is good air transportation; as you well know we don't like to drive, walk, train or bus our way across the country. Air transportation here is not as expeditious as we need; so far it's Phoenix by a nose, an elephant nose. Let's look over Amarillo."

The Mexicans

Just before checking out of the hotel, the call from Br. Angel came to them from the bus en route to Monterrey. When Bragg had finished the call, he had made his decision. He called the airport and cancelled the reservation to Amarillo and made reservations for Denver on a flight leaving just one hour later. Then he called Harry Foster and gave him the report he had just received from Br. Angel.

"That's an amazing story, Phil. I'll need a copy of that recording for the President as soon as you can get it here; use the Military courier. When we have had a chance to go over it, we'll give you a call back and talk strategy. This will require some serious work on the Agency's part, if it is as it appears, and I don't doubt it. Can you get that in the courier from where you are?"

"I'll call the nearest base for a courier."

"I'm sure you'll have no trouble, they all know you. Thanks for the report. Is there something else, Phil?"

Harry had sensed a little concern in Bragg's voice while they were talking about the report.

"You know, Harry, I've had this nagging worry that's been pestering me since talking to Br. Angel but I haven't quite been able to put my finger on exactly what it is. It started when I heard about where Br. Suarez was going and the more I've thought about it the more it's nagged me. But just now I remembered something I read about a lot of student unrest in Monterrey; all about the Jimenez people inciting the socialists. That's it; the students had trapped an older couple in their car and nearly tipped it over during one of their demonstrations. The old man died of a heart attack and the woman was in a coma."

"Phil, I think you need to get a tail on them right away; they don't have to know about it, but this is too important a venture to leave them on their own. We need to keep a watch on them while they're there, however you want to do it. I'd get someone on the way down there soon."

"You're right, Harry. That's front burner; we'll get right on it. I'll call you. Thanks."

Things Change in a Hurry

"That's it, Bea, it looks like Br. Angel has found out what they're up to down there. It's not about us guarding the border at all; it's about us tracking these illegals in places where they've settled in all over the country. Pretty soon we'll be getting actionable information and we'll have to be ready to send agents out on tracking operations. But you heard all that. Now I've got to get back to the office and get a cover agent down to Monterrey. Anyway, we might be through looking for the right city. Knowing what to expect, now, makes a big difference in where we locate the office. Flight access nationwide is the key for us along with a location central to the greatest influx of illegal aliens. Where would that be?"

"Phoenix."

"Yeah, either Denver or Phoenix, they make the grade for both points, but Phoenix does have the edge by being very near California. Still, Denver is a central location that could be helpful. For the time being we will stay put until I see what the operational data tells us."

"California has the most illegals, hands down, Phil, everybody knows that."

"Have you gotten involved in gambling without me knowing about it, Bea?"

"Phil, are you honestly suggesting - - - ? Are you inferring - - - that I would - - - gamble?"

"Well, Bea, 'hands down' is an expression used by experienced Poker players and that makes twice in two minutes that you used it; is that you, an experienced Poker player? 'Cause if it is, where are you keeping all your winnings?"

"Yeah, like I fly to Vegas while you're out walking the beat. Besides, what makes a Poker hand so good if it's down? You have to show it to win, I thought."

"That's the irony of it, Bea; when you know there's no way to lose, you can say for sure you've won the bet without even having to see the other guys' hands, get it? Hands down is face down on the table. But

123

you can only know you have a cinch if you've been able to remember all the cards and you know there's nothing on the table that can beat your hand and that's only because you're a good experienced gambler, so your lingo gave you away; now I know you're a big shot gambler. So, where do you keep the money, Honey?"

"Oh, shut up, Know-it-all. OK, then, hands up!'

"So, now you're a stick-up Moll. Really, Bea, I'm not sure I know you anymore."

Beatrice couldn't hold it back, she laughed like she used to laugh with Phil when they were dating, before diapers, schools and all the rest.

"Doggone you, Phil, I haven't had so much fun since I can remember. Now, cut it out before I pee my pants."

"Incontinence already? Diaper? Let's see - here, have one of mine."

"So, knock it off, General Bragg, remember who you are, a beast. Well, I can tell you right now, Phoenix is the winning hand, up or down; Denver's not even close – too many snow days."

Enough of the banter, Bragg cancelled the Denver reservation, called down for a taxi and they were on their way to the airport headed back to New Orleans.

CHAPTER 20
Rocky Mountain High

When Bob Crumpton got through to Carl Burkett, he found him in his cabin in the Wyoming Rockies talking on his radio patched through to his telephone service; He did that on all his trips – Carl was a Ham Radio buff.

"Bob. Man, I don't usually get social calls up here, but I'm glad to hear from you. I can guess what's on your NSA mind, that strange charter bunch, am I right?"

"Well, yes, Carl. I need to track it down if I can; did you copy the plane's call number?"

"I did. I wrote it down in my catch box. Do you want me to get it for you or do you trust my memory?"

"I trust your memory, but I'd appreciate it if you would go get it, buddy."

"I thought you'd say that. I'll have to jeep it on down to the lake. Let me call you back in ten minutes."

"I'll be here at my cell; same place you called me the other day."

@@

Mamie Dumont poured a glass of fresh-made iced tea and brought it to Crumpton. She touched his shoulder as he sat staring out into the trees of the back yard and broke through his reverie.

"Bob, I didn't mean to startle you; you've been out here for more than an hour and I thought you could use a nice glass of tea. It's fresh, I just made it; it's got fresh lemon juice, just the way you like it."

"Oh, thank you, Ms. Dumont; yes, I could use a cold glass of tea."

"Is everything alright? You look a bit worried."

"Oh, it's nothing, really. I'm just waiting for a friend to call me back."

"He must be having to find something; I know it takes me an hour or more sometimes to find something in my old desk in the front room when I knew for sure it wouldn't take more than a few minutes. I heard you on the phone about an hour ago, but I wasn't being nosey, I just knew you were talking."

"It's been over an hour. I expected him to call back in ten minutes. I hate to put a call through to him again; he must have gotten tied up with his hire – Carl makes his living hiring out to guide fishermen in the Rockies."

"Well, that's probably right. I expect he has to give them a lot of attention when they pay for it and you can't blame them for that. So, how's Rebecca doing, Bob? Is she still planning to graduate in May or are you going to whisk her away with you when you go to that border place?"

"I think she wants to finish that second degree right there at LSU, Ms. Dumont. She's worked real hard at it and I'm proud for her, but you're right; I'd like to whisk her away, like you say."

"Well, don't get in a rush, Bob; there'll be plenty of time for whisking come June." She chuckled when she realized what she had said. "What I mean is there's plenty of time for traveling; that schooling might be useful to her one day."

"I'm hoping we'll start a family and make a real home. I know Rebecca wants to raise children and I'm sure she'll be a great wife and mother; she's still got the home town blood in her veins, no amount of schooling can take that away. She can write books or research something while she's being a homemaker; she'd be a good author, I believe."

"I'm sure she would; she talks up a storm and she knows something about 'most everything, including the Bible."

"Well, I can't stand it any longer; I've got to put through this call to Carl. Just keep your seat; it's not a big secret."

"Oh, I'll just go back to my cooking, Bob; I wish I could sit out here all evening but I can't do it. I'll bring you some more tea in a few minutes."

"Thank you, Ms. Dumont."

The telephone rang and rang. He let it ring for a good two minutes, but no answer came.

"Well, he'll have to quit fishing in another couple of hours," he thought. "I'll give him a little more time. Those guys paying him can get pretty insistent on his time, no doubt."

The longer he waited, the more he worried. Ms. Dumont brought more tea and Bob read the whole book of Job while he waited; it always made him feel confident.

When he knew the sun had been behind the Wyoming mountains for at least an hour, he called Carl's home in Cody. His wife, Juliet, answered.

"Bob; oh, Bob, I'm so glad to hear from you. Have you talked to Carl today? I don't know what to think, he hasn't called all day."

"I did, Julie, I talked to him around noon, your time. He was going to call me back in ten minutes – went to retrieve something from the plane – but he hasn't called back. I've tried to call him three times and no answer. I don't want to alarm you, but that don't sound like Carl."

"I know it. I called Dad and he's getting ready to go up to the cabin, but it's so late, now, he'll have to wait for first light or he might get lost in those woods. He needs to get a plane; I think he's talking to some of Carl's pilot friends; they'll know what to do."

"Well, Julie, it looks like we'll just have to wait it out. He could be having radio trouble, you know; that's what I think it is. If he can't fix it, he'll be able to get aloft and call from the airplane in the morning; he can't get through from that lake site down in the mountains especially at night; the ionosphere is so high the signals get bounced all around the world."

"Oh, I know; he had radio trouble up there once before and he got a Ham to call me from Montevideo; maybe we'll hear from him tonight."

"Let's pray that we will, Julie. I'll be here waiting for first light. If there was something I could do I'd get a flight to Casper and hire a charter to your place in the morning."

"Bob, would you do that? Could you do that? Oh, I'd feel so much better if you were here."

He knew he had to do something to help Juliet; she was so frightened.

"I'll call the airport and see if I can get out there tonight, Julie; I call you right back."

He just got lucky. It was round-about, but Crumpton got a way to Casper on a flight out of Denver; a non-scheduled aircraft on a milk run and he might be able to get the pilot to take him on in the morning to Cody, if he could set his plane down on that airstrip up there. Ms. Dumont saw him off.

"Bob, it isn't everyone has a friend like you. I'll pray for you; I know God will bless you as you go."

He had three hours to make his flight out of the New Orleans airport, but he could do it. On the way, he called Juliet.

"God willing, Julie, I'll see you there at first light. All I have to do is find a ride out of Casper when I arrive there about 2 am your time, but I'll call you when I get to Casper."

"I'm so thankful, Bob. I just don't know what to do, but I feel better, now you're on the way. We're still waiting for a call; a relay from some Ham operator somewhere. It happened before, Bob."

Rocky Mountain High

"Just don't give up hope, Julie; hang in there. I'll call you in the morning. God bless you."

"God bless you, Bob."

The pilot of the flight to Casper from Denver, Davy Crockett, thought he was a little heavy for a set down at Cody, but he called ahead and found a free pilot with a light plane for charter. Bob gave Davy a big tip, but, best of all, on the way to Casper he hit upon just the right Bible message that convinced Davy to accept the Lord.

"You're right Bob, I feel lots better now. Minnie's been dogging me for years to get right with God; now that I am, I know why. This was a good flight for me and Minnie. I don't know why it took you, a stranger to convince me, Bob, but you're no stranger now, thank God."

"Send me a card now and then, Davy. I'd love to hear from you. I'll pray for you and you pray every day; that's important and read your Bible, you'll never regret it."

Fenton Stewart took him from Casper to Cody; he was there waiting for Bob when they touched down. In ten minutes they were airborne; they set down the light Cub at Cody Field with a couple hundred feet to spare, just as the day was breaking. John Burkett, Carl's father was waiting for Bob along with two other friends, ready to take off for the cabin at the lake. Juliet just hugged him and wept. So did Bob.

"We're gonna bring him home Julie. Whatever happens, Carl's going to be just fine, you know that. Dry your eyes, now and thank God for Carl and your life together."

At the cabin, there was no one. No plane and no people, just lots of fishing gear and camping equipment including the radio, which was in good operating condition. They searched the woods for hours and found no sign of them. The footprints led down to the lake where the plane tied down when it was there. It appeared that they had left in a big hurry and just disappeared.

"John, we need to call the Sheriff's office; something's wrong. This looks like maybe a high-jacking. Whatever it is, it don't look good."

The Mexicans

All that afternoon, the deputies searched for clues, but didn't turn up anything. There was a section of the ground that looked like there could have been a scuffle, but there wasn't any blood, so they couldn't be sure what that meant. At the end of the day the Sheriff was calling it a high-jacking and kidnapping because of the equipment that was left and the fact that no one had been able to call from the camp before leaving. They called in the FBI.

Crumpton called Phil Bragg and told him the whole story.

"Phil, I can't help but think this is connected to the sighting of the people and the planes in Canada that Carl told me about. He knew there was something wrong with that situation and I'm thinking they may have tracked him by his plane's registration, needing to silence him. I'm afraid they've done just that. They're nowhere to be found and the Sheriff is calling it a high-jacking."

"Bob, I don't know what to tell you; I know this is a terrible experience for you and your friends up there. I agree that it looks like something we could investigate, but without any more to go on than Carl's original call, you'd best leave it to the locals for now and wait awhile to see what might develop. The FBI won't be interested in a story about some Middle-east guys and not be given any way to track them. If there's a way to investigate this case, I'd say it's best right now to see where they can take it. On a hunch, I'd say drag the lake."

"I'll suggest they do that, Phil; thanks. I'll be back home in a few days if nothing turns up. Right now, I've got to stay with Juliet until she gets settled down. It's awfully hard on her and I'm one of their lifelong friends; right now, they need old friends, her and his folks both."

"I know that, Bob. Just let me know if there's anything I can do."

"Thanks, Phil. I'll be calling you. So long."

"Hang tough, Bob; so long."

CHAPTER 21
First Lights, First Awakening

"Play it again, Harry", the President knew he would have to open up a whole new file folder that would reside on the top of his desk and occupy a large portion of his planning time. They listened intently, each making prolific notes, study reminders of significant details in the report given by Br. Angel. The longer they contemplated the story, the more they worried that the country might be facing its greatest internal threat ever, or ever envisioned.

"It sounds like a very logical scenario for foreign agents to attempt to carry out, Mr. President, with the potential for a huge payoff; an army of potential invaders, but having the advantages of an insurgency – troops embedded in the population, unidentifiable, carrying out coordinated attacks at multiple locations all across the country. The potential for widespread and severe damage could be unending if the number of illegal aliens recruited were even a small percentage of the millions that are already settled in with bought or stolen identities. And especially if they're being well financed by a major foreign nation, like Iran."

"You know, Harry, they have a real ace in the hole with that income subsidy program for the families in Mexico; that could become their real arm-twister if and when they try to turn the workers into insurgents and use them as weapons. Think of the choices, Harry; either become a bomb yourself or be willing to let your family be killed and your home destroyed."

"I can't even imagine such a choice, Mr. President. But, of course, you are right. Many would willingly die to save their entire family, perhaps three generations under siege. It's the devil's work, for sure, but nothing that hasn't been going on with success in many places

The Mexicans

of the Middle East. But I have faith in our security people, Mr. President; we will defeat this threat in its infancy, now that we are aware of the plot."

"Yes, Harry, we will set out immediately to interrupt their plan and we can do so with the knowledge that they don't know they have been detected. Br. Angel is a genius in recognizing the importance of not disclosing any interest and then withdrawing from the towns immediately. He and Miranda appear to have hit upon a situation with good people. If that works out it can give us the edge on the invaders even before they have time to get their plot to first base. We will need the Security Council and the Intelligence Services together in the Board Room within two days; heads and first assistants only, Harry; the sooner the better."

"Of course, Mr. President; I'll get back to you with the date and time."

"Good. And thank you, Harry for staying on top of this."

In an hour Harry Foster had returns from his meeting call for 9am the next day; two were tentative, depending on air transportation back to town. He changed the time to 3:30 pm and got consensus. He informed the President.

"All members of the Security Council, the CIA, the FBI, Homeland Security and the NSA are on board for 3:30 tomorrow in the Pool Hall; that's street talk for the Board Room, Sir."

"Yes, Harry, I've been around the street; very good. Now, let's get the necessary copies of the telephone conversation transcribed so we'll have something to look at while we listen to the tape. But, for the time being, I'll ask for all copies to remain on the table after the meeting. And let's have copies of a Mexican detail map showing the locations where they delivered the groups of invaders; maybe we'll have an update by that time – see if CIA has gotten any more spotted before we meet so we'll know where they're operating right now. That may not be much help but it's good intelligence for starters. One thing, though, I like the way Br. Angel's reports are coming through General Bragg – he has the response teams, so let's continue that procedure."

"Yes, Sir; will do. I'll have your folder ready for you by 2 o'clock."

"All right, then. Thank you."

☯

John Smoltz dialed direct.

"Phil, John. We're in the Pool Hall tomorrow afternoon; you can guess what it's about, since you broke the news. The President would like to know of any new settlements the invaders have made since the first list, so get with that guy at the CIA for the latest; we'll need to get it to Harry Foster by 2pm. Also, when you call the towns down to Br. Angel try to get some sort of idea about how many families are involved in the villages, if he knows; just a ballpark idea for planning."

"Sure, John, I'll get him early and give him a little time to call back."

"Right. I'd hold up a few weeks on the selection of your operating location. We may get some thoughts on that from the meeting, you know, just in case."

"Yeah, I already put a hold on it, John. Right now I've got to get a guy down to Monterrey to keep a watch on the Suarez team. There's been some political activity there that's gotten nasty recently. Harry knows about it, too. I've decided on the guy to send; he'll get his orders as soon as I get back to the office."

"Good; we decided some time back to get approval on that and I sent your memo up; it's about time they got to it."

"Well, I was talking to Foster and recalled an article about a demonstration gone bad down in Mexico that resulted in the deaths of an elderly couple. He made the decision, himself, then and there. So, we'll get it done real soon. We're going to have some names and locations to run down within a week. I'm planning my teams small so we can get reports from a lot of towns early; we're going to need that early feedback to assess the long-term requirements as soon as we can. If this is as widespread as I think it is we may need to spread it out to the other Districts and add on some more agents as well. I think the

President can expect first reports within ten days, if not before, and realistic assessments of the risk level soon after. We're going in quickly and quietly, but we'll get the stuff we need."

"I know that, John, and I appreciate it, but I'd prefer to keep this in our own house for the time being – too much spreading around can let something out on the street. We'll probably have to bring the FBI in on it and locals as well, when it comes down to incursions. Let me hear from you tomorrow before 3pm, OK? Take care."

"OK, John. You're right; keep investigations in the Border District – I like it that way, too. Goodbye."

Phil Bragg called and got another ten towns, then placed the call to Br. Angel.

"Br. Angel, we've got a top level meeting tomorrow afternoon, the fallout from your report. I've got ten more towns for you; you ready to copy the positions?"

"Yes, Phil, just a moment, — now, I have the map before me. Go ahead."

Bragg read off ten sets of coordinates from his map where he had plotted them.

"You will find that they are all south and west of Monterrey and north from Aguascalientes to the border, a remote area of small villages, farming communities and rancheros."

"Good. We have a meeting here soon with our new friends. With God's help you will be receiving the first lists in the next few days."

"That's what we need; send what you can even if it's only a couple of lists, so we can get an idea of what the spread will be."

"We'll get them as soon as possible, Phil. Miranda sends her regards. Goodbye."

"Goodbye."

A little while later the plane set down at the Kenner Airport. Phil Bragg dropped Beatrice off at their house and headed in to his office. He called Misti on the way.

"Misti, pull the file on Captain Luis Caldera and see if he isn't a citizen of Mexico; I think I remember him having dual citizenship. I'll hold." (A short pause)

"Yes, General, Captain Caldera has both. Want to know the rest? He's big, a wrestler, ex paratroop Captain, served in a lot of hot spots in the Middle East and Africa, lots of decorations and — single!"

"Yeah, yeah, that's good enough; just put the file on my desk and tell him to be at the office in about an hour with his bag packed."

"Yes Sir, General."

Bragg had time to look over Caldera's background. He noted he wrestled in college as a heavyweight, 6 feet tall and 220 pounds.

"Not bad for a taxi driver in Monterrey," he thought. "He's 32, History and Law from Baylor, still single, sort of the Bob Crumpton kind of character. Six years, mostly in the New Orleans operations. Cited numerous times for interrupting illegal entry of people and weapons from Panama; captured two smuggling boats and one pirate operator; wounded twice by gunfire pursuing smugglers; knocked off a few himself; black belt martial arts, expert shot, prefers hand to hand, when possible. Clean record; scored high on his last internal investigation review. He'll do fine, since I can't send Crumpton."

Caldera knocked on his door and it opened for him.

"Come in, Luis, sit down. I see you have a bag packed. That's good, but I said that just to let you know it was an assignment and it was a hurry-up one. You'll have to make your way to Monterrey, Mexico and I'd like to see you there in a day or so."

"Monterrey, I know that town like my own back yard; I grew up on a farm near Saltillo, just down the road. What's in Monterrey?"

The Mexicans

"It's good you know the place so well, 'cause I'm thinking you need to buy yourself a taxicab and keep watch over some friends of our staying at the University Inn."

He went on to tell him the whole story of how Br. Angel and Miranda got the commission to do the work they're doing and how they had fallen in with the group of friends from the University.

"The thing that got me to call on you was a story I remembered reading about; some socialist students demonstrating and how the elderly couple were devastated, just by being in the way. Well, you need to know, the President of the U.S. has said clearly, these people, the Suarez's, are going to come home, play golf and keep dancing – no body bags, no arm slings, no black eyes, no messed up hair. That's what you are going down there for. Your background says the President wants you; what's more, so do I."

"General, you called on the right guy. What'll it be, Yellow or Checker? Maybe Gray Line?"

"You decide. Get plenty of cash to take with you, dollars and pesos. Here's all the dope on the Suarez team in this folder. These are some of the finest people you will ever meet in your life. I'll let you decide how you break the news to them, if you do; you may want to hold off awhile and smell out some of the friends. Just let me know how you decide to handle it when you get there and see the situation. It's all very fluid, right now. What's needed is the watch, the unseen protector kind of guy."

"Like I said, General, that's me. I'll take this stuff with me and memorize it. No one in Mexico needs to see these pictures and all the details."

"One more thing, Luis, we're using the secure telephone hookup. I'll call and let them know about you so they can get your name on the caller ID list. When you get on your way, use only the special line when you call me or anyone up here. Keep in touch and watch your back."

"I'll do that, General. This is the best assignment I've ever been given; you can frame it when we get back. Thanks for thinking of me. So long, General."

"So long, Captain and that's a deal; I'll frame your commendation for you."

He called Harry Foster.

"He's on his way, Harry; the best of the stock, name's Luis Caldera, dual citizenship, Latino. Monterrey's his old stomping grounds. They'll be in good hands, for sure. He can intimidate a swarm of polar bears to head south."

"Thanks, Phil; I'll pass it on to the President."

Then he called John Smoltz and gave him the same report.

"Nice move, Phil; no time wasted – the guys in the White House will like that. So do I."

CHAPTER 22
Boys, Dance With the Girls

The next day, General Bragg called all of his agents on conference call to explain that the Border District would remain at New Orleans for the time being and that he would be planning operations for many of his agents that might carry them on distant assignments for short periods of time and they should expect a call to meet at his office within two days. All agents acknowledged the call. Now he was ready to distribute the tracking assignments as soon as he received the first list of names and locations from Br. Angel's group. He set about determining the teams.

It occurred to him that an agent with a wife partner would draw much less attention looking over a city, than a lone agent or a pair of male agents working together; it made for a good cover. And since these first assignments were to be for location and assessment purposes, there would be no reason to anticipate trouble. He decided to send an agent's wife with him if she wanted to go, understanding the circumstances of the assignment but maybe not of the operation itself.

With that, he set up teams of two, beginning with the agent and wife teams he was sure of, Randy Jensen and Mandy, Ron Jensen and Amy, Jon Olafsen and Misti, Shep Turner and, possibly, Bobbie. The other teams comprised Bob Crumpton and David Solomon, Simon Pederson and Don Fletcher, Jim Franklin and Bill Dollar, Glenn Corbett and Paul Calvetti, Preacher Coleman and Bobby Norman, Burt Walker and Bud Wiegand, Dave Reilly and Moses May, Ray Leon and Fred Baskins, Carlos Ferrera and Niel Olafsen, Richard Brownlee and Jose "Flaco" Rodriguez, a total of fourteen teams for starters.

These would all be on loan from his New Orleans District operations, leaving that District a bit thin. He would have to start recruiting. His

The Mexicans

first thoughts were the women that had helped and proven themselves in the contact work in the Mississippi River operation. He decided to make a few calls to test the response beginning with Randy Jensen.

"Randy, I want to follow up on that last call and run something by you. These first operations will be mostly for identifying locations where illegals are working; there won't be any contact work except maybe incidental. How would you feel about taking Mandy with you as a way to stave off any suspicion that a two-man team might generate? I'm thinking of how effective the man and wife team was with your contact work on the Mississippi, a sort of human, ordinary look; know what I mean?"

"Well, General, I can tell you that Mandy would be delighted; you know how she is about this undercover work, she loves it. The only thing is, how well will her family take to it? They're real close, you know, and I'd hate for Mandy to worry about them worrying. I'll talk to Mandy; give me a little time to let it sink in and I'll call you back."

"That's fair, Randy. One thing, though, if she were to accept I wanted to put her on the payroll as a new agent in training, she's shown herself to be such a natural for this stuff. I'll let you decide; take your time, but I'm putting the enlistment papers in the courier, just in case."

"General, you sure have a way of making your point. How could Mandy argue with that? It's not as though she needed more confidence. Call you back."

Next, Bragg called Ron Jensen.

"Ron, I need to run something by you; it's about Amy. We need to augment our staff with new people for this assignment we're taking on – it's big, spanning the whole country. What do you think about Amy as a trainee? I was real pleased with the way she took on that inside job at the farm there in Natchez."

"Aw, sure, General, Amy's a real trooper. I don't think she'd be ready for prime time right away, but I believe she'd take to it right well. She was proud of what she was able to do for Randy and Mandy at the farm. And, too, her folks were pleased as punch then and would be now; I know them, they're real patriotic about this stuff. What'd you have in mind, I mean, what kind of assignments?"

"I want to use man and wife teams on these first tracking runs scouting out where the illegals are working. There won't be any real need for direct contact work, just nosing around like a couple on business or vacation, whatever works. The man and wife show will draw very little attention, not like a team of two men; everyone knows right away they're in the business. Tell you what, Ron; you talk it over with Amy and in the meantime, I'll send the recruitment papers over to you in the courier. Then you can make up your mind and let me know, how's that?"

"That's good, but I can tell you right now, Amy's going to flip right out of her mind; she's crazy about the Agency and the work. I'll let you know, General, and thanks."

Next, Bragg called Jon Olafsen.

"Swede, I got an idea I want to run by you; it involves Misti's new job as agent trainee, like I promised her a while back. Do you think she's ready to start out on this new operation? She'd be teamed with you to track down places where the aliens are working."

"Yeah, General, that would work out fine; she's been wondering if you really were going to make her an agent."

"Well, I am. There won't be any need for direct contact work, just snooping it out. A man and wife together won't attract attention like two guys in suits; you know, they'd look like any other couple."

"It's a good idea; this new work will be good training duty; snooping is the beginning of intelligence work, everything has to be dug up, sort of like a good hound dog, but I won't tell it like that to Misti. I can't speak for her, but I'll be happy to speak to her, is that what you want me to do?"

"That's it. You talk to her first since you're getting ready to get married. I'll wait for her to tell me what she's decided, then she can start filling out the paperwork. But the first assignment might get you before the marriage, if you keep putting it off."

The Mexicans

"No worry about that, General. Misti works fast when she makes up her mind. I'll call and talk to her, now, so get ready."

"I'm ready. By the way, what're you getting out of the locals there on that Black Bayou raid? We need to get our investigation cranked up before too long; there's questions we have to find answers for, like where'd that stuff come from and how did it get there? I know that little skiff may have brought some of it but I'm not inclined to think those guys would trust that much heavy stuff to a little fishing boat. We don't need to let the situation get stale."

"Yeah, General, I've been working my informers and I've got a couple of witnesses to a dump-size truck going in and out of that area, too big for any fishermen to need. I found the tracks, I think, but most of that's been obliterated a lot by the police cars. They're still playing out the investigation of what went down there; some of the usual outsiders are pointing fingers at the SWAT team and the dead count; they're crying overkill, but I'd have done the same thing if it'd been me. They had heavy stuff and we were all in the open trying to look inconspicuous with our six-shooters and badges. It may be a couple weeks before they get that resolved; meanwhile they're not ready to release anything. We'll need their report before we can get any warrants, so we'll just have to bide our time right now. I'll get my first report out to you today; it's about as ready as it can get up to now. OK?"

"OK, Swede, good report. Bye."

Bragg decided to hold off on any more calls until he and Misti finished her interview. Just as he suspected, he didn't have long to wait; Misti knocked on his door her signature knock.

"Come in, Misti."

"General Bragg, is it true? Are you really giving me the chance to become a super-spy? Jon isn't just kidding around, is he?"

Bragg just looked at her, not saying a word.

"I knew it, Jon was pulling my leg; wait till I get him, I'll pull his chain good."

142

"Now, wait a minute, Misti, the first lesson you must learn is to not assume and not to presume; both are likely troublemakers. You assumed that Jon was pulling your leg, but he wasn't; I want you to begin tomorrow as Agent-in-Training. Now, notice the first word is 'Agent', that's what I want you for. So, what's your answer? Notice I'm not presuming you'll want it."

"Yes! Of course, yes, you know how much I've wanted that; I only took the office assistant job to get into the Agency. Now, you've started my career! You're so great; you're the best boss anyone could have. Starting tomorrow! I'll get the paperwork done today before I leave. Oh, thank you so much, General Bragg."

"I'll need for you to join Swede on his first assignment of our Border operation and that will be very soon, within a few days. You'll be just snooping around together as a team, looking like man and wife on a holiday. Don't expect any danger, no contacts except maybe incidental. That's the whole of it, Misti. I'm glad you're going to be one of us in the field, an agent with a Lieutenant grade. Now go tell Jon you're on board."

"I heard that!" and she disappeared beyond the door.

"I love this job", Bragg thought, but he had really said it out loud.

In Cody, Wyoming, towards the late afternoon, the news was just breaking. Sheriff Tom Hastings called Carl Burkett's family first to give them time to prepare for the news reports of the scene at the lake.

"John, we found the airplane and all of the missing men. It was at the bottom of the lake out near the center, a quarter mile from the cabin. The plane had been scuttled. The men were tied in and had no chance when it went down. We don't know if they were alive or dead when it went under; the coroner will determine that. I hate to have to be the one to tell you, John. This is tough on all of us; we all knew Carl and loved him like a brother. Just so's you'll know, they let him carry his Bible with him; it was tucked under the straps."

The Mexicans

"Oh, God! Oh, dear God! How'm I going to tell Clara and Juliet and the others, Tom? I'm no good at this; I can't even hold myself together. Talk to Bob Crumpton, will you? He can carry the news to Juliet and Clara. Could you do that, Tom; he's good at these things."

John Burkett handed the phone to Crumpton.

"I'm here, Tom."

"Bob, they were all in the plane at the bottom of the lake; scuttled. That's the whole story right now. Carl went down holding his Bible under the strap. I gotta go, Bob; I can't stand to talk anymore. We'll see you later on, I expect."

"Thanks, Tom. I'll break the news to Juliet and his buddies."

"Bob," John Burkett asked him, "try to have Clara there when you tell Juliet; I'll be along in a little while. Would you do that for me, Bob?"

Crumpton put his arm around Carl's father, "Sure, John; you just sit here awhile and talk to God about this. I'll see to Clara and Juliet. Let me know if you need me."

That was one of the hardest things Bob Crumpton had been given to do in his life; good friends being torn apart inside, having their worst nightmares come true, tore his own heart to pieces. But Crumpton was strong even through his tears and he had a way of saying things, a way that calmed the spirit and brought a sense of peace. He often thanked God for allowing him to be able to do that.

Crumpton was at the scene to look for the slip of paper in the catch box of the plane, the one with an airplane's registration call numbers. No one knew the number, but Crumpton wrote it down and suggested it might be a clue. It was apparently a registration of an airplane out of Montana. He had a good lead, now, thanks to Carl. The FBI detached from the case, since it was clearly a multiple murder and outside of their jurisdiction.

Days later, at the funeral, Crumpton spoke of his friend and the Bible that he always had nearby, even as he went to meet God. Afterward they said goodbye to Bob Crumpton, teary-eyed, every one.

When Crumpton chased down the registration number in Montana, he found out that plane had been wrecked just two weeks before; the pilot was killed but no one else was in the plane when it blew up. The sheriff had closed the investigation.

"We don't have any reason to suspect foul play; it was determined to be a fuel leak."

The registration ownership was the Star Crescent Air Shuttle operating out of Billings. The owners of the firm's hanger on the private airstrip were listed as residents of Detroit.

"Now, why am I not surprised?" Crumpton thought.

He put his thoughts down in a memo to Phil Bragg.

"I believe the evidence points to an air link into Canada from Venezuela, through Mexico delivering terrorists to a point of exchange in the northern wilderness areas of the central Canadian provinces, at least one being in Saskatchewan. From the exchange point another waiting airplane takes the passengers into the U.S., possibly the Detroit area.

"What is known is that terrorists are flying teams into Mexican villages to control the families of workers in the U.S., mostly illegals, through cash allowances in order to arrange through them for their relatives to become employed by their terrorist counterparts at workplaces in the U.S. The airplanes originate from Venezuela delivering teams of agents into Mexico and some delivering teams into Canada in the wilderness areas. We know this because of spotters employed by CIA agents who have seen the planes and identified them by their registration numbers on the aircraft.

"We had an eyewitness to the transfer of a team at a lake site where charter sports fishing guides frequent. The witness, Carl Burkett, himself a charter guide, recognized the peculiar occurrence and reported it to me, having seen both the delivering aircraft and the waiting return airplane make the transfer. That witness recorded the number of the return airplane and stashed it in his plane's glove box, but before he was able to turn it over to authorities he was murdered.

The Mexicans

"Upon retrieving the number from Burkett's scuttled plane, I inquired to the Montana Air Traffic Control authority and found that the plane and its pilot had been blown up in an apparent accident. Tracing the plane's registration I found the owner's name to be the Star Crescent Air Shuttle operating out of Billings. The hanger property where the plane was housed was owned by individuals living in Detroit whose names were of Middle East origin, all noted below.

"It all points to an Iran-Venezuela nexus operating to import terrorists both for the recruiting of the Mexican laborers and for employing and managing them in their workplaces in the U.S. We have yet to plug the Canadian connection."

CHAPTER 23
New Faces and New Places

General Bragg could see a short window coming up in his schedule. Now might be the time to get a look at the Denver area, in particular the Colorado Springs area. He had worried about the problem of air transportation limiting their movements during bad weather. But, at the Air Force Base in Colorado Springs military aircraft were in and out of there regularly; their Ground Control Approach systems were very reliable, often flying even when weather had shut down the commercial airports. Then, too, it was close enough for a fast commute to the Denver-Boulder metropolis. His curiosity had peaked.

"Get your bag ready, Beatrice; we're on our way to check out Denver at last. You know how I hate dangling strings; we'll have another night or two away from this river muck."

"Sounds good, dear; we can use another trip out of this move business. I'll be ready just as soon as I can locate that last bag of secret things I bought from Veronica's Boudoir, you handsome hunk."

"Some secret; you know good and well you showed them off that evening in a special unveiling, saucy and a little naughty, I might add." Phil liked the nickname and he liked her planning habits.

Denver was having one of their heavy early season snowfalls when their plane approached the airfield. They would have to wait two hours for the winds to die down sufficiently for a safe landing. The roads were iced over with a layer of snow covering the ice. Traffic was snarled since no one expected the snowstorm and most of the cars hadn't had chains put on for the winter season. Two hours later they were able to get a taxi. Two hours later they were stuck on the interstate headed for their hotel and two hours later their taxi was abandoned and they were walking and rolling luggage the last two blocks to their hotel.

The following day was beautiful, bright and sunny, even warm in the sunshine. Phil and Bea relaxed at breakfast while he looked over the morning newspaper.

"I think this ice will be gone in a few hours; they salted it down overnight after the snowstorm passed. We ought to be able to get a car and look around probably by noon." Bragg wasn't concerned.

"That gives us a couple of hours to shop. I'd love to get a chance to skate outdoors. There's nothing like the real thing; I get so tired of skating in a circle all the time." Beatrice had ideas of her own.

A front page article caught his eye by its headline, "Four decorated cops get early out." It followed with the story of an Internal Investigation Unit of the State Police, under pressure from the American Civil Justice Union, determined that the four were guilty of using unnecessary force by shooting and injuring three suspects fleeing from a warehouse just before an explosion ripped it apart and demolished two small, low-rent apartment houses nearby. Eight homeless men who had taken refuge in the old dilapidated apartment houses were killed.

The injured suspects, they found, were illegal immigrants who had been employed storing heavy ordnance and weapons in the warehouse. They confessed to having mishandled live starter caps which fired and got the entire crate burning; they were running for their lives, barely escaping the explosions that followed. Their wounds were treated and they were turned over to the Immigration authorities who released the men pending a deportation hearing. The four cops were allowed to resign, forfeiting all pensions and benefits.

The FBI had been alerted and they were sending a team of investigators to determine what, if any, laws were broken by the stockpiling of munitions at the warehouse. A spokesman for the FBI issued a statement saying that the company that owned the warehouse was based in Detroit and had not been interrogated as yet but their lawyers have filed affidavits with the Federal Court stating that the property had been leased to a group of foreign individuals whose whereabouts are currently unknown.

"Now, isn't that a perfect example of American justice! The guys who can finger the operators of the warehouse are gone from the country, eight innocent men are dead, their mothers still praying for them to return home, the guys who faced the peril and managed to stop the bad guys for interrogation are out on the street, disgraced, and the American Civil Justice Union wins another case for the American people. Bea, I think we're gonna do some recruiting while we're here, maybe."

He tore the article from the newspaper and folded it into his shirt pocket.

"Phil, calm down. I can see you're seething under your skin, but don't spoil our day just from a newspaper article. What is it about, if I can be so bold?"

"Really, Bea, it's just more of the same thing we see going on around the country; good decent cops, honorable cops, being made out as the bad guys just for doing their jobs. I think the only thing that will satisfy the Wimp Party of this country is for all the cops to turn in their handguns and strap on a nightstick, preferably made of rubber. But, apart from that, the thing that makes this so interesting is that the criminal activity ties in perfectly with the sort of activity we are expecting to find in our Mexican Operation and probably is exactly that. If so, this could be our first opportunity to get some serious investigative work underway, right here in Denver.

"There must be evidence from that warehouse leading to people who can give us information, maybe on their entire distribution system. This is the second situation that has come to my attention in the last couple of weeks; Swede Olafsen ran up on a smaller instance of weapons and ammunition importing and storage down in his area on the coast. Before we even can get our new Operation going, they're falling into our laps. They must be really well staffed."

"Well, Phil, honey, this isn't a bad thing. You're getting a big lead dropped right into your lap and now we'll be able to stay here at the hotel, skating and skiing, for a week or longer while you look over the wreckage and check it all out. That could take a good while, couldn't it?"

"Bea, I'm not ready to get involved in an FBI investigation; those guys have their way of doing things. We'll just have to come in and work the scene when they've finished their paperwork. But, the good news is that there are four experienced investigators out on the street right now, right here in Denver, who know all about this situation. From what I read, these cops were watching that warehouse, probably the result of tracking a lead to the place. It wouldn't make sense for four State Patrol cops to just be cruising around an old warehouse area. Most of them are out on the highways; these guys have to be investigative officers. I'm going upstairs and get a number to call to get hold of them. We need to get them on our new team, if what I think turns out to be correct. How about ordering up a pot to the room while I work this thing for a few minutes? I promise it won't be long; then we'll be out scouting houses in Colorado Springs. And sign the check."

"I'm with you, dear; catch that waiter, right over there, for me, would you?"

Back in the room, Bragg called the State Police office and got the number of the State Police Benevolent Association. He called and asked to talk to the person in charge; a retired patrolman named Dewey Greene. He introduced himself and told Greene why he wanted to contact the men.

"NSA? Why sure we got their numbers. Do you want them to call you?"

"Good idea, Dewey, but give me their numbers, too. I'm staying at the Regency", he gave him the room number. "We'll be here for an hour or so, then back later for the evening."

"Bragg, was it?"

"That's right, General Phil Bragg. I appreciate it. Goodbye."

"OK, General; I know they'll be glad to hear from you. Those guys got shafted. So long."

Next, he called John Smoltz in DC.

"John, we have a situation here in Denver that I believe is directly related to our Border Operation." He recounted the report of the warehouse incident. "What's really interesting is the large amount of munitions that were stored there. If I'm right this could be a big break for our investigation. It looks like it may be typical of what's going on in the workplaces being operated in cities all over the country."

"Yeah, Phil; it could be the first fingerprints and it reminds me of Swede's Black Bayou incident you're investigating. But this appears to be a cut or two above that one; maybe a distribution point for the target locations."

"It does, for sure. The FBI is beginning to investigate, John, but I need to get a team in on that warehouse rubble right away to sift it for anything that might give us a clue how all of that stuff is coming into the country and where it's coming from. It could be the biggest set of evidence we'll ever get our hands on to use to develop warrants. The timing is important, John; can you talk with your friends at the FBI and get them to let us have a few days to sift through the rubble – not to keep it, just to make records of what we find, stuff that could be useful information, anything at all. The FBI can keep charge of it if they want but I'll testify as to the significance this scene has for our Special NSA Investigation. Harry Foster should have his hand in on this for us, too."

"OK, Phil; I'll do what I can but Foster can put the word to them with White House clout. I'll call him first. Are you going to be there for a day or two?"

"Yeah, John, I don't want to leave without getting these four guys vetted and maybe on the payroll; I'll call Bob Crumpton to come and head up the investigation for the sifting operation and get a good record of the evidence. We want to get to it right away, the sooner the better. That place needs a fine tooth comb, inch by inch."

"I'll get back to you, Phil."

The coffee came up; Phil signed the check, Bea poured.

"I thought you were going to sign the check."

The Mexicans

"Room Service doesn't speak to the restaurant; they run their own ship. The guy told me that. So, OK, big guy, while we wait, let me see that map of Colorado Springs and give me access to your laptop so I can get a look at some of what's on the market, there. I'm thinking Denver has just moved up a slot in the choices hierarchy; winter sports, you know."

"You could be right, Bea, you might just be right about that." Bragg turned to the sports page. "Let's see, The Bronchos, The Nuggets, The – hey, Bea, how'd you like to watch a hockey game tonight? This Denver team is right up there in their league; let's go watch a hockey game, it should be pretty exciting."

"I guess so, Phil; I like hockey. I like all the blocking and tackling; I don't like the mayhem and wrestling; that I can do without."

"We'll tell them before they start."

"I like curling, too; do they do that here? Phil, let's look at the ice skates! Let's do, let's look at the ice skates at the sporting goods store; we haven't skated in so many years, you'll have to pick my pretty butt up off the ice if you don't fall first. They're skating in the park; I saw them from the window, this morning."

"Hey! I caught that; and I remember that last time I hit the ice on my butt – it's hard. You're right, Hon, we can do a lot of things here that we used to do in the winter. Remember the garbage can covers down the hill? We can maybe afford to ski some now, if you're game."

"I'm always game, dear; as long as it's you and me."

The phone interrupted. "Hello, this is Phil Bragg."

"General Bragg? Are you the man that wanted to talk to the State Troopers?"

"That's me, Phil Bragg, National Security Agency. Is that you, State Trooper?"

"Correct. I got a call that you're looking to talk to some of us."

"That's right; I read about your situation in the morning paper and thought there might be more to the story. Maybe you and your friends can visit with me and talk while I'm here today or tomorrow."

"Yes sir, I'm sure I could. I'll call the others and make sure they know in case they don't get the word. What about tomorrow morning?"

"Let's say tomorrow morning, then, here at the hotel. I'll arrange a private room where we can have breakfast while we talk. You won't mind being on record, will you? See, I'm always looking for recruiting opportunities; so I only take statements that can be verified – all of it right up front. That sound OK?"

"That's fine, no problem."

"Tell the others to come at 8am and ask at the desk for the Bragg guest room. I'll look for you then."

"Yes sir; we'll be there early. Thank you, General."

Bragg hung up and called the concierge to arrange the guest room and the orders for breakfast to be taken at 8:05am.

"That's it, Bea; let's take a ride to Colorado Springs."

"I'm with you, General."

Two hours later, John Smoltz called.

"Phil, you have the go ahead to take the lead at the rubble site for as long as you need it. Harry Foster just now issued a recommendation memo in the President's name that the investigation there be considered an integral part of the Special Border Operations. The FBI will cooperate by making it all available to our team whenever you're ready. Call Judge Amory Johnson at the Federal Courthouse there; he has control. The FBI Operations Officer is Bill Drake, I think it's William Drake, so you can coordinate with them. Foster gave me their numbers; 'you ready to copy?"

"Yeah, go ahead."

153

The Mexicans

Smoltz read off the telephone numbers and spelled the names.

"It's in your court now, Phil; good luck"

"Thanks, John; I appreciate it."

An hour later Smoltz received an update on coordinates from the CIA, eight more, and delivered them to Harry Foster at the White House in time for the 3:30 meeting. Later they were sent down to Br. Angel. Foster had plenty to report to this gathering.

The drive along the ridge down to Colorado Springs was beautiful with scenic overlooks to take the breath away of those not used to these mountain passes. In the crisp, fresh mountain air Beatrice felt a sense of new life streaming into the body, a physical awakening of sorts, a renewal of energy. It was a common response to the mountain experience, that invigorating surge that got the creative juices flowing; that caused one to feel that whatever he would undertake just now would be attainable, even the highest peaks of the mountains.

"Alive! I feel so alive, Phil; it's so wonderful to see and to feel and to be a part of this beautiful snowy world of rugged beauty. Let's just stay here awhile, can we? You feel it, don't you, Phil?"

"Of course I do, Bea. At this moment I'm a world conqueror. You know, Hon, living in this environment must be the greatest way of keeping one's batteries charged. Have you ever wondered why the Northern climes have consistently produced the great economies, the great productive megaplexes that drive the creation of wealth and power? There's a dynamic undercurrent of creativity flowing from these cold climates; a drive that keeps the body moving and the mind churning and the soul satisfied. We'll settle here, Bea, we've been had. The Rockies made the decision for us today, so, let's just take their direction and go with it; no need to argue 'cause we couldn't win."

"Let's go down there and look at the places where we can have a little property with our home. I think you'd like to live in the country setting in the mountains, Phil. I can tell, you were born a mountain man, it just took you awhile to realize it."

Colorado Springs was a pretty town about sixty-five miles or so from Denver; an almost typical college town; almost, because the college was the U.S. Air Force Academy, a not so typical University with a not so typical student body. On a drive through the campus, though, it looked like any typical college campus, with lots of students lounging around, studying in groups, in pairs or singly; broken now and then by a squad of uniformed officer candidates marching from one assignment to another. But here, the standards of living, studying and training were based on a strict code of physical and moral conduct required of those fortunate enough to gain acceptance. The enforcer of discipline was an Honor Code that carried its own set of rules and strict punishments for those breaking the rules.

The discipline was tough military but the pastoral setting, the landscaping, the modern buildings and the great expanse of campus green all blended into a montage of beauty worthy of the beholder, should he happen to be a visitor on a first look or the President of the United States on a Commencement occasion.

Phil Bragg loved the place. He had several friends who were permanently assigned to the Air Force Base nearby, pilots who he had become acquainted with at various times when military transportation was assigned to him.

"You know, Bea, the social life here could be a real attraction for us. And the facilities at the Air Base would be available to us, just as for any active duty officer stationed there. The Post Exchange has incredible values; duty free on imported goods. I'm afraid you might become severely spoiled by the feting that often goes on for the wives of Generals. Do you think you'd like that? I mean, coming after all these years of relative obscurity."

"Well, that is something to consider. We don't have to decide right now, let's look at houses, OK?"

They drove the nicer areas of the town for the better part of the afternoon. Beatrice looked over some of the Open House offerings and was well satisfied as far as they went.

"These are all very nice houses, Phil, but let's get a Realtor to show us some landed properties; you know, like maybe ten or twenty acres on the fringes of the city."

They found the Realtor that dealt specifically in just such properties as that; it turned out that they were very popular with the higher ranking military officers at the Academy and at the Base. Beatrice found several properties that were just what she had pictured; well tended small farm settings, some with very upscale houses and others with the traditional country style house, full porches, front, sides and back. And barns; they all had picturesque barns, usually red barns. Those were the ones that Beatrice swooned over. By the end of the afternoon they had gathered up a small armful of brochures. If they settled here, one of those would be their new home.

They returned to their hotel in Denver and freshened up; then had a sumptuous dinner and watched the home team win their hockey game. It had been a very fun day. The bed was enticing; they settled down to a glass of Chablis, turned out the light and spoke softly for a long while before going to sleep. It was a really good bed.

The alarm went off at 7 am, just one hour before the 8 am breakfast meeting Bragg had arranged with the four Troopers.

"Bea, Hon, I sure appreciate you setting the alarm 'cause I clean forgot about it."

"You're welcome, dear, but it wasn't me; I didn't set the alarm. You can thank the guy who slept here the last time; he may have saved you from yourself. Anyway, we would have awaked in time for a quick shower and shave, surely. I've decided to have breakfast sent up so I can look over all these properties. Can I order anything for you for when you get back? Coffee? Tea? Me?"

"That's it, that last one. I'll have that one with all the extras."

"Well, I'll just order you a double."

CHAPTER 24
Anytime Anywhere Recruiting

Bragg entered the lobby at 7:55 and followed the concierge's directions to the private dining room where his breakfast meeting would be held. The door was standing open and all four of the former State Troopers were standing, ready to meet him.

"Good morning, gentlemen; my name is Phil Bragg."

The Troopers each greeted him and offered their names; Sergeant Reynaldo Vargas, Sergeant Maximilian Flores, Sergeant Felipe Delgado and Lieutenant Julio Cruz. They each gave the appearance of good officer material; men who were capable; early or mid thirties, well built, neatly dressed and clean cut, with an obvious military bearing that displayed an aura of confidence, both in the man and in the men.

"It's my pleasure to meet with you this morning. Here is my card. You may call me at that cell phone at any time. I'm here on a business trip; my purpose is to select a suitable location to set up a new District Office to direct a specific new set of Operations which I'll defer discussing until a later time. I didn't come here to recruit new officers, but I couldn't help but take an interest in your story. I'd like to know more about it, but from your standpoint. I'll turn on this disk recorder in a moment as we sit down to breakfast and have a relaxed conversation. Please feel free to ask and say anything that you wish to be made a part of the discussion, but we'll limit this meeting to business and personal background information; we can talk sports another time. I'll lead the discussion and let it flow from there. Each one of you has a story to tell and an individual point of view, so please be as open as makes you feel comfortable. Let's take seats now and, if one of you would like to ask the blessing, please do so."

"Thank you, General Bragg," Julio Cruz spoke first. "I will ask Rey Vargas to lead in the blessing."

Rey Vargas was usually called upon for group prayer; he always seemed to have just the right words. They all knew him as a devout modern Catholic, clearly evangelistic, evidenced in his outward offering of the Gospel message at opportune times. He often explained his lucidity in prayer;

"It is the promise of the Lord that a man need not take thought for what he shall say when he is called upon to speak for Christ because He would give him the words to say that no man could refute."

Bragg switched on the recorder.

"Lieutenant Cruz, would you like to begin and give us an account of the activities leading up to the incident that caused your dismissal from the Colorado Troopers?"

"Yes, thank you, General Bragg. The incident at the warehouse was the direct result of several weeks of investigation conducted by myself and these three men; all of us assigned as a team to follow a lead provided by one of our informants. The information given suggested some very strange activities taking place at a particular site where illegal aliens were employed by an unknown business interest. There was talk on the street of certain jobs being offered to certain Mexican immigrants, by name, and those hired speaking of some "serious firepower" being shipped in to a warehouse and made ready for distribution. The talk was becoming widespread among the illegals that had not been given offers to work. The pay was much better than usual at that place.

"When we began the investigation, we went undercover, dressed as trabajadores, workers, and we mixed in with the community using identities as illegals from certain towns below the border, places we all are familiar with. It worked very well, but to find the location of the warehouse, we first had to find out which of the aliens were working there and that was a slow tedious process of networking among the talkers on the streets; no one liked to speak names and we couldn't openly ask for names. We just had to stay active in the network, pass the cigarette pack and talk about other things, picking up an occasional piece of information leading finally to a particular rooming house where several of the employees were staying.

"After learning that, we set up a method of tracking the men as they drove away in the mornings, at first following on foot as far as one of us could go before losing sight of the vehicle, then positioning at that point the next morning and doing the same thing. We jogged as though we were just exercising, trying to lose weight. When we had tracked like that for a few days, we felt safe in using a car and switching off after a mile or two, then picking it up the next day in a different car to avoid any possibility of being made. In a week or so we had the location established. Next, we had to get inside and we did that during the night by trial and error, finally finding a jammed window that had not been locked, which we un-jammed to gain entrance. We had not obtained warrants because we had no physical evidence to suggest probable cause. That was wrong by the law, but we took nothing out of the place knowing that anything we took would be thrown out as being tainted. But what we saw there that night would be hard to describe and do it justice.

"There were crates stacked on steel shelving nearly to the top on one side of the building and on the floor at one of the work benches there was an open crate of Kalashnikov automatic rifles and another open crate of grenades for a grenade launcher. And at the delivery end of the place there were two half containers, shipping containers, setting there apparently ready to be opened and unloaded. We decided to back out of the place and take it slow until we could get an idea on how to proceed without the illegal entry. So, I turned in my report as it stood to the point before the entry and we kept up surveillance of the place from a distance."

"OK, Julio, but why did they blow the place up? I don't buy that story about someone mishandling the starter caps. They must have been trying to destroy evidence. What was that all about?"

"You're correct, General Bragg; the operators of the place didn't blow it; the guys who did it were pissed off at the owners for not hiring them. The story came out during the investigation. Those three guys were friends of the others that were hired, but when they went to apply they

The Mexicans

were told something about their families in Mexico not cooperating about something they had agreed to do, so they were not qualified to get a job. I guess there was a big argument about whether or not the family did or didn't do whatever they were supposed to do and these guys got real hot about it and started to attack the manager, three on one; so the manager pulls a gun on them and forces them out. In fact, we saw them being thrown out while we were parked down the street watching.

"None of this stuff came out in the official report of the inquiry; they were only interested in what we did as officers trying to make the arrests of the burglars. Anyway, after we saw the trouble starting we knew there'd be talk on the street, so that evening Felix mingled into his network where these guys hung out and overheard them bragging about fixing them at the warehouse that night for what they had done to them. See, they all knew there was illegal gun-running going on there and some of them were happy to see it get gone, they were fearful of what might happen to them when the cops got wind of it all."

He paused, seeing that Bragg had a question.

"Max, how about passing me that coffee pot or urn, I guess it is. – Thanks. OK, Julio, I get it, but why'd you shoot them?"

"Well, General, those guys had been drinking a good bit before they did what they did and we didn't want to hurt anyone, but they had got hold of some weapons and live ammunition from inside the warehouse and when they came out we could see they were armed, so we hollered at them to drop their weapons and wheeled down toward them. So, this one fool lifted his gun and fired at our car. Then the others started to panic and lifted their guns, all the time running away from the warehouse. We chased them three or four blocks and then the warehouse blew; man, did it blow! And it kept on blowing for five minutes or more. We knew we couldn't let them get away after that, so we returned fire to keep them pinned in the alley where they had taken cover.

"They took a couple of shots, just flesh wounds to the leg – we're all pretty handy with our weapons and we didn't want to hurt anyone bad, just keep them from firing on us and from trying to get away. Well, it all shook out OK down to the part where I said we tried to keep them from getting away. The Internal Investigators leaped on that after the ACJU intervened and put the blame on us for unlawful use of a firearm; the idea is that we are supposed to let them go if we can't stop them physically. After that, it was resign or be prosecuted and those guys go for the throat. So, we took the easy way out, and that's about the size of it, General."

"I get the picture. You were the fall guys to cover over a nasty situation the local police had let occur right under their noses. I guess you agreed not to make any of this story public and this room sure isn't public; that's kind of what I thought and why we're here in this room. I've still got a few questions, but nothing to cast doubt on your story. My interest is in the situation you men uncovered. If we can agree on your future as officers with the NSA, then we'll get much deeper into what it was that you came upon there at the warehouse. Right now, I'd like for you each to tell me if you would like to be considered for employment with us. You have to make the assertion before we can proceed. So, what say you, Julio Cruz?"

"General Bragg, I would like to apply for employment with the NSA."

"And, you, Reynaldo Vargas, what say you?"

"General Bragg, I respectfully wish to apply for employment with the NSA."

"And you, Maximilian Flores, what say you?"

"General Bragg, I too wish to make application for employment with the NSA."

"And you, Felipe Delgado, what say you?"

"General Bragg, I wish to make application for employment with the NSA."

"Very well, gentlemen, here is an initial application for employment with the National Security Agency. Please fill them out with these ink pens. Take your time, be careful to read the questions completely and enter your information completely as required by the question. Do not embellish or add any details other than what is requested. You will have opportunity to add personal history data to your personnel file in due time. But, let me inform you now that the only position available at this time is that of Investigative Officer with the Grades of Second Lieutenant, First Lieutenant and Captain depending on your experience as an investigative Trooper. Your service time with the Colorado State Troopers will be accepted for transfer to your account with the Federal Retirement System, and I will see to that. Now, do you have any questions before I leave you to your task?"

"No sir." "No sir." "No sir." "No sir."

"I'll return in thirty minutes. Order more coffee if you like, doughnuts too."

Bragg returned to his room, poured coffee and told Beatrice of the windfall he had just encountered for new officers. Then he called Misti.

"Misti, in an hour or so I'll fax you four completed applications for immediate employment; I will have written their pay grade on each. I want you to prepare Identification for each one and assign a badge number. Then, if you can get it done this afternoon, send the ID, ATM and badge as well as the usual set of forms to each one at their address on the application; also send them the bank deposit form. Use overnight express mail; I need to have them on the field as soon as possible, but not without Agency Identification. They'll be a part of our new operation and will work out of the Denver office when we set it up. Until then they will be operating on site as a team. Did you get all of that?"

"I think so, General. Four applications needing four ID's, four ATM's, four bank deposit forms and the other forms packet, and four badges to go with the ID's, all to go out by overnight express mail to the addresses on the applications. Will there be anything else, General?"

"Not at the moment. I've been here for a day and a half and have gotten only one call in that time; someone is surely smiling on me. We'll be back tomorrow, leaving at noon, so keep it together and we'll see you tomorrow afternoon."

"OK, General. Have a safe trip. Bye."

"Bea, would you like to meet our newest recruits? I'll be finished with them in a half hour or so."

"You go on, Phil. Just be ready to spend the rest of the day with me looking at ice skates for you and me and short skating skirts with bright socks and underpants for me."

"All of that last part, I'm sure. Just give me an hour to get back from down there and visit the chamber. Got a kiss for the old man?"

"You name it, I got it." She planted a big juicy one on him and wriggled all around.

"Baby, I gotta go!" He rushed out of the room to the elevator.

At the meeting room the new officer candidates had completed their forms and were waiting.

"Alright, gentlemen, let's see what we've got here."

He didn't find anything unusual. All were married, three with children, Bachelor Degrees, good colleges, good GPA's, eight, nine, twelve and fourteen years with the State Police, ages from 31 to 38. No arrests, no financial difficulties, home owners with mortgages.

"If these are all accurate, your employment will become permanent when the information passes the vetting process; that'll take about six to eight weeks. In the meantime, you will be assigned duty as a team right here in Denver. In the NSA we recognize pay grade by title of military rank, but we don't wear rank insignia. Cruz will be the reporting officer with the Grade of Captain. Vargas and Flores will start as Second Lieutenants, Delgado as First Lieutenant. Promotions can come fast in this outfit based on time in Grade but more so for outstanding performance, so you each are now in an excellent position to built a great career and I'm pleased to have you on my team.

"In a few weeks we will open an operations office in Colorado Springs. Until then you will work on site. Keep a mental record of your expenses; we don't want checks or credit card receipts or statements. We like to

The Mexicans

operate incognito without a trail of business that enemies can follow; we don't like surprises. You will operate with cash out of pocket, which you will replenish as needed by ATM withdrawals under a Company card and a pseudo name that will be assigned to the card. Withdrawals will be in amounts of two thousand dollars. You will be expected to develop informants using cash payouts judiciously, but when you find a reliable informant, be generous. Expenses will be reported once a month in general categories as you recall them. There's a form for that. Everybody with me so far?"

"Yes sir." "Yes sir." "Yes sir." "Yes sir."

"Your ID's, ATM cards and badges will be sent overnight express mail to your homes so you should have them in the morning; better stick around your houses until it's delivered. Also there'll be forms to fill out for taxes, insurance and the like. Personal weapons will be assigned on my next visit. In the meantime, use your own and record the registration number on this application – I see that each of you has already done so. Those weapons will be acceptable for NSA needs. Now, let me tell you a short story about the warehouse you are not familiar with."

Bragg gave them a quick briefer about the invaders in the Mexican towns and their plan to develop an army of illegal aliens to be used at some point in the future.

"All of this that you men have been involved with here seems clearly to be a part of the invaders' plan; we'll know from the investigation, but the word you picked up on the street seems to confirm it. Our assignment is given by special directive of the President, so you might understand where we stand in the scheme of things. What I want you all to do is continue to investigate this operation. Find out what has been done since the warehouse was destroyed. Those workers are either out of a job or the operators will have begun another operation somewhere else. Do your best to get a trail on where those weapons and ordnance came from and how it got here, so be watchful for replacement shipments coming to an alternate site.

"Now, you guys are known by the warehouse operators for what you've already done to them. Even though they may not know the whole story, they now know that you know a lot more than they'd like you to know. So, first of all, don't allow yourselves to become targets. I know that sounds like a given, but these are desperate men with a purpose that requires them to take great risks. It's important that we find out all that we can without tipping them off that we're tracking their activities.

"In a couple of days, when I return to New Orleans, I'll send Colonel Bob Crumpton up here to head up the Denver operations. He will contact you when he arrives and he will be responsible for being sure that the evidence is identified and recorded, photographed and documented, so keep everything clearly marked. I'll get with the FBI operations officer, Bill Drake, and Judge Amory Johnson to be sure they have all the information they need on each of you. You are my investigative team and we have authority for searching out evidence at the warehouse site and anywhere else that may take us. That's official just today, from DC.

"Now, Julio, I want you and one of these men to concentrate on the crime scene; I'll let the local police know that you're NSA doing investigative work. Get in there and sift through what's left to get a track on where all that ordnance came from and how it was delivered. We want names on shipping orders and receipts of delivery; that's big on your agenda. Get the name of the people who signed for the utilities then get the property records and the names of the principals – everything you can get, addresses, etc. Stay on that until you've gotten all the records and documents; photo the crates and cartons, anything that has a name or a lead of any sort; get it or get a good set of snapshots and use a good camera; if you don't have a really good one, buy one, your ATM funds will be here tomorrow. Clear?"

"Clear enough, General."

"For the others, we need you to do some street work. Go underground for a week or so, grow facial hair, dress like laborers, work up new identities, then buy a ticket from Juarez, Mexico to Denver, mix into a crowd getting on a Greyhound bus somewhere along the route and ride it in to Denver. Keep your ticket stubs that show Juarez to Denver. Hit the city like immigrants right in from Mexico and rent a room.

The Mexicans

Take pick-up jobs, mine the streets and the workplaces and don't take any risks. Find out where they've moved the operation to, because they will want to restart somewhere else nearby. Your families will lose you for awhile, but they can use some excuse like you're working out of town. Call me often; I want to hear from you and know that you are all safe. When Colonel Crumpton arrives you will begin reporting to him. Got it all?"

"Sure, General. No problem."

"This afternoon I'll stop by the Main Precinct and give them a heads up that you've been employed and will be investigating the warehouse for leads on the ordnance and the operators of the place; nothing more. We always let the locals know when we're operating in their area. So, who do I talk to there and what kind of reception do you think this news will get from those guys over there, Julio?"

"OK; you should ask for Major Carlson, Robert Carlson. He will take you to the Colonel, Colonel Frederick Lowery, Chief of Police, he's the guy you should inform. Those guys are pretty straight over there. Most of them were sick about the way we were shafted. I think the truth got around to them. They all know us or about us. We've been assigned to this area more or less permanently, not as a team but individually. I think they'll be pretty well pleased to see us come out of this thing in good shape."

"Got it. Hang around here a minute while I find a fax machine in the Conference Center."

Bragg found the concierge, tipped him big and got the fax. Within five minutes he was finished and back to the room.

"Now, one last thing before you all leave. Your pay will be delivered by courier to your houses every two weeks. The checks will be drawn on a cover company account. That will be your cover employer. When I return, I'll let you know the dates they will be sent, usually the first and fifteenth, and the time of the courier delivery. Your wives can deposit them to your accounts. If you'd like we will direct deposit to your bank, I'll have my office assistant send you the forms. Let me know if you need anything. If any of you need cash right now, I can leave you

Anytime Anywhere Recruiting

each with a couple of hundred, more if you need it, and charge it to your working capital. So, who needs cash? Don't be ashamed to speak up; I've been there often enough."

They talked among themselves for a minute, then Julio spoke, "General, we could each do with that two hundred, maybe two-fifty."

Bragg pulled a roll from his pocket. "Here's five hundred each. The ID's and ATM cards should be here tomorrow, but just in case, this'll hold you. Now, have we missed anything? I'll tell you what; be at your telephones, the ones on these applications, tomorrow morning at 10. I'll make a conference call to all of you and we'll talk about anything that comes to mind between now and then, so think it all over and anything you're foggy on, let's clear it up then. Will that time work?"

"That'll work", they all agreed.

"Deal. See you again soon. Julio, it's your ballgame and I really love home runs. Take care and don't underestimate this bunch we're dealing with; they're heavies, real heavies and they'd as soon cut off your head as look at you. Be careful, don't take unnecessary risks."

Then he was gone; Cruz and other men had their first team meeting in that room, starting with high-fives all around. Bragg first visited Judge Johnson and then Bill Drake, clearing the way for all that he needed to do. Next he called Bob Crumpton and arranged for him to come to Denver for a couple of days to meet with the new team and with Johnson, Drake and the local police.

"Just get things on an even keel, Bob, then leave it with Cruz and go back. They'll need a couple of weeks to complete the sifting of the rubble; I don't think there'll be any need for you to stay there while that's going on but you can judge Cruz's ability to handle it. Then you can decide if you still want to go out on the first foray."

After that he visited the police station and talked to the Colonel, informing him of the identities and grades of the new men.

"As you know, Colonel, the NSA has authority over investigating illegal weapons coming into the country. We're working in coordination with Judge Johnson and FBI Officer Bill Drake. Our first priority here is to get a look through that warehouse and pick up any information we can find. I've asked Captain Julio Cruz to get started on that right away. He will have the proper ID and will call on Major Carlson when he is ready to begin the investigation, possibly tomorrow. In a couple of days Colonel Bob Crumpton will arrive to take charge of our investigation. We're anxious to get this done quickly. Here's my card; call me for any questions that may come up. I appreciate your help."

"I'll see that your men have all the cooperation they ask for, General Bragg; thank you for taking the time to come by. Tell your men they can come to me if they need my help in any way; I'll be available."

CHAPTER 25
Things Begin to Shape Up

The first meeting at the University Inn took place in the suite that Br. Angel had reserved for the occasion. He expected the meeting to extend into the dinner hour so he ordered up heavy hors d'oeuvres, cold drinks and coffee. Afterward, they celebrated their first planning meeting with a champagne toast and good wishes. Carlos and Merced Pacheco hosted the meeting and introduced the group individually to Br. Angel and Miranda.

Pacheco opened the discussion with a statement of the problem, which everyone there already knew. They wanted to know what Br. Angel and Miranda had to say about it and what had brought them to Mexico in the first place. After telling of their long history with the Missionary Association, Br. Angel assured them they were not associated with the Mexican government, state or federal, and were not employed by the American government but had been asked to find out what they could about reports of foreigners invading Mexico, planning to enter the U.S.

"We were very surprised to learn about the support program directed at hiring Mexican workers; that's not what we were expecting to find. It was our intention to find out what we could about where the invaders intended to make their crossings by picking up information from local villagers who may have seen them or knew where they had gone. Now, we see a situation suggesting much more dire purposes. But by the grace of God, bringing us in contact with Carlos and Merced, we now hope to be able to gain names and locations in the U.S. where the workers are living and working."

"Will the police arrest them and return them to Mexico?" Felipe Echevarria asked the question.

The Mexicans

"It is not a matter of arresting illegal aliens; that is a matter for the people charged with immigration. Lately they have been reluctant to deport aliens without first having a hearing. But we are not here to police illegal aliens. Were it not for these foreigners, the workers lives would be no better off and no worse. We're here to expose these invaders and to find out their connections in the U.S., and we don't have a lot of time. Our intelligence source thinks they plan some sort of destruction by the end of the year; we think they plan to do that using unwitting Mexicans workers to prepare it and maybe help carry it out. That suggests the workers' lives may be in danger. When we learn what sort of work they are doing at their workplaces, then we'll know more. Have I stated the problem clearly; can you all see what we think is happening?"

"Why do you think the workers may be killed; do you mean that they may be used to carry explosives and be blown up?" Valencia Calderon asked the question.

"We don't know, but it's possible. What we do know is that Hezbollah does that sort of thing. If they could import their own suicide bombers, they wouldn't need to hire unwitting helpers. I ask you this; if they can hold the families in Mexico as hostages, to be killed if the worker doesn't do as he's told, well, what would you do?"

"Oh, I see. I hadn't thought of the families being used as hostages. Yes, that would be an insidious way to get the workers to cooperate."

"Anyone else?"

"If that is true and they are willing to kill, do you think it will be safe for our friends to compile these lists for you? Do you think they'll be killed if they are found out?"

"I would not think so; that would disturb their placid situation and might cause them to be investigated if the news got out of the village. Most likely, they first would warn them that their family could meet with an accident; something like that. We would know it when the list didn't come in, but instead, they might send us a fictitious list and then warn all their people in other villages of what we are doing. Your lives might be more in danger than the lives of your friends. Secrecy is extremely important for everyone."

"That sounds like what they might do. We'll have to warn our friends if they agree to help."

"Yes, certainly. And what about you people? Do any of you want to opt out of this work? You may do so, of course; we don't want anyone to feel obligated to us."

"We are obligated to our own people to try to stop this. The workers might all become suicide bombers if this is allowed to go on." Felipe Echevarria spoke up quickly.

"Yes, Felipe is right; we have no choice," Gomez Hernandez agreed, "This has got to be done and our friends will have to make their choice. They know what kind of people these are in their villages; they can imagine the results just as we do now. But, we should tell them what you said for their own good."

"Remember, this is all speculation on my part. You know enough to form your own opinions, now. Does anyone else have an opinion to express?"

"Br. Angel, let's continue; we are all of the same mind, I'm sure." Carlos Pacheco had heard enough.

"Alright, then; if we are all agreed, let's begin tonight. We need workers' names and contact information in the U.S., lists that we can pass up to our people who are waiting to act. Time is of great importance, so let each of you, before you leave today, prepare a list of contacts in the villages nearby, people who may be trusted to bring the names of the workers from their villages and their contact information, telephone and address, as well as the information of the local family. It may take them a few days to collect the information because we must caution them to be very discrete as to whom they talk to. You see how it is; we must speak with as few people as possible."

"Do you think it would help to offer a reward for their service?" Luz Cabrera asked.

The Mexicans

"I have enough money to pay expenses generously to your contacts for travel or for whatever else may be needed as the lists come in. How they use the money will be for them to decide but they must be secretive. Only those people who are truly worried about these intruders should be enlisted in this work. As I said, the one thing we need to see from each of you this day is a beginning list of contacts and their villages. Beyond that, we should have a good sharing of ideas and we'll set a date for the next meeting.

"Miranda and I will be right here to assist you in any way, including financially whether pesos or dollars. When you have information, even from a single village, bring it in and we will forward it without delay. Let me finish by telling you how gratified we are to have been accepted into your fellowship. Now let us thank God for giving us this meeting and ask His blessing on our work."

Br. Angel thanked God for all that had transpired since Miranda and he had been led to those people and he asked His safe hand to be upon every one of them and their families. Then he asked the blessing on their plans and all the work that they would begin to do. They all said:

"Amen."

Next, each of the group took turns telling their stories of what they had encountered and learned about the invaders and their activities; they specified the names of contacts they could trust in specific villages within a few hours' drive and some beyond. Everyone expressed confidence that they could carry out the work and keep it secret.

"We have a good set of plans, here; this is very encouraging. I would ask that we meet again Wednesday evening, that's three days from today. Bring the lists with you that you have at that time, but do not let that delay your bringing them to us individually if you can, as the lists come to you; Miranda and I would enjoy your company for dinner when you do.

Before you leave, let me share with you my plan for encouraging your contacts to do this work and also to enlist contacts in other villages to do the same. It will be in the form of cash for expenses and a savings account to build up as the work is accomplished so that they each will have a substantial sum to begin their own enterprises when the work is finished. And we will not forget you, our most important contacts, at that time."

Everyone was pleased with that; it would help in recruiting contacts. Br. Angel asked each person to sign a register and give a contact number. When finished, the register contained names of seven couples, including Carlos and Merced Pacheco. Others were Felipe and Montez Echevarria, Alberto and Luz Cabrera, Rolando and Valencia Calderon, Benjamin and Florence Valdez, Gomez and Thomasine Hernandez, and Ignacio and Sabrina Garcia. These were the seven couples of the University friends with whom Br. Angel and Miranda would spend the next few weeks gathering names.

The second day after that meeting the first lists of names and locations of the illegal workers began to flow in. Benjamin and Florence Valdez called late in the afternoon.

"We have the information from two communities where friends had come to us in the past few weeks. We have their reports and we can bring the information to you this afternoon if you want to move it forward; can we meet you there at the Inn?"

Br. Angel couldn't have been more gratified.

"Yes, yes, Benjamin, we will be here; come right up when you get here and we will have dinner together. That is very good news, indeed. We shall be expecting you then?"

"Yes; we should be there within thirty minutes. Goodbye."

"Fine. Goodbye, Benjamin."

"Miranda, we have the first fruits of our plan coming to visit soon. Benjamin tells me they have the information from two communities they have already gathered from their contacts. They will be here in thirty minutes. We'll look over the material and then they will join us for dinner."

"Oh, Angel, that is wonderful news. Perhaps that will be a good indicator of how well this will all work out. Let's order dinner up, we have plenty of dining space here in this suite. Don't you think we can talk more freely here than in the restaurant?"

"Yes, we should do that. I think I saw some menus in the top drawer of that desk. We can order dinner and look over the lists while it's being prepared."

Benjamin and Florence Valdez arrived as expected.

"Good evening, Florence, Benjamin, welcome."

"Thank you; you are most gracious."

"Well, it's our pleasure to have you, Benjamin; it's why we have taken the suite. Hopefully, we can get together with you and with the others often; one couple or many, it's a pleasure for us. Now, let's look over this work you have brought and share the blessings of this table; blessings the good Lord provides."

"Before you get started on anything else, Angel, let me pass out the menus. We should call down now for our dinner orders."

They ordered their selections and Miranda ordered the wine.

"So, now, let me show you what we have brought." Benjamin removed his jacket. "Now, here we have the community of Parras de la Fuente, about midway between Saltillo and Torreon. It is a fairly large community and we have in this list thirty-four names and their addresses in the U.S.; also the local information. As you can see, it is not in any particular order. Our friend drew it up from notes he has been making; he is certain it is good and complete. He had to work very quietly; the Council in that town has eyes and ears out everywhere these days."

"Yes, we've found that the other places we've visited. The Council pays the local authorities; actually, the locals would likely place themselves and their families in danger if they opposed those people. This work could be dangerous; we must pray for their safety every day. Now, I see there are many with telephones; that will be of help. And the family names back home could be useful when contacting the workers. I can assure you and your friend that these names will be kept in secret. And, what is this other list?"

"This list is of Sabinas Hidalgo, a quiet town about eighty miles to the north. It's on the old highway going to Nuevo Laredo. There has been a lot of drug traffic passing through this town and the local police have been involved in it all. It's been the subject of much scrutiny by newspapers in the past, but lately the drug traffickers have brazenly moved directly into the border city. That has been taking place all along the border; drug cartels have virtually taken over the governments of the border cities and are openly trading with dealers from the North."

"It's incredible how the U.S. is being taken over by drugs."

"Like the other one, our friend in this town has also been noting the names over the past few weeks; at first some were skeptical but now all of the families have taken the Council's payments. They haven't really tried to keep it quiet any more than they did when the drugs were being traded there. Many of the locals had their income from jobs with the drug dealers, so when they see an opportunity for money payments, they talk quite openly about it. Everyone in this town knows who is on the payment because everyone who has a relative working in the U.S. has taken the money. I guess you can't blame them for not asking questions, most of them think it is a legitimate program; but they don't ask."

"Well, this list is well organized, names, addresses, telephones and local family in nearly every record. Let me ask you, Benjamin, do you think that these friends of yours might have friends in other towns that they could recruit for this work in their towns? We would reimburse them and their contacts generously for expenses in cash while they helped with the work; pesos or dollars as they prefer. Obviously, none of us can go to the towns ourselves; we would never be accepted by the people and probably would be carried out of town in a box so let's be sure that there is satisfactory incentive for your contacts."

"Yes, that would suit them very well; everyone in the rural towns can use extra income. If they could be paid a certain amount for each town they turned in that would be best. You would not want to pay by the name or you might end up with too many names. And we would want to be very sure that we only take on good friends of good friends to do the work, people who are well known to be honest. So, yes, of course, that is the way to get into the other communities. And, I would advise, you there are many other villages, communities that don't show up on the official map."

"Oh, yes, but I have a set of maps that show just about every building, house and barn in every state of Mexico and it is all very recently compiled. As we proceed, we will check off those communities that we know have either been invaded by the Council or have not. And as long as we have the time, we will get to as many as possible. Money is not a problem and I want to assure you also that we have funds for all costs that you incur; you don't need receipts, your word is adequate. This is important work and we want to make it attractive for the workers."

"Well, I couldn't ask for a better offer than that."

"Very well, then, here is one hundred dollars in pesos for each list gathered by your friends. Tomorrow I will open a savings account at the biggest bank in Monterrey for each of them and deposit another hundred dollars into the savings account. He can count on that same two hundred dollars for each list he brings to us, so long as his information is valid and if he needs greater time in the larger villages, we will increase the bank deposit to commensurate him for the extra time needed, as much as one hundred dollars more. At the end of the work there will be an additional bonus for them in their savings. Do you think that a fair arrangement?"

"Yes, that certainly is fair, truly generous."

"The savings account will not bear his name as depositor, for security reasons, but he will be recorded as beneficiary. When we are at an end or he can no longer do the work, I will transfer the savings account to his name and arrange to have the passbook given to him by someone personally, here or at some meeting place. You will see and attest that the savings book is kept up to date with deposits that I will make and you will take a signature card for him to sign. And the bonus at the end will be generous. But the name takers must know that if their work does not bear up when it is verified by an investigator in the U.S., then the savings account will not be given to him; it is a payment for good work, not fraudulent work. You and the others who have helped will be rewarded as well."

He handed each of them an envelope with one hundred dollars in it.

"For your expenses."

While they were talking, the dinners had been brought up, the table set and it was all ready for them to sit down. Br. Angel asked the blessing on the food, the dinner guests and the work they were about. During the dinner conversation, Miranda asked Florence about their family. They had no children. They had thought of adopting one later in their life but had not found the time; it seems that teaching careers, research and writing textbooks had allowed little time for even a long vacation.

"Oh, I'm sorry to hear that, my dear. But you must have had a very active life instructing the children of others; and one can't relive the past but I'm sure you are living a full life as it is."

"Yes, we have much to do and this new work we've become involved with gives us a new reason for optimism. Who knows, perhaps there will be the possibility of a book in the future. In any event, it is a worthwhile project and I feel as though we have reason to thank God for the chance to do something more useful."

They learned the Valdez's were both educators and writers, in their late forties, world travelers during the summer, with a bent toward politics but with no desire for the Mexican sort of politics. They saw their future as indelibly written in the yearbooks of the University and the politics of the education hierarchy.

Dinner ended with ice cream and coffee, and their visit was at an end. They exchanged thanks and said their goodbyes.

"And please call anytime. We'll see you Wednesday at the meeting. Goodnight."

"Yes, of course and goodnight, my friends."

The Mexicans

Br. Angel and Miranda talked for more than an hour about their good fortune before going to bed. The next morning after breakfast Br. Angel hurried to the office equipment store to buy a good fax machine and returned to make his telephone call to Phil Bragg.

"Bragg, here."

"General Bragg, I have good news. We received our first lists of names last evening from two towns. There will be more to come soon, but I have these ready to send over the fax to you. Is your fax machine ready to receive?"

"That's great, Br. Angel. Yes, the fax is ready now." He gave him the number. "Go ahead and we'll talk later. Thanks."

The fax machine connected to the room telephone and he sent the lists, ten pages altogether. It all went off without a hitch. Next, he and Miranda walked to the large bank on the corner of the next block and opened two new deposit accounts in his own name and deposited one hundred dollars in each. Following that they were free to roam the city for an hour looking in the shops. They stopped for a cold drink at the farmacia, and sat at a table on the veranda, just off the street. It was a beautiful day and they enjoyed the freedom of just being out of doors for a little while.

"Do you know, Angel, this is almost like a vacation, now that we are settled into a nice hotel in a pleasant city. I hope we'll have time to visit around while we're here; there are many places of interest nearby. I noticed this morning while you were gone, the hotel has a guide for visitors and some of the places look very inviting."

"Of course, my dear. We are not tied down to a hotel suite. When we return we'll make a list of those places to visit and we'll see to it that we visit at least one of them each day, if they are not too far away. There are plenty of taxis to take us and we can have the hotel prepare us a box lunch if there happens to be a park or some such place where we visit. We'll picnic our way through Mexico in Monterrey. I'm all for it. And, if not the picnic, there's always arroz con pollo somewhere nearby."

"Angel, are you making fun? You sound like you're not serious at all about it."

"My dear, I am serious. We both need to get out and move about. A good walk everyday would do us good while we're here. I'm not making fun at all, it's just that I'm in a jovial mood after all that we've accomplished in just a few short days, and I feel very relaxed. Have I told you lately that I love you? Could I tell you once again somehow? Well, Darling, I'm telling you now."

"I remember that old song; it was a favorite of mine when we were dating. Oh, Angel, you are hopelessly romantic!"

"Yes, dear, I am; I admit it. This is very good tea, isn't it?"

"Oh, phoo, now it's gone."

"It isn't the best place for romance, sitting here just off the sidewalk of the main street in Monterrey."

"It is the very best place, just at this time."

"Miranda, if anyone is a romantic, it is you. Well, alright, maybe this is a good place for romance in English. Are you ready to go look at that tourist brochure?"

"I am. Did you pay?"

"I did. Let's go, mi amor."

So they returned to the hotel, the long way, around several other blocks, and looked over the brochure of tourist attractions.

CHAPTER 26
Some Things Get Settled

Now that he was done setting up the Denver team, Phil Bragg and Beatrice turned their attention to office space and houses. They first scouted the Colorado Springs area for office space near the University. There seemed to be an abundance of prime space available in a building that had architecture similar to the motif of the original University buildings. It had a little age, but it appeared to be well maintained, so he located the address of the rental agent on the GPS and drove over to see him. As it turned out the entire third floor could be rented for less that he was paying for similar space in New Orleans and they offered to include the utilities as incentive to take the space. And there was good parking and protected access to the parking deck as well as the building. He took a one-year lease on the space and signed it as agent for the National Security Agency.

"National Security Agency; that sounds familiar," the agent tried to recall where he had heard it.

"We watch over airports and places where stuff comes into the country, and a few other things. We try to keep a low profile so as not to frighten the local populace; I'm sure you understand. We have had scare groups get nasty and force us out of some places we've leased in other cities, kind of lower class cities, you know the kind. I don't think we'd have to worry about that kind of reaction here in this enlightened community but, just the same, it'd be best to not announce our tenancy. We'll post a business name that won't be likely to disturb anyone. All of our people working here will be very business-like and congenial. Let me leave the deposit in cash today and you can give me a receipt. We will do all our business in cash, if that is suitable."

"Yes, of course; cash works fine. Well, there's no reason to announce anything; you folks just move right in when you're ready. Here is the receipt for your deposit which can be refunded at the end of your tenancy. And I do appreciate it and want to welcome you to our community. I'll check up later on to see that everything is alright. Goodbye, General Bragg."

"Goodbye, Fred."

"Well, Bea, what about it? Do you want to take a shot at decorating and furnishing? I've got this floor plan to use. Maybe we'll work on it on the way back; then I can fax it to a local office furnisher and contract with them to give us a proposal. We'll look it over, make changes and let them deliver. Will that work?"

"I'm sure it will, Phil. Now, let's look at ice skates, OK? You promised."

"Here we go, dear, direct to the skate shop. I saw one in the hotel lobby; will that do or maybe we should go to that big department store?"

"We'll park at the hotel, look at the little shop in the hotel and go from there. Do you see that lever where that pointer says D for drive? You pull the lever down to the D and then you step on the gas."

"Like this?" And they were on their way.

They found the real modern gear that they both loved and paid too much for it, but they were ready to skate again after more that fifteen years. After a few minutes in the room to freshen up they made their way to dinner at the hotel restaurant for the city's best beef filet. They found the ice arena at about 8 o'clock and skated until shortly after 11 when the rink closed. The crowds were always light on weekday nights and so it was the organist's practice to play 'Goodnight Sweetheart' for about ten minutes and then they closed.

"Oh, Phil, I can't remember when I've had so much fun. You skated just like you always did, wonderfully! You never let me slip or even wobble the whole night. It was so much fun. We'll have to do this a lot more."

"I'm ready for it but right now I think I could sleep like a bear. Let's have a glass of Chablis and go to bed."

The next morning, Phil called his new recruits and they talked a short while. Everyone had a minor question or two. Phil encouraged them to develop their own strategy, but to keep their activities closely undercover.

"Julio, be sure these guys have what they need. Call me for any reason at all; I'll be looking forward to hearing from you. You guys will be hot for awhile, so use the made up alias and disappear into someone different on the street. Take care. Oh, by the way, we now have an office; check it out if you like, it's the whole third floor." And he gave them the address.

Before boarding the plane Bragg called John Smoltz and gave him a briefing on all that had transpired.

"I'm feeling really good about this situation, John. We've got our foot in one door and I think that door will begin to open to us and maybe give us a look at the sources of their weaponry and the methods of transportation and distribution."

"I agree, Phil. It could be a really big opening. Man, when you get your nose to the scent you track real close to the ground. New office and new Op team all in two days. Put it all in a report when you get back and I'll send it on up. Nice going, pal. See you later."

With Colorado Springs now the selected city, Beatrice could begin reducing her choices to two or three out of the eight properties on which she had taken brochures. Within a week she had her e-mail filled with property walk-through videos and neighborhood vistas. She spent hours going over and over the offerings and she whittled them down to three to choose from.

"Oh, Phil, just look at these properties I've picked out. Look at this country kitchen; it's just what I've always wanted."

"OK, Hon. Any one of them looks good to me, so you make the decision. This is your big event; one of the biggest in our lives. Just be sure of the one you choose, that's all I ask."

So they dined at Brennan's; Phil appeared calmly relieved and he left a big tip, always a good sign.

The two lists were at the office waiting for him when he arrived. After settling in, he turned to the lists, to enter them on his computer himself so that he could become familiar with the data, to get a feel for the information they would be working with. Once he got started he told Misti to hold his calls for awhile.

"This may sound strange, Misti, but doing this work helps me to think through the approach we'll take when we get to the point of contacting these guys; don't laugh, it's just the way I used to do it when I was working the streets."

"If you say so, General, OK, but I'm betting you never worked the streets."

"That's just a figure of speech in this business, Misti; didn't you know that? I guess you think your job as agent in training won't keep you working the streets a lot of the time. Face it, young lady; this is a gumshoe kind of business."

"Jon didn't say anything about working the streets."

"Jon may have sweetened the package a little; he wouldn't want to tell you something that would discourage you. Give the guy a break, he's looking for a partner and a wife all in one. But, hey, I've got to get started here, now, so hold my calls; I'm going to be busy."

"Gotcha, General."

Keying in the names helped Bragg learn the correct spelling of the Mexican names and practice the pronunciation. When he came to a name of a worker or a street or a town that he wasn't sure of he looked it up in his Spanish-English dictionary. It took nearly two hours for him to key the two towns into the program, but only an instant to sort the list down by State, city, street and house number. Then he printed the list to study the distribution pattern.

As he had expected, most of the workers were in the few States that had the greatest Mexican populations; California, Colorado, Texas,

Some Things Get Settled

Oregon and Washington. Others were scattered over the Southeast and in the northern States that had large cities. He would wait and see how it sorts out after keying the next set of lists before planning the first operations. They would focus on places with the greatest concentration of names.

"Misti, I've finished my street work, who's called?"

"Shep Turner and Randy Jensen both called."

Bragg called John Smoltz in the D.C. office.

"John, I just got a look at our first lists from two communities near Monterrey, sixty-three names in all. They're all over, but heavy in California, Colorado and Texas, also fairly heavy in Oregon and Washington. What we have is the name, address, telephone of the worker, and the name and telephone of the family in Mexico."

"Good, we can follow their telephone if they move; those guys will all be using cells. Well, how much else do you need before you send out the teams?"

"I'll give it a couple more days, say Friday. Br. Angel has a meeting of his group coming up day after tomorrow. There are seven couples in the University group, all married. He's pretty well satisfied that they will all bring the stuff in, so I'm looking for five to ten lists by tomorrow evening. It don't take long to key it in and sort it, so I'll have the work allocated to the teams Thursday and maybe call them in Friday morning for a long briefing. They'll move out then, over the weekend."

"Sounds like you'll be working with maybe 250 or 300 names, that's a good week's work just to find them with ten teams – have you got that many ready to go?"

"Yeah, John, I expect I'll have fourteen or fifteen teams; that'll work out to about 20 names per team, more or less. I'm sending wives that want to go as partners for appearance sake. They won't be doing personal contacts, just locating the place of employment; one, maybe two, places in a metropolitan area, I would think. Once they have the places identified they'll get records on the businesses, principals, financing, and all that. They'll pick up most of that from the property records. If it's like the places on the River, they'll have bought the properties and financed them through Detroit. What we really want to know is what's going on inside the places, but if we find that out it will be just luck, because we're not going to be taking risks, just observing from a distance."

"My guess is they'll all be something like the Denver warehouse; smaller maybe. All that sounds good, Phil; we'll need that kind of information when we go for the warrants."

"By the way, did I get authorization to beef up the personnel? I've filled the slots I have available with ex-police investigators from New Orleans; the file is full of applications and I called in a few of the ones that passed the vetting. Remember, we're trying to fill out a whole new slate for the Border District"

"Yes; you have authorization for the entire District staff, operations officers and support personnel. Are you satisfied with what you might be able to recruit from around there? I mean, we can transfer some officers in if you need them, they may be a little better trained that those ex-cops."

"I thought the same thing at first, but when I began looking into it I found these men to be well-trained and with good experience. This area has been pretty heavy in smuggling and drugs, you know, besides the illegal gambling, that's small stuff. The big stuff they don't like to turn over to the feds until they have the case made and then they like to keep it in State court just to keep it out of the national press. It's just politics."

"Yeah, politics and payoffs; what else is new?"

"No doubt, there are payoffs to keep things quiet. People around here have been that way for a long time because of the image thing and the tourists, but they're even more cautious now with the criminal activity increasing, lately. It just happens that they don't have the budget they used to have so they've cut back on the force with pension buy-outs and early retirement; some of those who left town didn't return to their jobs. But that's good for us because most of these guys all have plenty of experience and I think we can count on them to do good investigating work without the politics they're used to having to deal with."

"OK, Phil, I'll go along with that. Maybe we can pick up a few for the Texas District, as well; I'll let them call you about it so we don't infringe on your talent pool. Well, Phil, I'm going to get this report over to Harry Foster and I'll hear from you in a couple days. Thanks for the call, the progress looks good. That guy Angel is a whiz; either that or he has a bigger team than we can see, huh?"

"I guess that's a big part of it, John, but he's pretty formidable even without heavenly assistance. He's got these lists coming through the special line by fax, safe as can be. Talk to you in a day or two. So long."

"So long, Phil."

"Misti, get me Randy Jensen, please." (A short pause)

"This is Randy, General."

"Randy, I got your call, what's up?"

"Oh, I just wanted to confirm that Mandy is on for the long haul; sometimes I think she married me for the work we'd let her help us with. Now to be invited in by the General himself, well, you can imagine how she reacted; she'll be with me all the way. She knows there might be a little danger, but she figures we're on the right side of the fight and she likes the fight."

"That's good, Randy, she's one in a million, smart, brave and beautiful to boot. Tell her how pleased I am that she's coming on your team. I'll need you to be ready to go by Friday; look for a kick off meeting in the morning and I'll give out the assignments then. So, unless you hear from me otherwise, I'll see you both here about 8:30 Friday morning. Does that work for you?"

"I'm ready, General, and Mandy will be out the door ahead of me. See you then."

"Good. See you."

The Mexicans

"Misti, get me Shep Turner, please." (A short pause)

"Hello, General, this is Shep."

"Shep, I got your call, what's up?"

"Things are pretty quiet here, General except when LSU is on the court; then this town gets pretty noisy. Everybody's about sick of the stench from the river bottom, but I hear they've got the construction people ready to start filling and grading, now that the mud had dried out deep enough. They'll start by laying the chert or oyster shells, whatever they use for the base. What I called about was to give you Bobbie's answer about going; she says she's ready to join up and go. Since the auto rental agency has been gone, she's had a tough time just keeping up something to do, so this came at a real good time. I think she'll be a good partner for this kind of snooping."

"That's what I was hoping, Shep. Tell Bobbie I'm very pleased to have her with us. I'll need you both to be here Friday morning at 8:30. We'll have a briefing and pass out the assignments; you'll be on your own then, probably by lunch time. Does that work for you?"

"Sure, general, we're ready right now, except for the goodbyes. See you there."

Bragg then called each of the officers he had set out as team members to inform them of the Friday meeting and its purpose. At the same time, he asked each of the married officers to let him know by Thursday whether they would like to have their wife with them as their team member on this first assignment.

"But you need to realize that although the danger is minimal, it will still be a consideration. I want to offer this to you because I believe that a couple, a man and wife, out looking around in a city as visitors would not be as likely to attract the attention of any bad guys they might come near to; guys with guns who might be on the watch for government agents snooping around."

And he repeated his enthusiasm for the work done by the women working with his agents on the Mississippi River operation. By the time he had completed the final call, his day was about at an end.

"Misti, how about calling Swede and tell him to be here for the briefing? Have you gotten the new girl pretty well trained to take the office while you're gone?"

"I think so, General. Orella is a fast learner and since she clerked for Colonel Longmeier in Alexandria, the work here isn't new to her. You'll be in good hands while I'm gone, I'm sure."

"What was her last name, I forgot to write it down?"

"Burch, Orella Burch. I think she's from the Northeast somewhere, maybe Portland, Maine. No, I think she grew up in Bangor. I can tell you that a few of the single officers have been looking her over pretty good. She's really very pretty."

"I suppose nature will always be interfering with a good employee as pretty as she is. Well, I'm just glad she's also bright, got a quick mind; Brighton College wasn't it?"

"Yes, very impressive."

"Look who's talking. I'll be out of here in about thirty minutes. If you'd like, you can take off early and leave it to Orella to shut down. See you tomorrow, Lieutenant. Sounds good, doesn't it?"

"Really good, General. I'm going to make you proud for that. I guess I can tell you just this once that I love you." And she kissed him quickly on the forehead before he could dodge.

The General was nearly moved to tears, but quickly caught himself.

"If I could choose another daughter, Misti, it surely would be you. Now, go on and find Jon."

CHAPTER 27
Adding to the Ranks

"Harry, this is John Smoltz; I just got a call from Phil Bragg. Have you got time for this report?"

"Sure, go ahead."

"I'm starting the tape, here it comes."

He played the tape of his conversation with Bragg using a secure line while Harry Foster recorded it. That's how they filed reports up, using a secure line. White House advisers wanted first hand reports; no verbal skewing, omissions or extra emphasis, just the facts.

"OK, John, I have it and I'll get it to the President. Thanks."

Harry Foster knew this would be well-received, but he replayed it making some notes to be sure he had picked up all the details before taking it to the President. It was a good report and just what the President had asked for, good results in a hurry.

"The possibility of an enemy building up its forces in the country right under our noses; an armed insurgency, scares the hell out of me, Harry. Hezbollah, financed by Iran, poses a serious threat to the nation, far worse than a declared war because they fade in with the general population. How can our army fight that? It's prohibited by the Constitution."

"Mr. President, I have a report from General Bragg. It shows good progress."

"Bring it in, Harry."

Harry entered and inserted the disk.

The Mexicans

"Are you ready to hear it now?"

"Yes, go ahead."

He turned it on and the two of them listened intently. When it ended, the President said:

"Play it again, Harry." This time he took notes. "Thank you, Harry. This is a good report. Br. Angel has made good progress with this University group bringing in the names and locations. So now we can expect another five or ten towns to be reported by Wednesday or Thursday and Bragg's teams to be on the trail over the weekend. Excellent; this is better than I had hoped. Let's plan a Security Council meeting for Friday to let them know where they'll be working. We don't want any slip-ups with any of our people not knowing that these agents are out on the street."

"I'll arrange it for Friday just after noon. That's when the teams will begin to disperse unless something happens to get in the way; very unlikely. Say 1 pm, Sir?"

"That'd be my first choice, Harry."

"Right, Sir, I'll handle it and get back to you with the schedule."

"I can't believe it; maybe I'll have an afternoon nap."

"Why not, Sir; I'll stand guard," and he chuckled.

Foster took his exit and began getting the Security Council lined up. For a change, there was plenty of time.

☯

The last person Br. Angel expected to call him was Al Maldonado, his friend with the Missionary Association back home in New Mexico, but here he was on the cell.

"Al, how are you? I wasn't expecting a call from the U.S."

"I'm fine, Br. Angel and I'm in Socorro, getting ready to head down your way. I know you weren't expecting visitors but at our Association meeting yesterday, there was some concern over a couple of telephone calls from some little mountain towns down there near Chihuahua. The callers didn't identify themselves, but wanted to know if you were one of our missionaries. Since we hadn't heard from you, the Exec Committee decided to send me down that way to make sure you were alright. I was leaving anyway to go down to Chihuahua to visit my folks for a few days."

"That's fine, Al, but just this phone call would have been easier, don't you think?"

"I tried to tell them that a telephone call would be sufficient, but they insisted I visit with you to check on your safety; you know how they worry about some of the things that have been going on down there. A couple of them had you being held hostage and getting ready to make a deal for you. Those anonymous calls really shook them up. So, I'm on a mission to see that you and Miranda are safe and not being told what to say on the phone. I know it's maybe a bit silly, but just tell me where I can see you and I'll drive over Thursday or Friday and we'll have dinner."

"Well, I'm pleased to hear from you Al. I tried to call your friend in Chihuahua but couldn't catch him and since then we've been pretty busy. We're in Monterrey at the University Inn; it's a very nice place and the restaurant serves very good food so you'll want to spend the night here. Let me know when you'll be here and I'll arrange a room for you. Is Elena with you?"

"No, Elena's not with me; she was concerned about the kids and their school work, so she's staying to take care of all that and I'm alone on this trip. So, it'll take me a day to drive to Chihuahua, and another day to drive over to Monterrey; I'd better make it on Saturday, maybe Friday if I can get a plane out of the airport there at Chihuahua; sometimes they stop and sometimes not. Go ahead and get the room for me for Saturday and I'll call you if I can get away sooner, how's that?"

"Yes, that's fine Al. We'll be happy to see you. How long can you stay away? I might impose on you for a favor or two if you can stay for a few days. You have dual citizenship, don't you?"

"That's right, I'm a Mexican citizen. I can't promise you about that longer stay, but unless Elena objects, maybe I could stay awhile. We'll see. Let me get a flight down there if I can and I'll call you when I get the schedule, OK? Otherwise I'll have to drive, but I'll be there one way or the other."

"Fine, Al, we'll see you in a few days. Goodbye."

"Miranda, Al Maldonado is coming for a visit. The Executive Committee is worried about us."

And he told her of the anonymous phone calls.

"You see, it was a good thing that we left those villages; someone was checking up on us. That means we're probably in the clear after they got verification. But, do you know what I was thinking? Al could be the one we need to verify the contact workers in all these towns if he could take a few days with us, now and then. He's a Mexican citizen and he looks like a missionary or a traveling salesman. The Association won't mind lending him for awhile, now that they've sent him here. Anyway, it's a thought."

"Al is very good with people and he wouldn't seem out of place visiting in the small villages. Besides, he comes from Chihuahua, doesn't he?"

"Yes, Chihuahua is his home town. He'll be here probably on Saturday, maybe Friday, depending on if he can get a flight out of Chihuahua; they're unpredictable. I'll get him a room for Saturday; his Dad is getting over an operation, so he may need to stay there another day or two."

He called the desk and made the reservation.

The Wednesday meeting of the University group was to take place the next day at 3 pm in the suite as before. This time Br. Angel was expecting a goodly number of lists from the towns where the members had their contacts already established.

"Angel, my dear, do you know it has been weeks since you played a round of golf and, worse yet, weeks since you and I have attended a dinner-dance. I'm sure you must be anxious to swing your clubs at that poor little white ball, and I am just as anxious for you to swing your pretty little wife around a dance floor. Al can go golf with you if he stays with us awhile. Do you suppose that our new friends from the University play golf and maybe dance? Let's talk to some of them at the next meeting when they are all here; maybe we can arrange to get some fun and exercise, not that you aren't fun and you exercise sometimes when you get romantic, but you know what I mean, don't you?"

"Yes, I do, I miss my golf and our dancing and yes, I think we should bring it up at our meeting tomorrow. Everybody should like to play golf and dance. This afternoon we have our entertainment already decided. If you recall we are to take a walking tour of the University campus and devote some time at the library to see if they have anything about the villages that we selected. Do you still want to do that, because the tour bus leaves in twenty minutes?"

"Oh, I guess I can stand another long walk today. I'll be ready in five minutes and we can go down to the lobby."

The afternoon was pleasant. As they approached the University, they could see the campus teeming with students, some of them carrying signs demanding the tuition and fees be waived again this semester, but it all seemed peaceful enough.

"The Socialist movement is heating up here, Miranda. The Julio Jimenez influence is growing; they have funds coming from Venezuela. It's about what I had expected; just what Al Maldonado had told me before they left Socorro."

"They're dangerous people, I know. I remember those riots down in Oaxaca."

"I wonder what the Iranian invaders will do when the Jimenez movement finally comes to their villages, if they're still there when that happens. Double trouble, I expect; the Jimenez people have been talking and hatching plots to cripple the U.S. economy. That's what they really want."

The Mexicans

They continued their walk around the campus, then headed back to the Inn.

◎◎

The morning after getting his new assignment, Captain Luis Caldera had taken a flight to San Antonio, rented a car and drove to Laredo at the border. There he took a taxi to Monterrey where his room was waiting for him at the house of a law buddy of his who he'd roomed with at Baylor for seven years. He had made the call from the airport in New Orleans to Ignacio "Iggy" Menendez.

"I'm coming to visit you, Iggy. Better get the chastity belt oiled up 'cause you know how I adore Maria and she adores me, too."

"No chastity belt needed, Luis; I'll just clean and oil the shotgun. I got it for just such an occasion. You're not married yet?"

"Not yet, but I'm starting to get weak; time flies."

Iggy was so excited he couldn't finish his work at the office; he took the day off and went to buy a new bedroom set, art deco, a new desk and dresser and expensive paintings on the walls. This was his oldest friend and he couldn't have been happier. His wife, Maria, knew Luis since high school days and his two children had heard lots of stories about him. Maria knew just what to prepare for dinner; it would be baked chicken, his favorite.

When Luis arrived, he felt as though he was the long lost brother coming home. Ignacio opened bottles of his best wines, one red and one white. Maria called one of her good friends and asked her to come to dinner with them that evening.

"Luis, this is wonderful, it's been years since the time you came by after leaving the paratroopers. We've got a lot of catching up to do, but I want you to know that my good friend, Rita Juanita Garcia, will be joining us tonight so that you will have someone to talk to who is like you, single and good looking. You won't mind, will you?"

"No, of course not, Maria; any friend of yours will be my pleasure to meet, I'm sure. By the way, Iggy, do you know where I can buy a taxicab?"

"A taxicab; are you going to buy into a taxicab business?" It sounded strange to Iggy.

"Well, not exactly. I need one for my cover as a taxicab driver. It's part of my job assignment; you know I work for the federales, the NSA. It's why I'm here and it's all undercover work, it's what I do. So, what you know about me, don't talk about to anyone else, that is, if you like me alive 'cause there are bad guys out there who will make me a target if they learn about me."

"Well, I'll remember that in case you start getting frisky with Maria."

The doorbell rang and Rita Juanita Garcia joined them.

"Rita, this is Luis Caldera, our friend from way back. Luis, this is my friend Rita, Rita Juanita Garcia; we went to college together. Rita is a physical therapist, so don't try to arm wrestle her and watch out for her handshake; she likes to hear the bones crack; says it's just the realignment and it'll feel real good after a couple of weeks. Somehow Rita has managed to get by without buying diapers and pabulum, and that's probably a blessing for the pabulum-eaters that aren't laying there getting realigned."

"Wow, Rita, with friends like that, you must not have many enemies. I'm really pleased to meet you; and when was it that you took the Miss World trophy? Not long ago, I'll bet."

"Hmm, I haven't had that pleasure, but I have been offered the trophy wife award and had to turn it down; I was holding out for true love and he was bankrupt. You know, I don't often run into guys searching for a compliment, but I'll give you one, now that you've exposed yourself, illiterally." She touched his shoulder softly, "My, what a big bruiser you are; I'll just bet you wrestle grizzly bears on the rodeo circuit, am I right?"

"No, but I do a lot of damage to gummy bears when I'm really hungry. What're you doing tomorrow? I'll take you for a ride in my taxicab, high flag, for you. No kidding, I'd like to take you out for a ride; you can kind of show me around the new attractions."

She laughed hesitantly;

"What new attractions? Oh, I get it, you mean me. Ignacio, is your friend for real? I had him figured for busses or trucks, maybe, not taxis. Give me some help, here."

"Luis is putting you on, Rita. He's only out to buy a taxicab tomorrow, not make a living with it. It's just a tool for the real way he makes his living; give him the time and he'll explain it to you – that is, if either of you can cut the bull long enough to make friends."

Luis picked up a glass at the bar, "White or red, Rita Juanita?"

"I smell Chicken - that's boozer's choice, isn't it? So, OK, I'll have white, if it's Sauvignon Blanc or Chenin Blanc, otherwise Blush."

"Blush it is, White Zinfandel."

He handed her the glass and dropped a slight wink, sort of half-apologetically.

"Thank you, Luis; you have good manners for a bear wrestler. Who did you say you drove taxicabs for? Yellow? Checker? Independent? And what's your real game, bootleg booze? Unlicensed pharmaceuticals? Ladies of the night?   The works?"

"Independent. I'm just doing it while I'm visiting Monterrey. Sort of a part-time job. Where did you say you cracked bones? Hospital? Clinic? Morgue?"

"Mostly I do athletic rehabilitation at the men's gym; no, not really, I have my practice in the Medical Services Annex at the University Hospital. Come and see me, I'll give you a full body massage; you'd be surprised how it can relax you for days."

"I wouldn't be surprised. I'll try to drop by as soon as I find a taxicab and check in with my employer. If they don't have any trips planned, I'll come and see your office."

"And get that full-body massage?"

"Oh, I'm not sure of that; it'll depend on your rates, a half-body might be all I can afford."

"OK lovebirds, let's sit down to dinner. Mother has the kids for the night or they'd be up all night and never get to school in the morning. See how much trouble you are, Luis? By the way, you haven't seen your room yet. Take a look, it's the first one on the right down the hall, next to the bath. We can wait a few minutes."

"Come on, Luis, I'll show you where it is", Rita pulled him by the hand.

Luis whistled when he saw what they had done to the room.

"Wow, Maria, when did you do this? It's really beautiful."

"Yes, Maria, it seems more spacious now; the furniture is gorgeous," Rita fell onto the bed, "and the bed is scrumptious. I could fall asleep here, right now."

"Alright, kids, dinner's getting cold; you need to cool down, as well."

Maria called them back; her dinner was just great.

"This is by far my favorite; baked chicken, young and tender like this one. Gosh, Maria, you are really a great cook. No wonder Iggy's buying new belts every year."

"Who told you that? I've had a 32 inch waist since college."

"Yes, and a 42 inch belly. Don't lie, Honey, Luis can see, no one needs to tell him."

"Very funny."

After dinner, Luis and Rita walked outside and down the street a couple of blocks to a small park, where they sat on the grass and let their dinner settle. It wasn't long before they found common ground for conversation; Luis told her of his background and only that his work was something he didn't talk about. Rita seemed to understand and she responded with stories of her growing up not far from where they were sitting.

"Would you like to see where I grew up? Come on, it's only a few blocks away."

She led him down the narrow street about half a mile and then over several more blocks to a small white stucco house with a pretty garden and a family-size swing glider in the back yard.

"Grandmother still lives here; she knows I come back all the time, so she feels safe when she hears my voice."

Sometime later, they returned to the other house, but it was dark except for the light in Luis' bedroom.

CHAPTER 28
Working With Friends

When Br. Angel and Miranda approached the Inn, they noticed a nice new taxicab parked in front with the driver leaning his butt against the fender, a nice looking man, unusually attractive for a taxi driver, and he was watching them as they walked up. Just as they turned to go in and arrange for a car to take them on their visits, the man leaning on the taxi spoke,

"Taxi Mister Suarez? I work by the hour and the day; no meter."

They stopped when he spoke to them and turned his way.

"You will find me available at any time day or night. This is a new taxi, very dependable, just like me, and you can bet no one's going to disturb your peace while I'm around; 9th Degree Black Belt, Judo wrestling; 10th Degree, Tai Kwan Do; four year Paratrooper."

He lowered his voice and walked closer to them.

"My name is Captain Luis Caldera and I'm here to see that you are well guarded, with the compliments of the General."

"The General?"

"You might call him Phil; I call him General Bragg. But, let's not make a public conversation of it; just call me when you need me, taxi or not; here's my card."

Miranda knew a good thing when she saw it;

"Get in the taxi, Angel, this young man is another Bob Crumpton or Jon Olafsen, can't you see? Thank you, Captain Caldera, it happens that we have two visits planned for the afternoon and you may take us. May we call you Luis since your identity is not for public knowledge?"

The Mexicans

"Yes, Mrs. Suarez, I would prefer that. Where to, folks? "

Br. Angel quickly recovered from the surprise.

"Let us have a tour of the Public Gardens near the University Hospital. We can park and walk, it's such a beautiful day, and you can walk with us. I'd like to explain what we are doing, that is, what sort of business we are on, and the group we have taken up with. Perhaps you can do some background checks for us while you're not driving or wrestling bad guys."

They got in the cab and started off to the Gardens.

"You might be interested to know a little about my background, as well," Luis began, "I grew up near Saltillo and lived here in Monterrey for several years. I know the city very well and have friends here; in fact, I'm staying with an old buddy from Baylor University, that's where I got my Law degree."

"Does your friend practice law?"

"Oh, yes, Ignacio is a family man with a good practice. His wife is Maria and they have two small children. I'm not married, though I'm not opposed to marriage; I just haven't found the right girl. Maybe I've been in all the wrong places since college days. My parents still live on the farm near Saltillo. I haven't seen them yet since I came down. I just got in yesterday afternoon."

"Well, Luis, you've been a busy man this morning. How does one find a taxicab to buy so quickly in this city? It must require licenses and taxes and those things move slowly - oh, I guess I see; your friend is a lawyer and that's how things get done quickly, am I right?" Miranda was getting to like Luis.

"Well, not exactly. I found this nice new taxi parked out at the airport at the end of a long line of taxis waiting for a fare. So, I asked the driver if he owned the cab, since the old ones are usually owned by a taxi company, and he said yes. So I asked him if it was licensed to operate anywhere in Mexico and he said yes. Then I walked him away from the other drivers and handed him an envelope with fifty thousand U.S. dollars and asked him if he would like to sell the cab and the license and he said, "Heck, yes", but he didn't say "Heck", he said something like it.

"So I said, "let's go to get the license transferred and pay the sales taxes, make up a bill of sale and shake hands on it" and he said "Dang right", but he didn't say "Dang", he said something like it. So, we sweetened the clerk's cage a little and it was done in a jiffy. That's how we make things happen where I work, Mrs. Suarez."

"My goodness, that's a good story."

"I've got lots of good stories, but I know you two have some better than mine. Well, here we are. I'll park here in the lot and we can walk."

"Luis, we have about an hour, or so and then we'll have to return to the Inn. Our friends are meeting with us later this afternoon. They'll have some lists from the villages that we're waiting for. When we get them, we will fax them to General Bragg. He's waiting for them to distribute to his teams to track down the addresses and places of work. I don't know how much of this you have been briefed on, but that's basically what we're here for; collecting names and addresses of aliens in the U.S."

"I'd like to walk down that path over there, Angel; do you see the lilies all along the way? And that directory over there, I think, says something about an orchid nursery; let's go down that path." Miranda loved lilies and orchids.

While they walked the path, Br. Angel asked Luis if General Bragg had given him a special telephone number to use for calling him in the U.S.

"He did, yes, he gave me a number to use."

"Good, he prepared you well. Now, let me tell you about these people that I am working with here in Monterrey."

They stopped for a few moments while he wrote the names of the University group.

"Here are the names of the associates that are collecting the information we are pursuing. I think it wise that you remain unknown to them

The Mexicans

except as my taxi driver. I have not had a way to check out these people for security. It would be my greatest wish if you would do what you can to vet these people and their backgrounds so that we can trust them as legitimate patriots, not merely by their own word. Can you do that for us?"

"I can, yes. Give me a few days; I'll report the results to you, piecemeal as I complete each one. As a matter of fact, I have a friend who works at the University Hospital and my buddy Ignacio has good University contacts as well. I'll drop a name now and then and note their comments. Beyond that, I'll do the snooping I have been trained to do. If there is doubt, I'll find it out, you may be sure. This cover I have as a taxi driver allows me a good deal of mobility without raising suspicion."

"There is also the problem of trust with the ones who are preparing the lists. I will have their names and their towns but I don't know yet how to verify their information, except as the NSA officers work the names in the U.S. I fear there could be planted names that will allow the bad guys to know what is being done. Perhaps I am too cynical, but we are dealing with trained terrorists and their ways are devious, by nature. Somehow I would feel better if we had an agent who could check out those bringing in the names. If you happen across anyone suitable, perhaps we can hire them."

"I can't give you any assurance of that and it may not be a good idea to share the work with anyone we don't know very well. I'll give it some thought."

"You two just slow down now while I inspect these lovely lilies. My, but they are doing good horticultural work here; it takes very dedicated people to raise these specimens, they come from all over the lily world. We have just enough time to visit the orchid nursery before we have to return; where does the time go?"

"Now, Miranda, we can come again and stay the entire day. I'm looking forward to the orchids, too. Do you remember when we used to visit the rain forest in Puerto Rico where all of those orchids grew, many with their roots taking nourishment just from the air? Bromeliads, I think they were."

"Yes, I certainly do remember. It was El Yunque, or Junque, I think, the name of that rain forest. We went there so often we knew our way around without a guide. Maybe someday we will go back there. Now, just look at all the different varieties here; it is amazing, there is such diversity among the orchid family and they all are so delicate."

They stayed as long as they could and then walked back to the taxi. Luis was favorably impressed, too, though he had not thought of himself as a flower aficionado.

"I think I'll bring Rita up here; she probably knows all about this place. Rita Juanita Garcia, she's the girl my friends introduced me to, yesterday."

The University group was gathering in the lobby as they drove up. Luis held the door for them and took a good look at the friends. He would begin by finding out where they lived and what they did at the University; all instructors, he guessed. It was good to have an old fashioned snooping job again.

That meeting produced another eight lists from towns all within two hundred miles of Monterrey. Br. Angel explained his plan for paying expenses and a savings account for each collector and got the names of the eight contacts. He showed the passbooks to Benjamin Valdez, for verification, and then showed them to the others. They talked about gaining access to other towns through contacts made in the towns already secured. They agreed that there was some risk with that if the Group members themselves didn't know the recruited contacts. Somehow they would have to vet them, perhaps through a third person or a private investigator that could be trusted, one who wouldn't have to know the reason. They would discuss it further at the next week's meeting. Br. Angel continued:

"I think we will have to take the risk, putting the pressure on those we have already recruited by means of the expense money and especially the savings accounts. Any fraud that is uncovered will mean forfeiture of the savings account; that should deter any fraud. Beyond that, I may be able to get some help to verify the contacts that are not well known. We will talk about that again, but for now let us proceed with the recruiting through known contacts. Now, I have authority to offer

The Mexicans

you each a modest sum for your expenses; each of you please accept this one hundred dollars and we will reimburse you regularly each week as the work progresses."

Br. Angel passed out one hundred dollars in U.S. twenty dollar bills to each person, each man and each woman. They were all very pleased; the next meeting was set for the next Wednesday at the same time.

"But, remember, also, that as lists come into your hands, should you be able to bring them to me immediately, I will appreciate it. Please call us at any time you would like to visit; Miranda and I would love to have lunch with you. We are here most of the time, but we try to get out for a walk or a visit to an attraction during the day. Your company is always welcome; perhaps even a game of golf. For now, I will arrange to submit these lists. Thank you all for coming and we look forward to your next visit. Now, please let us join in prayer for the safety of each of us and for the blessing of God on the work that we do. Carlos, would you like to lead us?"

Carlos Pacheco was a man of growing faith; he offered the prayer..

When the guests had departed, Br. Angel looked over the lists and found them to be suitable for transmission. He dialed the fax number for General Bragg, with his fax machine connected, and passed the lists; it all took about five minutes. Then he and Miranda went down to the Inn Restaurant for dinner.

"God has surely blessed us this day, my Dear, more than I could have anticipated."

"He calls His people to service by unexpected means, bringing together the needs of some with the meeting of those needs by others. It is the mystery of God that He unveils according to His good will. We are truly blessed to know there are Angels all around."

"We shall find a Church meeting place this Sunday, Miranda, where we can worship with true believers. Tonight we will pray for God to lead us to that Church."

On Saturday afternoon, Al Maldonado arrived by taxicab from the airport; the schedule turned out to be convenient for him to leave

Working With Friends

after his father had recovered sufficiently for his mother to help him with his needs. He called up from the lobby to Br. Angel's suite.

"Al, you made it; I'm so glad you could come. You have the room number?"

"Yes. Angel, I'll be up to see you as soon as I get my things settled in my room; give me fifteen minutes."

When Al arrived at the suite, Miranda had already ordered up a pot of tea and a plate of cookies. They exchanged greetings and sat down to chat.

"Angel, I'm very relieved to find you in such nice surroundings. Some of us feared you might have gotten bogged down in one of the remote villages. Tell me how you are doing and what keeps you here in Monterrey."

"Al, it's a long story, but perhaps we will not have to go into a lot of detail. Let me ask you, my friend; if you found a good enough reason, would you be able to spend a week or two helping on a very special project?"

"Perhaps, Angel, but it's a little surprising to be asked such a question. To be sure, I will be available to help you if you need me. But can you give me a bit more to go on before I call Elena and tell her?"

"Yes, of course, but it would be better if you were not too explicit when you tell Elena; I think you will understand when we finish this conversation. Let me say, first, that I have known you and your family for what - about twenty years? And in that time I have found you to be a loyal and trustworthy friend. Because I know you that well, I can speak candidly of this project we have taken on. Please keep everything I tell you confidential, extremely confidential."

"Certainly, you can be sure of it."

"Some eight months ago I was engaged in a rescue effort down in Louisiana; you may remember I was gone a good while, several times. Miranda was a part of that work, as well, and it took us to the White House in Washington. Eventually, from that first visit we were asked to be part of a much more discrete operation and this venue is our share in that operation. We have gotten off to a successful start but there is much more to be done before we can put it down. Are you aware of the Council of Unification?"

Al shook his head slowly.

"I didn't expect you were; I will have to begin at that point. Let us pour another cup of tea."

That began a recount of the whole story for Al. Br. Angel knew Al Maldonado to be a trustworthy man of unflinching faith. He would accept it all simply because Br. Angel said it was so. When he had finished, right up to the present, he explained what he would like Al to help him with.

"There are a number of communities that I would like you to visit, perhaps in the guise of a teacher from the University doing research on adequacy of classrooms and quality of teaching in the remote villages. Spend a day interviewing school teachers and parents, but watch for any indication of the Council of Unification having been in the town. Do not appear to be judgmental, but inquire of the program when you find them to be there in the village. If possible, recruit a person that may be able to prepare the list of families. If they express an interest tell them we will pay expense money to start, with the promise of a substantial reward when they bring us the completed list."

"How bad are these people, Br. Angel? I mean, will I need a way to defend myself if they don't trust what I'm doing there and maybe want to get rid of me?"

"I know it sounds risky, but really, the Council seems to be more of a shadow than a danger to visitors. They seem to prefer to remain out of sight, at least when there are visitors. Leave as quickly as you can complete the contact. Call me frequently in public view and I will call you back, so the people of the village will see you as a man connected, a man of obvious importance. These are the nine towns I would like you to visit. As you can see these are all to the west of Chihuahua over to the mountains. Only Buenaventura has been completed. We know the Council is present there and at Cuauhtemoc and Guerrero. I will provide substantial pesos and dollars to meet all your needs."

"I'll need transportation; an important writer must have an automobile."

"Monday morning we will purchase an automobile; perhaps not so new and shiny, but a late model in good condition. It will be bought in your name and paid for. Your efforts will be well rewarded, as well. Monday we will open a savings account with twenty-five hundred dollars for this trip and the same for any others you may choose to undertake. When we have finished you may keep the automobile; perhaps your mother can use it."

"I'll call Elena. She will agree to two weeks, I'm sure, but if it is to extend much beyond that I will have her come to Chihuahua. The school will allow the children to take their lessons and tests on the computer."

It was settled, then. Elena agreed and decided to take the children and fly to Chihuahua in a day or two.

The next day was Sunday; they found a church and spent much of the afternoon visiting with members of the congregation and a family that asked them to share their dinner. They identified themselves as members of the Missionary Association in New Mexico and learned that the church also supported several missions in villages in the northern states; so they made a generous contribution and also asked for names of families in the villages that their missionary workers might be visiting. These they would give to Al as contacts along with the names of the church members who gave them the names.

From then on, they met regularly with the church for prayer meetings and Sunday services. Br. Angel was asked to bring the message the next Sunday, which he was glad to do. The church visits filled an important place in their lives for the rest of their visit. Luis was Catholic and attended church with Rita and his friends, but he visited the Baptist church with Br. Angel and Miranda for evening and mid-week services.

CHAPTER 29
Sneakers and Snoopers

"Phil Bragg, here," answering his telephone.

"Luis Caldera, General; I'm using the special security line, ready with my first report from the border assignment."

"OK, Luis, go ahead, you're on." He clicked on his recorder.

"I'm set up with a taxicab cover and I've made contact with the Suarez team. We have exchanged understandings; I'm acting as their driver and they agreed to let me know whenever they are about to leave the Inn, even if it's just for a walk. Today we drove to the University Gardens and walked for an hour. I'm working the backgrounds on the group members as my first assignment for Br. Angel; that will take a few days."

"Sounds good, Luis; I'm glad to hear you've gotten set up so quickly. Where're you staying?"

"I have a room with an old college friend and his family, Ignacio and Maria Menendez, at their house. He's a lawyer, she raises the two children; these are people I can trust. Just so you'll know, I've been introduced by my friends to a girl, a chum of Maria's named Rita Juanita Garcia. I'll be dating her while I'm here. She a long time friend of both Iggy and Maria from childhood; she has a private practice as a physical therapist, also she's very nice. She's a little confused about my job driving the taxi. Eventually, I will have to trust the three of them to know my purpose here, but I don't think there will be a problem with that; they are all educated people, very discrete."

The Mexicans

"Well, you weren't asked to sign a pledge of celibacy. Take good care of the Suarez's and let me know how things are going; regular reports, two or three times a week. With the telephone system we have there's no reason not to call as often as you like. The folks in D.C. worry about those invaders finding out we're tracking them, so they like to hear from us."

"Yeah, I'll keep contact, General. They're having their meeting at the Inn right now, so you should be getting some stuff over the fax in an hour or so. I'll be here keeping watch. If there's nothing else, I'll sign off now."

"OK, Luis, thanks for the report; so long."

He passed it up to John Smoltz.

"John, here's the first report from Luis Caldera in Monterrey. Ready?"

"Ready, Phil, go ahead with it." The recording went through in a few seconds.

"Got it, John; I'll read it right now. Thanks."

Bragg replayed the recording to be sure he had gotten all of the details. He'd leave it to Luis to check out his acquaintances. His teams were lined up and ready to go out Friday morning. That gave him just one more day to get the towns organized for assignment. He decided to stay late to get the fax from Br. Angel. Bud Wiegand's wife, Susan, asked to join him on this first expedition; that set well with Bragg since Susan was an ex-police lieutenant from the New Orleans force. That put Bobby Norman teamed with Burt Walker, a good match, ex-cop and ex-Marine.

Within an hour the fax turned on and began to generate the transmission from Monterrey. As the lists came in over the fax Bragg started to smile; then as they just kept on coming, the smile got wider and wider.

"Eight lists, there must be more than two hundred names here." He called Beatrice.

"Honey, I'm headed home now with my computer; I've got some work to do, maybe you can help key in some of these names."

I'm ready, Phil, but dinner's starting to get cold."

"Give me five minutes, then warm it up – dinner, I mean."

"Smarty. See you in fifteen minutes."

Before he could get gone, Br. Angel called to see that Bragg had received the lists.

"They look good, very good. We'll be working them starting this week end. My first concern now is that these people making up the lists aren't making them up out of their heads, or the telephone book."

"I've been concerned about that too, Phil, and I've offered them a plan to pay expenses as the lists come in, but also a sweetener; I'm putting a substantial dollar reward into bank savings accounts for each one, to be turned over to them at the end of the project, but only if their data turn out to be valid; the question of fraud will deny them their nest egg."

"Not bad, not bad. I think that'll work with a good payout."

"How would you feel about a hundred in pesos for a list and another hundred in dollars in the bank account? I control the passbooks in my name and the group sponsor verifies it to them each week. I think it's a good offer and the group members each get $100 expenses each week and the promise of a bonus at the end."

"I think I'd be making tracks. Sounds to me like a really good scheme. I guess you've met Luis; he called me with his report."

"I want to thank you for that consideration; yes, Luis is a very impressive young man. We will sleep well with him around, for sure. Miranda loves him; he's kind and speaks well."

"I'm glad you both like him; he's first rate. John Smoltz and Harry Foster send best regards. I'll let you go, but call me anytime. I'm always thinking of you; that's a serious situation you're in down there.

Just stay safe, my friend, you and Miranda."

"Thank you, Phil, we'll keep you informed. Our next group meeting is in one week, but more lists will likely come in before that with these expenses being paid. Goodbye for now."

It was late and Beatrice would be losing patience; he left on the run. Bragg would spend another two hours at home keying information into the database and then sorting it by location. When he had finished he had all ten lists like he wanted them. He was ready to allocate the names to the teams in the morning.

"Beatrice, with all your physical and intellectual assets, how can it be you're such a great homemaker? This dinner is outstanding and you kept it nice and warm; just right, even though I was an hour late. I'm telling you, Babe; you're too good for me, and I know it, too."

"Whatever you're after, Phil, dear, the answer is yes. I just love it when you talk romantic."

The next morning Bragg was prepared to report the town count and names to Harry Foster. He pushed the number.

"Harry, I have the lists in from Br. Angel. Are you ready for the report?"

"Ready, Phil, go ahead."

"We have a total of ten lists, representing ten villages, and a name count of two hundred eighty seven. Our teams will be on their way tomorrow to visit the principal cities first. We should have some returns by midweek. The cities we will be operating in are Seattle, Portland, the large cities in California, Las Vegas, Denver, the large cities in Texas, St. Louis, Cincinnati, Cleveland, Chicago and Detroit. There are other names, one's and two's, scattered in the principal cities of most of the other states, a few in agricultural towns, but we won't take on any of those until we get more names. In short, it's just as you would expect."

"It sounds good, Phil."

"Our first forays will be to get the flavor of what's going on. I expect these teams to come back with good, actionable information, but we won't move to interrupt any of the terrorists yet. They're gonna want to get their ducks lined up before pulling any triggers and that will take some time. It's a coordinated operation they're trying to pull off, large and scattered. If they pull one trigger they'll be giving up the others, they know that. We are moving to verify data on this first outing; Luis is doing the same in Monterrey verifying the University contacts. Br. Angel has set up a plan for paying expense money but also bank savings deposits to build up during the operation; the plan is to head off fraud by using the big carrot for the end game. I'm thinking that was inspired planning on his part. That's the report for now, Harry; as I get more data, I'll let you know."

"Thanks, Phil; I'll pass it along. Give Br. Angel and Miranda our best regards when you talk to them. Goodbye."

The President heard the report and was pleased to have it ready for his meeting that afternoon.

Phil Bragg returned to the task of allocating towns to the teams. He first selected the states they would go into, then he allocated the volume of names fairly evenly for the teams, range of 16 to 22 names using the city counts and keeping the distance between towns as short as possible. He decided upon what seemed like the fairest and swiftest way to get to the cities he had selected.

"I'll let that simmer awhile and go back to it later this afternoon; maybe I'll have an inspiration by then," he thought.

Two weeks ago Misti Fontaine and Jon Olafsen had announced their wedding day; they were so excited when they sent out the invitations that they carefully read the magic words on each one as they prepared the mailing:

The Mexicans

*"Mr. and Mrs. Charles Pender Fontaine are pleased
To announce the Marriage of their daughter,
Misti Michelle Fontaine to Mr. Jon Erik Olafsen
Of Shelby County, Alabama,
Sunday, November 7th, 2006 at Eleven o'clock A.M.
At the Living Waters Baptist Church of Metairie
In Metairie, Louisiana.
Your presence on this blessed occasion is graciously requested."*

Now they had to make a serious decision that they really didn't want to make. The problem stemmed from the timing of their departure for this upcoming assignment. Friday they would get their orders and they would then be expected to make travel arrangements and be out of town that same day or the next day, that would be Saturday. But they had arranged their marriage to take place on Sunday. It was too late to change that.

At the time they made the wedding plans they thought they would be leaving the week following the wedding, not before Monday, but the lists had come in faster than anyone expected. Now, they would have to either delay leaving for their assignment or change the wedding to Saturday and it was a little late for that.

"OK, Misti, I'm going to call General Bragg; they went in and put the question to him. If he doesn't want us to wait for the Sunday wedding, we'll just have to cancel the church wedding and have a private wedding by the pastor Saturday morning, then leave that afternoon. What do you think, Honey; do you think I ought to call Phil?"

"Yes, anything."

Misti was near to tears as she gave up the planned wedding. She thought of all the friends they would have to contact and the disappointment. Her mother would be the most distraught.

Jon called General Bragg and explained the problem.

"What? That's not a problem! You'll keep your wedding plans and we'll have everyone delay their flight plans until Sunday afternoon or Monday morning. We're not in this business to ruin lives by having to imagine what might have been, just to avoid the one day delay. Besides, we've all been waiting for the big day. I'm just very sorry I forgot to remind the others of your date, but we'll take care of that little oversight in the morning. So, here's the game plan: We meet in the morning, make travel plans for Sunday afternoon after the wedding and arrive at our assigned towns on Monday, or as near to that as possible. Now, get on with your lives; Beatrice and I will be there at, what time? 11 am, right?"

"That's right, General, 11 am Sunday at Living Waters Baptist Church in Metairie."

"Done. Now go and wash those tear stains off your face Lieutenant Misti Fontaine, soon to be Misti Olafsen. The big event is just two days away."

"Oh, golly, thank you, General Bragg; I just knew you'd set it right. Did I tell you, I love you? And I do right now more than ever."

When they had left his office, Jon turned to Misti,

"How could I have been so stupid? Honey, I'm sorry, I've been taking orders for so long, I guess I forgot that General Bragg is really Phil Bragg, a nice guy and a good friend. I ought to apologize to him, too, for discounting him like that. Call your mother and see if she invites us for dinner; I'm feeling a little homesick."

Bob Crumpton was in Baton Rouge spending the evening with Rebecca, their last time together before he was to leave on the assignment. He had been given a choice by Bragg to stay and handle calls from the others as they reported in; after all, the Border District was really his, even though it was still being operated out of New Orleans. But Crumpton was a man of action, a leader, and he loved to be on the street when something new was going down; he wouldn't have given up a street assignment on this first operation for anything; anything, that is, except Rebecca. And that's why he was hurting to tell her that it had been his decision to go; he wasn't sure that she would take that very well.

"I know it's selfish of me to want to be in on this first Operation of my own District; I've been putting off telling you but I decided that you trust me to do what I have to do, even if it means being gone from you for a week. Besides, mid-terms are coming next week and you'll need me to stay away so you can study and make those A's. But really, Sweetheart, I need to get my feet wet on this assignment so I can know what we're up against; truth is, I've got to do more than just get my feet wet, I really need to swim in that water."

"Oh, Bob, I know you have to go and I don't mind that you take your turn on the street to start it off. That's your way and it's the reason I fell in love with you. When I sat with you on the porch over at Mamie's that afternoon, when I talked with you for the first time, I knew we would be lovers, even soulmates. I loved your masculinity; I loved your background, your bashful, self-effacing ways; the horse breeder from Wyoming, the decorated Captain of the Army. You were just exactly the guy I had hoped would walk into my life before I finished college; before I started some mundane job and boring way of life as a working girl. I needed you in my life. And there you were, right there in real life, not just a dream!"

"It was the same for me, Rebecca, the very same feeling; a dream come true."

"I haven't forgotten that feeling, Bob; I'd never known it until then and it hasn't left me or diminished, not even a little, since that first day, it's just matured more after getting to know you. You're mine. Mamie thinks you're hers, like a son and I guess I can share you in that way; you are, you're like her son. With me it's that feeling that makes two people into one, the feeling that can create a beautiful life together with beautiful children. Just stay safe, Bob; I'll be here waiting for you to come back. Just call me whenever you can."

Bob couldn't speak, he was so touched by this confession; Rebecca hadn't opened to him this way before now. Theirs was a love affair that hadn't needed confessions of feelings of the heart. They knew how each felt about the other simply by their closeness and the way they looked into each other's eyes. They cooed and they whispered sweet phrases and they sparked a lot on the porch at Mamie's house; they had learned a lot about each other, and confessions like this, putting it all into words, were not expected. But now, here it was, openly expressed. Rebecca felt that Bob needed to hear it; now he could keep the words in his heart forever, but especially while he was out on assignment. Now that he had them she felt relieved.

Crumpton was a student of literature and he knew how to turn a phrase, some very moving phrases. But when that beautiful prose from Rebecca came to him in the spoken word, there was just nothing in his experience that could compare. Nothing he had ever read or written had so much impact on his life as that heartfelt confession. He knew that his best efforts at writing the words of lovers were just like tinkling glass when compared to the feelings expressed by Rebecca, just then.

"I don't know what to say, Sweetheart; I've never had to respond to such a beautiful confession of love from the one I love. I think I'll just have to let it linger awhile before I mess up the feeling with any of my words. Let's go have dinner at Maubie's and dance tonight."

"Yes, I'd love to; let's go there and dance tonight."

CHAPTER 30
Scouting Orders

At 9:30am ET in D.C. at the White House the President was attending a meeting of his Security team that he had directed Harry Foster to arrange. Attending the meeting were senior officers of the NSA, the FBI, the CIA and Harry Foster.

"Gentlemen," the President began, "we are here to explain a situation that we have uncovered concerning the security of the country. Mr. Foster will give you a background briefing on what we have found out so you'll all be aware of what we are facing. Go ahead, Harry."

Foster took about ten minutes reviewing the information they had received that caused the President to begin the Mexican investigation and to initiate the Special NSA District to act on intelligence that came in from Br. Angel's work. Then he described the situation they had found in the villages and the techniques that had been used to get the names and locations in the U.S. He took several questions and then turned it back to President Cooper.

"You see now what we are up against. I consider this invasion of our cities to be potentially disastrous, but we're moving quickly to put a stop to the terrorists in their tracks. Operationally, we have a set of teams deploying this weekend, today in fact, across the country to investigate locations and people that we have gotten from the Mexican effort. These NSA teams will be conducting their investigations at every city where we have determined terrorists to be at work, but this is just the first of several forays.

"These teams will work in complete secrecy; no local contact with any of your people, a completely autonomous operation. If need be, they will contact the local police for information, but they are there to gather information and observe, non-contact. You will need to inform your people of their presence just so there are no misunderstandings. Mr. Foster has the list of cities they will be operating in during the next two weeks. Above all, make sure that there is no breach of security on the matter. Be very clear to everyone; the lives of our people will be in danger; these are Hezbollah. The agents will continue with additional forays until they have investigated all the cities where these people are operating; each week more and more information is coming in from Mexico. That's it. Any questions?"

"What if some of the NSA agents contact our people? Do we tell them to cooperate or do they run it through channels?"

"Good question. Yes, cooperate after verifying the legitimacy of the person. If there is a question about the person's legitimacy, no, not until your guy gets a good verification and that means the person may have to be delayed. These NSA people all have normal ID's. But, in any event, don't waste time. The agent might have been mugged, so you have to use good judgment before you detain."

"Can you give us a clearance number that will be able to verify the agents?"

"Yes. Harry will give you the numbers of Phil Bragg and Bob Crumpton; one of them will always be at their number. If there are no more questions, I'm out of here. Thank you all for your help."

@@

That same Friday morning at 8 am CST in New Orleans the officers were arriving for the assignment meeting, several with their wives and partners, ready for this first foray across the country. They had been prepared and knew what to expect in a general way. There were stand-around chats between agents that hadn't ever worked together on assignment before this one. Some were new faces, recently recruited from the old New Orleans police force. "Their loss is our gain," Phil Bragg would tell them as he introduced the new agents. The meeting started on time at 8:30.

"Let me start this off by reporting an amazing coincidence that occurred on my visit to check out Denver as a possible site for the Border District office. As I looked over the morning newspaper at breakfast, I came across this front page article that hit me right between the eyes."

He went on to recount the entire two-day series of events that brought him the four new agents and the decision to take an office in Colorado Springs.

"So, you can see, we have a leg up on this operation because now we see the actual activities in progress that we are working to intercept. And, remember, this was just Denver, one city, and pure luck that these guys uncovered it and we read about it. Well, now you are all caught up on the new office and new agents so I'll get on with the thrust of the meeting."

General Bragg spoke for an hour on the specifics of the operation they were embarking on. He described the work going on below the border to collect the names and locations, the payments going to the collectors, the group of local patriots that had come upon the scene and how it had all occurred. All of this was to give the officers and wives a fair understanding that the information would likely be accurate.

"We need to do two things if we don't do anything else on this first time out. First, we need to know where the illegals are being employed when they are recruited by the terrorists, and as much information as possible about what might be going on at the work place and who owns it.

"Second, we need to verify every name on these lists that we can. If you have a name and address and you can track a guy from that address to the workplace; I'd call that a good name. Some may have moved and we need to trace them if possible by their telephone numbers. What we are after in verifying the names is to determine if the guy taking the names is giving us good information or if it's mostly junk. We need to know that so we can weed any bad ones out of the group they've employed in Mexico. But let's be sure when we crucify someone that it's for real; that it's clearly fraudulent work. If we raise flags that aren't for certain, if there's some doubt, then the others working on the name gathering could get real pissed at us.

"Those are the two primary objectives of this operation. It's just good snooping; all you officers know about good snooping, you trained on it, most of you cut your teeth on it. Whatever you do, avoid encounters with any of these people. We don't want to expose you and we don't want to expose what we're doing, either here or in Mexico; lives may be snuffed out in a few minutes with a telephone call. Keep your distance carefully. Any questions?"

"Are we OK to contact local police, property records, utility records and the like?"

"Absolutely; if you need to identify yourself, do it to get the information we need. Just be sure it's only with official agencies.   Anyone else?"

No one spoke.

"Alright; now here are the assignments. First off is the wedding of Swede and Misti Sunday morning at 11am at the Living Waters Baptist Church in Metairie. If you don't have an invitation, you don't need one. See Misti or Jon; they'll tell you how to get to the church. It'll be over by noon and you can stay for the reception unless you have a flight to catch. I hope I didn't mislead anyone by suggesting we get out of town tomorrow. The truth is, I forgot about the wedding, like a dummy. So, be there if you can, it's a beautiful occasion for two of our beautiful officers. Oh, yes, Misti is our newest Operations Officer. Most of you know the undercover work she and Swede did for us in putting away those terrorists operating right under our noses, last summer. Now they're together on this trip as a team.

"Seattle and Portland assigned to Randy and Mandy Jensen. The Bay area includes San Francisco, San Jose, Oakland and points nearby, assigned to Jim Franklin and Bill Dollar. Sacramento, Stockton and Modesto assigned to Ron and Amy Jensen. Los Angeles area assigned to Simon Pederson and Don Fletcher. San Diego and southern California assigned to Ray Leon and Fred Baskins. Las Vegas and Phoenix assigned to Glenn Corbett and Paul Calvetti. Boise, Salt Lake City and Cheyenne assigned to Bobby Norman and Burt Walker. Dallas and Ft.Worth assigned to Carlos Ferrara and Niel Olafsen. San Antonio, Corpus Christi and Austin assigned to Richard Brownlee and Flaco Rodriguez. Houston, Galveston and Beaumont assigned to Bob Crumpton and David Solomon. St. Louis and Kansas City assigned to Shep and Bobbie Turner. Cincinnati, Cleveland and

Columbus assigned to Dave Reilly and Moses May. Chicago area assigned to Bud and Susan Wiegand. Detroit and Lansing assigned to Jon and Misti Olafsen.

"If any of you want to switch assignments, see Bob Crumpton. That's it. Keep a close watch on your backs, look incompetent, act stupid, ask directions if someone finds you snooping around, and don't go with anyone anywhere, unless it's to church services. Call me every day. You're on your own now. I'll see you at the wedding Sunday. Good luck and God bless you."

The next meeting of the officers was at the wedding.

"It's amazing," Misti would later wonder, "how those big tough gorillas can choke-up and some actually weep at a wedding."

But, those who were there, even the gorillas, knew it as something very special; they felt common kindred to all NSA officers, but these were two of their friends. This was the joining of two of their own together in the sight of God; joined into a new life as one, one flesh, and blessed by the words read aloud from the Bible. It touched hearts and made it easy to shed tears.

By Monday they all had reached their target cities, taken their rental cars and had settled in their hotel rooms. Many had gone out to walk the streets to get oriented to the city they had studied by map on the flight out. Randy and Mandy walked up the hill from their hotel on 5th Avenue where they were staying, into an area of low rental rooming houses and apartments. Four of their names lived on this street, Madison Street and two on Marion Street, the next street over. After walking eight or nine blocks up Madison Street they found the addresses and a crossing street, 14th Avenue, where another two lived a little further away, two on Seneca Street and four on Cherry Street.

"Mandy, let's leave the other streets for another day. It looks like this is the area where the immigrants are congregating. Did you notice, the houses are old but they look to be well maintained? The city seems to be conscious of appearances, even in the low rent areas."

The Mexicans

"I'll bet these places aren't as cheap as we think; it takes a lot of money to keep up these older places like this, and the sidewalks, too, they've been fixed. No trash on the streets, old cars, but no toys, cats and dogs in the yards, but no kids. Typical of an old rooming house area. I'll bet they have a good police force here."

Their next step would be to visit the library and try to get the landline telephone numbers for all of their addresses from the City Directory or the Cross Reference Telephone Listing. On returning to the hotel they inquired of the downtown library and found it within walking distance, a few blocks away.

"Gee, Randy, this weather up here is just right for walking. We've gone a couple miles at least and I'm not overheated at all. Try that in New Orleans!"

"It's a lot different 'cause it's more than a thousand miles further north. But it's a beautiful setting with all the water around and the mountains in the distance. One thing I want us to do while we're here is to take one of those ferry boats over to Whidbey Island. I read about that place in a novel recently. If you look down there in the bay, you can see the ferries coming and going. I think I'm going to like this place."

"Just wait until it's rained a week or two straight. But, I want to drive over to Mt. Rainier before we leave. Do you think we can drive up it?"

"Well, I would think so. The skiers get up there in their cars so there has to be a highway leading up to the ski lodges. We'll have time; we'll take time to look around."

They found the library and the Reference floor and finally found the City Directory.

"Sure enough, Mandy, there's the first house number and it's got the telephone number; I'll read it off and you write it down on the list."

Then he found the next rooming house listed and read off the telephone number to Mandy. The Cherry Street numbers were there but no telephone numbers. The 14th Avenue addresses had numbers. They continued through their list and found most of the numbers.

"OK, let's find the Cross Reference Telephone book. They're usually big black books with green pages – that looks like it over on that table."

It was and it had all but one of the numbers.

"Not bad for starters, about ninety-three percent. I'll take that success rate any day; that means the data we have been given are actual addresses and not fictitious. I'm ready for a cup of that Starbuck's coffee; the little coffee bars are all around this town."

"Randy, do you know what time it is? It's getting on to five o'clock."

"Big deal; we've got all evening to do what we want. You come with me for the coffee and I'll take you to the best restaurant in town at about 7:30 or so."

"You're on. I saw a Starbuck's shop over there by that big department store a few blocks over, I think it was on Fourth Avenue. Come on, we'll walk that way."

The coffee break was just what they needed. After all that walking they had earned some relaxing. Then they walked back to the hotel.

"Do you want to share a shower, Mandy? The bath stall is big enough for a basketball team. I won't bother you, I promise."

"You might change your mind when you see me do my little wiggle and maybe rub against your leg, Hon."

"We can try to ignore each other just this once."

"Honey, I've lost that battle every time."

"Come on in, it's great!"

"It is great! It's so refreshing…oh, oh, Randy, don't forget, you promised."

"There's just something about being three thousand mile from home that makes me feel completely free. What'd you say, Honey?"

A little later they took a taxi to a good seafood restaurant on Elliott Bay a few miles north near the Ballard section of the city. It had been

The Mexicans

recommended by the concierge and it turned out to be excellent. Clams and crabs were the specialty; a real delight for a visitor not used to the seafood of the Pacific Northwest. But, Randy had his mind on the task of locating the place where the aliens were being employed.

"Mandy, I'm not sure we have to call these places to verify names. Our priority is to check out the addresses and locate the place where they're doing their work; like that warehouse in Denver. Do you recall what those Troopers told Bragg? They followed from the houses on foot tracking them until it was far enough away to introduce a car from a side street to pick it up and follow to the workplace. I'd guess that took several days.

"What if we picked up some sweats and began a regular jogging route at 6:45 in the morning up Madison Street past the rooming houses and over 14th Avenue and then back down Cherry Street, the same route we walked today. I'll bet we could pick out a different car to follow each morning and after a few days we'd have the workplace identified. I mean, just think, we know these guys on our list are working for the Iranians, or Hezbollah, whichever, so by tracking a car with the right number of guys coming from the right address we'd have a good probability of a hit."

"Yes, that can work, and we can be sure of it when we track at least two cars from different addresses to the same workplace. By the end of next week we should have the workplace identified and the deliveries that come into it and maybe out of it. We'll do the jogging in the morning, if we can find some sweats tonight and get a fix on the direction the car follows and then next morning wait for that car further up the street on a cross street and fall in behind it as it passes. That's good, Randy, at least for starters."

"OK. Let's finish up here and see if we can find a clothing store open in one of these shopping centers; maybe one stays open after 9 o'clock, I hope."

The taxicab drove them to a department store in a large mall and waited for them, thirty buck worth, while they found their sweats and jogging shoes and light warm up jackets. Then the driver returned them to their hotel. On the way back, Randy asked him about the neighborhood they were going to jog, whether it would be safe.

"Don't go too much farther up past 15th Avenue and don't go down around Yesler Way. It'd probably be safe enough, but once in a while there's trouble; I try not to take calls or drop offs late at night up that way. But during the day, I go there all the time. The people are just as nice as can be, but the night clubs can get rowdy and then there's the characters walking the streets. I can't complain about rowdy, though, after a couple of stints in Baghdad."

"Tell me, Erik," he read the name off the driver ID on the visor, Erik Nielsen, "do you drive as early as 6:30 or 7 in the morning?"

"I start pretty early and sometimes drive pretty late; this is my cab, I just take calls from Yellow."

"Well, if it's OK with you, we'll take your card and call you for our transportation needs while we're here. I'd rather use a cab than a rental car. That will include mornings at about 6:30."

"I can handle that."

They arrived at the hotel. Mandy wanted to have a word to make it a little more personal.

"Erik, this here is my husband, Randy and my name is Mandy; easy, huh?"

"Randy and Mandy, I can remember that, OK. So, just call me a few minutes before you want the ride or you can give me a time and I'll put you on my trip schedule."

"Well, then put us down for 6:30 am starting morning after next, that's Wednesday; same for Thursday and Friday. You don't mind tailing a car, do you, because that's what we'll be doing?"

"Fine with me, Randy, as long as it's legal."

"It's legal." Randy passed Erik a hundred dollar bill. "Keep the change. See you Wednesday morning at 6:30 if we don't call before then."

The Mexicans

"You got it, Randy."

They were both exhausted after a busy day. Sleep came quickly at 11pm with the alarm set for sweats time, 5:30am.

CHAPTER 31
They're Not All Bad Guys

Bob Crumpton and David Solomon had decided that they would pass themselves off as workmen, dressed as stevedores; they wore jeans, boots and light sweatshirts, with a rolled up cotton skullcap. They were looking to find a rooming house near the Port of Houston. After scouting the surrounding area in a rental car they found several streets that showed up on their list of addresses; that would be the area they would hole up in and watch the morning activity on the street until they decided who to follow to work in the mornings. The area thereabouts was a rather seamy warehouse section where low income workers and pensioners stayed in old houses converted to rooming houses, some with boarding privileges; many had signs posted with their offerings.

"This looks like the place to hole up, David."

They had located a house fairly clean on the outside with a few older model cars parked on the street. They were lucky to get a direct flight from New Orleans that dropped them in Houston with plenty of daylight. They had set out their route on board the airliner, using the address information they had along with a very detailed city street map. Now, having been here only two hours or so, they had found the target area to begin checking. They parked their rental car several blocks away near the Port yard operations and walked back to the rooming house. The evening was pleasant, but the daylight would pass quickly and catch them in a very worrisome industrial area, so they hurried and had their weapons stashed in their belts. At the door were several Mexican men loitering on the porch, talking. They knocked on the door, and then one of the men offered to get the lady of the house for them. Soon he returned with a husky German looking woman with a German sounding accent.

The Mexicans

"Vhat do you vant?"

Crumpton spoke, "We need to get set up with a room and some meals, Ma'am. Expect to be here for awhile if the job pays out."

"Vhell, come in und see der room. Two to a room, two meals und a sack to go, no sack on veekends. It'll be two hundred a veek, forty a day. No alcohol in da house, no schmoking in da house, lights out at 11 o'clock." Mrs. Gruenvald ran a good house.

The room was satisfactory; "We will move in tomorrow about noon."

They paid for one week and got a receipt. The day was getting dim as they left. On the way back, they were approached by a small group angling over to them from an alleyway. They stopped, drew their pistols and walked directly toward the group. Without a word, the men hurried off, cursing. The car was safe and they drove away slowly up to the highway, headed back to the motel they had picked out and checked in for the night.

"We're a little too white looking, Bob; we need to let the beards grow. That was a little too close for comfort down there by the Port; I'd hate to be making out police reports but it's better that getting dead."

"You got that right. Let's get some dinner; I'm hungry like a walrus."

"Gimme a minute to flush. Walrus? What do you know about walruses; do walrus swim around in those trout streams back home in Wyoming?"

"I saw a movie one time and the walruses ate up a whole herd of seals; man, that was brutal. That's how hungry I am, so button up your fly and let's go. Are you sure you don't have prostate problems?"

"Don't be funny; at my age? Just a little slow sometimes, that's all. My wife thinks I'm prostrate enough. I'm ready, let's go."

Next morning they found a well worn old car that advertised "mechanically perfect" and gave it a spin.

"Not bad, Bob, the motor and transmission run good, the oil level's right up there and clean. I'd say we could trust it for a couple weeks. Sure is a sorry sight to look at, though."

"This is just what we need, David; it'll blend right in. I'll drive it to the rental agency at that big hotel downtown; you drive the rental car and we'll turn it in. Then we'll check out of the motel and see if our two names show up at the rooming house. We'll just have to listen and try to pick out the names. If the list is right there's two guys from the same village supposed to be living there and we know their names; that ought to give us someone to track in the morning. Then, when we have those guys' workplace pegged, we can stake out a few more of these addresses and see if we can get more tracks to the same workplace; that'd cinch it, unless there happens to be two workplaces, but we'll have to figure it out as it develops."

"The other thing we have to do is find out who owns the property and maybe where their deliveries are coming from, if we get lucky enough to see a delivery truck."

"Yeah, and if we still have time we go to check out Beaumont and Galveston; that's a big bite to chew; we'll need a little luck. First things first, David, let's get a bead on the guys at this house. Keep your ears open and don't talk unless you have to; just sully around and listen. You still smoke, so you can sit out on the porch while I sit around the TV room, how's that?"

"That suits me; the television shows are getting too hoary for me, you know? Filthy language, sex or sex innuendo, bad guys win, preachers are either rascals or funny kinds of fools. The end days are coming, Bob. When the number of apostates begins to exceed the number of new believers, I believe the Messiah will return for His church."

"When the Saints go marching in, I'll be there. Do you know that old Gospel song?"

"Yes, I do."

He started singing a chorus of it and Crumpton joined in. By the time they reached the rooming house they had sung that one and two others. As they opened the doors to get out in front of the house, they were both saying "Amen" loud enough for the porch sitters to hear. The small group of Mexican men responded to the blessing:

"Amen", "Amen."

The Mexicans

They welcomed Crumpton and Solomon with smiles and handshakes. At that point they realized they were among their own kind; they looked different, they talked different, they came from different places, but they were all of that one kind, the ties that bind believers as one.

At dinner that evening, Mrs. Gruenvald invited the new arrivals to introduce themselves first, and then the others to do the same. Crumpton stood and said:

"My name is Bob Crumpton. I'm from Wyoming where my family raises horses for rodeo and show. I'm here hoping to earn enough money to buy my fiancé a nice wedding set for our marriage next June."

"My name is David Solomon. I'm from Louisiana where I have a wife and two children. I am here because of a job that brought me here. I'll be here for two weeks until that job requires me to join them to return."

The others stood one at a time and introduced themselves. Crumpton noticed that the names of two of the men matched those on their list, Jose Menendez and Benito Leon. He and Solomon etched the men in memory to follow in the morning. But, during the dinner the men were very open with the new arrivals because of the feeling of camaraderie with their Christian brothers. They spoke of their background, being from the small village of Guerrero and told of the good jobs that they had found. Crumpton sounded interested,

"That sounds like a good job. We're only getting $9.75 per hour. Does your job pay more?"

"Yes, we are being paid $10.50 per hour, a very good pay for an immigrant; we are very fortunate."

"Where do you work? Do you think they might need anyone else?"

"I don't know but you could go over and ask. It's over on Clinton Drive a little ways past the Interstate 610, maybe a mile."

"What time do you go to work? Maybe we could follow you in the morning before we go to our jobs; we start at 8 o'clock."

"Yes, you will have time; we have to be there at 7. If you want, you can follow us there. The office workers start at 8, so you may have to be late to your job."

"That's OK. We'll go there the next day and we can tell them we need to be an hour late. It'll work out fine; thank you, Jose."

"De nada, amigo. No problem, my friend."

So that was the fastest locating they could hope for, ever. The next morning after breakfast, they followed Jose to the warehouse and got the name and address, all the information they needed to find out the property owners from the property deed record. Before leaving they took down the license tags of all the cars parked at the lot. They left to retrieve the owner information recorded on the property at the Property Records room at the Courthouse. The owners were recorded as Star Crescent Assembly Inc., a Detroit company. The lien holder was recorded as the Muslim Bank of the United States, also in Detroit. The principals of the corporation were listed by name and city. It was all very legal and proper and the property taxes were paid up to date. Crumpton purchased a photocopy of the property record.

"OK, David, now let's take our list and visit these other addresses later this afternoon when they get off work and see how many license tags we can match up. And I think we'd do well to start matching these tags at the Galveston addresses. I got a feeling the Galveston aliens are living there with wives or girl friends doing domestic work in those beach hotels; it'd be foolhardy for the Iranians to set up another workplace that close to this one."

"I can't argue with that."

It was almost too easy for comfort. The tags were parked near each of the addresses.

"Bob, I believe we've had some help on this project; you're pretty smart, but there's got to be more to it than that."

"There's no doubt about it, David; the Lord answers prayers. You and I have the power of prayer and it's inspiring. You know, David, I don't wonder where our good thoughts might come from 'cause I know what the Scripture says, but it amazes me the number of folks who think there's no source for their thoughts but their own mind; inspiration to many is just a phenomenon without explanation.

"Have you ever asked an unbeliever if they believe we send space probes into the heavens to explore the planets, to do the things their engineers ask of them? Every one of them will tell you, yes; they don't doubt the ability of man's mind to do it, not for a second; to control the activities of the probe, to give it thoughts that cause it to change direction, to accelerate or decelerate, to view a moonscape or a planetary body and to take pictures and send them back to earth. They are willing to accept man's ability to communicate and influence his creation, but scoff at the suggestion that God can do the same things with His creation."

"I've never posed that question to anyone, but I can see how the allegory is compelling. Inspiration is undeniable except to the one who is blinded to any matters concerning God and creation. It's a powerful thought you have there, and could open up some minds if they would think about it."

The next morning at breakfast Crumpton asked Jose;

"Jose, do you think the company you and Benito work for might have another place where they might need workers?"

"I don't know, but I don't think so. Nobody ever says anything like that."

That was good enough; they didn't think they would have more than one workplace in the same city.

"David, I think we can move on to Beaumont. Let's keep our room here for the time being and commute until we can find a place there. We'll have to tell Jose that we couldn't get time off to go by and apply for a job at his workplace."

The Beaumont and Port Arthur area was about one hundred miles over Interstate 10 near the Louisiana line. There were just three names from that area; conceivably they might be commuters to the Houston warehouse but they would find that out. There was a lot of shipping in and out of the port city, a likely place for a distribution warehouse.

Now that they had a name for the company at the Houston warehouse, it could be that they would be using the same name here and other sites as well. If so, they might be able to track the operation site by that name. Crumpton decided to call Phil Bragg and let him distribute the name to the other teams.

"Hello, Bob, how are you doing?"

"We've hit it lucky, General; got our workplace located and the name of the owners. It may be a common name being used around parts of the country. I thought you might give it out on a conference call as a lead for the others."

"Good, Bob, let's have it and we'll get it out right away."

"It's The Star Crescent Assembly Inc., a Detroit company, wouldn't you know? The principals are all Detroit addresses and the lien holder is the Muslim Bank of the United States. If they can't find a telephone listing, maybe they can locate the name and address from the Water Department billing files. But, listen to this, General; once we got to the workplace we copied the auto tags and drove past the addresses on our list in the afternoon after the workers had time to get home. It was a snap; I mean just a matter of driving the street and checking off the auto tags in order to verify the addresses. Tell them that, too."

"Sounds pretty simple; if you have the name of the operator, you get the utility address of the workplace; you can even guess at something with 'Star' and 'Crescent' in it. When you locate the workplace you copy the auto tags and verify the lists from the auto tags parked on the street. That's a winner, Bob. I'm sure it'll be useful for some of the others."

"That's it, so far. We're on our way to the other towns. With any luck we'll check out this whole list by the end of the week. So far, so good. I'll call you when we have anything else to share."

"Thanks, Bob. You could have passed this around on your own."

"I wanted to let you; maybe I'm shirking my duty,"

The Mexicans

"I appreciate it. Take care."

They called the Beaumont Police and reported in as NSA agents:

"I'd like to come down and pass something by you; maybe you can help us on a search."

"Come on down, Colonel; you're always welcome here anytime." Major Paul DeShane greeted him.

When they finished their visit, they had the address of the warehouse of the Star Crescent Company from the utility records. They would have little trouble finding the warehouse about ten miles out of Beaumont in an industrial area off the highway going to Port Arthur. They thanked Major DeShane and drove over to the location.

"David, all we have to do now is write down all the license tags parked around this place."

"I'll get them; give me your binoculars and stop over there away from the front of the place."

By five-thirty they had verified the legitimacy of the three addresses and were headed back to Houston.

"Score two, day four. Tomorrow we visit Galveston and maybe wind it up."

They were almost too late for dinner but Mrs. Gruenvald was kind to hold it over for them and they let her know how much they appreciated it; they drove to a nearby shopping center after dinner and bought her a two pound box of chocolates. Mrs. Gruenvald wasn't used to such kindnesses and couldn't hold back her emotions. Maybe for the first time in years, she shed tears of joy, just to think that these poor men would show her such a kindness.

"Vhat can I say; you are too good to me. Dhank you, my boys, dhank you vedy much."

Later that evening Mrs. Gruenvald served hot chocolate and coffee to all of her "boys" along with her very best chocolates. David Solomon asked the blessing on the food and on the house and on everyone in it.

At the Galveston addresses they found car tags from the Houston workplace. By the end of the day they had verified the tags to their three addresses on their list.

"That's the end of it David. We go home tomorrow."

The next morning at breakfast they excused themselves from the rooming house.

"We have been called to take the return job to New Orleans. But, we'll probably be back in a few weeks. Thank you for your hospitality, Mrs. Gruenvald. And thank you all, friends, for the good company. We'll see you again, I hope."

"Vaya con Dios, amigos."

Juan and Benito were sorry to see them go; they don't get many friendly Gringos at the rooming house.

Crumpton parked the car in long term parking at the airport with their telephone number taped to the window, in case they were overdue in returning. By 3:30 that afternoon they were setting down at Kenner airport outside New Orleans.

Weeks later, with no reason to return to Houston, Crumpton wrote out a bill of sale for one dollar and sent the keys and the parking ticket to Mrs. Gruenvald along with a note to give the car to Juan and Benito, or keep it for her own.

CHAPTER 32
Who Are These Good Folks?

Luis rose early, usually beating the sun up, and he did this morning in Monterrey. As was typical these last few days, his first thoughts were of Rita Garcia, quickly followed by his responsibility for the safety of Br. Angel and Miranda. This morning he had no schedule except to get started on the vetting of the members of Br. Angel's University group and he had an idea how he would begin. He got cleaned up and dressed, then called Rita to see if she would have breakfast with him at a little café near the University.

"OK, pal, we've done the dinner and the luncheon, now you're trying for breakfast; what next do you have in mind, a bedtime snack? It seems to me you're a little presumptuous for a taxi driver." Rita liked to kid around.

"It's genetic, I'm afraid. I have no control over my presumptions. I presumed you would know that by now. Not only that, but I have a genetic presumption that tells me you are ready for breakfast, so I presume you'll be ready when I come by there in about ten minutes."

"Well, you can try it if you like, but I may not be able to wait that long; if not, I'll order for you at the café; what's it, a wrap with eggs, cheese, sausage, onions and peppers, did I get it right?"

"That's it and hot chocolate. See you there in ten minutes."

He stopped by the kitchen to greet his friends. He took a few minutes to run his vetting job by Iggy to see if he had any connections to get a standard background check, quietly.

"Sure, Luis, we can start on it this morning when I get to the office; we run background on everyone we do legal work for. Give me the list; it'll take two or three days, no longer, and these people do a thorough job, quietly."

"My man, Iggy! I knew you'd be good for something besides a bed and breakfast. Really, I appreciate it and I'll pay you in cash; what do they charge?"

"I'll let you know, it varies."

"OK, I'll run off this list; just a minute."

He hooked the laptop up to the printer and left the copy with Iggy.

"These are all University people; I'm mostly interested in their politics and any connections to the Jimenez bunch or any other groups active in the country; that would be great. I'm having breakfast with Rita. See you tonight. Bye Maria, you pretty thing."

"Move along, Luis. All this time and you haven't even said my name."

"Waal, shucks, Ma'am," he did his John Wayne pose, "you know how jealous that husband of yours can git. Why, I couldn't be the first one to speak, he just might jerk my toupee right off my head. No, Ma'am, I ain't looking fer no trouble. B'sides that, with yore permission, Ma'am, I gotta go. Good day, Ma'am."

"Git."

He found Rita at the café with a cup of coffee and his cup of hot chocolate waiting for him.

"Mmm, that's good; sweet, like someone I know."

They passed some small talk and then he got serious just about the time their breakfast was served. He told her of the University group that his friends were associating with and asked her if she knew any of them. She looked over the list.

"I know or have heard of all of them but this Pacheco couple. Are they from around here?"

"No, they retired a few years ago and are running a guest house in Buenaventura. Do you know anything about any of the others that would cause you to be cautious of them?"

"Well, the Echevarria couple is not from here; they're Cubans who immigrated here to teach at the University. I think they are math and physics instructors. Every year or so they take a sabbatical leave of absence and return to Cuba. They do their writing and research there in Havana. That's all I know about them. They write quite a few books, mostly text books, some on economics. They're very intellectual people. I don't know about their politics; probably leftist, maybe even Jimenez supporters. There are quite a few of them at the University. Give me a few days to ask around and I'll find out more about them; their personal lives and such."

"That'd be great, Rita. See, I have a responsibility for the safety of a couple who are here on a special assignment that is very secret; even I don't know the full story. But they are very nice, an elderly couple and they are missionaries; that is their usual work, this assignment is a special undertaking. That's all I can tell you, but it is the reason I need to vet these people they are associating with, for their safety; that's my assigned responsibility and the reason I'm here. I know I kid around a lot but I'm really a very serious guy. I'm a Captain in the NSA and I'm looking for Major if all goes well with this operation. But, that's not the only reason I do my work; I love what I do."

"I'll get what I can for you on these people, Captain, soon to be Major Luis Caldera. I'm glad you told me this; I feel I know you a lot better. NSA makes sense; it fits you well."

"Do you like what you know of me?"

"Yes, I do. I like your character, even when you sometimes act like a character."

"That's what I wanted to hear."

"Look, I've got an appointment coming into the office in a few minutes, so I'll have to go. I'll call you later. You can give me a lift, though."

Luis paid the bill, left a tip and drove Rita to her office. "Man, what a girl," he said it out loud. He decided to call in a report to Bragg and to ask him to vet these names through the FBI.

The Mexicans

"Bragg here".

"Luis Caldera, General. I'm trying to vet these people who Br. Angel is working with; the University group, he calls it. I've got two local checks going, but I'd like to get a wider range check on one couple. Can you run a check for me, like the full plate, I mean?"

"I'll do what I can; what have you got?"

"Two names, their a couple teaching at the University here. They're Cuban citizens who came here several years ago to teach; they go back each year to Havana, supposedly to do research and write books on math and science. The names are Felipe Echevarria and Montez Echevarria, man and wife. I don't have anything on them but with all the Jimenez influence gaining favor, I wonder where they might fit in. The others are all locals and seem to be well known."

"I'll get back to you. Is everything else OK with the folks?"

"All OK, General. We've had daily activities that usually take a few hours, even hit the golf course; that Angel got me for a twenty, but Miranda kept score so I made out like I wasn't all that sure there wasn't a little bias there. They're really good sports; it's fun being with them. There are more lists coming in tomorrow, so you'll be hearing from them then. I think they're enjoying the work. He has a friend from Socorro coming by to check up on them; one of the missionary people, Al Maldonado; he comes from Chihuahua. He'll tell you about him. That's about it."

"Ok, Luis; let me know how you come out on the vetting. I'll get this one moving; it may take a day or two. Take care."

"Thanks, General."

Before the end of the day, Luis got a call back from Bragg.

"Don't get into any more checking out on the Echevarrias. They're protected; understand? They belong to some of the other guys. Just let them do what they want to do; they're untouchable."

"I get you, General; they're clean. We ignore them. Thanks."

"Good work, Luis. It was like a bomb over at the other place; big surprise. No sweat, just keep digging around, but in other yards. We got good marks from this. See you."

Luis called Iggy and Rita to drop the Echevarrias from the vetting list.

"They're cleared."

❦

Br. Angel and Al Maldonado picked up a very nice used auto with low mileage and clean; nothing very nice, not a lot of extras, but in good condition. Br. Angel provided the cash and Al paid the money, purchase price and huge taxes and got the receipt and registration in his name. Br. Angel deposited the twenty-five hundred in an account for Al and gave him a goodly supply of pesos to use in the villages and a supply of dollars. They met with Luis for lunch and told him of Al's venture.

"In truth, it's the job Miranda and I had initially started on when we came down, but didn't get beyond the third town. Al will determine if the Council is at work in the village and if so, he will find a family that will agree to be the list provider; he will offer a good reward, an advance of one hundred dollars in pesos and a telephone number. His cover will be that of a University professor researching the quality of rural education facilities and the opportunities for new teachers. Now here, Al, is a list of friends of ours at the church we've been attending and the names of their friends in some of the villages you may visit; they might be helpful.   God always provides people we need when we pray for His help. Do you believe that, Luis?"

"I believe that, Br. Angel. I'm very happy for you, that you now have help to do the scouting work. I've begun the vetting of the Group, by the way, and so far it all looks good. I have two sources at work on it and we have cleared the Echevarrias and of course the Pachecos, but we are just beginning to clear the others. Perhaps another couple of days and I'll be finished."

"Well, my friends, I'll take my leave now to allow enough time to drive to Chihuahua. It's a good ten hours; perhaps I'll make it by midnight. I'll call you as I stop along the way, Angel. Pray for me every day, won't you?"

"Yes, of course, Al; God is with you my friend. Call often. Goodbye."

And with that, Al Maldonado began his venture into the rural villages.

"Luis, can we visit the gardens again, this afternoon? It is so lovely."

Miranda was feeling down; she always felt a loss when a friend departed on a mission.

"That's a wonderful idea, Mrs. Suarez; we could all do with a good walk. And let me say, if I may, you truly have a very fine friend in Al. I've only just met him but I have a really good feeling about him; that he will succeed in all that he does out there. In time I'll get to know him better and that will be my pleasure. Are you ready?"

"Ready, Luis; let's go."

CHAPTER 33
Everybody's Making Progress

Julio Cruz and Felipe Delgado began their investigation of the rubble where the warehouse had been standing; today it would be work boots and heavy clothing to protect themselves from cuts and abrasions from things falling on them and from them falling on the rubble. They carried canvass bags to stow anything they came across that might hold a clue – virtually anything with wording or numbering, even residual fragments. Much of what was recognizable was metallic; parts of gun barrels, gun magazines and residue from the larger stuff.

They rescued anything that would give evidence as to the make and model of the weapon or ammunition. It was slow going, but they had laid out the space in ten foot square sections using yellow tape. They took photos of each square before disturbing it and again after they had exhausted the space. Each square took several hours to examine; the whole job would take about a week, but they were not in a hurry; they didn't want to miss anything of informational value.

"Julio, I'm confused about what I'm finding on this piece of metal. It looks like it came from a shipping container; you know, the big ones they carry on railroad cars and transport ships. It seems to be the corner of the container and it looks like a handler's mark, maybe at a Port or a transfer point. Look at this a second; see the first record appears to be noted in Asian style characters, maybe Japanese or Korean. Then below that one is another in English and it looks like maybe Sydn— and the number 9 2, could be Sydney. Then, just below that is another Sy—y and the number 9 31, could be Sydney again with a different number. The number could be the checker's mark or maybe a date. The last one is Seat— and the number 10 8, probably Seattle."

"Yeah, that's what it could be; this container may have come from Korea or Japan, we can find that out, and it went to Sydney and then

The Mexicans

Seattle. It appears like the shipment came from Sydney, Australia; I wouldn't have expected that."

"Neither would I and that's what's confusing; the two Sydney marks. If the container had been loaded and shipped at Sydney, the old marks would have been cleaned off and just one mark would be on it. What it looks like is this container was sent from maybe Korea to Sydney, remained on the dock and then was reshipped a few weeks later to Seattle. Maybe a mistake or maybe the original point of origin was purposely lost from the shipping trail when a new shipping order was cut. Do you remember what General Bragg told us about the Iranian invasion from Mexico?"

"The word was that weapons would be bought from Korea. You know what, Felipe, this looks like it was a way to hide the point of origin, maybe so it wouldn't be suspect. Australian stuff probably goes right through, but Korean stuff probably gets a chance for inspection. I think you've found what we're looking for, or at least a good shot at it. We don't want to let that metal get away from us. Let's get an 'evidence' tag on it, front side and back and get pictures. And lets save any other fragments of that container we can find; those evidence experts can piece it back together if they have enough pieces. So let's save any pieces, big and small. Maybe we'll have a good size pile of it by the time we get through here."

They rented a truck with a large covered trailer and brought it to the warehouse site and loaded their bags of items into the trailer as they proceeded. At the end of the day, they parked the rig in the police parking deck where there was an entrance guard posted night and day. By the end of the second week they had completed filtering the warehouse wreckage and the trailer was loaded to the ceiling with metal pieces and whatever scraps of wood or paper that had escaped incineration. Many had writing or markings on them. With a little luck, the scraps could provide reliable evidence by the time the experts got through studying it all. They turned the trailer over to a team sent down to the Air Force base at Colorado Springs, set up and working in a secure hanger.

During the week Cruz and Delgado had copied the property records. The company name was the Crescent and Star Development

Corporation, out of Detroit. They owned the building and the lien was held by the First Muslin Bank of the United States. General Bragg had been kept informed of the work as it proceeded and he passed the Company name out to all of the operating teams; that was two different names, but merely a juxtaposition of the first two identifying words.

Meanwhile, Rey Vargas and Max Flores had entered the illegal alien community, bearded, sweaty and ill-dressed. They had done well at networking the streets and had found two potential informants who they were in the process of checking out by starting rumors on the street. By speaking between themselves where others could overhear and then waiting for the rumor to get back to them through the informants, the informant should report it to them. It worked quite well, returning the rumor by the end of the next day. They rewarded the informants for the rumored information with ten twenty dollar bills, then explained their business in a few words and promised to keep the informants safe from any trouble with the immigration police as long as they cooperated and brought them good information. The informants were happy to be on the right side of the law.

"What we want is information on what the operators of that warehouse are doing with their employees from the warehouse, where they're setting up and what company name they'll be using. Names and locations are what we want, so keep your ears on and meet us back here on Monday, same time. Information is worth up to five hundred depending on what it is; no less than two hundred. But if it turns out to be bogus, the deal is off and you go home; like to Mexico."

Vargas didn't pull any punches.

"You got it, boss; that's a good deal." They called themselves Ferdie and Carlos.

@@

When Randy got the information from Bragg about the Star Crescent Company, he paid a visit to the City Water Department and asked for the location of that customer. The clerk hesitated for a moment so Randy showed her his badge. She squinted at it, glasses lying on her desk, then;

The Mexicans

"Of course, Lieutenant, just one moment."

In a few minutes she returned with the address. Randy thanked her and she saluted, sort of, as he left.

Later that morning, Erik drove them to the location; an old warehouse down in an old industrial area off Old Marginal Way. There they copied down the auto tags, recording them on the paper the girl had given them that contained the name and address of the company. Now they had a couple of hours to kill before the employees would begin returning home.

"Hey, guys, I've got an idea." Mandy was getting hungry. "What about a picnic lunch in that park out by this big lake, here on the map? I saw a Wal-Mart somewhere back there. We can pick up a picnic basket and some cold cuts and rye bread and mayonnaise there. And cold drinks and fruit, too. Erik, do you think we could find a nice place by the lake?"

"Oh, I think so; that's Lake Washington. That park, there, isn't real close to the lake, but I have a friend who is pretty well off, he's got a big house on the lake shore. He won't mind us using his picnic area down a little ways from his house. It's a good idea; we can be there in twenty minutes even stopping at the store."

"I'm for that, Mandy. Lead on Erik."

It was a beautiful lakefront residence and the lake was peaceful. The picnic lunch was good and they fed the scraps to the ducks along the shoreline; that was fun. Erik waved to his friend who appeared on the rear deck. They rested on the grass for a half hour before they even thought of leaving.

"Please give your friend our thanks, Erik; this has really been nice and the lake is so beautiful." Mandy was captivated by the splendor of it all.

By the end of the day they had matched up the addresses with the license numbers copied at the warehouse. Job completed.

"Tomorrow, we head to Portland for the next two days, one day to get the location of the workplace and the auto tags and do the match-up on the addresses. Friday we finish up and head back."

"Wait a minute, you said we could go look at Mt. Rainier and go across the Bay on a ferry to Whidbey Island." Mandy wasn't in any hurry to leave.

"Tell you what," Erik offered, "how about I take you to Rainier and Whidbey tomorrow? We'll come back by way of Mukilteo; there's a nice restaurant there; we can hit it just at dinner time. I'll pick you up at 9 and we'll make a day of it and catch the Interstate back."

That was an offer Randy couldn't refuse.

"Then you drop us off at Sea-Tac and we fly to Portland. Friday we do the investigation and Saturday we finish up and head back to New Orleans. Let me call for reservations on the late plane to Portland." He dialed it up and got the schedule.

"There's a flight leaving at 9:15pm arriving in Portland at 10:25. That means an early dinner. We'll make reservations from the hotel tomorrow morning. When we arrive in Portland we'll rent a car at the airport, do the investigation Friday and make airline reservations Friday evening for New Orleans."

"That'll work, Randy; tomorrow is our day off. Hooray!" Mandy loved it.

Before leaving Erik, they confided in him as to their purpose and asked him if he might like to do some investigative work in his off duty hours.

"What we need to know is where the shipments are coming from going into the workplace. Do you think you might be able to scout the place out for us and pick up on the delivery truck, then follow it back to it's warehouse? We'll pay you for your time and trouble; in cash, like maybe a thousand now, another one later. You can't tell, Erik, you might like this work; it could be your initiation into an exciting job."

"I know a lot of folks in the trucking business; in fact that's what my friend there on the lake does. He owns a big interstate trucking business; mostly picking up from the Port of Seattle and from railroad container traffic coming into the city. If he wants to do it for me, I'll bet he could get a manifest of all destinations going out of the Port, addresses and all."

The Mexicans

"I can't think of anything more efficient than that. We'll take pictures of our IDs and Badges for you to use if you think it might help. Then call me whenever you come up with something. We'll be coming back before long to extend our investigation, probably in a week, maybe two. Here's the guy we report to, General Phil Bragg", he wrote it down with his office number, "just in case you can't get us; he'll know who you are.

"So here's a thousand, now; you'll miss some time on the meter and you might need to buy some help, we'll send up another thousand by mail when you call us. By the way give me your full name, mailing address, telephone numbers and e-mail so we can contact you and we'll have to get you vetted; is that alright with you?"

"Sure, anything you need. I'm glad to be helpful; maybe it'll turn out to be something."

"Could be; that's sort of what happened to me. Well, we'll catch you in the morning at 9 and head up to the mountain."

They were at the hotel, now.

"Good deal, folks. See you then; goodnight"

෴

When Jon and Misti Olafsen began their investigation in Detroit they were well aware that the terrorist activities throughout the Louisiana District were controlled from the Muslim community in Detroit. They naturally expected to encounter a wary attitude in the Muslim areas and hoped they would be able to avoid any footwork on the streets there. They took a room in the hotel at the Renaissance Center, a convenient location at city center, near the Detroit River. Here they would have access to any of the low rent areas surrounding the downtown quickly using any of the major highways including a cross-web of Interstates.

From reading the reports of Reggie Halbrook, Olafsen knew that Hamtramck, the town situated close to Detroit downtown, provided a large segment of low-rental rooms and some with board so he was not surprised to find that was where many of the addresses on his list were situated; that would be an ideal place to begin, not far from downtown. He had ordered a rental car to be delivered to the hotel and it was ready, so they had transportation to get around the city.

When they checked in they were ready for dinner, so they decided to try the place that had been recommended by Phil Bragg. After settling their bags and freshening up they called for their car and drove to the sea food restaurant, not far from the hotel. They were amazed at the size of the Alaskan king crab appetizer, but the real surprise came when they began to taste it.

"Oh, Jon, let's just order another platter of crab and a big salad, this is unbelievable. Well, alright, maybe a tureen of the lobster bisque, shrimp salad, and we'll split another platter. General Bragg said it was almost too good to believe."

Early next morning they started out before breakfast to begin a surveillance of the street on their list that had the most addresses clustered in close proximity, hoping to make a lucky guess and follow a car to a workplace. The car they decided to follow had three Latino men riding together. The destination was a warehouse two blocks off of Woodward Avenue that stood in an area that appeared much like a destruction crew had leveled the buildings that must have been there at one time. They watched from a distance as several other cars arrived with Latino men. By 7:30 the arrivals stopped.

"It looks like they begin the job at 7:30; that means they'll probably get off at 4 this afternoon, maybe 3:30 if they get free lunchtime. We'll copy down these auto tags and see if any more of them show up near our addresses this afternoon. If they do, we'll know this is the place. Can you read the number on the front entrance over there?"

"I can't quite make it out, but you can drive over that way and I'll be able to read it."

Amy was able to get the number and they knew the street name.

"Now we'll go by the Detroit office and get someone there to look at the property records for the name of the owners and all that."

Mike Murphy received them cordially.

The Mexicans

"Any foot soldier of Phil Gramm's is a friend of mine; you're in good company here. What can I do for you?"

"We need the property records for this address; can you call over there to someone and get us access?"

"I can do better than that; I can call over there and get the information over the phone."

"That'd be good, but I need to get a copy for the file."

"Yeah, well they can have it ready for you. Give me a minute."

Murphy placed the call to a number in his computer file and made the arrangement while they waited.

"It'll be waiting for you in a half an hour; here's where you go."

He wrote down the address and directions to get to it.

"Can you have a cup of coffee with me; we'll make a fresh pot?"

"Mike, we're trying to get back by the end of the week and we're pushing it, so let us take a chit and turn it in a little later in the week if we have time; I'd really love to."

"OK, Swede, but I'm holding you to that chit; come back anytime."

"Sure, Mike, and thanks for the help. I'll put you in for a raise."

They picked up the property record copy and looked at the names.

"Boy, Misti, honey, I think we made a hit on the first time out. This is Muslim all the way; Crescent-Star Processing Incorporated, all local addresses and all Alibaba names. Let's go have some breakfast back at the hotel Grill."

"I married the best teacher in the Agency; Jon, you're so smooth in everything you do. Before long I'll be married to a full Colonel; everyone knows you."

"Heck, Misti, in this outfit, everybody knows everybody, or they talk like they do. But I'll take that eagle anytime you can arrange it. Thanks for the confidence; it's one reason I fell in love with you. And I do love you, Sweetheart."

"Oh, I'll bet you used to say that to all the girls. Better not have! I love you too, I sure do."

That evening they made a home run on the auto tags and cleared the whole street. The next morning they would take another street and check off the tags. By the next afternoon, they had most of the Detroit addresses checked off. As they drove the last streets the next morning, they swung back by the warehouse to check for any new tags and there, waiting to unload, was a tractor trailer rig just opening his doors, with a Canadian license tag.

"Misti, it'll probably take them an hour to unload and reload any stuff they had to move out of the way. Let's run down to that Coffee House we passed near the last intersection off the Interstate and get some breakfast to go, then get back here in time to follow this guy. Copy down that trucking company name and address and all and we'll check them out."

Fifteen minutes later they were back on site eating breakfast and waiting for the truck to leave.

"Jon, if we follow this truck, he may make another delivery, like maybe at Lansing, before going back to Canada; that'd give us that workplace, too."

"Hope so. But we need to follow him into Canada, if we can get through the border guard without losing him. I'm calling Bragg; he needs to know if we go out of the country." He dialed it up.

"This is Bragg; go ahead Swede."

"General, we're on the tail of an interstate delivery truck that's licensed in Canada. I'm planning on tailing him to his next destination here and then back to his home base, wherever that is. Is that OK with you? I mean, we may get interrupted at the border."

"That shouldn't be a problem, but if they try to detain you, show your ID and tell them to call Jerry Johnston in Detroit; he's the Canadian

The Mexicans

liaison with the NSA at that port of entry. When you tell them that they'll probably let you go on and take down your auto tag. I'll call Johnston now and he can alert the tunnel that you may be coming through. That's a really good lead, Swede. It'd be good to track that distribution point; it's likely to be pretty big. Call me and let me know how it goes."

"Great, General; I was worried about losing the guy at the checkpoint. We're on our way; the truck's coming out of the warehouse now. I'll let you know. S'long."

The truck turned toward the Lodge Freeway; they followed onto the Lodge and off to flow into I-696 at Southfield headed west, then onto I-96 headed toward Lansing.

"This'll take about an hour more, then we'll see if he stops at Lansing or keeps on to Grand Rapids. Look at the list and see how many addresses we have in Lansing. I don't remember seeing any at Grand Rapids; that one may show up on later lists. Anyway, this guy is in the middle of it all so wherever he goes is a point of interest, to be sure."

"We have eight addresses in Lansing on just two streets. I guess we'll get those tags today and check them out at the addresses tomorrow, unless this guy beds down for the day in Lansing. He may be on a long run; maybe he'll get up and go somewhere else in the morning."

"We'll see; you could be right, he's pulling a big trailer."

Misti had brought along a few favorite CD's for times like this; she put in her favorite by the Bee-Gees and they listened to the music. Towards the end of the second time through they started onto the western bypass. In a little while they dropped down off of I-96 and continued for a mile or so to a railroad bed with a spread of warehouses. The truck pulled up to the loading dock; they continued on, then circled back by the car parking lot and wrote down the tags on seven vehicles, most of them old model cars. They found an address on a sign that had been stripped off the building and was laying face up in a ditch by the road. They drove on down the road and parked headed back toward the warehouse. There they waited for the truck to make its next move. Misti put on an Eric Clapton CD. Jon liked the guitar work on this one and they held hands.

"Jon, we've got to begin dancing together more often; I love this music."

"I can't dance, Misti; you know that."

"That doesn't mean you can't learn; even your folks dance a lot. You're just too bashful to try."

"I know, I know; maybe one of these days. Let's just drop it for now and follow this truck."

Jon could get irritated when he was pushed. Misti knew when to stop.

A half hour later, the truck moved out. They let him get out onto the main road into the afternoon traffic before they pulled out, then maneuvered into position a few hundred yards behind. He headed to the eastbound ramp of I-96; they followed him up the ramp. Soon they took the right turn onto the eastern bypass.

"It looks like he's headed for the barn. Let's get our IDs ready for the tunnel station. No hurry, we've got an hour or more."

The Eagles were on their third time through the CD when they entered the tunnel and the music dropped off. The officer at the inspection station looked at their IDs, smiled and said;

"Welcome to Canada, Major; welcome Lieutenant; proceed on, please."

The truck had been flagged through the adjacent lane, but Jon caught up by the time they had exited the tunnel into Windsor, Ontario. They followed out highway 401, turned off at London onto highway 23 and headed north. At Stratford they turned west onto highway 8, going about thirty miles to a farm road near the town of Rodham where the truck entered through the gate and drove a half mile or so, as they watched, to a large metal storage building where they could see a railroad spur terminated.

The Mexicans

They could see this was an active farm with access roads passing through the fields and much heavy farm equipment stationed about at various locations. Men were coming back from the fields to the large farmhouse and the several large barns at the central operations area. The sign at the gate read "Crescent Farms" and gave a Post Office box number at Stratford. That was the best they could do. Jon noted the mile marker near the farm road entrance. They took a few snapshots of the place and headed back to the hotel.

"We'll see if we can get a property record on this place; maybe that guy, Jerry Johnston, can give us a hand with it. I'll call Phil and give him a report. How about you driving us back, Hon? I'm getting a little edgy."

They stopped at the next intersection and changed seats. Jon called Bragg and gave him a run down on events of the day.

"Do you think that guy, Jerry Johnston could help us with a copy of the property record for that farm?"

"Why not give him a call in the morning? He knows about you and your investigation and those guys are usually cooperative; we work together on cross-border activities. That's a good day's work, Swede; it looks like Misti is bringing you some good luck, or maybe it's just good sense. Anyway, it all looks good. Don't get too confident, though, after all that tailing today, they may have made you. I think I'd change cars and hotels tomorrow. There's no need to take any chances; you can only see your side of it. So stay safe and remember there's two of you. Call me again soon. Take care."

"Thanks, General; I'll call him in the morning and we'll do those other things, too. I appreciate it. So long."

Dinner was French onion soup and steaks at one of the best steak houses in the Midwest, another recommended restaurant.

"I think I could get used to this, Jon."

"Well, don't forget about all that good stuff down home; red beans and rice, blackened Redfish, crayfish etouffe, okra and seafood gumbo, yum; I'm ready to go back"

"Quit acting smart, Swede."

Next morning, they got started early and checked off addresses to auto tags on the remainder of their list in Detroit. They would check off the Lansing addresses in the afternoon. After breakfast, Jon made reservations at the hotel on Grand Boulevard; still a good location for their work and close enough for another night at the seafood restaurant. Next, he called Jerry Johnston and asked for the copy of the property record for the farm. That was easy; he would send it over to the hotel by courier. They changed cars for a complete makeover; this one a small sports car.

At the hotel, they told the desk clerk they were expecting a piece of mail to be delivered; it was valuable and they asked it be kept in the hotel safe until they came to pick it up. After settling into their room, they lunched at the hotel restaurant.

Next, they headed for Lansing to get the property record of the warehouse there; no problem, just two dollars for a copy. That property was owned by the Star Crescent Packaging Corporation; all principals were familiar names from the Detroit location. At four o'clock they positioned themselves on the street near the largest number of addresses on the list. Within an hour they had verified all the house numbers to the auto tags. That took care of the list.

"It looks like we can make airline reservations to go home tomorrow unless you want to take a look around up here for a day or so." Jon was in no hurry.

"Let's talk about that at dinner; I'm not sure what we could do if we stayed."

"They always have major league sports in this town. How about catching a basketball game; they have a home game tomorrow evening. Then we can leave the next day."

"OK, if I can't think of anything else. Let's get a paper and see what else is going on; they used to have Broadway shows during the season, but I don't think they come here anymore. Maybe there's something at the Renaissance Center. Basketball is fine, maybe hockey; we'll see."

The Mexicans

"Whatever basketball suits you will be fine with me, Hon."

@@

The next set of lists came in on Wednesday as the University group gathered at the suite for the weekly meeting; another eight lists, but there was no assurance of additional lists to be forthcoming. Most of the reliable friends of the group had brought lists of their own home villages and a few neighboring as well. Hereafter they would have to rely on friends of their friends in other villages; a network that has yet to be tested; the group worked hard to embolden their village contacts to recruit reliable friends; it wasn't so easy, but they were making progress.

Br. Angel took care of the business end, distributing bank passbooks with savings deposits and expense rewards to the group members. American dollars were always a good motivator, but especially now, as the group members were able to distribute expense money and tell their friends in the villages of the passbook savings waiting for them; passbooks that they had seen for themselves.

Next, Br. Angel informed the group of the scouting mission he had sent Al out on and the area he was to cover. When he made that announcement, several group members offered to contact acquaintances in those villages Al was going to be visiting. Br. Angel would pass the information on to Al; six names in all with perhaps more to come from friends of the group during this next week. The meeting broke up with a prayer, led by Carlos Pacheco; everyone went their way.

"Eight more lists, Miranda. We're doing well."

@@

General Bragg was really pleased and a little surprised to receive another eight lists. Br. Angel reported on the week's progress, Al Maldonado's scouting mission and the new contacts that had come in; and he expected to have another set of lists to send next week. These lists and the ones next week would provide the basis for the next team assignments.

Bragg entered the lists to the residual names which gave a total of two hundred eighty two names. Eliminating the sparse ones left nearly enough names for the next foray, even without those expected to come in the next week. Well, that would be just about the right timing for his teams to be ready to go out again.

By the end of the week all of his teams were either on their way home or close to it; some with a few loose ends to track down next week and some encountering resistance from local politicians. Some of the Water Boards out on the west coast were refusing to cooperate. They told the agents that they would have to have a court order to get that information; that the information was private and personal. So, with the help of the Governor's staff and the Attorney General, warrants were being obtained to force the Water Boards to give out the information to the NSA officers. All the west coast teams expected to have completed their work by Wednesday, barring any intervention from the American Civil Justice Union, protectors of the Constitution. So much for national security.

The most unexpected problem showed up in Kansas City where Shep and Bobbie Turner's investigation ran into gangland 'wise guys'. Shep had developed an informer on the street who claimed to be able to put him onto the address of the warehouse that employed a dozen or so illegal aliens and the guy who hired them to work. When Shep acted on the tip and began snooping around the location, he was mugged in a hallway and dragged into a room where the thugs began drumming him for information, thinking that Shep was a snitch for a Chicago mob that had been trying to move in on the lucrative gambling and prostitution business they had with political protection.

When Shep finally agreed to write down the names of the mob bosses in Chicago, he took out his poison pen and squeezed out several doses to the three guys handling him. They fell unconscious for a couple hours during which he called the police, informing them of his identity and what had happened to him. When they arrived, the mob guys were still out on the floor and were taken into custody. Shep filed a complaint and gave his statement. The judge allowed his statement to be used in place of his personal testimony when the men came up for trial and he was allowed to leave. The men were tried and released.

The Mexicans

When he reported the incident to Phil Bragg, Bragg's response was simple.

"Get that snitch of yours on the right track; he seems to know the wrong bad guys."

Shep and Bobbie completed their lists when the information came in from Crumpton's team. They found the Star Crescent Assembly Corporation on the utility books and everything fell into place; they were through on the following Tuesday, headed for home.

Of the California assignments, Ron and Amy had found good cooperation from the central cities they had to work, much the same results as had been achieved elsewhere.

Jim Franklin and Bill Dollar had finally gotten through the political hang-up; the firewall that the utility commissioners had thrown up to them by refusing to divulge the locations that they had presented for water department records in the San Francisco area and the surrounding cities of San Jose and Oakland.

"Just an extra three days time. What if the Governor had been one of theirs?" Bill Dollar wondered at the politics out there.

"What I can't understand is why the ACJU isn't taking it on; I guess there isn't a big constituency of citizens for the protection of Water Users' addresses. Good thing the Governor still has some say so out here. He ought to clean house."

"You can't stop progress here on the left coast, Jim. We're now one nation, divided by socialists, with libertarian justice for all." Bill was a little cynical, too.

"A house divided against itself cannot stand. Who said that, Abraham Lincoln?"

"I think he was paraphrasing the Lord, when he walked the earth, speaking to the religious leaders of Israel of the time."

"Well, those two ought to be enough to cause some of these people to wake up before it's too late."

"The Jews didn't, and I don't think they would have listened to Abe Lincoln, either. So many things are changing, Jim; people don't believe like they used to."

"Yeah, I know. I was just as bad as them until you and I were on the battlefield back there on the Mississippi River bank. But it takes a really bad situation to cause you to realize where you stand with God; how far you may have drifted. A guy is really blessed when God shakes him up and sends someone to open his eyes."

"I'll never forget that night at the river, Jim."

CHAPTER 34
A Higher Calling

"Good morning, folks, it's going to be another beautiful day, I think. Where do we go today for starters, Br. Angel?"

"Good morning, Luis. Let's go by the bank first and make these deposits. After that, we'll turn control over to Miranda."

While Br. Angel was in the bank making deposits, Miranda waited in the car with Luis Caldera. Luis took the opportunity to talk to Miranda alone.

"Mrs. Suarez, I'm sworn not to tell Br. Angel this news, but no one said not to tell you; the State Department is vetting you both for some reason I'm not aware of. It looks like they are interested in your background. This sort of thing from State often is requested of NSA officers as well as FBI and CIA and many others, looking for details of a person's history, and it usually means they are thinking of a person to fill a position of some importance; a position involving international relations which is their bag, of course. I was asked to return a profile of you two including everything I knew of your background during the times I have been associated with you, which is limited to this assignment."

"My goodness, Luis, do you suppose it is just a late inquiry concerning this assignment? But this assignment is by Presidential Order, so that wouldn't be it, would it?"

"No, not likely; this has something to do with the State Department. They have to know of anything that might be embarrassing if it turned up during an assignment of some sensitivity, which is really all assignments from that Department. I wish I could tell you more but that's all I know. Of course, if you were to divulge it to your husband it wouldn't break any rules since your name was not included in the blackout."

The Mexicans

"I wonder if something that happened many years ago might bear on the result of the vetting. It's interesting that it come up now, just two weeks before Angel is to meet in Albuquerque for his annual martial arts recertification. There is only one incident in his background where he completely lost control of his emotions and caused injury to a group of men who were bent on attacking me. The judge decided his martial arts expertise made his arms and legs deadly weapons. He could have been cited for his actions but instead it was deemed to have been a citizen's response to unlawful conduct by the men which placed my life in grave danger. That is the only incident I can think of where he was charged and brought before a judge."

"That sounds like quite a story; especially as it applies to such a pious man as Br. Angel. I never would have thought him capable of that sort of combat."

"It was really bizarre, Luis. As you know, there have always been people hateful of men like Angel; a missionary and a man of God who is very vocal in taking his calling to those who need to hear it. Well, on this one occasion, he sort of struck out, so to speak, when he suggested to a man he had recently met that he should believe in the Lord and be accepted into the family of God. The man actually cursed him and accused him of trying to force his belief in what he called fantasies and fables on others. He was very distraught and left in a huff.

"Well, later on that day, while I was returning from shopping at the grocery, that same man and two others approached me as I was about to enter our house and forced me into the living room and pushed me to the floor. They ripped my clothes off and began beating me. Then, just as one of them began to rape me, Angel called to say he was on his way home, as he always did. They forced me to answer the phone and to just say I'd call them back. Instead, I told Angel I was being raped. They struck me so hard I nearly passed out. Then they talked between themselves and decided to take me with them to an old house near some railroad tracks.

"As they were taking me out to their van I was able to scream out and by God's grace a neighbor heard and took down the license plate number of the van. Soon afterward, Angel arrived and found me gone. The neighbor rushed to him and told him what they knew; they had called 911 for the police and given them the license number. Angel was a very young man at that time and something about the situation caused him to revert to the trappings of his Indian heritage. He threw off his shirt and splashed war paint that he had as a keepsake on his body and face and began to hunt the van.

"The van's tires were muddy and left tracks leading out of the driveway and Angel followed them. He guessed they would stay on the main road going that way, headed for the low rent end of the city. As God seemed to be leading him, he spotted the vehicle parked in the alleyway behind the house where they had taken me about twenty minutes before. Angel rushed to the house and broke through a window to find the three men taking turns at me on the floor. I shudder to recall those moments; I was terribly distraught and in shock.

"Angel was like a savage, his face distorted and blood red. The veins on his neck and shoulders were throbbing and standing out like blue cords; I was almost as much afraid of that image as I was of the men holding me down because I didn't realize it was Angel, seeing him in that condition. I didn't see it all, but he left the three men helpless on the floor with their legs broken, shoulders and hips dislocated, cracked disks and the one had a broken neck and nearly died.

"Angel told me he was sure that he had been ordained at that single time in his life to execute the wrath of God; he told me that later, when he was back to normal and I was in the hospital bed. He felt that he was actually the arm of God's vengeance called upon to execute justice and to wreak destruction upon those men and he still believes that to this day. It has never happened again, but Angel has never felt more secure about himself than he did on that day, knowing that God had led him to me in time to save my life. And he has never missed one of the annual martial arts meets to maintain his standing as a master of the arts, the highest degree of the black belt. We've since been blessed with three children."

"That is a remarkable story, Mrs. Suarez. I'm honored that you would share it with me. Thank you for your confidence, it will be safe with me forever."

The Mexicans

Br. Angel returned from the bank and they drove over to the park for a brisk walk.

"Br. Angel, I would like to be gone for just a few days soon to attend my annual martial arts certification meet in Albuquerque. It's just two weeks from now; perhaps it will be a convenient time for you and Miranda to return for a visit at that time as well; otherwise I must remain here with you."

"That's interesting, Luis. I have that same meeting to attend. We can make the trip together and visit Socorro for a day or two before returning. It would be a good time to take a break from our project; the lists may be slower coming by that time. I'm pleased to know that you are maintaining your certification in the arts; it's been a source of great personal satisfaction for me over the years."

"I'm sure it has; you must tell me about your experiences some day. I'm sure you have many fascinating stories to tell."

"Oh, no; not so many as most, but some for which I continue to thank God."

After they had their walk and returned to the hotel, Miranda broke the news.

"Angel, I learned something today from Luis while you were busy at the bank. He told me that we were being vetted by the State Department. He knew because he had been asked to give his statement, which he did. The instructions were not to tell you of the background check being conducted but they said nothing about me, so he thought that was tacit approval that he could tell me. He was not told the purpose of it but he suggested it was not likely to be concerning this assignment since this is by Presidential Order, so it must be for some other task that they have in mind for us."

"Oh, my; I can't imagine what it might be. Perhaps it's just routine, such as is done by employers when they hire a new employee who handles money. Let's not try to make something out of it, Dear. If there is something to it, we will find out in due time. Still, I can't imagine what it would be about; we have a lot of work remaining right here."

☙❧

Al Maldonado was making good headway on his rounds of the villages he had set out to visit. He had verified the presence of the Council in Cuauhtemoc and Guerrero, and had made contacts with local families as he conducted his research on education in remote towns and villages. More of interest, he had found the people becoming concerned about the demanding attitude of the men from the Council and they had begun to wonder at their visitors' appearance and speech, obviously foreigners. With that concern growing, it was not difficult for Al to find the family willing to join in the work of finding out what was being done in the workplaces of their relative's new employers.

He left them with half of their expense money. When they had collected the information, they were to call Al and he would meet them to take the lists and give them the remainder of their expense money. So, with recruits established, Al was finished with the first two villages in the first two days and moving on to El Sueco. It was then that he received the names of friends of the University group who lived in the villages he had yet to visit, including El Sueco. But before going there, he stopped at his family home in Chihuahua to spend a day or two with his wife, Elena and their children who had just recently arrived to be with him.

The next day, he was not surprised to find the Unification Council had not been to Chihuahua, a much larger city and one where they may have expected more questions from the local citizenry. Apparently they didn't want to expose themselves to the better educated people of the better policed cities. He spent the rest of the day in Chihuahua, calling in his report to Br. Angel along with the names of the families he had recruited, rather easily.

Early the next morning he set out to begin the work at El Sueco and Nueva Casas Grandes, both smaller towns. The friend in Monterrey had called ahead of him, so Al's visit had been expected. Soon he had verified that the Council was in the community, though they rarely were seen in public. The people were pleased with the money the Council was giving them, but Al learned some of them were disturbed by the officious attitude of the Council members who had told them not to discuss the arrangement with others. No matter, Al's contact knew the ones who were receiving the payout and could put together a list within a day or so and would deliver it to Al in Chihuahua. Before the end of the day, Al had finished his work in El Sueco and he drove on to Buenaventura to stay the night at the Pachecos' guest house where they were expecting him. He called in his report to Br. Angel and enjoyed the evening, a good dinner and the beautiful view. Manuel Pacheco agreed to accept lists if they were to come to him.

The next morning Al drove about forty miles on the country road to Nueva Casas Grandes, a small village in a valley in the foothills. The people of this village were slow to respond to his survey questions and it was late in the afternoon when he encountered the Quinones family where the husband was more self-assured and willing to talk openly.

"So, you have a son who is of school age, Mr. Quinones?"

"That's correct, I do."

"What do you think of the education your son is getting at the schools here?"

"He's not getting any, now. We buried Jaime three weeks ago."

"Oh, I'm so sorry, so very sorry, but I didn't know. They told me of several families up here on this farm road and I just came to talk to all of you; forgive me, I would never have called on you if I had known."

"It is alright; you didn't know. We are very sorrowful but it is God's will. Jaime quit school to cross the border into the States and go to work; he was big and strong for his age. So he went up to the crossing, high up to mountain pass to go down the pass and across the river. Up there, a farmer, Jesus Trujillo, let him ride down on his hay wagon and cross over at Palomas, but they stopped Jaime at the border and made him go back because he didn't have identification.

"Two days later Jaime got a ride hiding in a truck; that coyote stopped in the desert and wanted money. The others paid but Jaime didn't have money so they shot him dead and left him there in the desert. A Texas farmer found him and took him to the border crossing where Jesus Trujillo sold his hay. When Jesus Trujillo came there he saw Jaime and he brought Jaime back here and we buried him three weeks ago. Some of the people in the village don't know it even yet, but he's gone."

"That is a very sad story, Mr. Quinones; I will pray for God to send comfort to you and your wife. Do you have other children?"

"Oh, yes, my first son, David, works in the U.S. He made it across last year so Jaime wanted to find him and go to work where he works. My second son, Tomas, is in the American Army. They let him join and he will be able to become an American citizen when he finishes his time. God has blessed us with three sons and two daughters who live away with husbands and children, now."

"Since you have a son working in the U.S. then you must know about the work of the Council in the village."

"I know the Council, but I don't take their money," Quinones bristled a bit. "I don't know where the money comes from. They don't say and so I don't want it; it may not be clean money. People talk about them, but they take the money even though they don't trust them. Those Council people stay to themselves too much and they don't want to be seen. There's something wrong with that; they hide themselves and remain out of sight when people come from out of town. They stop whatever they are doing and quickly go indoors until the visitors have gone. I can't trust people like that."

"It seem very strange also to many other people. My employer doesn't trust them, either."

"Just as today; since you are visiting, none of the twelve council men has been on the streets of the village. They do not wish to be seen by outsiders and that is very unusual for government officials; the people wonder at this."

That provided Al with sufficient confidence to pursue the subject. Until now no one had been willing to say a word about the Council; this old man was the only one with courage to speak. This could be

Al's only opportunity; he showed his missionary identification and gave Quinones his card.

"You see, Mr. Quinones, I am here to gather information about the purpose of the Council's work. My employer is acting on behalf of a government agency that is working at this moment to determine the truth. You can be of great help to them in this effort merely by providing the names of the families that have been contacted by the Council and the whereabouts of the relatives living in the States. The relatives working in the US may be in danger; these people are not from the government of Mexico or the US, in fact they are in Mexico illegally from Iran.

"There is risk for you to help us here, but if you don't, I don't know who will. To help you, I am able at this time to leave with you one hundred U.S. dollars, in pesos, with an additional hundred when the list of names is turned over to us. Would you do it; write the names addresses and telephone numbers of the relatives in the States and the family here? The workers will not get in trouble if you give the names, I can promise you that."

"I could do it, yes, but it may take a week to gather all of the information without causing concern. Yes, I will do it if I can be assured that my son will not be arrested."

"Your son will not be on the list because you didn't give the Council his name, so your son will not be a part of this; just leave his name off the list and any other families that have not been taking the money; their relatives are not doing illegal work for the Council in the U.S. but the others are. As I said, the relatives working for the Council in the US will not get into trouble if we have their names, but right now they are all in harm's way."

"Then I will do it."

Al counted out the money and gave Mr. Quinones his telephone number and instructed him to deliver the list to Mr. Pacheco at the guest house in Buenaventura.

"Mr. Pacheco will be expecting your visit."

His business completed, Al returned to Chihuahua where he called Carlos Pacheco, telling him of the arrangement with Quinones. Then he reported to Br. Angel and made his plans to leave in the morning for Ciudad Jimenez and the other three villages.

"I'm really pleased with these results, Angel, and I'm confident that I can finish the remaining towns just as quickly. I have contacts in Ciudad Jimenez and Hidalgo del Parral and the other two are nearby. Elena had worried about me doing this, but now she's very proud of my accomplishments; four villages and four contacts recruited."

"Al, you were cut out for this work; we are all proud of you. God is certainly with you, my friend."

CHAPTER 35
Speedboats, Fishing and Intelligence

Erik Nielsen took his new opportunity seriously when Randy passed him the thousand in cash; it wasn't the money that gave him the enthusiasm; he was doing well enough driving his own cab on his own schedule. What got Erik's interest, his excitement, was the idea of being a part of an NSA operation, the kind of important work that he had always hoped for but could only dream of, until now. After spending four years in the Army Rangers, he thought he had found a lifestyle that suited him very well and he nearly stayed in for a career. But, unforeseen circumstances kept him out longer than he anticipated and would have lost his rank, so he lost his enthusiasm.

While he waited for the next semester to begin at the University he took up driving the streets in a taxicab. Soon he was able to buy his own cab and that modest bit of success was enough to keep him satisfied for awhile. But now he could see the possibility of an exciting new career in his future, a lot like what he loved about the Rangers. It all depended on him coming through with the goods that Randy was looking for and he knew he could get it from his friend.

"Frank, it's me, Niel. Have you got a minute for me?"

Frank Heinkle was his friend on the lake who owned a large interstate trucking company.

"Yeah, Niel, why don't you come on by the place? I'm just here doing some home work until the races get started."

"Great, I'll see you in ten minutes." He was parked at a hotel downtown.

Frank had been a good buddy in the Rangers, but had no intention of staying for a career; his family was in trucking and his dad wanted to

The Mexicans

get him into management so he and his wife could start taking time off on their yacht. Frank had the knowledge and enthusiasm to keep the business expanding and it did well, nationwide. But one thing about Frank; he never forgot a buddy and Erik was his buddy.

"Come in, Erik; you know where the beer's at. Make yourself at home. What's the occasion? You've got that wild look in your eyes again; getting ready to add another cab to your stable?"

"No, man, it's bigger than that; I'm headed for a career in the National Security Agency as an operations officer if I can pull off a cinch assignment for starters, but I need your help 'cause I think you might have what I need and it ain't money."

"Well, the NSA sounds like something you'd be good at; grab a chair and tell me about it, and where do I come in?"

"I need to find out about shipments coming in through the Port that are being delivered to a warehouse owned by the Star Crescent Company on Marginal Way. I need to know where the shipments come from, like what ship they were offloaded from, and where the container was loaded on. Can you do that for me?"

"You just need to get a copy of the manifest for the cargo going to Star Crescent; that'll have the port of origin and the port of delivery and the dates and who did the shipping; the whole string of shippers, custody and transfer agents. I can handle that. Gimme a couple days, so it don't show up on anyone's radar. What else? Get us a couple more beers and let's sit out on the deck; the unlimiteds are running today. World class, they're from all over; Australia, Europe, the US, even a new guy from Japan; I think they have about a dozen entries – it's a big one. Come on, I'll make the call and get your thing going before the boats get started."

"Hey, that's the best offer I've had in weeks."

Before the end of the next day Frank had copies of all the shipments going to the warehouse over the past three months delivered on his fax. Erik called Randy. In a few minutes the fax in General Bragg's office was spewing them out; his fax machine was high speed over a secure line.

When Bragg had a few minutes to look them over, he knew this was the evidence he needed to get warrants on ships in port, trucking rigs, railroads, and all the points of destination. With this guy in Seattle getting the goods, they could track deliveries coming off ships at the Port of Seattle to any of the locations they were investigating. It just might be all of them.

"Randy, get your man, Erik Nielsen on the phone and let me talk to him; you just hit the home run that may have won us the World Series for smarts. We'll see if he can keep the stuff coming and get him on the payroll."

By the time General Bragg finished talking to Erik, he had hired him as a new Operations Officer; only subject to being vetted.

"You'll be getting the whole package within a few days, just as soon as I can turn Randy around with it in tow. He'll be returning up there with a short list of other points of interest; we believe they all may be coming through that Port. If you need anything in the meantime, call me here and we'll get it to you overnight. Do you think your source can handle several more delivery points for you? I'll be glad to come up there and visit with him if you think it'll be helpful."

"That would be good, if you can; he can probably handle it but he'd salute when you walk in and that would help, like big-time."

"I'll be there with Randy tomorrow night if we can see him the next day. Call me back and we'll get our reservations."

In a few minutes, Erik called back.

"Frank says come on up; he's looking forward to it. The day after tomorrow we'll meet at his place on the lake."

"We'll be there tomorrow night; I'll call you when we know the schedule. You can meet the plane. That OK?"

"That'll be fine, General Bragg. Thanks for calling and thanks for the job."

"Don't mention it."

The Mexicans

Bragg got all the reported warehouse locations and names together; made a set of copies and began to gather up the paperwork for the new employee.

"Orella, I need for you to get me the whole bag of material for a new Operations Officer; you know the stuff. I'm leaving tomorrow morning, early. Can you do that? The guy's name is Erik Nielsen; that's about all I know but that's enough for the ID and the debit card. Put it all in the package, options and insurance and next of kin; all of it. I'll need it by the end of the day."

"I'll have it ready, General Bragg; how does he spell his name?"

"Call Randy Jensen for it."

He called Jon Olafsen.

"Swede, did you get that name and address from Mike Murphy on that Canadian place?"

"It just came this morning; I'll bring it to you."

He called his remaining teams to urge them to fax their workplace locations and name to him by the end of the day, if they have any to send. The others he would call for from Seattle and get them faxed up there.

The next morning General Bragg called Erik Nielsen. When they arrived at Sea-Tac Airport, Erik was waiting for them.

"Taxi, mister?"

Randy made the introduction and they headed for the hotel suite where they held the pre-employment interview, which Bragg recorded on disk. Erik was given his ID and badge and debit card. Bragg went through the whole run-down; cash for everything, two thousand per pull on the card, recruiting informers, legal necessities of the different activities.

"The whole nine yards, Erik; it's all on this set of papers in this binder, titled "New Officers Handbook". Read it tonight and we'll talk about it tomorrow when we have time."

"Yes sir, I can get that done tonight."

"Good. Now, Lieutenant Nielsen, I'll switch off this recorder and we can get on our way to your favorite restaurant for dinner. On the way, we'll stop by your favorite ATM and you can try out that card; don't forget your password, it's 'GoTigers'; that's Orella's doing, she's an LSU fan. Ready, Randy?"

"Right behind you, General."

At dinner, Erik gave them the background on Frank Heinkle.

"As good a friend as a man can have; I'd trust him with my life."

"He sounds a lot like us, Erik. I don't suppose he'd be interested in a permanent job; not with all he has going for him."

"Well, you can't tell about Frank. If he wants to he can turn the business over to his brother to manage. His dad probably wouldn't object; he's an old war horse himself - not so old, though."

"Hmm; not so improbable; some guys just like this kind of work."

"Some just love it," Randy gave his own point of view.

The next morning Erik picked them up and drove out to the lake house. Bragg couldn't believe the beauty of the setting.

"Erik, there must be hundreds, maybe a thousand of these big lakefront estates on this lake. It goes for what, eighty or a hundred miles of shoreline, all just like this. I've never known anyone who lived like this; it's too much to imagine, too beautiful to describe."

"You ought to be here in the summertime, General; it's to die for."

They met with Frank Heinkle; a cordial, well-bred man; educated at Seattle University's Liberal Arts School and their MBA program. Frank loved the time he had spent in the Army Rangers, but he also found a lot of pleasure in running the family business. He liked to make decisions, mostly because he had the kind of self-confidence that breeds leaders.

The Mexicans

General Bragg spent a long time describing to Frank and Niel the extent of the Border Operation, the background, the Presidential Order establishing it, how this work ties in, and he mentioned the unusual Canadian charter fishing connection. He and Randy gave an exciting account of the Louisiana Operations on the Mississippi River; it was that kind of thing that interested Frank.

"I don't normally talk about operational methods to new recruits, but in this case I feel compelled to be more open, since I'm asking for your help. Truth is, what I'm asking you to do requires some very important intelligence gathering, no warrants, and you're carrying the ball. I'm talking myself dry, Frank; I guess I'll have another beer, if you don't mind."

"Hey, General, this place is yours; it's here for you, just like I'm here for you. I'll get you another beer, but feel free to make your own way around here; I don't keep any secrets." Frank brought Bragg another beer. "Let's sit out on the veranda, guys; the sun's warming it up out there."

By the end of the afternoon, the conversation had covered the top NSA management, their own backgrounds, wives and families and Frank had insisted that Phil stay over for a day of fly fishing on the Snoqualmie River. He couldn't turn that down, so, before returning home, he and Randy learned the art of fly casting; they caught and released their limit of natural trout. When they made their goodbyes from the place on Lake Washington, the list of locations was in Frank's hand, plus two others that had come up by fax.

"I'm going to get this work done for you and any more that you need me to handle, but about your offer, give me time to think it over, Phil; I wouldn't want to turn it down and regret it the rest of my life. It's very tempting."

"Take your time, Frank. I appreciate your help on these places and more as we proceed with the work; you can't know how much this is helping. And I'll take you up on another day on the river one day soon; I had a great time; learned a lot, too. We'll keep in touch. Take care."

"You too, both of you come back when you can."

Erik drove them to the airport and watched them off. He couldn't help but feel left behind as he saw his new friends leave. "I wonder how it is in Denver," he thought. He kept his taxicab as a façade, now; not wanting to explain his change of business even to his friends, yet. Early the next week, Frank called Erik to come and pick up the documentation on the shipments. He had gathered it up on a few of the known locations. Erik faxed it all to General Bragg.

CHAPTER 36
The Denver Connection

Bragg had most of what he needed; the rest he would have to take up with the intelligence agents in Australia. It seemed that all of the weaponry must be coming through the Port of Seattle, shipped from Sydney. The original port of shipment to Sydney was lost; that lading manifest stopped at the first destination, Sydney. Loading at the Port of Sydney began a new shipping record. The records at Sydney would have to be accessed to determine the port of first departure and the shipper information. He'd need John Smoltz to get that connection underway, so he called him and gave him his report on the Seattle shipping records.

"Wow! Phil, we're moving along really fast. That's nice work, give those guys a raise – no, make it a high-five, they all just got raises. That can come after we get this operation in the can. It's mighty good work so far, especially now, with the Seattle connection pinned down. Give me a few days to get the connections in Sydney; then you can send one of your guys down to get the documents. I'll let you know; those guys down there are always very helpful."

"Fine, John, I'll be ready to go on it whenever you say. Thanks for the good words."

"Say you're going to take the vacation trip yourself? Well, I can't blame you for that; someone's got to sacrifice. I'll let you know."

Next on his agenda was Bob Crumpton.

"Bob, can you come in for a minute?" He did.

"Glad to see you back, Phil. How'd it all turn out up there?"

"Oh, it was great, Bob; I got my limit of trout – the guy's a trout fisherman and he had the right spot pegged; sort of a private place on the bend of the river. It's all natural mountain trout. But the big thing is that we'll be getting copies of the manifest records for all the shipments into the Port of Seattle that go out for delivery to our locations – all of them, yours, Swede's, all of them from all the teams. The ones we've gotten so far all came through Seattle by way of Sydney. We can expect the rest of them to come in next week; there're still a couple of teams that haven't finished up yet, out there on the California coast. Take a look at this documentation, Bob; this is what we should have on all the locations. We'll have to see what he can do for us if we turn up any other ports of entry in places we haven't been to yet."

"Boy, we can pin them down all the way with that; start to finish. One thing, though, most of these shipments seem to be going to distribution points. The workplaces probably won't be much help."

"You know, you're right. Dang, I missed that! We need to get our guys to hang around a day or two at the workplaces to maybe pick up a truck delivery and follow it back. Without the distribution points, we can't get the shipping documentation, unless it's carrying the workplace as the destination."

"I'll make a point to get that to the teams; we don't know how the distribution channels are set up; but they're probably central to a large group of cities. When we identify a distribution point, we can maybe follow a truck out on his run like we did at the River. We'll need a few more teams to be able to allow more time for following trucks."

"Yeah, let's do that. If we need more teams we'll borrow a few more from New Orleans; we've hired a dozen just this past month. Randy's recruit up there is a good find; Erik Nielsen; we'll bring him down for training with you. Good background, college, Rangers, talks well and seems to have good instincts. His friend is a big wheel in trucking; major operator, lots of drivers hauling stuff cross country. His name is Frank Heinkle and he can get copies of any documents coming through that port, maybe even some of the other ports. He's ex-Ranger, too; they were buddies and still are. He'd be a darn good recruit if he decides to come with us, he's really considering it. Truth is, he'd probably be a lot better satisfied as an NSA officer, you can tell he's a Ranger at heart. Graduate MBA, Seattle U."

"General, you've got a real knack for recruiting; you're finding them everywhere you go, Denver, Seattle, where next?"

"I'll be taking a trip down to Sydney to pick up some documentation on the shipments. It looks like Sydney is just a re-loading port to keep the port of origin off the shipping manifest that comes to the States. John Smoltz is getting the contacts lined up for me; it'll be another couple of days. You want to spend some time in Denver, now? Maybe you can do some recruiting up there at that Air Force Base."

"I'm ready, General; my bag's always packed. When do you want me to leave?"

"I'd like for you to get cleared on anything you have going here; turn over the Texas cities to Solomon and give him a mate. You'll want to think over the wives; we may have to expect a little more risk now that we've been to town once. Someone's almost bound to have been made, out of all the teams, and I'm a little reluctant to stretch our luck. But talk it over with them and do what you think best. Let's aim for the second foray the end of next week; you can get back here to send them out on Friday.

"Between now and then we ought to be setting up that Denver office and meet up with the recruits. Those guys found a whole shipping container blown apart in the wreckage of the warehouse and were able to recover the pieces; the team from DC is reconstructing it now. What's so important is the marking on the upper corner of the container. It turns out that the load checkers always put their mark on every container as they load ships and as they unload ships. The marks can be partially read on the corner piece they recovered and it looks like that container in Denver had been shipped into Sydney and right back out from the dock without being repacked."

"A convenient way to reship and dump the paperwork trail."

"Yeah, except they didn't know about the loaders' marks and we do. The first mark is made in oriental-type word blocks, you know, either

The Mexicans

Korean or Japanese, possibly Chinese. I'm betting on Korean. You might be able to get that much of it in your initial operation report without waiting for them to finish rebuilding the whole container; we'll need the whole thing re-pieced as much as possible for evidence, but that shouldn't slow our investigation, so get what you can. Take pictures and get an interpreter who knows that Oriental script.

"As for the new agents, Cruz and Delgado are still in suits; Vargas and Flores are still working the streets undercover as illegals. They've hired a couple of informers and verified them, maybe by now, so they'll have found out if anything is being done to rebuild that workplace. You can read the recruiting report in the file here for their addresses and telephones. Try to work those guys in on the next foray, if you can. I'll be here until I hear from Smoltz, but let's get you on your way if we can, before I go. I'm going to take Beatrice on this trip; no need to miss out on Australia, she's always wanted to see Australia."

"OK, Phil, I'm ready to take over the Border District. When do you think we ought to make it a permanent relocation, maybe when we finish this next foray? The lists will be coming in a little slower now, I'd guess."

"I don't know, Bob. I'd hate to interrupt an important investigation just for moving the office. Let's sort of mosey along on it, you know; whenever the time is right. Let it find its own good time, no one in DC is pushing to make the move anytime soon. How about if you plan to settle in up there while the teams are out on assignment this next time and let them report to you there in Colorado Springs. Maybe you can recruit one of the wives to handle the office.

"You might want to move the teams after this next foray, but let's give them plenty of leeway if they need more time. You may find that they all are ready to go just to get away from the smell of this Mississippi riverbed; I would. You can decide after talking with them; I'll withdraw from that decision. But, while we're in transition, I'll stay here with the remainder of the Louisiana District, 'cause when I give it up, this District goes over to Fuzzy Longmeier."

"But you still will have the oversight as Adjutant. I'll work the move along like you suggested, Phil. But, jump back in when you see a need to; that won't bother me a bit. I'm a willing student; I know I've got a lot to learn and I'm just glad you'll still be there to keep oversight control, whether you move to DC or to Denver."

"You're more than ready right now, Bob; I've known that for some time. Hold on a minute while I get Swede Olafsen in here." Then, "Orella, if Major Olafsen is in the building ask him to come to see me, please."

"He's here, General Bragg, he just came in."

Jon Olafsen knocked and entered. "I'm back, General."

"Good. We need to send you and Misti over to Lake Charles to pick up on that Black Bayou investigation. Ten to one that load of weapons and ordnance came from that Beaumont-Port Arthur warehouse that Crumpton and Solomon worked; it's close enough to truck over to Lake Charles and then down to the fishing shack. We need to verify that and find out what the target was. I'm thinking they must've used that submerged boat to carry the stuff off somewhere and stash it for whatever they had in mind.

"You know, Jon, it wouldn't take a whole lot to disrupt the Intracoastal Waterway if they were to blow up one of those mile-long log booms and cause it to dam up the channel. I'm no expert but it seems to me there's very little current flowing there to keep the destruction from piling up. Worse, it could be an oil barge along with the logs."

"You're right, General; or one of those ocean going coal barges from the coal mines in Alabama. It'd be like a huge rock pile and slow things down for awhile. Maybe no permanent damage, but it could stop shipping through that channel for a month or two; more if there were any freighters beached or scuttled at the same time."

"Hey, it could be bad. Clean up any loose ends and get down there and get what you can from those guys; they ought to be able to release it to you by now. We've got what's left of this week and next week to work that up before we take the next foray on the lists."

"I'll be there in the morning. That'll give me a weekend to snoop around and get some answers. I'll call in next week. See you, Bob."

The Mexicans

"Yeah, Swede. By the way, I'm heading over to Colorado Springs to start up an outpost. How will it suit you and Misti to make the move after the next foray; that'd be about three weeks, or so."

"We're sitting on 'go', Bob; no problem at all, we've been looking forward to a change of scenery."

"Good, Jon, that's good. I'll let you know for sure by the time you leave out on the road next weekend. Take care."

೦೦

The university group met again on Wednesday afternoon bringing in another 8 lists from retired friends some of the group had tracked down. The older people, it seems, were much more likely to take a personal hand in stopping an invasion of terrorists on the continent. So, the web of contacts continued to expand to more and more remote villages; all likely places for the Unification Council to be found at work.

Br. Angel distributed the expense monies and they reviewed the bank savings deposit books. Some of the accounts were beginning to look very good indeed. Clearly, the incentive plan was working.

As they broke up the meeting, Miranda engaged Montez Echevarria in conversation privately while the others departed, in order to keep her and Felipe in the suite for a talk with Br. Angel:

"My friends, I wonder if you might do me a great favor. You see, I have an obligation to attend to in Albuquerque for a few days, beginning at the end of next week. I will have to be away for a week or so, but I would like the work to continue so as not to lose the good momentum we have built up these first weeks. For that to happen we will need another couple in the group, perhaps yourselves, to take charge of the lists that are brought in. I wonder if that would be too much of an inconvenience for you; hopefully it would not distract you from your normal duties."

"But, Br. Angel, why did you pick us?" Felipe wanted to reject the idea. "Why, among all of the friends, would you wish us to take this responsibility?"

"I understand why you would ask; actually I thought a great deal about who to ask. It soon became clear that, of all the friends, you two seem to be held in highest esteem; perhaps because of your distinguished positions as Adjunct Professors at the University. But, more than that, I realized that the others were obviously much closer, more of a cohesive group, most likely because of their common backgrounds in this region and at the University. To select a couple from that close group of friends could possibly cause that couple be set apart, seen as having received a special distinction, an honor without any justifying merit, perhaps even engendering some envy. No, I feel it best to play upon your strength as a couple already set apart. Do you see how it becomes you for the task?"

The Echevarrias looked at each other, but could not seem to find a valid reason to excuse themselves from the assignment. In a few moments Felipe answered.

"Well, your logic seems incontestable, Br. Angel. We will accept the task, but you must make clear to the others, without harming any of the relationships, why it is best that we be selected for the task; that it is not an honor of distinction in any way, but merely because we are, as it were, sheep of another fold."

"Of course, Felipe; we will avoid any misgivings on anyone's part, by providing a clear explanation. And I want to thank you for taking this assignment for me. At our next meeting, we will visit the front desk and explain that you will be using the suite in my absence."

"Very well, then; it is agreed. Goodnight, my friends."

"Yes, goodnight to you both and God bless you."

Br. Angel could see Miranda was relieved, too.

"General Bragg's teams will be going out on their second investigation during the week we will be gone so it will not hold up their work to delay the transmission of the lists that come in for a few days. These people can be trusted, don't you think?"

"It would seem so, Angel, but – who knows for sure?"

The Mexicans

It was a sad day at Mamie Dumont's house, but Mamie kept it hidden in her heart so that Bob wouldn't feel too badly about leaving. But she knew that he would come back; probably not permanently, his job was much too worldly to allow him to settle down with Rebecca in Slocum or even nearby, but a boy returns often to the place where he is loved. And she knew in her heart that hers was a home that Bob loved; he had told her straight out that he loved her as though she were a second mother; she often recalled how he told her that.

"Now, Bob, don't you fret about it; a man like you with the responsibilities you have has got to do what he's got to do. You know that, after all the years you've been a man under authority. I know you worry about me when you're gone; I can tell it when you call home, it's in your voice. But don't worry about me; you just keep calling when you can and come to see me and all of your friends here, because you know we'll be waiting to see you coming up that drive; we'll be watching for you every day. You have Rebecca to come back to, and your marriage is coming along soon; that's enough to keep us all around here looking for that day with hope. You know, we all live in hope, but ours is a hope that comes from knowing it's a certainty, just as we know the certainty that the Lord's coming for us soon. We know you'll be back because you've said so."

"Ms. Dumont, you know just what to say every time something upsetting comes along into our lives. This is one of those times, but every word you just said is the truth. We'll be keeping time together for as long into the future that God lets us walk the earth. And if my time comes before yours, just watch for a sign, because I'm sure God will allow me to let you know that I'm safe, and dry your tears."

"Did you see all your friends at church and tell them?"

"Yes, ma'am, everyone who was there and everyone at the gas station. Now I'm going to visit with Rebecca for dinner and then I'll be heading to Denver. I'll let you know when I can come back; I won't be gone very long on this trip, but next time it'll be for a lot longer."

"Well, you're all ready to go, so I won't keep you. Tell Rebecca we miss her at church; I guess she's doing well there at the University. So give me a kiss and you'd best be on your way or you'll be late taking Rebecca to dinner. I love you, Bob, like my own son."

After a long embrace, Bob drove away to take control of his new District.

When he arrived in Denver the next day, he took a rental car and a room in a smaller hotel where most of the traveling salesmen stayed, preferring to maintain a low profile and modest appearance. His first calls were to the new recruits to arrange a meeting the next morning. He settled in at the hotel and found a good restaurant; then he prepared for the meeting in the morning and turned in early.

At the meeting, he asked to be brought up to date on the investigation. Julio Cruz told him about the large rental trailer sitting in the hanger at the Air Base.

"It's loaded with hardware and wooden items; all pieces of the remains of the weaponry and ordnance cases, but the biggest find was the rubble of a shipping container that had been left in the warehouse, apparently to be unloaded. The team from D.C. is piecing it together to determine its origin, but we already know it was from Korea by the loader's marks; we took photographs and had them interpreted at the Air Force Base by a Korean-American pilot. It was shipped out from Pusan, South Korea. Also they're preparing an inventory of weaponry as they sort out the pieces.

"We have another briefcase full of scraps of paper items that we've been sorting through; so far we have come up with about two dozen names; in a lot of cases we can't tell if they're names of people or businesses, but we're a long ways from finishing the job. All of this is in the last report I sent to General Bragg. The warehouse rubble is still quarantined as a crime scene and there's still a few ten foot squares we haven't finished pawing through. I'd give it another week or so to finish up our initial look, but we've tried to be very thorough. Some of the experts can maybe find more evidence when they get to it. We'll turn this stuff all over to them after we get what we can and take pictures of it."

The Mexicans

"Good, very good. I'll get a look at the hanger and see what they might have found, but that Korean writing sounds to me like hard evidence. General Bragg is headed to Sydney to get the manifest documents on the shipment from Korea to Sydney; pretty sneaky guys, but we'll have the goods on them with the manifest papers and your hard evidence right off the container. How about the relocation of the workplace; do we have anything on that, yet?"

"Yes, we do, Colonel. Vargas and Flores have gotten right into their house. They've developed two informers, one of them is a leaderman on the job which is sort of like a foreman; it means they trust him with information. We've tested them for phony rumors and they passed OK, so we feel pretty safe with the stuff they're giving us. We have the address of the new location in Boulder; apparently the heat's too hot to restart in this town. The best we can estimate is they'll start with a shipment coming in toward the end of next week. Meantime, they're calling the men to work Monday putting up scaffolding and shelving and some other prelim work.

"Most of the men don't like having to make the move; apparently there aren't any really low rent rooming houses in Boulder like these in Denver, but it could get expensive, commuting by car. Right now most of them are thinking of loading up in cars, like six to a vehicle and leaving earlier. We also got the names of the people running the operation. They're about what you would expect; Middle-east types from Detroit. We'll keep these guys on the street until things are settled and we've gotten the shipment information."

"Good, real professional; I appreciate your work. One thing I want to stress; we need to follow the delivery truck back to his distribution point, that's really important so we can get the shipping manifest – we have to have the delivery address and that means getting the place where the trucks work out of."

"OK, Colonel; we'll follow it when it comes and get the location."

"Right. I'm getting ready to open the office in Colorado Springs and start bringing some of our teams in here on a permanent basis. Right now, I could use someone to man the office and handle the telephone and fax traffic. We get some e-mails too. Do any of you have someone to suggest; like someone with a little education and knows how to talk to people intelligently? No disrespect intended to those that don't."

"Delgado's wife has a college degree; I'm not sure how smart she is, you can see she married Rey; that ought to tell you something. Maybe Rey wants to speak for her."

"No, man; I don't want to speak for her; she'd never get the job if I had to speak for her. She can come in and speak for herself. What I do know is that she's gnawing the furniture for something intelligent to do, since I'm about the only one she can talk to while I'm undercover and that's only now and then, plus she don't put me high on the list of intelligent talkers. I don't know why, I got two years of college studying in the Air Force through the Armed Forces Institute. It's enough to get a second Lieutenant's stripes."

"You mean the Lieutenant's bar?"

"No, man, I don't drink that much." Ray liked to act up, now and then.

"Rey, I think we need to get you off the street; it may be rubbing off on you. Maybe if Margarita got the job she'd quit chewing the furniture and you two might start a family like the rest of us wetbacks; how about that, Colonel?"

"I'll leave that one alone, Julio, but I'd like to talk with her; maybe we'll take care of two problems at once. What do you think Rey?"

"I think she'd love to take the job, Colonel; I'll tell her to call you."

"Good, that'll be fine; the sooner the better."

The next morning, before he had left the hotel, Margarita Vargas called asking for the interview.

"Have you got transportation?"

"No, Rey took it; he had to go to Boulder. I can meet you at the supermarket a few blocks away; better not come here."

"Give me the location, I can find it on the map. I'm driving a blue Pontiac rental; how about in a half hour? We'll drive to the office in Colorado Springs and talk. If it works out you can fill out the paperwork while I make a visit. Can you spend a few hours down there today? I'll buy your lunch and we'll pick up what we need for the office; that should take most of the afternoon."

"I can spend the whole day if need be; no problem. I'll call Rey and let him know."

"OK then; I'll pick you up at the supermarket; I'll flash my blinkers a few times. Where is the place?"

She gave him directions; he finished his coffee and paper and started out."

After arriving at the office, Crumpton left Margarita to complete the employment forms while he visited the hanger to view the progress for his report. The work was slow but there was no way he could speed it up. He took pictures that showed a number of nearly reconstructed weapons and ammunition cases. The shipping container had been partially finished on the end that contained the loaders marks; more good photographs. He took statements from the experts as to the quality of the materials and the percentage of finished product they expected to achieve; nearly seventy percent. Before leaving the hanger, he called his report to Bragg, en route to the airport with Beatrice.

For the remainder of the day, he and Margarita made the rounds of the office supply stores and the Post Exchange to pick up some initial office supplies and some computer equipment to be delivered and installed the next day. By four o'clock they were ready to return to Denver.

CHAPTER 37
The Sydney Connection

Beatrice couldn't believe Phil would take her to Australia on a business trip, even if he was paying for her fare and expenses himself. He'd definitely changed since that last promotion.

"I guess you feel like you've arrived at the top, now, and can do whatever you please; is that it, General Bragg?"

"That's it. Don't forget your bathing suit; it's still summer down under and we've got a beachfront room. Just remember to stay within the shark netting and don't feed the alligators; keep your feet out of the water when we go on the swamp ride. You've arrived at the top now, Babe."

"I'm getting one of those string bikinis; you know, the kind that disappears in the full moon and you have to shave where it tickles. You'll like that, Big Guy."

"Just what I had in mind; they have those for us big guys, too. I think they call it the hammock."

"Well, if you're planning to wear that general's star on the hammock, maybe we'll just take last year's suits and save the money."

"Last year's suits are last decade's suits and I'm for that, but I still get to wear the star."

"No star."

"You drive a heck of a bargain, Love."

"Now what, we start talking Aussie?"

"They don't have a copyright on that term of endearment, Love. I may take it for my own."

"Anyway, you don't pronounce it 'Love', it's 'Luv'."

"That's what I said; 'Luv'."

"I'm ready to go, Luv; let's get this show on the road."

It was a long flight to Sydney; fortunately the airliner had good movies to watch and decent food and they enjoyed both along with a quiet two-hour nap. Beatrice brought some snapshots of the grandkids; it was time for reminiscing.

"Phil, you haven't looked at these snapshots of the kids, yet; we just got them on the e-mail yesterday and I ran them off on the photo-print. They're pretty good; Haley's getting so big and pretty, and Megan looks just like you; doing her own thing, she's a natural leader. Marie just puts that big smile on her face and poses every which way, like she was making a movie. Here, you ought to look at them."

"Oh, yeah; these are really good! You know what; they always take their best pictures when they're at our place. I hope they'll be able to visit us as often in Denver as they do now. They're going to love that farm you've got your eye on; that'll bring them out faster than anything. I wonder when Number Two Son might decide to make a few, too. Oh, don't tell me, I know; it's their business, not ours; it's up to them if they ever do."

"Now, Phil, I happen to know they've been trying for two years to have children, so you need to stop nagging; just leave them to it, they'll start a family pretty soon, if they have to get clinical help to do it. At least I hope they do. I can't think about that; this book I'm reading is getting exciting. Phil, you ought to read this one; you won't believe what it's about."

"What's the name of the book?"

"It called 'The Genesis Riders: Angel on the Bayou'."

"I heard someone was going to write about that. Sounds good, but I wonder if they got it right. I'll read it on the way back. We're nearing Sydney air space; it won't be long now. I feel like we should be getting ready for bed, but it's just now morning here; guess we'll try out some of that jet lag for the next day or two."

"Oh, Phil, I couldn't care less; I'm just glad to be getting here. How long will you be over there at the Security Offices? You know how I hate to be all alone on vacations."

"I can't say for sure, Bea. I'll call this guy from the hotel and then maybe I'll get some idea. There are some matters of protocol that I'll have to watch, but the rest of it is just getting the copies of the documentation and making sure they're certified by the government security agency, and signing for them, of course. My guess would be two hours or so unless they want something more from me. Here we go down, now; we should be on the ground in twenty minutes."

The hotel room was gorgeous and the beachfront was inviting. Beatrice took to the chaise and umbrella and a Pineapple drink that threatened to put her to sleep. Phil Bragg showered and changed clothes, slurped dark coffee and took a taxi over to the government building that housed the Ministry of National Security where he met with his counterpart, the Undersecretary, all according to protocol. General Smythe escorted him to the office of the Minister of National Security, George Powers, where he was introduced to a small group of officials from various branches of government who had an interest in the matter; Lord Stafford, foreign ministry, Lord Burroughs, trading ministry, Lord Skilling, justice ministry as well as Lord Powers. Powers began the talks.

"General Bragg, thank you for this visit. We place a great deal of importance to the problem your agents have uncovered. Frankly, we have been aware that re-shipments were occurring through our ports, but with the protections we give our business interests to operate quite freely here in Australia, we've had no evidence with which to proceed against these trading companies. Now, perhaps we can make the necessary case for warrants to examine their cargo as it arrives. We have the documents covering the particular shipment you have identified. Its Port of Origin was Pusan, South Korea. With this, we are taking steps to ask the government of South Korea to stop shipments from North Korea to our ports that are not inspected; we don't wish to be unwittingly involved in this sort of dealing; they understand our position. There is just one additional piece of evidence we will need to put these people out of business through our courts. That is the point of delivery of the weaponry and evidence of the weaponry that was involved in this shipment. Can you help us with any of this, General Bragg?"

"In fact, Sir Powers, we have a unique situation that promises evidence of both the weaponry and the actual shipping container itself recovered within a warehouse in Denver."

He went on to explain about the explosion and the materials that have been found in the rubble.

"Our experts are reconstructing the container, piece by tiny piece; fortunately there is one large piece that tells the history of the loading docks; beginning with on-loading in Pusan, off in Sydney, on again in Sydney and off in Seattle. The manifest documents are being gathered at the Port of Seattle at this very hour. They will show the transfer and delivery point from Seattle to Denver. With that, we have the hard evidence of the loaders markings on the container in the Denver warehouse, itself protected as a crime scene, and the container itself reconstructed complete enough to serve as irrefutable evidence. I believe you will have your case for a court warrant."

"Excellent, excellent; those are exactly the sort of things that we need. We should be obliged if you will provide the full documentation of your investigation."

"But, may I request, Sir, that you withhold mention of these things to the Koreans until we have completed our work and have made our move to invade the workplaces and arrest those responsible for this illegal terrorist activity. If the perpetrators were made aware of our intervention in their plans they would proceed to inflict as much damage as they could before we could act to stop them. Secrecy at this point and for the next six weeks is imperative. I hope you understand my concern."

"Of course, General Bragg; we will hold all of this information in closest confidence until we learn of your successful intervention. We are most appreciative of your work in this affair. What you have told us today is precisely what we had hoped when we were informed of your good fortune with the warehouse recovery in Denver. We can rely on you, then, to provide us with certified photographs of the warehouse rubble, and the reconstructed container and weaponry, General Bragg?"

"You may, indeed. Our officer in charge of the Denver operation is Colonel Robert Crumpton. Colonel Crumpton called me as we boarded the flight down to inform me that he has personally observed all of this and will have the photographs prepared by the experts from Washington who are there piecing things back together."

"Hmm; indeed, I have heard of Colonel Crumpton and his exploits with you and your band of brave men on the Mississippi. Very competent hands and we are very grateful indeed, Sir."

All of the others in the room followed on with "Hear, hear!" General Bragg was feted for an hour as the men there each wished to have their time to speak with him, personally. He hadn't expected such a reception and felt truly humbled by these men of political power all fawning over him and the stories of his exploits.

"Gentlemen, my Lords, thank you for such a heartfelt welcome; I am truly honored to be with you, just to be in the presence of such dignitaries." The photographer was taking pictures of the gathering. "I shall remember this occasion for all of my life."

The business was accomplished. He called John Smoltz and gave him the news.

"I'm going to take a couple of days here to relax on the beach. Crumpton will be back from Denver on Thursday; the teams will be sent out Friday afternoon, all going to new cities. He'll give you the list of cities."

"We'll need that list to pass along to the other agencies. Take all the time you need, Phil; you and Beatrice enjoy yourselves. Share a couple hours with the folks in church on Sunday."

"John, that's the best word of advice I've heard from you that I can remember. We'll do that and I thank you for the reminder, I really do, because without it I might have overslept and missed the best part of Sunday. Truth is, I've had a lot to be thankful for lately. So long for now, John."

CHAPTER 38
Out on the Road Again

Bob Crumpton had the itinerary all set for the Friday meeting with the teams but he wanted to keep it less obvious so he rented a conference room at a hotel that held a lot of business meetings using the name of the Association of Welded Pipe Manufacturers, out of Chicago. He arranged for all the usual amenities, coffee and rolls to start it off and catered lunch to finish it up as well as posters in the lobby to direct the attendees to the meeting room. He instructed the agents to wear a business suit, park at the airport and arrive by taxi carrying a briefcase. Everything was planned so as not to show the force gathering and dispersing from the office where he worried they might be watched.

"It wouldn't be the first time", he thought. Then he wondered if he might be getting phobic about it. "Nope, they're everywhere."

All of the team members from the first foray were present except Bobbie Turner who had excused herself from this outing to return to Lafayette and get their things ready to go to Denver. Her parents, Mr. and Mrs. Beauchamps had planned to visit Colorado Springs with Bobbie and to help her look for a nice house; she would have a whole week to look. Shep knew he would love anything she picked out, especially with her mother there to help; they both had good taste for houses and furnishings. Whatever she chose would be their home, just so long as Bobbie was pleased with it.

So, Crumpton sent Shep Turner on the team with David Solomon his old partner; a good match. Except for that one, the teams would be matched up the same as on the first foray with two replacements but the itineraries would be altogether different. He gave out the assignments at the hotel Friday morning after working all day and night Thursday to have them ready in time.

The Mexicans

"OK, here we go. Randy and Mandy go to Jacksonville and Orlando. Leon and Vargas go to Tampa and St. Petersburg. Franklin and Dollar go to Atlanta, Macon and Columbus. Ron and Amy go to Oklahoma City, Tulsa and Wichita. Pederson and Preacher Coleman go to Birmingham, Memphis and Huntsville. Fletcher and Chuck Knight go to Baltimore and Wilmington. Baskins and Delgado go to Charlotte, Raleigh and Winston-Salem. Corbett and Calvetti go to Pittsburgh, Harrisburg and Scranton. Norman and Flores go to Nashville. Walker and Nielsen go to Chattanooga and Knoxville. Ferrara and Niel Olafsen go to Savannah, Charleston and Columbia. Brownlee and Rodriguez go to Indianapolis, Ft. Wayne and South Bend. Shep and Solomon go to Milwaukee, Madison and Davenport. Reilly and Moses May go to Minneapolis, St. Paul and Duluth. Bud and Susan go to Richmond, Portsmouth and Norfolk. Jon and Misti go to Rochester, Syracuse and Buffalo. Does anyone have any questions?"

"Yeah, who gets Miami?" Calvetti wanted Florida.

"You get Miami, Paul, when we get some names for the place. I guess the Cubans aren't willing to share with the Mexicans; we'll have to send you down there just to find out if they have an operation there. If so, it must be manned by Cubans. Let's see if someone can come up with an answer off the street about that area. We'll have to know before we finish this investigation and before we make the raids. OK; the names we know of so far all include the Star and Crescent in some configuration. But, let's watch also for the Spanish equivalent, maybe Estrella y Luna or any other permutation you can imagine. And then it may be something with Muslim or Persia, you know, whatever you can think of if you have trouble finding the Star and Crescent configuration and let me know when you find a new company name.

"OK, now, pay attention. We may have missed some distribution points on our last foray. The only way we can get the distribution points is to follow a delivery truck back to its yard. That's something we overlooked, but fortunately two teams used your heads and picked up on it so we got two. This time we want you to stay on the watch a little longer, an extra few days, and see if a delivery truck shows up, but don't make it obvious, we don't want to take any risks of being made. Everybody get that?"

"Follow the trucks back to the home base", Reilly spoke up.

"That's right. Now, I don't expect we'll have any problems like we did in California, but you never know what these protectors of aliens will do to keep you off the trail. Handle it like they did in California; through the Governor's office; that's where our Agency carries the budget clout. Call me if you need anything and take extra care. They may have made someone on that last trip, so be careful; the word may be out. Keep moving when you're getting tags at the workplace; don't stop and look like tourists taking pictures. Now, there are a dozen or so QREs on the table over there so go ahead and make your reservations. When you leave here take a taxi back to the airport in twos or threes. God bless you all."

Next, Crumpton called John Smoltz to let him know where the teams were going to be working.

"OK, Bob, I got it. I'll alert the other agencies and pass it along to Harry Foster. Good work, four hundred names, that makes a total of around seven hundred, so far, out of what, forty-two villages they gave us so far? Well, we know they have ten or twelve invaders in each village, so that's maybe five hundred that we know of, maybe a thousand by the end of the year. That means another month at the rate we're going. I don't expect that we'll get every village, but it's a good probability we'll have all our cities identified; I'd hate to make the incursions and then find out we missed any; sort of like that paddle-wheeler on the Mississippi."

"Yeah, I've thought about that, too. Both times when we put the list together we've had a few singles or just a few in some cities that we didn't want to go out on, not enough to be sure it wasn't just a mistake. When we get to the point that we don't have many singles left over, we'll know we've probably hit all the towns where they have workplaces; there'll be a few errors in the data. I'm thinking one more foray and then the incursion; that'd be near the end of the year. But, man, that's going to take one heck of a coordination effort and bunches of troops."

"I've been working on that; it'll be big, but we can put it together starting from right here in DC. We'll need most of our District officers along with the FBI and the local police SWATs to get a large enough

The Mexicans

force. The key will be sequestering the forces for a day or so without outside contact and without being spotted. We'll do it, Bob, and I expect you and Phil will have the controlling hand in it."

"Hey, I'm for that. I know it's going to take some organizing; Phil's good at that."

"Yeah, he is. OK, Bob, keep me informed and thanks for the update; got to go." Smoltz hung up.

Monday morning, General Bragg was back in the office telling the story of his meeting with the Australians and their time on the beach and visiting the outland.

"We had a great time and saw things in the flesh that we'd only seen on the National Geographic Channel, and I mean both on the beach and in the outback; you know, they have very liberal attitudes toward beach attire down there."

Crumpton brought him up to date on his team assignments, the Denver operation, the office secretary, the office outfitting and his plan to have all teams transfer to Denver as they return.

"Nielsen, Vargas, Flores and Delgado are each teamed up with a regular out on this foray. Br. Angel is in Albuquerque for his annual martial arts recertification tournament and Luis is there too for the same reason. Luis will return Thursday and Br. Angel will remain in Socorro for the remainder of the week and return to Monterrey on Saturday. He left the store in the hands of the Echevarrias to hold the Wednesday meeting and take in the lists. His friend Al Maldonado is out on the circuit getting lists; it all seems to be moving along well, but he noted some restless activity by the Jimenez people brewing in Monterrey. I gave a full account to John Smoltz and have a report ready for you to look over."

"Well, Bob, it sort of looks like you have the Border District in hand. We got really good marks in Australia for all that work the new guys dug out of the rubble at Denver and the work in Seattle by Randy's recruits. Those guys Nielsen and Heinkle were a Godsend, getting those shipping manifests. I'm hoping we'll hear from him this week on all those other locations I took up there to him. When I left there he had all of them on his list, even the late ones from the west coast. I'm guessing this next batch of lists should bring us the rest of the workplaces. After we finish that foray and get the shipping documents, we'll have all we need for the onslaught; boy, that's going to be huge. Smoltz will have to plan that one from DC and we'll be a part of that, too.

"Yeah, he gave me an idea of what he had in mind for that; everyone sequestered for a couple of days at various locations before the countdown; then the incursions all on zero hour. I know that's going to be big."

"A lot is depending on this being carried off to a T; we can't miss anything on this one."

Br. Angel called Al Maldonado to advise him of his visit to Albuquerque for his certification tournament. He gave him the new names of village contacts the University group had since brought to him.

"I'd like for you to visit around farther south, down to Zacatecas; there are perhaps five or six more towns that can be reached within a day's drive. I'll try to be back in Monterrey next Friday. You are doing such good work, Al, and I suppose the lists will be coming in by that time, yes?"

"Yes, Angel; I can start on those towns next week. Elena is enjoying the vacation in Chihuahua, so my time is unrestricted. Carlos Pacheco has agreed to pick up some of the lists as they call in completed. Others are bringing them to Chihuahua. Have a good visit and I'll see you next weekend."

"OK, Al; goodbye for now."

Next he called the NSA office in New Orleans where he found Bob Crumpton in charge.

"Did you receive that last set of lists I sent yesterday morning?"

"I did, Br. Angel. The teams just went out on their way; nearly four hundred addresses on this foray. These will be new cities, so we're getting much more widespread across the country. By the way, as these teams return in two weeks, we'll be operating out of the new office in Colorado Springs and you can send the lists to me there; Margarita Vargas is our office assistant. I'll let you know the new telephone and fax numbers after we get them installed next week."

"Fine, Bob; I'll call you before I leave Socorro. Please give my regards to all my old teammates."

"I will. Thanks for calling in and I hope you enjoy that tournament. Be compassionate, treat the other guy's bones with respect, but especially your own; we can't afford to lose you even for a few days. See you later."

With the work all in good care, Br. Angel and Miranda made reservations for the flight to Albuquerque by way of San Antonio, an active flight corridor. The next morning he called Luis and he drove them to the airport.

"I'll see you in Albuquerque for the start of the rounds on Monday, Br. Angel."

"Yes, and plan to visit with us in Socorro afterward, if you should have time."

"We'll see; Rita Juanita may have something to say about my time, so I will have to let you know about that; you understand."

"Yes, of course, Luis. We'll try to return to Monterrey next Friday to send in the lists."

"I'll be back here before then. See you on the mat."

As they waited for their flight, Miranda called Patsy Perez in Socorro to ask her and Fred to meet them at the airport and to have dinner with them at their favorite restaurant.

"Miranda, how delightful to hear your voice. Yes, of course, Ben and I will be there to meet you; it may be just a little after five but you'll need a few minutes to get your bags, anyway. Hey, tell me, have I ever, ever turned down a dinner out?"

Their connection in San Antonio went through without any delays and they were in Albuquerque by late afternoon. Ben and Patsy drove up just as they exited the terminal and it was all hugs for several minutes. Dinner and a lot of conversation took up the next two hours; Patsy had to tell Miranda how she had taken good care of the dogs and watched the house like a hungry hawk. When they got to their house, they were ready to sit for about an hour before getting ready for bed.

"Angel, dear, it is so good to be back home; I feel like I'm just waking up from a long dream. Can we stay until Saturday?"

"We'll see, my dear. There should be no urgency to return Friday, so, yes; we'll change our return flight in the morning. I'm ready for bed, aren't you?"

"For our bed; yes, by all means", her eyes were twinkling.

"My dear, have you been snacking on your 'Friskies' again?"

"Oh, Angel, I love it when you speak Romantic."

CHAPTER 39
Things Can Get Good – and Worse

When the tournament was progressing, Carlos and Merced Pacheco were on their way to Monterrey for the Wednesday meeting, stopping at El Sueco and other points along the way to pick up the lists that were ready. Al Maldonado had arranged for several lists to be delivered to his house in Chihuahua. Carlos picked up the lists and another at a house in Ciudad Jimenez, then they spent the night with friends at Torreon as was their usual custom; but that night was not a good night for sleeping.

"Carlos, what is all that noise out there in the street? It sounds like those people are very angry."

The socialists loyal to Julio Jimenez were out in force, demonstrating and demanding that the town's mayor and council meet with their leaders and negotiate a list of grievances they had prepared.

"I'm afraid it is those Jimenez activists. I read that they were coming north; it looks like they have decided to disrupt the peace here in Torreon."

The crowd was carrying torches and signs and their leaders were speaking through a bullhorn. They wanted to address the conditions of the town's poor; they wanted jobs, welfare, health care and protection from the local police who they claim were inflicting injury on the poor people who gathered in the streets wanting work and wages. They warned that they would not stop the disruption in the streets until their demands had been met. It looked like it would be a repeat of the insurrection that had been put down in a bloody struggle with the army in Oaxaca only a few weeks ago.

The Mexicans

"Carlos, what will we do if this is still going on tomorrow morning? We won't be able to leave the house and it might get worse. Carlos, I'm really scared."

"Don't worry, dear, we're safe. Try to get some sleep. I'll set this alarm to go off at four in the morning. If it has settled down by then we will get up and leave quickly before they wake up and start again. Don't worry, dear, we'll be alright."

Carlos and Merced awoke before daylight. The noise was gone; the streets were calm for a period, but they couldn't know for how long. They arose quickly and slipped out of town before the rioters awoke to resume their troublesome demonstration. Their car was unharmed and the drive to Monterrey was peaceful in the early morning hours. But later that morning from their room at the hotel they watched as a similar demonstration of students took to the streets and moved on to the University campus where they became disruptive; by early afternoon the University had dismissed all classes and, with the help of the police, had barred the entrances to the buildings with steel angle irons bolted into the mortar. They would use these irons again and again in the months to come.

The Pachecos worried that the group might not be able to meet, but before the clock approached 4pm, the police had managed to contain the violence within the confines of the campus using force of arms. They were allowing the students to mill about and shout obscenities at them while their leaders met with University officials to talk. In the end, more than two dozen of the ones inciting the violence had been suspended from the University campus and would be given an incomplete for all classes in which they were enrolled, but no one was arrested. That suspension would be the seed for the riots to come during the next days and weeks.

Felipe and Montez Echevarria had been escorted from the University by police along with the other professors during the disruption, but a small group of dissidents followed them to the hotel, shouting obscenities and attempting to spit on them as they entered. By 4:30 the others had arrived and brought their lists. The television was flooded with news of the student uprising. Felipe opened the meeting.

"I'm afraid this trouble may last for days or weeks, like that uprising at Oaxaca. We had better finish our work here and leave before it gets dark and they start again. Please let me have the lists and there is an envelope here with expense money for each of you. We will meet again next Wednesday." Felipe worried for the safety of the others.

"Yes, it's best not to stay tonight." Carlos Pacheco described the situation they had encountered at Torreon. "We should leave the hotel while it is still daylight."

Felipe distributed the expense money and displayed the bank passbooks with the savings deposits Br. Angel had made for the last week's lists. Those he left in the suite along with the lists. They all were anxious, concerned about the safety of the city with all the disruption going on. The Echevarrias were last to leave, but by then it was starting to get dark.

"Felipe, maybe we should spend the night here. This could turn into an all out insurrection as long as the money to support it keeps coming in from Jimenez; eventually even a Cuban-style revolution could result if a strong leader emerges."

"We could be in greater danger here. Let's go quickly while it is still light."

They emerged from the hotel parking garage in their car and drove down an alleyway to avoid the crowds gathered in the streets.

"I love you, Felipe."

"And I love you, Montez, my love."

The next morning, the television station reported that the slain bodies of Felipe and Montez Echevarria were found on one of the streets in a lawless barrio, Las Casas del Rio, a slum-ridden section near the open discharge from the waste treatment plant. They had been tortured, their bodies slashed open and a cardboard banner was posted over them with three letters scrawled on it in blood; C I A. The University group would never meet again after that.

That morning Luis Caldera awoke to the news of the slayings on the television. He had arrived back in Monterrey late Wednesday evening

311

and realized as he drove to his room that things were not going well and perhaps the end of the work was at hand. Carlos Pacheco had called him from Torreon Wednesday night to warn him of the dangers at Monterrey, but this news was shocking. He called Br. Angel with the news; he and Miranda wept over their friends when they heard the gruesome manner in which they had been slain. Luis said he would scout around and make a determination of the situation; whether it would be safe for them to return by the end of the week. He asked that they remain in Socorro until he had made an assessment. Luis then called Phil Bragg to report the conditions that were developing.

"I'm really concerned, general; we have disruptions in Monterrey and nearby Torreon, and the slayings, not by accident, I suspect. Someone was out to kill the Echevarrias and this was their cover for the murders. The police say it appeared as though the students had done it. Well, I don't believe that for a minute; the student protests have never taken an anti-American stance and have never murdered anyone and labeled them CIA agents. It was clear from the sign on the bodies that it was a political murder. These were Castro's goons who had preferred to eliminate them on Mexican soil and place the shadow of guilt on the students. It's true these student uprisings are incited by the Jimenez people trying to undermine and weaken the federal government, but they are not yet ready to take on the CIA in a war. Castro may have wanted them to handle it, but they probably turned him down; that's the way my friends here are reading this whole thing."

"I think you are probably correct, but where does that leave the Suarez's; do you think that the Castro people would mistake them as CIA because of their connection with the Echevarrias?"

"Well, I wouldn't know that without more time to investigate, but I do think we should pull them out now before something bad happens; remember, they have been here for several weeks and meeting regularly with the Echevarrias. The others have already made it clear that they will not meet again; Carlos Pacheco made that point very emphatically when I called him earlier today."

"What about our remaining work in the villages; do you suppose that is also in jeopardy? But that work has been kept in the clear; no one in Monterrey has taken part in any of the surveys at the villages."

"I think the village work is far enough removed to be safe to continue; Pacheco thinks so, and he will continue to help with the gathering of lists if he is asked to do so; he's very dedicated to the cause. And Al Maldonado; he has never attended any of the meetings in Monterrey and in fact has met only once on an afternoon here with myself and the Suarez's. Al is now visiting towns south of Torreon, recruiting contacts in each town and arranging for the lists to be delivered to his home in Chihuahua, those he does not pick up himself. He has done a remarkable job and could perhaps be relied on to finish the work. Also, without the University group, there is the possibility that Br. Angel might wish to stay on at another location."

"When is Br. Angel returning?"

"He had planned to return this coming Saturday, but I asked him to delay until I called him back after assessing the situation. I would like to make a suggestion, General. Let Br. Angel return as planned to gather up his things; then I will drive him to meet with Maldonado. They can outline a plan to complete the remainder of the villages east of the mountains leaving that work to Al and myself, shadowing him. Br. Angel and Miranda then can return to Socorro. I would feel it much safer for them. Al and I have not been a party to the Monterrey meetings, so we should be unknowns to the Cubans or whoever the assassins are."

"Luis, I don't expect we will need more than another two weeks from today to the point where all workplaces will have been identified by at least one name from the lists; right now we are getting close to saturation of cities. If Maldonado will stay with you for that long, let's go with your suggestion, then shut it down two weeks from today, we'll want the last of the lists in here on that Thursday, no later. If everything looks good we'll make our move against these workplaces two to three weeks after that, so be ready. I'll call Br. Angel and lay it out to him. One more thing, Luis; see if Al Maldonado is interested in working with us as an agent. It sounds to me like he has a talent for getting information out of difficult situations. What do you think of him?"

"From what I know of him, I think he has the potential, if he is willing and can adapt to the physical action that is often required of the work;

The Mexicans

sometimes good men are just not compatible with the military aspect, the firestorm side of it. But, Al is showing a natural talent for the work as an investigator. I wonder if he will be able to leave his missionary job and take his missionary talents with him on the road with the new job. From what I understand, Br. Angel has done a lot of missionary work on the road; those guys seem to find the ones that need the message, almost like they'd been sent to them, and maybe they are."

"Well, Luis, here's your chance to develop your recruiting record for the Agency; talk to him about those things and see if you think he's a candidate. If so, see if you can sign him up; right now I'm looking for all the good recruits I can find. If he agrees we'll fax you the forms and mail the ID and debit card by courier if they have secure couriers down there. The hardware we'll assign to him when he gets back here."

"Couriers operate here, General. Your courier up there can arrange it; it just might cost a few more bucks. OK; if that's the plan, I'll get my things ready to go on the road for a couple weeks. After that, I may be getting married before coming home; Rita Juanita and I are engaged. It seems like we've been waiting for each other all our lives. It's amazing, General, how God directs you to the one He has planned for you, if you pay attention. Think back on how you and this situation here brought Rita and I together. I don't think it was by chance."

"I don't really believe much in chance, either. I think it was Einstein who said that God doesn't play dice with the universe. That would surely go for people, as well. I know they use probability statistics to study physics, just as though there were random effects controlling it all. But what they get turns out to be a range of probable solutions and that only means that the eventual truth is given by only one from within that range of answers. There is a most likely one, but even that one they can't be sure of. Even though the fuzzy math may allow them to make computations that work out, the answer is always fuzzy. The question remains, who determines the selection that gives the true answer? It's not the computer."

"Yeah, General; that's Quantum physics, using probability distribution. It's scientific but it's indeterminate and one wonders at how the calculus of indeterminate equations can reliably predict a resulting effect. The Bible tells us that the wisdom of this world is foolishness with God. Just think for a moment; where do our thoughts come from? Do we just create them out of what we have learned over our lifetime? I don't think our mind's creativity can be explained that simply. I believe God influences us, especially His own people, to accomplish His purposes. Look back on your own life and see if you don't see God's hand in many of the events you would credit to chance if you didn't know better."

"I'm hooked, Luis. I know there are influences, spiritual influences; perhaps angels, perhaps devils, but for Christians, more often it is God's spirit. I read about the madman who Jesus encountered and the thousands of evil spirits in him saying "we are legion". He evicted them from the madman to enter into a herd of a thousand swine, and the mad swine drowned. By that account, I can see how a body might be under many influencing spirits besides our own, so, yes, I think you are right; I'd like to think that I was chosen to play a part, unknowingly, in your meeting with Rita, and that it was God's doing. But take a little advice about married life; don't let your love get lost in all of the momentary situations that can overshadow your love life, be true to that love and trust your faith. We all need to place a high priority on the things that can reinforce our faith, and love is our homework. If I can I'd like to attend the wedding, Beatrice and I."

"You have an invitation right now, General, and I'll send you the first formal invitation when Rita has them ready."

"Good; we'll be there. Now I'm going to call Br. Angel and talk this over with him. If he agrees, we'll wind it up down there in a couple of weeks. Let the CIA worry about those assassins; you take care."

"I'll do it, General. So long."

Bragg called Br. Angel and gave him a briefing on what he and Luis had decided.

"The situation down there is likely to get worse and we'll have enough names with what Maldonado is bringing in, so we need to give him an itinerary for the next two weeks and send in the last of the lists by Thursday of that week."

"That is a good plan, General. I'll return to Monterrey alone. It will take just a few days to arrange it with Al and then I'll be back in Socorro by mid-week. Let me tell you what else I had occur just today. A courier packet arrived this morning sent to us from Washington. An official with the State Department, Donald Brubaker, an undersecretary, is requesting Miranda and me to visit there next week, by official invitation of the Secretary. I don't know what it is about, but I suppose the vetting they did a while back was related to this."

"I think they will ask you to accept a position as an envoy to the Mexican government. I heard something to that effect a month or so ago. You are becoming a celebrity in the White House, Br. Angel. Whatever it is, it will be a dignity that few of us ever receive. Just the invitation is a compliment. So that is all the more reason for us to pull you out of the survey work; you can finish up down there on Wednesday and still be in Washington on Thursday."

"Yes; that will work. Let me tell Miranda and then I'll call Luis and Al."

"OK, Br. Angel; I'll let you go. Give my regards to Miranda."

Br. Angel made reservations for his Saturday morning flight to Monterrey, connecting through San Antonio. Then he called Luis in Monterrey and, after that, Al Maldonado who was in Juan Aldama securing a contact. They would meet in Zacatecas on Tuesday, allowing Br. Angel time to transfer the ownership of the bank accounts to the contact people who earned the reserves. For the rest of the time, Al's work would continue by paying double the initial expense payments at the time the lists are received. He requested an additional supply of pesos to give to Al. Then he was ready to talk with Miranda, reluctantly, because he would have to leave her in Socorro for this trip.

After he explained the revised schedule, she spoke before he could get it out:

"Angel, I don't think it would be wise for me to join you on this last trip, if that is alright, Dear. You and Luis will be very busy and I would have very little to do; and the possibility of disruptions in the streets really scares me after what happened to Felipe and Montez. I really think I should stay here and get things caught up so we can go to Washington when you get back. Is that alright?"

"Of course, my dear, of course. I should have known you would beat me to the punch; you always seem to be able to read my thoughts when I have disappointing news to bring. I will miss you and I know you will miss me, as well, but it's only for a few days. You will have time to get caught up with the many things we have neglected. Why don't we have some friends over tomorrow afternoon? My flight leaves at 9 am Saturday."

"Let me decide what to have; it will be nice to have dinner at home with friends, if that's what you would like."

The last part of that sentence struck him as a little too obvious. "I have a better idea; let's spend a quiet evening at home, just the two of us."

"Oh, Angel, you have the most romantic ideas. Yes, that's good, just the two of us."

"He's made us, Simon; that's the same guy that was hanging out at the side entrance to the warehouse. He's the one who watched us taking down the tags and he wrote down our tag; I saw him do it. Now he's checking his note to see that the tag matches our tag. We should have changed the car last night."

Simon Pederson and Preacher Coleman were working the Huntsville venue a little too closely.

"Go over there and tell him he's under arrest and bring him over here; see if he comes."

Preacher Coleman walked over to the man and called to him not to move, that he had to answer some questions. The man looked like he was about to run down the street to his rooming house, so Coleman pulled his pistol and the man stopped in his tracks with his hands in the air.

"Don't move; we want to talk to you", Coleman warned the man pointing the pistol at him. "Come over here to the car."

The Mexicans

When the man moved toward the car, Simon got out and opened the rear door.

"Get in here while we talk."

The man sat in the back seat as directed, obviously frightened.

"How much money do they pay you at the warehouse?"

"They pay us $8.25 per hour; it's good pay. I am satisfied and I don't want any union."

"Why do you think we are from the union?"

"Who else; you are the only ones they have told us will be trying to get our names and where we live. Isn't that what you are doing?"

"Why do you not want to join the union? You could be making $12 an hour in the union."

"No! They will turn us in to the INS if we talk to the union."

"What if the union says they will do the same?"

"You don't know how much trouble you will have if you do that. These people will do anything to keep people from the outside from coming in; anything. And they mean it; they will do bad things to you union people. You should stay away."

"We have found out what we want to know. Maybe we will wait until there are enough workers to make it hard on them. Don't say anything or they may fire you for talking to us about it. You can go now, but we may be watching this place another time."

"Thank you; please just leave us alone, just leave us alone."

"That will be up to you. Don't tell them about this talk."

The man returned to his rooming house; Pederson and Coleman had all they needed to know, but they were a little worried about this encounter and they reported it to Colonel Crumpton. Crumpton put out the warning to the other teams:

"Two of our guys just got made today; they reacted with good sense and caused the guy to believe they were union organizers watching the workplace and following them home to find out where they lived. They hit it just right because the employer had warned the workers about talking to union organizers and getting fired if they do. Keep that little ploy in mind in case you get in a similar situation. But, the important thing is don't get made. Don't remain in any one place when you're watching the workplace or the residences; keep moving in the car and change the car everyday; use a taxi occasionally if you're just scouting. Take moving pictures from the car so that you can read the tag numbers later.

"A few more cases like this one in Huntsville could bring the death squads out on us. These guys are serious and they are bad. Don't give them any reason to notice you. And watch your backs to see who's watching you. Be careful and remember; these guys are an integrated organization, just like us. They talk; they pass it around. One bad move by one of us could put the other teams in trouble and kill the whole advantage of surprise that we need to be successful. Don't be the guy who spoils it."

After that, no one questioned who they were reporting to in the Border District.

CHAPTER 40
Dissidents and Incidents

Saturday morning Br. Angel packed a small bag, enough to take care of his needs for four or five days, and turned to say farewell to Miranda. He had never in all the years of his marriage managed to control the tears from welling up in his eyes when it came time to leave Miranda, even for a short time. This day was no exception and as he looked down into her imploring brown eyes, Miranda gently pulled him down to her and kissed the tears away, but no matter, more followed.

"I'm sorry, my dear; I can't control it. You know, I love you so much."

"Yes, Angel, I know that; you are my very tender hearted husband and I love you for it. Hold me very close, then leave quickly while I get busy in the kitchen doing something. These times of leaving are very difficult for both of us but soon will be the returning and the joy that it brings. I will turn to God for solace and He will honor my prayer and keep you safe. Now, Angel, leave quickly. Then hurry back; hurry back to me."

"My dear, you are always my great strength. I think this shall be my last trip without you; we have given up enough time away from each other. I'm trusting that our next calling will be you and I together; we will see to it, Miranda, we will see to it. Farewell; yo te amo, mi esposa, my love."

"Farewell y te amo, mi amor, my love."

Br. Angel's connecting flight in San Antonio was on schedule. He called Luis to tell him his arrival time and Luis was there to meet him at the airport.

The Mexicans

"It's good to see you back, Br. Angel, but I want you to know right off that after watching you in that tournament, I'm very reluctant to lose you as a partner. You went through your matches and disposed of your opponents as fast as anyone in the younger classes; I was very proud of what I saw, I can tell you, very proud."

"Well, thank you, Luis. Coming from you that is indeed a compliment. I couldn't help but notice the look on the faces of your opponents when they saw who it was they were about to encounter on the mat. Yes, we would make a good team; I'm sure of it."

"I hate to change the subject, but we will have to be wary as we near the hotel; there have been quite a few small bands of disrupters out on the streets looking for trouble, so be prepared. I'm not sure who is putting them up to it, but Jimenez is catching the blame."

"Why? Do you not think it is his doing? If not, who else might it be?"

"I wouldn't be surprised if it were the drug cartels and the smugglers trying to take advantage of the fear the people here have for the Jimenez activists. By keeping the violence going here in Monterrey, they provide cover for their own illegal activities up along the border. Most people are more disturbed by the Jimenez outsiders than they are about the drug and smuggling gangs - they don't operate around here. But it is easy politically for the federal government to place the blame on the Jimenez outsiders, so they aren't doing much to try to stop these street gangs. It's getting to be just a big political football while the drug runners and smugglers continue to operate openly in the cities they control."

"So now you think we have three groups to avoid, counting the Iranians. Well, the sooner we get out of Monterrey and only in the villages, the better. Al is not having any trouble; apparently his cover story about educational conditions is working out well. Nevertheless, we will be safer and the whole Operation in the states will be more secure when we finish the village work. General Bragg said we might have it well enough documented with one more foray around the country."

"That's right. Another two weeks to finish up here, then another two weeks for the last foray at the same time the D.C. people put together the incursion teams. I'd bet we'll be knocking down the doors in about five weeks, maybe six. That's what I'm looking for."

"I'll be praying for you, Luis. By the way, did you set the date for the wedding?"

"The invitations go out Monday; it's Sunday, December 3rd at Santa Ignacia Catholic Church, here in Monterrey. After that, I expect we will be in planning and preparation for the incursion, then the quarantine, and then the count-down."

"One thing I've wondered, Luis; how do they get the doors knocked down at exactly the same zero hour. It seems that the teams must be dispersed at differing distances from their targets; that would mean it will take a longer count-down for some than for others."

"Oh, that's easy. As part of the preparation the teams all make a series of dry runs from their place of quarantine to the target to determine the exact time it will take to make the move. They will know the planned time of day, so the traffic should be the same as they encountered on the dry runs. The Count-down is then set to begin with the team at the point farthest away in time and each team sets their departure time in accordance with the time remaining in the countdown that they will need to reach their target at zero hour. See? It's just good planning and a little math."

"I should have guessed that."

Luis pulled the taxi up to the hotel entrance; as he came around to open the door for Br. Angel, a small group of young men approached them from around the corner of the side street; they appeared to be intoxicated and spoke very loudly. One of them asked Luis scoffingly,

"Is this the taxi that goes to the CIA office? We want a ride to the CIA office right now."

Another two attempted to open the rear doors but Luis always kept them locked, especially when Br. Angel was in the car.

"You men are drunk; I don't take hires from drunks. Get your hands off the car and get out of here if you don't want to get hurt."

The Mexicans

"Look! He wants to fight," and the man pulled a knife from his belt.

Before he could use it, Luis had thrown him high over his hip and he crashed onto the pavement; the knife went spinning into the gutter. The other two young men rushed Luis attempting to overpower him, but within a few seconds they were both on the pavement, as well; one flipped high, head over heels and the other nursing a rabbit punch to the kidney and a chop to the back of the neck; that one easily could have cost him his life had Luis preferred it.

As those three were taking their knocks, the other two young men watched Br. Angel step out of the taxi and move toward them.

"Wait, young men; let me speak to you."

He intended to ask that they leave them alone, that they had no desire to fight with them, but they turned and ran back down the side street to where their car was parked. With his gun drawn, Luis waved the injured men off to join their friends.

"Tell your boss there's no CIA here, only black belts and pretty damn good ones, too. Now, get going and don't show your butts around here again unless you want to spend the rest of your life in a wheelchair. Get!"

They got the message.

"I'll pick you up in the morning whenever you're ready, Br. Angel. We had better leave as soon as possible; it looks like they made the connection with the Echevarrias and us."

"Yes, I think so too. I'll be ready at about 6 o'clock; will that work out for you? We can have breakfast here and leave soon after. I'll call Al and arrange to meet with him. I will have to sign the passbooks over to the contacts and you and Al can deliver them, or mail them as the case may be."

"If Al's at Chihuahua that will be a full day's drive for us, but it will be safe up there. The last I heard from him he was down below Torreon; that's only a few hours' drive. Have you selected the final group of villages for us to visit?"

"Yes, I think it would be well to go west from Chihuahua over to the villages near Hermosillo; there are several towns within two to three hundred miles. It's over the mountains but that will be better than going farther south. I'll leave you with the locations where the Iranians were dropped off and you can select whatever towns are easiest to reach. The ones we have already surveyed are checked off."

"OK, then, I'll see you here at 6 am."

Br. Angel made the call to Al Maldonado before going to dinner. Al was relieved to know the work was coming to an end. He had made his last contact at Fresnillo today and was now headed back to Chihuahua.

"I'll be driving until about midnight unless I get sleepy and stay somewhere on the way, but I really don't think I'll need to stop. You will be driving most of the day tomorrow to get to Chihuahua, so we'll expect you about dinner time?"

"Yes; we'll check in at the hotel and call you. Perhaps we can meet Monday morning at about 9 o'clock?"

"That's a good time. We'll get the work planned out and there should be a few lists coming in also. Maybe you can return on Tuesday."

"That would be good. We'll call you tomorrow, Al. Drive safely."

He called Miranda and told her the plan, then went down to dinner. While he waited to be served, a man sitting with a lady at a table nearby stood and came over to where Br. Angel was seated. He asked if he might sit down for just a minute.

"Yes, of course, please sit down."

The visitor introduced himself:

"My name is Eduardo Fortunado. Please forgive the intrusion, but I couldn't help seeing that encounter you and your driver had on the sidewalk out there; neither of you seemed to be intimidated by that gang of roughnecks. Were they attempting to rob you? I wondered because as many times as I've visited this hotel, I have never seen such a brazen attack on a guest right there at the entrance. My wife

The Mexicans

and I were so relieved to see that your driver was perfectly capable of defending himself."

"I'm sorry; let me introduce myself. My name is Angel Suarez Rivera. I have been in Monterrey on business for several weeks now. Fortunately, my business is at an end and I will be leaving soon. I'm afraid these disturbances will continue and may even become dangerous. But, the taxi driver has been on call for my needs and I was delighted to learn that he is a master of the martial arts; certainly that was a rare public display, there on the front walk. And as you have observed, we are none the worse for the encounter; but I want to thank you for your concern and please convey my thanks to your lovely wife for her concern, also."

"What caused me greater concern was the recent murder of two visiting professors of the University, a man and his wife; Cubans, Echevarria I believe, was their name. Those two were marked as foreign agents; do you suppose they might have mistaken you for another foreign agent and tried to kill you out there tonight?"

Then it became clear to Br. Angel; these people were, in a very discrete way, suggesting that a connection had been made between the Echevarrias' visits to his hotel and himself. But, why? Were they CIA operatives, perhaps suggesting that he should give up his work in Monterrey and leave the area?

"But who would make such an assumption? Yes, that is certainly possible; one can never tell what others might assume in error. In any event, that is not my concern; those poor people must have been engaged in activities that the killers didn't like, whatever their motives."

"Of course, you are right. And I am relieved to hear that your business in Monterrey fortunately is ending. Forgive me for interrupting your dinner and please have a safe journey from here, when you leave. Goodnight, Mr. Suarez."

"It has been a pleasure to meet you. Your concerns are valid, of course, and I thank you again for coming forward with them. Goodnight to you, Mr. Fortunado."

Sunday morning at 6am, Br. Angel had his bag packed and was seated in the restaurant when Luis Caldera walked in and joined him at his table.

"Good morning, Br. Angel, did you have a restful night?"

"Yes, Luis, I am very well rested. I can see by your eagerness to get the day underway that you also are well rested."

As he spoke he watched Eduardo Fortunado and his wife enter the restaurant and take a table in sight of theirs. Fortunado, seeing that Br. Angel had noticed them enter, nodded a greeting and sat down. Br. Angel made the slightest gesture of acknowledgement in return. By those gestures, Luis could see there was something he should know about.

"Do you want to introduce me to your friends?"

"I think not, Luis. There is more to that couple than meets the eye. I'll tell you the whole story as we drive. I'm not sure which side they represent, but I suspect they are agents investigating the killings of our friends."

"I expected as much. If their side is island based, we should be very devious in our departure route; I'll have to think about how best to do that. If otherwise, then our departure would eliminate one of their chief concerns.'

'And what would that be?"

"Two more in the body count."

"Oh, yes; that would be of concern."

They each ordered a heavy breakfast, intended to hold them for the day, except for liquids. Afterwards, Br. Angel paid the bill and they paid a last visit to the suite for restroom privileges and to gather up the luggage. For appearance sake, Luis carried the bags to the taxicab while Br. Angel checked out and paid his bill which was substantial, in cash, pesos. They made a stop at the bank for ATM cash; several drawings for the needs of Luis and Al Maldonado.

The Mexicans

Next, they drove to the airport and stopped for a time in the departure lane, then, with Br. Angel stretched out on the rear seat, they departed and Luis drove to Ignacio and Marie's house watching for tailing cars all the way. There he entered and remained for ten minutes or so, watching for any cars moving in the neighborhood. Only one passed by, rather slowly, and continued down the street out of sight. That is when Luis quickly departed the house and drove to the highway headed north in the direction of San Antonio. When he came to an opportune intersection, he took a less traveled street back to where highway 85 headed out of town to the south. Again, after a few miles he took a detour to meet the highway headed east to Saltillo, the direction they intended to go.

"We should be on our own now, Br. Angel, unless they have air support, which they don't. In about ten hours we'll be in Chihuahua feasting on arroz con pollo. Now, tell me the story of the two people at the hotel."

"You know, Luis, I'm convinced their sole purpose was to let me know we were in the way. When I sat down to dinner last evening, the man came to my table and introduced himself as Donaldo Fortunado. He began by recounting our encounter with the young thugs that he and his wife had observed. We spoke briefly about the disruptions and then he made mention of the Echevarria killings, suggesting that the thugs may have been put up to it by someone thinking we were CIA agents, as they were. He didn't suggest any reason to make that connection, but it was clear that he wanted me to know that they knew we had been meeting with the Echevarrias. I dismissed it as foolishness and told him we'd had an enjoyable stay conducting our business and that it was coming to an end. He inferred that it was the best thing for everyone that we did. After that, we had little else to talk about and he excused himself."

"He's got to be CIA. They don't want others like us muddying up their water; they may even blame us and our work for getting the Echevarrias killed. He was clearly an important spy. I don't think we have anything to worry about from those goons that tried to intimidate us on the street; that was probably the Cubans wanting us out of the way to further discourage the CIA from investigating them; they don't know what's going on, they're just used to getting tough with people they can't control. The boss of the operation just wants to do the most damage he can before going back to report to his chief in Cuba. That'll be the end of their foray into Mexico now that they've killed the spies they uncovered.

"Your visitor was there this morning because he had to keep you in his sights; he'd have been tailing you to the moon until you got out of town. Right now he's slapping high fives with his spotters who probably had picked you out at the airport, coming back from Socorro. They probably were watching when you got on the airplane in Albuquerque to come back here. They've got the budget to keep up with everyone on their list."

"Well, now we're done with them, I hope."

"We're done with them."

They switched off driving the long distance to Chihuahua; stopping to fill their canisters with coffee in Torreon and buying a sack of snacks at Ciudad Jimenez. Br. Angel got in a few short naps while Luis drove, but they generally kept the conversation going to stay awake while driving.

"Br. Angel, what would you think about Al Maldonado as a candidate for an officer with the Agency?"

"I was wondering when General Bragg would spot him for recruiting; that man has a gift for identifying brave men of character. Well, Luis, I've known Al for more than ten years, since he joined the Missionary Association. He's much younger than Miranda and I, but we have had a close friendship with him and his wife Elena most of that time. They are very nice people; trusting and trustworthy, always agreeable to be a part of the workload of the Association. You saw that here when I asked him to help me for a time on this work. He didn't hesitate, but called Elena to be sure she would not be opposed, knowing the possibility of danger. It meant a serious adjustment for the children's schooling, but Elena worked that out, too, arranging for home study and testing by computer attendance. I could not ask for a more dependable partner, with the possible exception of you, Luis."

The Mexicans

"Hey, I already knew that last part."

"Ah; I said that was a possible exception. The only thing I don't know about Al is how he would react under fire, never having seen him in such a situation. If I were to guess, I would say Al would be steadfast and would exert whatever force were necessary to save lives. Al is a powerful believer in Scripture and he knows that those men of God were also men beholden to the laws God gave them. The archangel, Michael, fought with the Evil One with all the weapons at his disposal, as did Abraham, Moses, Joshua, Barak, Gideon, David and many others, against the enemies of their people. We can view that as a priority with the Lord; defending against the works of the devil with whatever force God gives us. Al Maldonado will not flinch in the face of death. He will make an excellent Operations Officer. Whether he will see that as a calling for him, I couldn't say, but in your shoes, I wouldn't hesitate to make him the offer."

"That was what I needed to know, Br. Angel; you expressed that point beautifully. I have always felt that God had ordained my work as an Operations Officer so long as the purpose was noble. I would not hesitate to withdraw in any situation that my convictions told me to oppose. I believe that the Spirit of God will let me know by way of my own thoughts, when any matter does not meet God's standard."

"You can depend on that help when the time comes; I'm sure of it. I have had the experience on many occasions; enough to know that God does not leave His people without guidance."

"I'll present the question to Al. I expect he may talk with you about it."

They arrived at the hotel just before 8 pm, checked in and cleaned up for dinner. True to expectations, the day's special dinner was arroz con pollo, Br. Angel's favorite, asada and tortillas. Next morning they got started at 7 am, after sleeping an extra hour. They had agreed to meet with Al at 9 so they had plenty of time.

Al's family home was modest, tidy and well kept; there was a small vegetable garden in the front yard. Elena showed her usual love for Br. Angel with a kiss and welcomed Luis. The children were very impressed with Luis and his good looks and athletic appearance and Luis clearly enjoyed being with them. Br. Angel thought how Luis had many wonderful days coming to him now that he was getting married to a good woman. They would have a big family and Luis would train the children well in all the sports and in the Word of God. Elena introduced them to Al's mother and father, then settled them in the living room where Al soon appeared.

"Good morning, Br. Angel, Luis; welcome to our home. How are you both?"

"We are well rested. It's good to see you, Al; you're looking well. So, how is the work progressing?"

Br. Angel was interested in forwarding the lists to Crumpton.

"The work has been progressing very well. I'm amazed, the local people have been receptive and willing to talk when they find that I am interested in improving their education system. Once they have accepted me, usually after an hour or so of talk, they begin to talk freely about almost anything going on in their community. I seem to hold an attraction for these poor people of the villages. And it's true; I do have a serious concern for them and their condition. They are all so hopeful that the U.S. will allow them to enter legally and take jobs."

"Conditions here are very difficult for the uneducated; I've seen that and my heart goes out to them. Tell me, Al, have you encountered any opposition from local constables or any activity by the Jimenez demonstrators or any others?"

"Not in the villages; things remain calm in all of the villages I've worked thus far. With the federal government so weak in the rural communities, it is the locals who wield the power and they want most of all to maintain the social order. The people appreciate it and particularly since the Council has been freely distributing largess to many of the families. But I think we have pretty well worked the south areas. Below Zacatecas there are many larger cities, but we have seen that the Council avoids visiting those cities where they are not as able to take charge."

"We should turn our attention for the next two weeks to the west, across the mountains to the Hermosillo vicinity; then we will have completed the work and should have the lists faxed to Colonel Crumpton by Thursday after next. So, you and Luis will work together until that time. How does that sound?"

"That sounds good, excellent; we can do it."

"I have brought you a fresh supply of pesos; you probably have been using your own. And I will leave the bank deposit books with you and Luis to arrange their delivery to the contacts. And, with that said and done, I will have completed my work here and shall take my leave tomorrow."

"Well, it is surely time for us to bring this work to an end and leave Mexico, with all of the disruption increasing throughout the country. I'll be pleased to return with my family when the time comes and that will be less than two weeks."

Luis spoke up;

"Al, I have a question to put to you. Perhaps while Br. Angel is refreshing his coffee cup, you and I can move to the porch outside and talk about our work. Will that be OK?"

"Of course, we can go sit out there now."

CHAPTER 41
Meanwhile, Back in the Field

Ron and Amy Jensen had completed their work in Wichita and found an unexpected bonus; a railroad distribution warehouse less than two miles from the railroad yard where the shipping containers were unloaded from the train. Quite by accident they happened to be observing the workplace from a quarter mile away using a telescopic VCR when a tractor-trailer rig came on the scene and entered the delivery entrance. Amy saw the rig approaching and warned Ron to begin rolling the film. They got a tape of the rig and its identification, name, location and tag. When the rig left the warehouse two hours later, they followed it to its terminal, a modest in-state delivery operation recently taken over in bankruptcy by an investment firm located in Detroit, the Crescent & Star Development Corporation.

Ron and Amy interrupted their local observations for three days to follow deliveries dispatched from the truck terminal. A single rig was used to deliver to Kansas City, Oklahoma City, Ft. Worth, Tulsa and Little Rock. They got VCR tapes on all of the locations, including addresses and business names. Then the deliveries stopped completely; apparently they had emptied the contents of the shipping containers from the last rail shipment and would wait for the next shipment. Ron called Bob Crumpton to report their find and the evidence they had gathered on tape.

"That tape will be good evidence linking the delivery operation with the shipping manifest and to a lot of workplaces. With it, we go from the port of entry to the railroad delivery point and to the local workplace operations in those cities and perhaps others at the end of the chain. This is evidence of the entire connected distribution channel. It couldn't be better and it corresponds to the distribution operation coming in from Canada and from the one in Texas the others ran across on the first foray. Great work by an observant team - and you got names at all of the facilities; I'll get this out to all the teams; it just shows, there are terminals to be found at other locations. Take care of those VCR tapes."

"Yeah, Bob, I'll see if I can find a military courier and get them off to you; there's a base around here, I think."

"That'd be best; use the military courier. Take care, Ron, and thanks for the good report."

They still had a week to go, but they didn't mind that; they had plans to look around Tulsa. There were two excellent Universities with award winning architecture and great sprawling campuses. There was the Museum of Art that housed the largest collection of Remington paintings and sculpture in the world; Misti had looked forward to this visit since learning of their assignment.

"Ron, you have got to see the things this man Remington has done; you won't believe it. He has these paintings of old west characters and horses and when you look at the painting from anywhere in the room, the horses eyes follow you and look straight at you, no matter where you are, and it's the same for the rider. If you start from the far side of the room and walk to the other far side of the room, the eyes are watching you every step of the way; it's just incredible. He's done that with a lot of his works. But it's not just the illusion that makes his work so valuable; it's the beautiful characters and settings that look so real. The Indian wars and the clouds of dust from the herds of buffalo and horses and the gunmen shooting; it's all so lively and realistic."

"OK, Amy, I'm game for the paintings, let's go there after breakfast and spend a few hours; then we'll find a good restaurant and later we can catch a basketball game; both of these Universities have good teams."

"And let me tell you about the sculpture. There's a horse galloping and its hooves are completely off the ground except for the tiniest spot of a single hoof that keeps it in the air and not falling over; it doesn't even look like it's touching, but it is. You'll see; it's fantastic, how he could have done it, not just to one horse, but to a whole lot of his sculptures. Most of them look like they're defying some law or other of gravity or motion or just credibility. I went down to see the display of some of the work when they came on a circuit show to LSU. You're really going to be amazed at this Remington art."

"Well, after all that, I'd darn well better or you're likely to leave me there and go off mad in a taxi."

"Oh, you know I wouldn't do that. Ron, that breakfast was so good. I haven't had breakfast in bed since I can remember. And the coffee is really good, too. Can you pour me a little more?"

"Well, I'll just do my best, Honey; hold your cup a little closer – a little closer – a little more - - -don't you just love breakfast in bed?"

"I do, Ronnie; I surely do."

"Amy, you know I hate that name, but - - oh, well."

@@

Bob Crumpton decided to try another idea with Frank Heinkle at the Port of Seattle terminal; he called Phil Bragg to make the call, since he was trying to hire him.

"Phil, we just got another distribution point from Ron Jensen in Wichita. I don't think we told Frank Heinkle about this problem with addresses on the delivery documents coming into Seattle. We only have three, now, including this one I just received from Ron, the one in Pecos and the one in Canada. Why don't we see if Heinkle can check for the names that we have found at the workplaces, besides the addresses; either one or the other could be on the document. I'm sure we must be missing some of those distributions points."

"OK, Bob, I'll call Heinkle right now; I've wanted to get back with him on it. Maybe that's why we haven't heard from him about those others we sent from around the country. Look for Star Crescent or some such configuration of name; I'll get back with you, Bob."

Bragg called Frank Heinkle and got his voice mail.

The Mexicans

"Frank, this is Phil Bragg; how about giving me a call back when you can? Thanks."

He called Crumpton.

"Bob, give me all of the name permutations you've come up with so far; I'm not sure my notes are up to date."

"Sure thing, Phil. I'll fax you a copy of my list; I've got it right here in front of me. Let me know if you can't read it."

He had Margarita fax it to Bragg.

Later on, Bragg got his call back from Frank Heinkle. He explained why the delivery addresses may not have been the ones on the shipping document.

"Can you check just for these names and get us a copy of the shipping manifest and the delivery order, no matter what address it carries?"

"I see your problem. These terrorists are breaking up the containers in a delivery warehouse and trucking out the orders for the local workplaces. Yeah, I think we can do that, Phil; we can get just about anything you need from these documents since they put it all on the computer. Do you still want them there in New Orleans?"

"Just as well; I'll need a copy for my records and I'll fax them on up to Bob Crumpton in Denver; he's handling the operation teams. You may get a call from him sometime; he's Colonel Robert Crumpton, but he'll call himself Bob. He's my kind of officer. By the way, I'm still looking for a few good men to fast track. Things are getting heavy all over and that Seattle area could use a back-up Operations Director right now for the Northwest states. If you're at all interested, that'd be your responsibility in a short time after a few high profile assignments. Think about it and let your brother do the easy work."

"I'm seriously considering it, Phil. You just sweetened the pot 'cause I'd hate to have to permanently give up my place here on the Lake for Peoria or Roanoke; know what I mean?"

Meanwhile, Back in the Field

"I can't say I blame you for that. Give it a year of two on the streets and then backup in Seattle for a few years and I'll have you heading up the Northwest District Operations; you can count on it."

"I'll make the decision by New Years Day."

"I'll take that meeting; it's on my schedule right now. I'll have a list of names to you overnight; there's more than one. I'll let you go now and Frank, I sure do appreciate your help on this operation; it's heavy and it's going down before New Year's Day, but that's a trade secret."

"It's safe. Talk to you when I get the documents. So long."

He called Orella to his office.

"Orella, fax that list of Star Crescent names to Frank Heinkle when it comes in; Crumpton's sending it. Also, I'm expecting a package of documents from Frank Heinkle in Seattle. If they come while I'm gone, make a set for Crumpton and send them to him on the courier."

Next, he called John Smoltz in D.C.

"John, I just want to update you on the guy in Seattle I told you about, Frank Heinkle. I've about got him on the sign in sheet, but I had to promise him a Northwest Operations District in Seattle in maybe five years; isn't Jim Carlson retiring about that time? I think he can be ready by then with some heavy work over that time. I know you don't like the homestead kind of District Manager, but you've got to let a little time for the Agency to get in his blood; it will, he's one of the rare breed."

"Phil, that's why I put you in as Adjutant; to make those things happen. I'm all for it; I remember Carlson's date is about that time, so, OK, if you want it. The California Operations are way too big to be handling the Northwest states, too."

"Do me a favor and send him an early Christmas card; I'll fax you his name and address."

"Be happy to, Phil; send it on, I'll start a file."

337

That evening Phil and Beatrice took a long look back over the farm properties they had selected as potential settlement locations; then they looked them over again. Neither of them said much, just sort of looked at each other for help. Beatrice broke the silence.

"Phil, you know how I love the mountains. The fresh mountain air is so invigorating and the winter sports are so exciting when your blood starts to warm you up from the inside; that's when the weather seems almost summery with the sunlight on your face and your sunglasses fighting off the glare from the snow banks. I wonder, do you remember the times we spent in the mountains in northern Virginia when you were called to DC for days - sometimes a week at a time?"

"Oh, yes, I sure do. We had a great time in those Shenandoah Mountains; Front Royal, isn't that where we stayed? Yeah, I remember it; I'd slip out of DC after lunch and bring my work with me so we could have the afternoon on the horse trail. It really wasn't all that far on the Interstate. Lots of those smaller towns were an easy distance from the city. Why? What're you thinking, Bea?"

"Oh, Phil, I don't know about pulling up and going to a place where I don't know a soul, except some of your agents. The idea of rank recognition and special privileges at the Air Base and all that is sort of a turn off to me; I mean, I'm really not like that, at least I don't think I am; do you think I'm like that, Phil?"

"No, Bea; if you were I probably wouldn't be as mad about you as I am. You're the sort of person who takes position more as a bother to be overcome around the ordinary folks, rather than a badge of privilege. I wondered about that when I saw your reaction to the subject when I raised it out there in Colorado Springs. I thought then that it might not be the best thing to do, moving out there. But, the alternative is DC and the pomposity of the high echelon up there is unbelievably elitist; oh, not everyone, Smoltz and Janie are good home types and there are others, I know. But there is one big advantage to DC and that is that you can choose to avoid the elitist crowd and pick your friends from among your neighbors and your associates who think more like you do. When you're the big dog in a small yard like Colorado Springs, you don't have as much freedom of association and that could get boring, maybe even distressing over time."

"Phil, let's take a week in the mountains of Virginia and look things over before we make any hasty choices. Is that OK? Can we go off for a week now before this big operation of yours gets to the point where you can't?"

"You bet, Babe, and now's the right time. Smoltz will love to see us looking around up there. I'll arrange to go right away; Crumpton's got the reins of the Border District, now. The planning for the big showdown will begin soon and this will allow me to take the starting gun in hand; I want to direct the planning for that operation myself. Start packing, Bea; I'll have reservations to leave here day after tomorrow."

"Yeah, man, I heard that!"

The next day their flight sat down at Washington International Airport, where they had a car waiting for them. By four o'clock they were checking into the motel at Front Royal.

"Phil, this is the view that I've always remembered. Pour us a glass of Chablis and let's sit out on the veranda for about an hour while you call Smoltz and tell him you're here. This place has a great restaurant, too."

He poured the wine and called Smoltz.

"John, we're in Front Royal and we'll be looking around for a place over the next few days. I'm yours, Denver is Crumpton's; when do we begin the planning for the invasion?"

"Glad to hear that, Phil. Now that you're here, we'll get the legs under that operation. Have you got the week here?"

"I'll take the week here; got Bea, got my ears, and Orella knows where we're staying. What about Monday morning; is that soon enough?"

"Monday's fine. We start around here at the crack of dawn – 9am sharp."

The Mexicans

"Bureaucratic excellence. See you then."

"Babe, we're free for the weekend; let's call that big Realtor in the phone book and see what he's got for sale."

He dialed it up and arranged for a tour of several small properties in the morning at ten o'clock.

"Phil, you are remarkably efficient. Can you pour me about half a glass; we'll stay here taking in this lovely mountain view for another half hour; then I'll hit the tub and soak for twenty minutes before we go down to dinner. You have the bathroom until then."

"Bea, you are remarkably instructive."

The next afternoon at 3:45 they were initialing an offer on a twenty acre property with horse stables, a mountain view and a five acre lake. It had a house, too; 4200 square feet and a four car attached garage. Beatrice fell in love with it at the first look.

"Ride 'em, Cowboy. Phil, we're made for this place. Let's get another look at the house. Oh, don't look so smug. So, maybe it was your idea but you had to sell me on it."

CHAPTER 42
Diplomacy Rules

The modest twin engine propeller aircraft seemed to stutter a bit as they climbed to 18,000 feet for the flight to El Paso from Chihuahua. These days it was fortunate that the plane actually flew on schedule; you could never know for sure until the plane left the ground. The uncertainty in the country was never greater than it had become over the past few months because of the disruption taking place in the cities by the political supporters of Julio Jimenez, the Venezuelan.

But on this bright Tuesday morning, Br. Angel was aloft on schedule and observing the rural countryside from the shady side of the flight. He was on his way home, having successfully transferred the final weeks of list gathering to Al Maldonado and Luis Caldera. He was well satisfied that the matter was in good hands. His work at the task was ended; he would turn his sights now to new venues with new adventures to be determined by his next employer, the U.S. Secretary of the State, Phyllis Morales.

He recalled meeting Ms. Morales on his previous meeting with the President and members of his Cabinet, he and Miranda together. Ms. Morales was personally very cordial and she showed a special interest in his relationship as missionary and confidant to the Indian nations. She seemed fascinated by the accounts of his rescue of the lost airmen in Louisiana and again with Miranda on the high seas approaching South Korea. Perhaps that meeting may have influenced her to consider them for a State position in Mexico City to help improve relations there; after all, that is what envoys usually do. Whatever it turned out to be, both he and Miranda were looking forward a new adventure; Miranda loved adventures.

Before long, they arrived at El Paso. He called Miranda to tell her he was back from Mexico and that his current involvement there was now ended; that caused her to issue a great sigh of relief, loud enough for him to hear.

"Hurry home, Angel, my love. Thank God for letting it all work out to the good. I'll meet you at the airport; hurry home Angel, my dear."

The return to Socorro was joyful; but thoughtful as well, recalling the many weeks of work they had managed to accomplish.

"Miranda, looking back it just seems incredible how a situation that was for us at its beginning, filled with unknown people and unknown risks, could over a couple of months, gradually turn itself from a scattered puzzle of questions into a beautiful montage, the pieces moved into place by circumstances that we hardly had any control over. This was not a work of ours, my dear; we were at best just parts of the puzzle, not designers, not architects, not engineers, not movers of the pieces. The puzzle seemed to work itself through to completion. Don't you see it?"

"Oh, Angel; you are too deep into abstract thought today. Yes, we were only a part of the puzzle, but that's the best we can ever attain to. We are only a part of the puzzle of our own lives; we don't even shape our own lives, not really. We take actions, make changes, turn wheels, bad or good, but our efforts are but a part of the result; the force that shapes the events and measures the time and makes the substance of our lives actual, real, is the will of God. Any good that results from our efforts is given by the will of God and it is He to whom we give the glory, if there is to be any glory from our lives. It is all about God in our lives, isn't it?"

"Yes, my dear, it is. We are saying the same thing but you said it best."

There was a gathering of friends waiting for him at their home as he and Miranda arrived from the airport. The friends had prepared a luncheon of special foods; they all knew his favorites. The remainder of the day was spent in the yard and on the deck, sitting around with friends, talking. Somehow they all had guessed that he was involved in something important; something involving the government. No one spoke of it outright, but there was an abundance of allusion, enough to cause Br. Angel to change the subject on occasion.

However, now that the Mexican mission was over, he openly acknowledged that he and Miranda would be leaving the very next morning to go to Washington D.C. for a few days. Fortunately, he could rightly tell them that he had no idea what the people there had in mind when they asked them to come. Regarding Al Maldonado, he was able to tell them that his father had survived the operation and was recovering very well; they expected that he would be back home in another two weeks.

Later that evening as they packed their bags they realized that they had no idea how long they should expect to be in Washington. They decided it would be a brief visit; perhaps three or four days at the most. He had been told to expect the military plane to pick them up at the Albuquerque airport at 9:30am. They both lay awake in bed that night in anticipation, wondering what the future held for them. Eventually, they decided to leave it in God's hands, whatever it might be, whatever it might bring. After that, the stress of the day caught up with them and they slipped off to sleep, holding each other very close all through the night.

Br. Angel saw Miranda reaching down to him as he approached the rim of the mesa; he released his mule and took her hand as she looked deep into his adoring eyes and helped him effortlessly up to the mesa top where at once the light was so bright and his eyes so clear that he could see the love and the grace and the eternal truth abounding forever over timeless wonders. "Of course", he thought, "it was always so." Then he realized his prayer was being answered as he knew it would be; Miranda and he were as one, ordained to be so, then and now and forever, and the Light was a part of them just as they were a part of the Light, as one. And amazingly, the great love in his heart that had often welled up in his eyes left his eyes dry now and instead, shone so brightly on his face that he glowed from the joy of it. And, he thought, "Of course – there are no tears here in this place; no more tears, ever."

The next morning, the military jet that picked them up in Albuquerque landed at Andrews Air Force Base where they were met by a Colonel who escorted them to the waiting helicopter that carried them to the helipad at the White House grounds in Washington. There, they

The Mexicans

were met by Ramon Diaz, assistant to the Undersecretary of State for Mexican Affairs, who had contacted them earlier.

"Good day, Mr. and Mrs. Suarez; I am Ramon Diaz, and I am pleased to be at your service. The Undersecretary has asked me to see to your accommodations at the hotel and to arrange for all of your needs. He looks forward to meeting with you at a dinner in your honor this evening hosted by the Secretary Phyllis Morales."

They were greeted at the hotel by the hotel's liaison that saw to their bags and escorted them to the Guest Registration, where they initialed the registry, and then up to their suite on the twelfth floor. Ramon Diaz attended them as they settled into the suite. The accommodations were splendid and well-appointed.

"Mr. Suarez, our schedule calls for me to return for you at 6:15 and escort you both in the limousine to the White House where Undersecretary Alfred Romulus, will brief you on a proposal for your consideration. Should you accept, it will be announced at the dinner by Secretary Morales. The President will attend the dinner and will welcome you to the White House. Here is my private telephone number; call me if there is anything that you need, anything at all; I am here at your service while you are in Washington."

"Indeed; you have been most helpful. Thank you, Mr. Diaz."

They had time enough to settle into the room, attend to shower and bathroom chores and then relax for an hour before getting dressed for the dinner. Ramon Diaz arrived right on time and soon they were at the White House being escorted into the guest reception area to meet with Alfred Romulus.

"It is a great pleasure to meet you, Br. Angel and Mrs. Suarez. I have heard many stories of your adventures and your missionary work; such marvelous dedication to duty. Please, let us sit down for a few minutes while I explain a situation we are faced with that we hope will attract your interest."

"The job of introducing the impending situation here and the required accompaniment in Mexico to the Mexican government would be the

Diplomacy Rules

task of a special Envoy acting through the auspices of a Presidential directive representing the State Department with the power to speak officially for the Secretary. That Special Envoy we hoped would be you, Br. Angel, with your wife, Miranda as Assistant Special Envoy. Your initial appointment would be for four years, under the normal protocol of the Department and so there would be other matters to come, but those are not of our immediate concern."

Romulus escorted them to the White House dining room where they were seated at the places reserved for honored guests. Sharing the table with President Cooper were Harry Foster, National Security Advisor; William George, Homeland Security; David Brent, Interior; Phyllis Morales, State and Alfred Romulus, Mexican Affairs. President Cooper gave the official welcome to the honored guests and acknowledged each of the government officials. Then he asked Br. Angel to ask the blessing, and he did.

Next, Secretary Morales read from the Presidential Letter of Appointment.

"These days are days of special circumstances. The President of the United States, in recognizing the importance of maintaining good relations with our neighbors to the south, does now appoint Angel Suarez Rivera to the diplomatic post of Special Envoy to the government of Mexico. Ambassador Suarez will solidify understanding and participate in joint planning for the good of our two nations as we face a surreptitious enemy poised toward destructive activity. Joining Ambassador Suarez, the President appoints Miranda Davida de Suarez as Assistant to the Special Envoy. These envoys will speak for the President in matters of special significance and importance facing our two nations."

"Mr. and Mrs. Suarez, we welcome you both into the family of the State Department and I look forward in anticipation of the enhanced relations that your work will bring about to our continuing relations with the government of Mexico. I would like you to attend with me tomorrow morning a meeting with Senor Carlos Lopez, Ambassador to the United States from Mexico, in the Executive Conference Room of the State Department for the purpose of introductions and the announcement of your appointments as Special Envoy. We shall begin

The Mexicans

at ten o'clock. And now, I would ask each guest to join me in raising my glass in a toast to your success and good health."

With that, the dinner began. By its end the attendees were all suitably impressed at the comportment of the Suarez couple. They would clearly be an enhancement to the Department's Ambassadorial team. President Cooper bowed out early to attend an important conference, but Secretary Morales remained to the end, clearly elated by the magnetic presence her new associates had brought to the table.

The meeting with Mexican Ambassador Lopez went well, he being aware of the history and background of these two people as international figures. He had also learned of their recent visits to Monterrey and the surrounding communities although he was not clear as to their purpose there; his contacts told him they had been on a mission for the Central Intelligence Agency, something to do with Cuba. This new appointment as Special Envoy was a bit bewildering and he wondered, "Special Envoy for what?" He would have to call on his contacts in the city to find out their purpose.

"I am indeed pleased that President Cooper has taken this step to solidify our relations with the addition of a special envoy. May I ask when you intend to take up your place at the American Embassy? I must be sure to mark the date on my calendar and be there for the welcoming celebration."

"That has yet to be established; we are just now becoming aware of the Appointment, but I can assure you that you will be among the first to know that date when it becomes known." Ms. Morales answered the question and put it to bed.

That's the way it went, pare and thrust, for a half hour with little if anything divulged before its time. Secretary Morales was very good at diplomatic fencing. When she had had enough of Senor Lopez, she excused herself and asked Br. Angel and Miranda to make time available to attend a briefing at the State Department. At the briefing they would be given their Identity papers conferring the Diplomatic status that they will need to move in and out of the country without restriction.

"We are ready to hold the briefing this afternoon, if that will suit your timetable. Should you wish to remain in the city over the weekend, I would enjoy having you here for all or part of next week to show you around and be sure that we make all of the correct introductions in the various branches and agencies of government, but that will be up to you; we can arrange to have you back for a later visit, if you prefer."

"Let us continue with your plan, now that we are here; whatever is necessary, our time is yours."

"Very well, then. We will send a car for you at the hotel at, say 3:40, and the briefings will begin at 4 this afternoon. In the meantime, I will ask Alfred Romulus to prepare an itinerary for next week and we will plan events by that schedule. Is there anything else I can help with just now?"

"Just one thing, perhaps you can refer us to a Christian Church nearby."

"Let me have Ramon Diaz get with you on the favored churches; he attends regularly. I'm afraid I can't be of much help in that area; I rarely attend."

"Oh, I'm sorry, but, yes, that's really not unusual. Many of the great leaders of history were at first unaware of the source of their calling. Would you be surprised to know that the Bible tells us that you were personally selected for the very important position you hold; that your destiny as a great world leader was determined by God's personal selection; by His calling? Has that idea never been offered to you? Forgive me, I don't wish to lead you into a discussion that you feel uncomfortable with."

"In truth, it hasn't. I have always thought that success was based largely on one's ability to learn and to draw upon that learning to determine the ways that things and ideas should develop and then to take direction from that understanding. I must admit, I have always believed in the ability of man to formulate his own destiny using the power of logic."

"Of course; the mind of man is magnificently created in the image of God. Developing ideas is an act of creation beginning with imagination; but for us, we must then deal with a material existence to finish what we have imagined to create. We believe that God is the Creator and therefore not constricted by a material world; He creates using only the imagination of His mind and directs using only His will.

"I have heard that many times and it seems so ephemeral, so unreal. For me it's hard to imagine that sort of spiritual influence. I must deal with reality."

"Incongruous, isn't it?, that we can create a space probe and send it off on a course it takes that we have given it, all the time sending to it thoughts for it to enact. On its journey it makes millions of decisions; when it arrives at the destination that it has in mind, it looks about and decides to take pictures and to move about to areas it finds attractive. Then, it decides to send those pictures home; sometimes it changes its mind and takes another course of action. Eventually it decides to return home and it does the things it needs to do to make that happen. We are geniuses in making such a creature and controlling it without tethers or wires. How then is it so difficult to credit the same intelligence to God and His ability to influence His creation without using tethers or wires?"

"Thank you, that's an interesting thought; perhaps we can talk more of it sometime. Now, I'll have to go to meet with some visitors. We'll see you this afternoon at four. Goodbye for now; Mr. Diaz will be here shortly to take you to your hotel."

"Oh, that really won't be necessary. We like to walk and it will be a good exercise; I'm sure we can remember our way to the front exit. But thank you, just the same. We'll see you at four."

CHAPTER 43
Collegiate Activities

Ahmed al Hamdi, the Iranian assistant manager of the Oakland workplace, called the workers to a meeting early Monday morning; he called it a "management conference". Many of the employees were still a bit fuzzy from their weekend revelry and were glad to have a little more delay before beginning their routine activities of sorting, weighing and repackaging materials from the shipping containers. Al Hamdi's title was `facilitator'; that meant that he made things happen. Today he intended to make something happen, alright; something these employees hadn't counted on. He gathered them into the lunchroom, shut the door and began to speak.

"You men have been employed for about three months. During that time, most of you have been paid about $400 a week in cash money with no taxes taken out and no records kept for the Gringos to harass you with. Also, during that time, your families have received about $125 or more a week that you had been sending home for them. Altogether, most of you have received nearly $7,000 cash for you work during the time we've been operating this place. You have done good work and you have been paid well. Now comes the time for an additional operation that will require your help, but also will put an extra $200 into your pockets. We have deliveries to make nearby of some of these materials that we have been working with. That is what we will do together this morning, you and I."

Here again was another respite from the usual boredom; everyone brightened up.

"We'll visit the University so you must first be made to appear as students, so we have jeans, t-shirts and sneakers of the style and brand that most of the college students wear, ready for you to put on. Before

The Mexicans

that we will let our hair stylist cut your hair in a style popular with college students, and you will shower and put on fresh underwear. So, let us begin that part of the operation now, half of you go to the shower room while the others line up for a trim by the stylist; you six go to the shower room, you others line up over there."

The men were a little bewildered; they hadn't expected this sort of public exposure. Many expressed their confusion and worry.

"Don't worry; the task will be accomplished in two or three hours. Besides; no one in this town cares if you are legal or illegal. The police will never stop you unless you break the law and you won't be seen breaking any laws because I'm going to be leading you there and leading you right back here. So, just relax and let's get going."

Al Hamdi spoke good clear Spanish, unlike most of the terrorists brought into the country; he had been born and raised right here in California and educated at Berkeley. In an hour the men were all dressed and clean looking. Al Hamdi indicated a row of typical student bookpacks, common to the college campus at Berkeley.

"Each of you pick up a bookpack and place it around your shoulders the way they are carried; you've seen them being worn all over town. These are a little heavier than a load of books but when you tighten the shoulder straps you will find them to be comfortable. We are going to the college campus at Berkeley. We will go in two vans. Inside the vans are six books of the English language; you will each take a book.

When we arrive we will drop you off in pairs, near a building entrance with a bench to sit on. You will remove your bookpack and begin looking at your book. When there are no others around, you will enter and place your bookpacks behind the door marked "Utility Room", up against the wall, then exit thebuilding; these are very large buildings. Then you will wait on the bench for the van to return to pick you up in a few minutes. So do your job and then continue studying your book. If anyone passes by, don't look up or they may wish to talk. Do you all understand?"

No one spoke; they all just nodded their heads, hoping this would be over soon.

"Alright; we have two family-size vans parked in the alleyway, through the rear door; everybody head out to the vans and get in, six in each van, and take your book. I will be in the first van. We will drop off the men in that van first, two at a time. Then I will get in the second van and we will drop the others off. When we have done that, we will circle back to the first men and begin picking you up. Now, let's move out to the vans."

Soon they were entering the Berkeley campus. The vans took the road that passed nearby the residential dormitories; two men were dropped off at each of six very large residential dormitories. Most of the students were either in their classes or over on the quad. Very few milled around the dormitories. Within twenty minutes the men were picked up and the vans were exiting the campus. Back at the workplace, each man was given his bonus of $200 in cash. They were instructed to change back into their own clothes and to fold and place the student attire in baskets. That was the end of it; they were all relieved and pleased with the extra money.

At two-thirty a.m. that night, when the campus was soundly sleeping, six dormitories were heavily damaged, each by two blasts of explosives. Between the blasts and the fires that ensued, few students on the lower floors escaped with their lives and limbs intact. On the higher floors, those who were not killed by the explosion either chanced the flames in the stairwells or jumped out of windows to avoid the flames. The buildings burned for hours before the three fire departments could extinguish the flames.

Very little remained for the fire marshals to investigate; most of the debris that did remain had been badly disturbed by the rescue effort and the body recovery operation. Traces of explosives were located, but none contained any tracers to identify the source or the manufacturer of the material. Nothing unusual had been reported that night or the previous day. The death and destruction was very democratic, equally distributed to dorms of every description and ethnic predominance.

The college spokesmen discounted the idea of terrorism, saying that it looked more like the work of some right-wing nuts who have been expressing hatred for the liberal attitudes of the school for many years.

The Mexicans

Why, they asked, would terrorists want to kill and injure hundreds of peaceful students, all of them anti-war, anti-military, anti-NRA, anti-ROTC, pro-European Union, pro-Muslim, pro-immigration, amnesty, and just about every other correct 'Pro' and correct 'Anti' issue that mattered to anyone?

It didn't make sense to try to blame it on terrorists; better look closely at the Military-Industrial groups, the Ultra-right Conservatives, the neo-Nazis, the white supremacists, the KKK-style hate groups, the Republicans. They're the ones that would do something like this, they said. The major newspapers picked up that theme and ran front-page articles and editorials on the disaster and speculated on the Cooper Administration's likely complicity for days. The liberal anarchists had a new issue, now, and the liberal world was ready to promote their version of events.

CHAPTER 44
A Single Incident or A Signal Incident?

The Berkeley event opened a lot of eyes. Phil Bragg could see the handiwork of the Iranian-Hezbollah insurgency from Mexico in its beginning stage. Where he had been rather certain that the internal uprisings would be well-coordinated, this event appeared to discount that theory. Was It a single incident, perhaps meant as a signal to others around the country that the time for the coordinated action was nearing, or was it the act of a single impatient hot-head ready to go? The location, he thought, would have some bearing on why the event took place.

The college administration could be expected to turn their backs on any suggestion of terrorist complicity in the destruction. Until an objective investigation could be conducted the facts would not be known, perhaps not even then. The truth would be stifled politically to some extent, discounted even, by the masters of the school itself; those most affected. An investigation would take many weeks; long past the time they were expecting the major coordinated act to occur, at the New Year. They clearly could not focus on any investigation at this point.

Bragg met with John Smoltz to analyze the event prior to Smoltz having to meet with Secretary George to discuss Homeland Security's presence in the Berkeley investigation. Smoltz was expecting him to give him some ammunition for that meeting. He called Bob Crumpton to get that ammunition.

"Bob, I need the reports of our foray into the Northern California locations; the whole thing, including the problems the guys had with the uncooperative locals. Also, send me the tracking results of the container shipments coming through Seattle. Fax it to me at the D.C.

office. I guess I should tell you, I'm of a mind now to make my office here and begin the planning for the big thrust. Smoltz is meeting soon with William George and he'll need all the help we can give him on that area around the Bay, so take a little time now and get me a package."

"OK, Phil; I'll get it on the way before the end of the day. I guess that was sort of a "fire for range" thing they pulled off up there in Berkeley; maybe wanting to see what kind of response they'd get. Well, I think they'll all get a surprised response in a few weeks. Man, that was tough; so many of those students' lives ruined, even wiped out. From what I've read in the papers, they think the Ku Klux Klan did it. I guess that idea came out of that sweet smoke curling up around their brains. But, to change the subject for a minute, that's a little cruel isn't it; you taking the D.C. option, I mean? I thought Beatrice was crazy about Colorado Springs."

"Bea don't call the shots, Bob. No, I'm sorry, that was misleading; we were both a little hesitant about that place after thinking it over, maybe a little too much brass posturing around there, you know what I mean? We got to thinking about this rural mountain property around Front Royal that we had looked at some years ago and it all sort of fell into place. We made an offer on a place Saturday and they accepted yesterday. Anyway, you've got the ball down there and that's a good thing; too many cooks –, you know the way it goes. I'll be visiting often and I'll need you here for a few days when we get incursion planning underway. So, keep your reports coming to me up here as well; I'm not sure how long it'll be before we can get back to New Orleans to arrange the sale of the house and the move, the time line is sort of blurry right now. What else is new?"

"Well, Phil, we're getting good results from the teams so far. They should all be back by the end of this week. There are a few good stories coming out of the guys in the early reports, but as far as I know right now, they're all safe and sound. Our coverage is good; the only places we don't seem to have any names coming in from is that lower Florida peninsula. My guess is they're leaving those alone because of the Cuban population outranking the Mexicans for jobs, either that or they're operating their home boys from Cuba, but we can't do anything about that, unless we can get the leads some other way, maybe by the shipment papers, now that they're watching for names."

"Yeah, let's look over those shipment manifests and see if there are any going to those blank spots. I'm of the opinion that they're probably satisfying themselves with not having to deal with the mixed bag of Latins, but we'll only know for sure when we check the paperwork; so let me know what you find. Thanks Bob. Talk to you later."

That afternoon the fax arrived and Bragg put together a presentation for Smoltz. Toward the end of the day, Secretary George called Smoltz and asked for a meeting at ten in the morning, Wednesday. They stayed late putting it together. The next morning at the meeting, George was placated but far from satisfied.

"What do we know, John? What do we know? Does this mean that our plan to take them down all at once on a particular date requires that we wait while they blow up more of our campuses? I'm of the mind that we move our date up and take them down as soon as possible. What do we really know about this campus operation and is it going to spread across the country while we wait for our date to take them down?"

"It looks like it was probably initiated when someone in a local politician's office dropped the word on the street about our guys checking out the water records; the leak went out almost before our guys had gotten the address they were after, we've confirmed that much by way of an informant. This is probably their way of thumbing their noses at us, at both ends of the transaction; I guess they think we're stupid."

"Well, we're not stupid; they'll find that out in spades. We'll move up our date for the incursion; lets be sure to have it ready for the week before Christmas, that's coming up real soon, just a couple of weeks."

"We can do that, Bill. What about it, Phil?" Smoltz was scratching for help.

"We can be ready before Christmas; not a problem, Mr. George."

"Beat that date if possible, John. These guys are Muslim fanatics and that day may be a flag day for them but it doesn't necessarily mean they'll hold off until then. This Berkeley job makes me wonder how well coordinated they are and it doesn't give me much confidence. Phil, I'm darned glad to have you up here and your Border District under command of Bob Crumpton; this arrangement makes good sense to me. Things are looking good for us; you've got enough evidence already for a blanket warrant. Now if we can just keep the Aussies quiet until we make our move, we should have a good hand going in.

"I can take this report and digest it for the President, but I may need your help in that meeting, so keep your ears on in case I call on short notice. I'm going to promise him a December 13th date; that gives you two weeks from tomorrow. Give me a progress report next Wednesday, John. And thanks a bunch for all you've done and all you are doing, the both of you."

That ended the meeting with William George. They felt like at least they still had their stripes as they left.

"That was at least a long field goal, Phil; George isn't an easy man to bargain with. Let's get the outline you put together on the desk and start laying the bricks; we've got a lot of them to lay to get this thing built and ready for the incursion by mid-December, now at the 13th we lose over a week's time. But I think he's right about that; these people we're dealing with are into a religious war, something we've never known before. They may be getting antsy the more they hear about Jesus on the television. Doesn't it make you wonder how they can be so full of hate?"

"It does, John, but they've been blinded to the truth from the day they were born; that's all they get in their schools, growing up. For them I'm afraid it's already too late. OK, John, I've got it right here. You can see by the shading on this map that they're operations pretty well cover all the principal cities. See how wise they are, John? Just a few workers at many small sites so that no one gets concerned about what's going on at the warehouses; to the unsuspecting, they appear to be skeleton crews just keeping a few things moving and the place in repair.

"But, that's good for us; we go in with a lot fewer men and with the element of surprise; with any luck, we should shut them down before they can detonate the stuff; you can bet they'd like to kill the workers and themselves – no witnesses. That's what we have to put together; plenty of firepower with minimum troops and a lightning fast entry through the door. We won't have time to move in any equipment besides a battering ram and it needs to be a big one to break through those warehouse fire doors; six men, like a pall bearer team on the run."

"Yeah, now what about the locations; have you got them all covered?"

"From the counts we have right now, there are 76 workplaces and 10 distribution points, not counting the two in Ontario; those we'll have to coordinate with the Mounties; do they still go by that name? Anyway, we'll have to provide marshals in support on those two. That gives us 86 known sites so far and maybe another couple of distribution sites we haven't found yet. So, let's plan on 88 for our side of the border and 2 on the north side, better make it three. From Crumpton's talks with the Mexicans at Houston, there will probably be four or five terrorists at a site and about twelve workers.

"The workers will drop to the floor right away, but the others will resist. Two or three will probably be in the warehouse and two or three in the office, at the most. I figure 12 men to each team, four through the front door and the rest through the warehouse door with the ram; we'll need to control the materials inside immediately and blast anyone who tries to get to it; we don't want any Berkeley moments."

"OK, Phil; that gives us 12 times 88 plus the marshals; nearly 1100 men. Where do they come from? Have you got that penciled in anywhere?"

"Well, John, you know there are SWAT teams in most if not all of these cities. We'll start the plan with four of our agents, four FBI agents and eight or ten locals, plus two marshals for each of the Canadian sites. FBI will have oversight, we will have investigating priority, locals will have judicial authority through federal warrants. The rules of engagement must be simple; anyone not responding to an officer's order to fall on the floor face-down will be subject to the officer's self-defense use of firearms if they make a move to take up arms, and they will be subject to physical battering until they respond to the officer's order. The usual order for engagement of militant antagonists should apply here."

The Mexicans

"OK, Phil, I believe we can arrange that mix of manpower alright. I want to add another man from our staff to each team as coordinator; the voice that has authority to perform. We can have no discussion of authority from the time of quarantine to the entry; there must be only one man in control of keeping the team ready for action. Let FBI have oversight, but we can't allow an FBI hotshot to interfere with preparatory and timing moves; we have to have the voice of authority to make it all happen by the numbers. It's our responsibility and it will be on our butts to get it right; that means it's your butt."

"I'm for that, John; my say so, my responsibility. The only thing I won't have nailed down when this comes off will be this fly's ass that's buzzing around my ear." He took a futile swing at it for the sixth time.

"OK, then, start making the calls and bring me in when you need me, the Secretary, too; he's in on this."

Bragg settled into a vacant office for the interim; telephone, fax, computer hook-up and a desk with chair and side chair.

"What more could a guy want?" another thought that came out through his teeth, unknowingly.

"Was that me talking? Gotta settle down." He called Beatrice for a few moments of comfort.

"It's getting heavy around here, now, Hon. Time's a crunch, so I may be a little late tonight."

"No sweat, Big Hunk; I'm here for you, whenever. I'm ordering up spaghetti and meatballs; just give me a call when you leave. Relax, Phil, you're the man; they all know it, just like I do. But I love you, they just like you. I love you, capital Big Time. See you when you get here, dear."

That's all it took. He arranged for some clerical help and put the young officer to work getting up a list of the Chiefs of the police departments that had jurisdiction for all of the addresses he had on his list. While that was being prepared he passed around an e-mail to each of the District Directors, now under his authority, requesting they each forward to him a list of six distinguished officers, "distinguished by fire, not politically", which he would review for special assignment under his command, selecting a few, not all, of those submitted. He gave no other indication as to the type of special assignment, and he wanted the lists on his desk the following morning and he wanted the men ready for deployment on December 10th.

Towards the end of the day the list of police chiefs was brought to him, including full name, rank, title, date appointed to the job, office telephone, fax number, cell phone number, the number of men under his command and the number of SWAT equipped officers. Bragg was astonished at the detail.

"Greg, who told you to dig up all of this information on those calls you made?"

"No one, General Bragg; I printed it off a secure site on the Internet that police chiefs have set up for their own use, for sharing information. I learned about it several months ago when I needed some similar information; one of the friendly chiefs let me in on it and got me a clearance to access the site. Most of those guys are good about cooperating with us when we give them a little respect."

"It's good, Greg, real good; who sent you here to help me? And give me his number."

"Major Harrington; he runs the office pool of assistants." He gave him the number.

Bragg keyed the extension.

"Harrington, this is Bragg; can you come here for a minute?"

In a minute, Major Harrington knocked and entered.

"Don Harrington, General."

"Major Harrington, I'll need this man assigned permanently to my office. His title will be Assistant to the Adjutant. And notch him up a grade; this isn't a job for beginners."

"I'll prepare the paperwork for you right away, Sir."

The Mexicans

"Now, Greg, see if you can get me the number of the Director of the FBI; I'm sort of out of my usual waters here, so I'll be depending on you for a lot of detail including contact information to most of the law enforcement and Justice Department officials."

John Smoltz had already been in contact with the Director about the incursion, so Reginald Dwyer was not surprised to get General Bragg's call. He had designated Stanford Turner as the FBI's leading agent to direct their involvement in the NSA operation, with oversight credentials. Bragg spoke briefly with Turner and promised to fax him a copy of the plan, including all details, within one week; also Turner could expect information to flow to him from various police jurisdictions across the country;

"All are cities where operations will take place on countdown, December 13th. Deployment will be quarantined and will begin December 10th."

Before leaving for the day, Bragg dictated a letter to go to each individual police chief on the list now-Captain Fred Burroughs had prepared for him; the same letter to go to all Chiefs. In it, he asked that each jurisdiction prepare a team of officers, preferably SWAT conditioned officers, to be available the week beginning December 10th for deployment the morning of December 10th to a meeting, the location to be announced at that time, to undergo quarantined training and preparation for a special operation.

No further information about the assignment would be announced before that meeting, except that the Police Department of the location will have jurisdiction over the target of the assignment. He asked that all correspondence be addressed to him and a copy to be forwarded to the Chief Coordinator, Stanford Turner at FBI headquarters in Washington. All correspondence will be confidential, need to know basis.

By 6pm he was finished with his work. He called Beatrice.

"I'm just leaving, Sweet Thing; see you in about an hour. How about the restaurant there at the motel? See if you can get us one of those tables overlooking the gorge. You set the time; I'm for anything."

"Oh, Phil, you know how I love it when you talk romantic; I just melt like a little ol' Stepford wife. Hurry home, Big Guy."

Phil hurried down to the garage and hurried to where he had parked the car; and he hurried home.

"Romantic? Big guy? It must be the mountain air; so who's arguing?"

The beauty of the mountain scene from the restaurant was always stunning; memory couldn't record the magnificence, you had to see it with the eye. Beatrice was equally stunning and radiant. Phil never had to be reminded of the blessings he had been given; he knew in his heart that God had brought them together and that it was through His blessing of the marriage that he and Beatrice would always be anointed as one flesh by that very first institution God established for mankind. Phil Bragg was a man completely fulfilled since that day not so long ago that he found his way to the Lord on his knees at his bedside. And now he had nearly completed his first full reading of the Bible, studying a chapter or two every night.

"Phil, you're looking so pensive; are you happy that we're here?"

"Bea, I'm happy being here, but I'd be happy anywhere as long as you are there with me; after all of our years together, I still love you as I always have."

His cell interrupted their moment. The student dormitories at Duke University had just been torn apart by multiple explosions.

"Honey, I'm going to have to interrupt our dinner for a few minutes; why don't you listen in while I make a phone call, I'll dial you in for this call to Bob Crumpton. I'm sorry, it's awfully important to do this just now."

He called Crumpton. "Bob, you've heard about Duke?"

"Yeah, Phil, just now; I'm ready to get on it."

"Good. Get a competent crew over there just as soon as you can; use military aircraft under my authority, or John's or William George's, whatever it takes to get the wings. We'll put together an incursion

The Mexicans

to go into whatever locations you have identified in that area. We're going to respond in heavy force; we're going to put these guys on notice that we can make a move on them in hours, not weeks. When I hang up I'll call the FBI coordinator to get a dozen of his guys ready to go in; then I'll call the local police chiefs and have SWAT teams on site within an hour after we give out the address or addresses. Right now, I'm going to take a doggie bag from this dining table in paradise and board a military aircraft at Andrews in about an hour, however long it takes me to drive over there. On the way I'll report to John and George. No bull, Bob, I need you at the Duke location before daylight. Give me the addresses you have in that area; have you got them available there?"

"I've got them on my laptop; you read to write?"

"Just a minute . . . . ., OK, go ahead." He copied two addresses, one in Raleigh, one in Charlotte. "We'll go in on the both of them; I'll see you at the Tri-Cities airport in a few hours."

"You got it, General. I'll call you when we're on our way. I'll be bringing Shep Turner, he's back and Swede, he's here, Niel Jensen and Burt Walker and Bud Wiegand, too and a few others are back; counting me, I can muster a dozen guys with the two that are in that area already. Now I gotta move on this; so long."

Bragg called FBI Agent Stanford Turner at home and Chief Vaughn Medford in Charlotte and Chief Harrison Franklin in Raleigh. Turner would get his dozen from the local area and Franklin would recruit a dozen SWATs and another dozen officers from Raleigh and Durham. Medford had all the men he needed in Charlotte.

Next he called Smoltz and George; they were delighted at the response.

"Go for it, Phil, and use my authority in any situation you need." To William George, Bragg was his kind of man.

"That's it, Bea, we're on our way; you don't mind driving, do you?"

"I'm with you all the way to Carolina, Phil; you can explain it to John and them however you want, sabe?"

"I'll take that deal, but you've got to take orders from me; is that clear?"

"Clear. We're on our way, Big Guy."

"Dang, I love it when you talk romantic, Sweet Thing."

CHAPTER 45
Beginnings of Diplomacy

Br. Angel and Miranda were enjoying an eventful week in Washington; meeting people, attending briefings and luncheons, and a two-day seminar on State Department protocol and persons of interest In Mexico, Cuba, Central America and South America. It was a lot to commit to memory but they were given descriptive notes and photos to help in the memory work. During the pleasant evenings they walked the downtown streets and shopped for the clothing needs they hadn't expected when they left Socorro with only three days' supply, but that was a large part of the fun; the stores offered much that wasn't available in Albuquerque and so they splurged a good bit and kidded each other about breaking their budget.

By week's end they were full of it all, the meetings, the diplomacy, and the shopping was even becoming boring; they were ready to emerge with their new wings as Special Envoys. His one request was easily granted; for Luis Caldera to be assigned to his offices as U. S. Government Liaison and Al Maldonado to be employed as Executive Assistant to the Special Envoy. He would arrange the paperwork when he arrived in Mexico City. He called each of the two men immediately when the authorizations were signed by the Secretary.

"Luis, you're now assigned as Government Liaison to our new Consulate in Mexico City; you'll have to turn in your silver bars for a gold leaf, can you agree to that? I don't know how I could get along there without you."

"That's a no brainer, Br. Angel. What did Ruth say to Naomi?"

"She said, "Whither thou goest, I will go; … thy people shall be my people and thy God, my God." (Ruth 1:16)."

"Well, that's what I say, too. Rita and I will be ready for the move; when do we go?"

"You can start packing. Miranda and I will be there 11:30 Monday morning for the airport reception."

"Watch for me; I'll meet you. Thanks for the good news."

Next, he called Al Maldonado, still in Chihuahua with his family, preparing to return.

"Four years in Mexico City as a U.S. diplomat? Me? That sounds like a dream job; you know we'll be there just as soon as we can get our place closed up in Socorro and catch the next plane from Albuquerque – no more than a week."

"I'll leave the papers at your door as we pass through; fill them out and send them back in the envelope. Your first check will be waiting for you in Mexico City and expense money."

"We'll see you in Mexico City."

"Miranda, things are really looking up for us, now. This has been an exciting week, don't you think?"

"Ten days, Angel; I didn't think I could do it, but I did! And I feel confident about it, too. You must be very proud of me," she smiled up at him, coyly.

"My Dear, I don't recall ever hearing you fish for a compliment before this; are you learning the dark arts of diplomacy so soon?"

"How can one avoid it in these surroundings? When can we go back home, do you think?"

"We'll leave in the morning. Tonight we'll go to the hotel and we'll have another evening just like the last time we were there."

"Oh, Angel, I just love it when you talk romantic. I've thought of that night so many times and now we can relive it all again; it's wonderful."

That evening they traced the steps they had taken the last night of their previous visit; the walk to the hotel where the dinner-dance was featured on Friday nights, the wonderful dinner and the romantic hour on the dance floor, the appreciative eyes of the guests as they watched the obvious delight they shared in each other; all the highlights of that special evening were revisited this last night including the walk back to their hotel, though they missed the salutes of the White House guards this night.

"My darling, you were wonderful tonight." Br. Angel sung the words of the song.

"Oh, Angel, I just love it when you talk romantic; it's almost like our wedding night all over again."

"Yes, my dear; almost, with only the enhancements of time to make the difference, but even at that, it's almost like being in love for the first time; you are still so lovely, so beautiful as on our first night of marriage. The romance never gets old; when I'm with you, my love, it's just as always, the same now as then."

"Oh, Angel, I just love it when you talk romantic; can you help me with this zipper?"

CHAPTER 46
Practicing Up For the Big One

In the early morning hours after General Bragg had begun his plan of intervention, his aircraft set down at the Raleigh-Durham airport. He and Beatrice were ushered into the suite he'd reserved at the airport hotel. Soon after, Bob Crumpton rang his cell phone saying his plane was on descent to the airport and his men would be ready to deploy immediately. He had with him ten agents, and the two agents who had just scouted the cities, Fred Baskins and Felipe Delgado, were waiting to join them at the airport.

"Bob, I'm sending you to lead the go-in at Charlotte. You'll take a plane from this airport with half of your guys and meet with Stanford Turner, FBI, and Police Chief Vaughn Medford at the airport there. When we have good daylight and the places are operating, we'll go in on a count-down. Take one of the guys who knows where the place is at, OK?"

"Got it; you'll call me for the start of the count-down?"

"Yeah, I'll make the call to you. I'll lead from here. Done deal."

Stanford Turner had arrived at Charlotte about the time Bragg had landed at Raleigh-Durham. His agents had been instructed to meet him there and they organized for the deployment, two sites, half of the dozen agents for each site. He called Bragg and reported ready to proceed. Bragg asked that he send his Raleigh group to meet him at the Raleigh airport using whatever aircraft were available and he would send Colonel Crumpton and six of his team to join Turner at Charlotte. Crumpton would have the location of the site in Charlotte; one of his men who knew how to get to it would lead the way. He gave Turner the name and number of Chief Vaughn Medford in Charlotte.

The Mexicans

Next, he called Chief Harrison Franklin in Raleigh who was ready and had his SWAT team waiting. They would meet up and prepare for the incursion. Crumpton's plane landed and deployed half of his team to Charlotte along with Delgado to lead the way. Fred Baskins would lead Bragg's team to the Raleigh site.

In an hour Bragg's team was ready. He called Crumpton who was nearly ready in Charlotte.

"OK, Bob, our countdown will begin at 7:30 and we'll make the breach at 8:10. Will that give you enough time to get to the site there?"

Crumpton asked Leon and got a nod, "Easily".

"Yeah, Phil, that'll do; we can make it with a few minutes to spare."

"That's it, then, Bob. We've got about twenty minutes here before we start out. Call me if you need anything; otherwise, hit 'em hard and knock down anything that don't give up. God bless you and keep you safe, you and all your guys."

"Thanks, Phil. You take care and God bless you all."

At 7:30 Bragg's contingent, twenty-two strong, loaded into the SUVs and began the drive to the workplace about a half-hour away. Crumpton loaded his teams, twenty-one strong, into the vans and headed to the Charlotte site.

At 8:06 the SUV's in Raleigh and the vans at Charlotte rolled into the parking lot just outside the workplaces. Stopping near the warehouse entrances, they waited briefly to get their final reminders of the plan, then came the command:

"Move out and move in."

At 8:10 steel ramrods broke the warehouse doors open and boots kicked in the front doors.

"Hands in the air – get on the floor - face down. Now!! Now!! Now!! Get on the floor! Now!!"

Shots were fired. The SWAT teams led the way into the warehouses at the same time the front offices were ripped open.

"Get on the floor. Now!!"

The men in the Charlotte office attempted to reach their weapons and fire; Bud Weigand was the first to fall shot in the chest and legs.

"Hands in the air! Hands in the air!!"

Burt Walker sprayed the one who felled Weigand through the neck and shoulders; blood gushed to the ceiling.

"Do it again and get the same, you assholes – go ahead, you do it too, asshole!"

The rest of the enemy froze in place, hands up high.

"Now, kick your weapons over here and get on the floor, face down. Do it! Do it, Now! Dammit, do it now!!"

They kicked the weapons forward and fell to the floor face down, prone and still. The FBI moved forward to take the men into custody. It was too late for the shooter.

"Bud, stay still while I tie off your bleeders; you'll be fine, just lay still, Bud, just lay still."

Walker tore off his shirt and made tourniquets of the sleeves to tie off Weigand's leg wounds and stuffed the rest of the shirt into the chest wound, holding it in place with pressure, stanching the blood flow.

"Let's get the ambulance here!" he shouted, "Someone call the ambulance; he ain't got all day!"

Bud Weigand and Burt Walker had been best friends since their early childhood; they were like brothers which made it very difficult for Walker to keep his composure.

"He ain't got all day, dammit!"

The Mexicans

"Ease up, Burt, the ambulance is on its way; I can hear the siren now. Just keep up the pressure on that chest wound until the medics get here. You're doing fine; Bud's going to be alright. Dear God, bless this good man and his friend. Help us here, Father; help us, now, I pray."

Colonel Crumpton's quiet response gave the room an air of calm; it was as though God's presence was with them and they began to feel at ease, especially Bud Weigand, comforted by that presence. Soon the ambulance arrived and the medics attended to Bud.

"You'll be alright, Bub; they'll patch you up quick as we get you to the emergency room, maybe five or six minutes. Just hold on; you'll be fine."

Bud knew it was bad, but he wasn't afraid; he winked at Burt and nodded.

"I'm just glad you're here, Burt; stay with me no matter what." Then he told the medic "It's Bud, Doc; you got it pretty close, but my name's Bud. I appreciate your help, Doc."

On the way to the hospital, Bud Weigand fell unconscious. He was pronounced dead at the hospital. Bob Crumpton spent the rest of the day with Burt Walker, reading the words of the Lord from the Book of Mathew. It was one of the most difficult days of his life, comforting Burt Walker, but they all knew Weigand to be a true believer.

It all went off without a hitch at the Raleigh site; no lives were lost, just a few wounds. All the people from the site were rounded up and arrested by FBI Agents, then loaded into SWAT vans and carried down to a special cellblock at the Sheriff's jail.

Crumpton called Bragg when he had time to break from Burt Walker for a few minutes and reported the results at the Charlotte site.

"We lost Bud Weigand, Phil, our lead man on the break-in; he never flinched. His buddy, Burt Walker is really down. I'll stay the day with him before starting on the paperwork."

"Oh, no; my God, Bob; gee, I hate to hear that; that's really bad. Bud was as good a man as I've ever known. Walker's got to be hurting bad. Bob, we've got to have an honor guard at his funeral; let's not forget to have that in place and let's be sure to have a big turnout for Bud. Kalamazoo, wasn't he from Kalamazoo? Can you make the arrangements? See if they can make it on Monday. I want to breach that Oakland warehouse on Wednesday morning, and we'll do it for Bud. I've been having a lot of recriminations about not taking them out when the Berkeley thing went off and I'm pretty sure the locals won't know where to look without us to tell them."

"I'll get it done, Phil. We'll all be there to salute Bud; count on it. Give me the details on the Berkeley event when you can get a little time. We'll just head out there from Kalamazoo after the funeral and keep our armbands on for the action. I guess Stanford Turner will arrange the FBI team, but maybe we ought not to disturb the locals until it happens; know what I mean?"

"Yeah, you might be right; we'll tell them what we did. Why don't you give Turner a heads up and give him the Oakland location while you're there with him so he can get things ready. We'll settle it today; ask Turner to call me."

"OK, Phil. We'll make the motel arrangements today for Monday night in Oakland. I'll use this same team we brought up here, that way we can keep it less well known, the less movement, the better; these guys are just getting warmed up."

"Right. Well, Bob, we had a little better result at our breach; just a few wounded. I guess those Iranians were still a bit woozy at 8:10am; they seemed to think the place was being robbed. I guess they thought no one would ever catch on to what they were doing. OK, so when you get all the paperwork finished give me a call; I've got mine to do here, too. Now, let me talk to Burt for a few minutes."

"Walker here, General."

"Burt, I wish I was there with you; I really can't speak the words to express my sorrow. Bud was my kind of guy, a true man and faithful;

not afraid of anything, including death. I know he was your closest friend, buddies for most of your life. Now, it's going to be really difficult for you to pick up and get back on the circuit without Bud. Take whatever time you need. We're all going to keep you in our prayers. But, let me give you a little encouragement, Burt. Brotherly love such as you had with Bud doesn't go unseen in Heaven or without regard. One day when your suffering eases and when you least expect it you'll get a visitation; maybe in a dream, maybe by an apparition of Bud, or maybe by an angel in the flesh. I've known good men who have told me of their encounters in incidents like these. Faith and love can overcome the great divide. God respects our broken hearts, Burt; watch for that visit and when it occurs you'll know then that your love has overcome your pain and your grief. Take care, now, and remember that Bud is alive, only out of the flesh. Scripture tells us that "to be absent from the body is to be present with the Lord" (2Cor 5:8). I'll be seeing you, Burt."

"Thanks, General. I know there's a lot I don't understand but maybe one day I will. So long."

After that experience Burt Walker began to read the Bible in hotel rooms; he was drawn to the Book of Ecclesiastes, "that's a strange name", and soon he could see himself more clearly.

Bud Weigand was buried on Monday. His funeral was attended by all the NSA Agents of the Border District and the Louisiana District, as well as most from the Detroit office. Phil Bragg, John Smoltz and William George were there from Washington. Stanford Turner and the FBI agents who participated in the raid in Charlotte with Bud were there with armbands. The Marine Honor Guard, representing his military service, attended with the Colors and Secretary William George ordered a twenty-one gun salute.

General Phil Bragg gave a stirring eulogy, Major Burt Walker spoke for his dear friend and comrade through his tears, and Colonel Bob Crumpton gave a Gospel message, noting the words of the Lord that "Greater love hath no man than this; that he lay down his life for his friends" (John 15:13). The Border District agents departed the graveside for the airport, wearing their black armbands. Bud Weigand was truly honored that Monday and Susan was grateful for it as she tearfully accepted the flag.

Federal warrants were obtained by Stanford Turner and the teams breached the doors of the workplace near Oakland wearing the black armbands they had worn for three days. All of the Mexican workers dropped to the floor on command. Three of the Hezbollah attempted to resist and paid the ultimate price. No other injuries were incurred. Bob Crumpton took care of all the paperwork and agreed to remain and appear in court at the arraignments. Major Jon Olafsen returned to Colorado Springs and took charge of organizing the last foray across the country; those last lists would be waiting for him and his agents; they'd have no time to waste. Crumpton had a lot of respect for Swede; he knew he could make things happen.

William George called John Smoltz.

"John, this makes two attacks so far. What about stationing a watch at each of these locations to spot any more activity like this before it gets done? I'm getting heat on this now."

"We talked about that, Bill. Three things; one, the watchman would likely be spotted because it would have to be a 24-hour effort. That might cause the whole herd to panic and go off like thunder. Two, the likelihood that we could figure out an event beginning is questionable; I mean, these guys come and go, delivery trucks arrive and leave often enough to cause us to wonder and maybe pull the plug on a routine delivery. Three, we'd have to have warrants for every site individually and that would take days or weeks and the word would be out on the street in no time. Once we make a move on a place the whole set of them would be informed and we'd just be making a guess. How could we hope to stop one of them from dialing out when they see us? Don't you see how much we have to lose by trying to watch them and then outguess them?"

"I got you on record, John. It's a good argument. I'll copy it and use it. I agree."

"Thanks, Bill; this has been a real burden, this whole question of surveillance."

375

The Mexicans

Months later, Burt Walker was stopped by a young man on a crowded street who asked directions to the nearest Baptist Church. Incredibly, the young man looked amazingly like Bud Weigand, his eyes softly smiling, but he gave no indication that Burt was someone he knew. They stood over against the building and spoke quietly for a few minutes. The young man's presence imparted the most calming feeling of ease and contentment that Burt could recall ever having felt, certainly not since the shooting incident. He was from out of town, but needed to find a place to pray for a short while. Burt walked with him to the church building and then felt the need to join the man inside the sanctuary. It was as though it had all been planned ahead of time. They prayed together silently for several minutes. When Burt opened his eyes the young man was just leaving through the front door; he turned and smiled, then was gone. After that encounter, Burt Walker was a changed man and he never once feared death.

CHAPTER 47
Big Changes in the Making

The work was coming to its end. Luis Caldera and Al Maldonado had worked straight through the weekend gathering up every outstanding list; finally they had them all. To be certain, they spent over an hour checking all of the villages marked off on the map to the original lists they had in their files. None were missing, all were complete. Then they faxed the last set of lists to Colorado Springs and received the confirmation of the counts. Exhausted, they turned in to bed ready to begin a changed way of life in the morning, Monday. Neither could say that it had not been an exciting experience and rewarding inasmuch as they had been able to accomplish all that had been hoped for and more; they had completed the work in half the time that had been expected, thanks to the initial work of Br. Suarez in setting up the procedures. Everyone had been paid generously and had been very grateful for the bonuses they had distributed. They kept careful records of all that had been done and the names and contact information for all of the workers.

As Al and Elena were preparing to return to Socorro, the phone call came from Br. Angel in Washington and their lives were once again turned about. But this time they were to be in the employ of the United States Department of State, living in the diplomatic village in Mexico City and working in the American Embassy, Al holding down the job with Elena maintaining the very important position of diplomat's wife.

"Is this amazing? Elena, is this amazing? Here we are, instead of returning to Socorro to resume the very important work of the Missionary Association, we are returning to Socorro to settle things and then turn back again to Mexico, but this time with diplomatic dignity. I feel a little like a turncoat. Elena, we will have to be sure to voice the concerns of the Lord in all matters that we are involved with. This shall be an opportunity for high level missionary work. Right?"

"Yes, of course. Wherever we go, whatever we do, that shall always be a part of our responsibility, even apart from the Association. It is our obligation to the Lord and we will not fail our obligations. And at the same time, we will be together for four years, maybe more; oh, that will be the best part for me, having my husband with me at home every night. I'm anxious to get back down here and settled in Mexico City."

Al's father was just about back to normal. He and Al's mother were happy for them as they packed their things and prepared to drive home. By mid-afternoon they were on their way to spend the night in El Paso.

Luis Caldera called Rita in Monterrey and gave her the news. Rita was unbelieving at first; it was the sort of assignment she had never dreamed of, the wife of an executive liaison attaché at the American Embassy in Mexico City, and a house in the American diplomatic village where security guards made certain that the village was not entered by outsiders without Embassy authorization. She responded about like Luis expected.

"You're kidding me, I know you're pulling my leg, so give it up and tell me what you really called about."

"Honest Injun; no offense to Br. Angel, but that half-breed just got off the phone and I'm not the one to call him a liar, mi esposa, cause in some ways he's bigger than me. It's the real thing; he's the Special Envoy and I'm his military liaison, Major Luis Caldera."

"Ow! Major! Wow! Looks like I got a good deal when I let your talk me into being your wife. I may even get a chance at a big diplomatic career of my own; then I wouldn't need your silly gold oak leaf to get respect; I wouldn't be just an unemployed physical therapist. I wonder where an attractive girl like me goes to apply for one of those diplomatic jobs. Could you find out for me, Sweetie?"

Rita was elated and her hopes now were turned to beginning their family; she was head over heels in love with Luis, though she tried her best not to show the extent of it. Even so, Luis had a good idea that her often flippant remarks and satire were a soft cover-up for her true feelings. She had given herself away on many occasions and Luis knew that Rita loved him just as he knew that he was crazy in love with Rita. They had been married for less than one month and here they were, embarking on an adventure that few people had opportunity for; life as a diplomatic couple; hopefully to be a diplomatic family; he would have to work hard on that and he knew that Rita was as anxious as he to begin the family.

"I already have, love. There just happens to be a job opening for a 'diplomat-in-waiting' and you've got all the right attributes. That's where you say all the right things in public, but you're just 'in waiting' for your private time when you get to say all those things you've wanted to say all day long, but couldn't say in public. You know the sort of stuff I'm talking about, like "I'm so proud of you, Baby, getting promoted to Major and taking me to the best place in Mexico to live and raise a houseful of kids and I'm just 'in waiting', wondering when you're going to tackle me right here on the rug and begin with a big sloppy kiss?" You'd know how to do that diplomatic job really well. Why don't you try it out; go ahead, say it."

"I can't remember all the words, but it sounded just right, so, ditto."

"Oh, Baby, I just love it when you talk romantic."

"I'm thinking of a boy for you and a girl for me to start with; is that OK, Sweetie?"

"That's just right, Baby; and with God's blessings, it'll come true, for those of us who love the Lord."

Luis and Rita loved the Lord.

The brass band played the Star Spangled Banner as Br. Angel and Miranda walked the stairway down to the tarmac from the U.S. Air Force jetliner, arriving to official fanfare at Mexico City. They were welcomed by Alfredo Coronado, the Minister of International Affairs who had been instructed to prepare a diplomatic reception at the

The Mexicans

airport for the new Peace Envoys from the United States and to escort them to the Presidential Palace where President Vicente Calderon would personally welcome them to Mexico.

The national media were all on hand for the welcoming event, televisions panning on Br. Angel and Miranda as they descended to the welcoming stage set up for the event just a few yards from the plane. With the plane showing the flag and colors of the United States in the background, reporters doted on the couple:

"And best of all is their ethnicity as Americans of Mexican heritage living in New Mexico and their background as lifetime Christian Missionaries to the world's poor, the weak and the disenfranchised. Theirs is a story of Mexican attainment; educational, cultural, theological and recently political, in the greatest nation of the world. Now, proudly we hail them as personal emissaries of the President of the United States to the people of Mexico."

It was a popular story and it was carried nationwide. The Honorable Alfredo Coronado escorted them to the stage where two senior military officers walked them each up the stairs and to their seats behind the dais. There in the periphery of the crowd Br. Angel caught the eye of Luis Caldera and waved. The official in charge introduced Senor Coronado who spoke brief introductions.

"It's my pleasure to introduce Brother Angel and Mrs. Miranda Suarez, arriving to our country as personal emissaries of the President of the United States; Peace Envoys who will reside in Mexico City during their term of appointment. Brother Suarez and Mrs. Suarez, it is my distinct pleasure to welcome you to Mexico in the name of the people of Mexico on behalf of Presidente Vicente Calderon. I look forward to a most pleasant and fruitful association with you as we pursue together our good purposes under the auspices of your government and my government and in the interests of the peoples of our two nations. May God be with you in all that you do. Welcome, friends of Mexico; Bienvenidos!"

Following the applause of the welcoming party, Br. Angel said simply;

"Thank you, Minister Coronado; it is with sincere goodwill that we undertake our new duties here in your beautiful country. We look forward with great anticipation to a fruitful relationship with you, your president and your good people. May God bless the peoples of our two nations, together on this bountiful continent where He has placed us as neighbors. We are delighted to be here, Mrs. Suarez and me; thank you so very much."

The official party moved swiftly in the limousines through the city to the friendly waves of the people lining the way. The reception at the Palace was a very dignified affair; the red carpet was laid out for them and the Palace Honor Guard stood rigidly at attention while the band played the Star Spangled Banner and all of the attendees stood in respectful silence.

The television cameras and the battery of microphones were all in place to share the event with the nation and even the world. President Calderon waited a brief moment after the band played while the Honor Guard displayed the colors of the United States and Mexico, side by side; then he did a turnabout and retired, marching toward the stage at the rear of the palace hall while the drum roll followed his steps. The drum roll ended as the President approached the couple across the stage, shook their hands individually and with a flowing gesture, invited them to walk with him to the podium where he gave a formal welcoming speech identifying them by their diplomatic credentials.

"Angel and Mrs. Suarez, welcome to Mexico. Let me express the gratitude of the Mexican people that such a distinguished pair would be devoting their service to the betterment of relations and understanding between our two countries."

He expressed his personal gratitude to President Cooper for the appointment of the new Envoys and his personal appreciation to each of them for their service.

"I am confident that your presence in Mexico, bringing with you the goodwill of the American people, will greatly enhance international relations and the goodwill of the peoples of both nations."

After a few further words, referencing their ethnicity, the President ended with the traditional Mexican welcome,

"Bienvenidos, Amigos."

Br. Angel responded with a brief acknowledgement of the kind welcome and his expectations of good relations to continue between the nations as the result of the goodwill of the people of both countries.

Miranda spoke eloquently about her life with Br. Angel in the service of the Lord as missionaries to impoverished people in New Mexico and elsewhere, wherever they were led. She implored those present to open their own eyes and to see others as the Lord sees them and to extend the love of God to those in need of comfort and care. She spoke of children that were in conditions of poverty without hope and children that had been thrown away before breathing their first breath that God had prepared for them.

"It is all a matter of love, for love brings goodwill and kindness and tender mercies, the very blessings of God, himself. I thank God for the spiritual goodwill that comes from people of the family of God and those willing to deny their own pleasures to raise children in loving families under His guidance. There is no spiritual poverty in the family of God."

Interrupted by applause, she then repeated her comments in perfect Spanish and drew a standing audience and another resounding round of applause. She bowed gracefully and waved.

Miranda stole the show, you might say. Her presence and composure, along with the message she brought connected immediately with the news media who featured her with close ups and extensive reporting on her beauty as a woman of maturity and charisma. Br. Angel was beaming with pride through it all and the formal state dinner that followed while Miranda displayed her natural talent at interpersonal relations with the many diplomats and their wives present at the event.

Before the evening ended, Br. Angel had been invited to a private meeting with President Calderon for the purpose of establishing an initial agenda by which they would begin conversations and prepare for negotiations on a number of topics that had been of concern to both nations. Br. Angel undertook his very first effort at diplomacy during the fifteen minute meeting.

"Mr. President, I am greatly honored to come before you as spokesman for President Cooper on a number of matters that he views as being of critical importance at this time in our relations; matters that the President assigned to me in confidence with only a few others of his staff and cabinet in attendance. Such is the import of our assignment. Let me, if I may, take just this few minutes to elaborate briefly on the item of immediate concern. There is occurring at this very moment an invasion of Mexico by numerous teams of Hezbollah; Iranian terrorists transported into your country by private plane from Venezuela, whose activities are directed at the United States. The United States has an impending action planned to defuse the activities of the terrorists working within the U.S. and those within Mexico; that action that will require your cooperation."

Br. Angel went on to briefly describe the activities of the so-called Council of Unification in the remote villages of northern Mexico and their planned coordinated insurgency by undocumented Mexican workers throughout the United States.

"You have witnessed their attacks on the campuses of the University of California at Berkeley and at Duke University. This is the most important item on the President's agenda inasmuch as it will require your immediate cooperation in preparing to arrest very soon the terrorist teams in the villages where they are established. Time is very short; we should meet privately for a full discussion within a day or two at the very least, Mr. President. In the meantime, please maintain this in confidence."

"You should see Alfredo Coronado to arrange the time for our meeting. We will meet tomorrow afternoon or Wednesday morning; you have my assurance of our confidence. Is there anything else?"

"There is, but this single item is what we must direct our attention to at the moment. We can take time for the other items after this situation is under control. Thank you for your consideration."

Later that night, as they prepared for bed, Miranda spoke softly to her husband.

The Mexicans

"Oh, Angel, my dear, you made me so proud tonight; I'll remember this day in my heart forever."

"My dear, we both know who is the star of this team and I am greatly impressed; I have to tell you, though it may seem untimely after so many years, I was entranced by your magnetic presence among all of these people. Where have you been hiding all this time?"

"Perhaps in your very large shadow, my dear Angel; just where I have always wanted to be, in your loving shadow. But this eventful life can be a bit tiring, don't you think? Let's go to sleep now; Kiss me, I love you."

"Yes, it is a bit tiring, but very exciting, as you say. I'm ready for sleep, too. I love you, my lovely; I do love you very much."

They kissed and held on for a long moment, then drifted off to sleep. There, Miranda stepped lightly down a bright path more beautiful than she could ever have imagined, hand in hand with Angel, and she looked up into his eyes with love and whispered softly, "Oh, Angel, I just love it when you speak the words of eternal love."

Tuesday morning Br. Angel arranged the meeting with President Calderon for 3:30 that afternoon. Then he called Luis Caldera.

"Luis, it was good to see you at the airport reception; I'm sorry I was not able to talk with you there; the schedule was not mine to revise and the events left no time to spare. I hope you will be available to meet with me this afternoon at the Presidential Palace."

"I'm here to support your needs, Br. Angel; just say the word. Rita understands the necessity for being available at all times in this diplomatic world."

"Very well, then; I will need you to join me in this meeting. Bring with you the lists of names that we compiled during our operations in the villages; we will need all the evidence we have to convince Calderon of the presence of these invaders. Do not bring any names of the people who we employed to get the names; we don't know what sort of security exists in the Presidential Palace. Do bring the list of villages where the Iranians were dropped off, and the maps. You have all of that, do you?"

Big Changes in the Making

"I have it all. Do you wish the list of the University group as well?"

"No. We know that the University group had been identified by the Cubans and probably the Jimenez people, too. Let's do nothing to confirm that connection with us. It could put their lives in danger. No names of those who worked on the project should ever be divulged by any of us except in a court of law and then not without informing the workers beforehand. Destroy all money transactions; we will have no more need for any of that. Our focus will be only on the Iranians and the immigrants working for them in the U.S."

"I understand. I'll be there quietly, as a shadow diplomat, unless you call upon me."

"Dear Luis, I can't emphasize enough how your presence and your confirming testimony about your involvement in the villages will be a critical part of our presentation. Without you, I would be without a witness, so don't underplay your importance in this entire diplomatic mission; you are privy to it all. Al Maldonado will be helpful, but your testimony as an agent of the federal government directly involved in the whole operation is essential."

Later that day, Br. Angel and Luis, seeing that others were waiting in the alcove for the meeting to begin, spoke privately with Vicente Calderon and asked him to defer inviting his two Ministers into the meeting for about thirty minutes. Calderon instructed the two, Alfredo Coronado of International Relations and Federico Dominguez of National Intelligence to await his call. Following introductions, President Calderon asked Br. Angel and Luis into his private meeting room.

"Now, Mr. Suarez, please describe the discrete details of the item of President Cooper's concern. Then we will ask the others to join us."

"Mr. President, certain of your people have kept us informed of an operation currently taking place, begun early last fall whereby the Iranians have established a base in Venezuela that they use for transporting invaders, Hezbollah and Iranians, to settle in small bands of twelve in remote villages of Mexico. Ten or twelve such teams had been delivered at that time and many more have arrived since then. Our friends knew only that their purpose was to enable

The Mexicans

terrorist attacks in the United States. President Cooper asked me to investigate and I did. Major Luis Caldera joined me in the work as did another of my associates.

"What we found was startling; a plan involving the local families of illegal workers in the United States and the workers themselves. The so-called Council of Unification is offering a monthly income payment to the families here in Mexico, substantially the same amount of money that the worker relative has been sending back to them from the U.S. This Council, in groups of twelve men, then tells the families to communicate information to the workers; they must leave their jobs and take new jobs in certain cities at a higher rate of pay to be offered to them by their collaborators in the U.S. They are told that the money payments would continue in Mexico so long as the workers retain their jobs at the new locations.

"They work in warehouses where they package weapons, ammunition and explosives shipped in by freight containers. The ordnance is to be used very soon – even before Christmas, very soon now. The Mexican workers were not told what they would be doing; apparently they do not know the purpose of the munitions. It is continuing to this day and we have documented the names of the Mexican families and the workers in the U.S. over the past two months. We believe that we now have compiled a complete list of the workplaces, though not a complete list of the workers, and there are forty-two villages in your country that we know of where the Council is working."

Br. Angel stopped briefly and Calderon spoke.

"But this is incredible. We will move against these men here in Mexico immediately! They must be stopped."

"Mr. President, it is extremely important that word of this does not get beyond this room until such time as the FBI and the National Security Agency finalize plans for a coordinated incursion at all locations across the U.S. and, at the same time with your cooperation, incursions in the villages here, so that no opportunity will be afforded them to use the explosives before they are arrested. I can tell you that it will not be long but there are other things that must be done before that time; the last of the workplaces must be located, that will take the rest of this week, and all of the evidence gathered must be presented to a federal court to obtain the entry warrants. If word were to get out of this room the entire operation will be brought to naught for lack of surprise. It must be understood here and now that release of any part of what I have presented will cause the deaths of many Americans and working immigrants and will severely damage our relations for years to come. The damage done in the U.S. will be incalculable."

"I understand. Then what is it that you wish for us to do now?"

"Simply be advised of the urgency of the situation so that you will be able to make your move against these invaders on a one-day notice. Major Caldera will provide a list of all villages that they now operate in and any others that they invade, up until the day of incursion. The day and time of the operation and the list of villages will be given to you at least twenty-four hours beforehand. I will personally inform you at the earliest moment and you can direct us to the official to whom the information should be given."

"Agreed. Well, then, let us continue to the other matters; I will call in my ministers in waiting"; he smiled at the unintended diminutive.

Then Calderon held a brief discussion with Alfredo Coronado and Federico Dominguez, instructing them:

"You will maintain contacts with Br. Suarez and Major Caldera during these next weeks and be sure that every convenience is afforded them and their families during their resettlement in quarters. Assign security teams to them for immediate service upon their request, and be sure that all matters are handled with care according to normal diplomatic protocol."

The President wanted to be sure that Suarez and Caldera heard him say it.

CHAPTER 48
The Dynamics of Change

The huge freighter cut back its engines to reduce speed as it approached to within thirty miles of the California coast, headed for port at San Francisco harbor. The crew was more than ready for a little shore time after the long ocean crossing from Australia, and shore time didn't get much better than at San Francisco. The passengers, too, were weary of the time spent crossing the ocean on the freighter. These ships were nothing as pleasant as a passenger ship where the cargo walked and talked and danced and partied their way across the ocean. The cost of passage was much less on the freighter, and that usually was the deciding factor. But the cheaper fare came with more restrictions, less freedom of movement, and table fare that could hardly be called sumptuous. The pleasure of the voyage depended a lot on both the purser's spending policy and the strictness of the captain's moral standards. On the Pacific Empress both the policy and the standards were known to be tight.

It was early in the morning with daylight just breaking before sunrise when Francisco Arroya wheeled the big trunk to the rear of the lower deck toward the main loading platform. It was here at the stern that all rotting, stinking and particularly disgusting refuse that might bother the passengers was cast down to the sea bottom to disgust the sea anemones and others. There was no big secret about how to dump bad smelling trash; just bag it, weight it down and "give 'er the old heave ho." But that wouldn't do for this item on Arroyo's hand truck. This big trunk was being treated a little differently; it had been outfitted with a series of floats that tightly encircled it and in addition, there was a set of large red balloons attached to the top of the trunk lid, unusual décor for a piece of disgusting, stinking trash.

The Mexicans

Through the doors opening onto the rear landing platform, Arroya wheeled the trunk to the exit gate; there he opened the gate, then pitched the trunk load forward slightly so he could slide back the lip of the hand truck, freeing the trunk. Next, he hooked his left foot securely around the deck pole and very carefully gave the trunk a shove so that it slid freely along the shiny wet steel deck right through the open gate and into the ocean.

"Perfect shot; just like that eight ball, straight into the pocket."

When he turned from fastening the gate, Reynaldo Guzman was standing with a puzzled look on his face.

"What's that all about, Arroya? You got something against that trunk?"

Surprised, Arroya just shrugged and started back inside with his hand truck.

"Captain said to dump it; it stunk like dead polecats. You ever smell a dead polecat, Rey?"

"I never seen a polecat; don't know what a dead one smells like – like a dead dog, I guess."

"Worse than that; dead polecats smell lots worse than dead dogs. My old man could smell one a mile away; when he did, he always made me go find it and carry it to the dump. He wouldn't let me bury it 'cause a dog would dig it up; nothin' can stop that smell. Anyway, we're shed of it now."

"Why'd you float it? It's just going to stink up the ocean and maybe float to shore in a few days."

"Captain thinks it might be a dead body. He had a dead body once in a freight container and it made him sick so bad he had to go to the hospital for some medicine. This time he called a fishing boat to come and get it and take it to the Coast Guard to see if there's a dead body in it. They can find it OK with that big red balloon. Hey, don't let no one know I told you! The Captain might get pissed off; he talked like it was a big secret, he didn't want the passengers to know about it. Some of them might want a refund or something."

"Now what would I be doing talking to the Captain?"

"No, I mean don't tell nobody; he'll get mad as hell at me if anyone says anything. Just forget about it, OK?"

"Yeah, yeah, OK. C'mon and give me a hand with the laundry."

The freighter was long out of sight of the trunk when the "Lucky Ketch", a fishing boat, approached it, slowed to a drift and came alongside of it. They used a trawler boom to secure it, raised it and swung it onto the deck. Two men down in the hold raised a few floor planks and guided the trunk, still hanging from the boom, into position. They stove it in the subfloor beneath the floor planks in the hold, then filled the hold with fresh fish and dry ice. Then they headed in toward the marina to unload the catch.

A few hours later, after they sold their catch, a fish market van backed up to the slip where the fishing boat remained tethered and opened the sliding side door while the deck hands rigged up a come-along to raise the trunk up and out of the hold; four of them muscled it off the fishing boat onto the gangway, then carried it to the van and slid it in through the side door. The boat captain walked up as they finished the chore and took an envelope from the driver of the van.

"It's all in there", the van driver said. "Count it if you want."

The captain opened it and flipped through the bills.

"Looks like twenty thousand, here. Where's the other five?"

"They didn't tell you? The other five is my commission. I got it right here in my pocket." He showed the captain a pocket with a pistol shoved in it.

"You bastards never keep your word." He turned and walked off.

The van drove along the wharf to the street while the fishing boat captain and the fishermen all held up middle fingers in salute to the van driver. "Up yours, asshole! Up yours!" they shouted, each one a little less wealthy than they had expected.

The Mexicans

The van drove alongside the Bay down the Embarcadero to the Bay Shore Freeway and kept south until it reached South San Francisco, where it disappeared into a garage attached to an old house. The driver closed the garage door, double padlocked it and set the alarm system on before walking into the house where the others were waiting for him.

"Got it," he said and opened the refrigerator for a beer.

The guy with the phone made the call he'd been waiting to make; after two rings a voice answered.

"Yeah?"

"Got it," he said, and waited a moment to hear the response; then he closed up the phone.

◎◎

Ali Jeruselim, Minister of Intelligence for President Alhaminijah, rapped twice at the door of the President's private study.

"Enter," Alhaminijah responded.

Jeruselim opened the door to where he could be seen standing in the doorway and asked,

"My President, may I have one moment? I bring good news."

"Yes, yes, come in, Jeruselim and shut the door. What do you have for me that is good news?"

"Yes, my President, it is indeed good news I bring; news of the delivery of the great weapon to the shores of America. It is now at rest in a garage south of San Francisco, near the San Andreas Lake where the great earthquake rift is located. Our operatives are ready to execute judgment on the day that you desire it be done."

"Good. The time is approaching that we will give the order."

"Just this morning we were informed that it is safely in the hands of our brave warriors at San Francisco. There will be an immense explosion, a nuclear explosion that will be set off directly in the earthquake rift valley of California; it will be the end of the city of Satan, the very seat of evil. The city will be judged and destroyed like Sodom, and all living things in that evil city will be purged as salt purges from the ocean, invading every living piece of flesh. It will be a glorious day for you, My President."

"This is a part of the Mexican invasion plan, but the control groups in Mexico know nothing of the great weapon; the weapon is in the hands of a special force of warriors who will give their lives to Allah as they bring down His wrath upon the evil city."

"The same plan, the same glorious plan for destruction, My President."

"The two separate operations have not been in contact with one another, nor does either of them know about the other. The invasion operation will draw the internal defenses of America to respond to seventy or eighty attacks, coordinated all across the country, Ali. While they are scattered and confused by the many smaller attacks, our warriors at San Francisco will deliver the great weapon and position it in the midst of the San Andreas rift and detonate it at my command. The disaster will throw the country's leaders and the people into shock and disbelief. Other invaders then may take their vengeance out on the great Satan at that time and make the destruction of the country complete. From thenceforth there will be no more America."

"It is very imaginative, very imaginative. When you give the order to deliver the great weapon, it will be my great honor to make the phone call that will relay your order, as Minister of Intelligence."

"Yes, Ali. Keep your peace; you will hear from me. Speak of this to no one. Thank you, Jeruselim."

"Thank you, My President."

After Ali Jeruselim left Alhaminijah's study, he was driven across town to a Mosque where he reported to the Ayatollah Kalmeshti, his real boss.

"Come in, Minister Jeruselim."

"I am at your service, my beloved leader. The great weapon has been delivered."

"There have been many rumors about what that man, Alhaminijah, has been plotting, Jeruselim, but nothing has been presented to me about any orders to carry out the devious plan. We tend to dismiss much of what we hear as simply words, the result of exuberance by the people who worshipped him."

"Alhaminijah will resign, I am sure of it, my great leader."

"Alhaminijah will not get off so easy by his resignation. We will bring the man to justice in our Court over this insidious plot and all of those who were a part of the plot and the cover up of the plot; the work of a barbarian. This plot will be exposed and the weight of justice will be brought to bear on the necks of the plotters. I leave it to you to uncover the names of all those who are involved and you must begin at once. These sorts of acts do nothing to further our plan for world leadership that is in the making. The international media would destroy us if this were to be placed at our table. Get the evidence on all of them; our Court will exact justice on these barbarians."

"I will have it well documented, Ayatollah Kalmeshti, my great teacher, and very soon."

Very well, then; let me hear from you, Jeruselim; I will be available to you at any time you need my direction."

@@

Ambassador Ali bin Alsheiki was dispatched immediately by Ayatollah Kalmeshti to Mexico City where he presented his credentials to President Vicente Calderon. Calderon, in turn, immediately called him into private session;

"I am pleased that you are here, Ambassador bin Alsheiki."

Calderon's demeanor was dutifully respectful but clearly his manner was stern.

"Now, my first order of business for your attention is this; I wish that you give me an explanation of why Iranian agents are operating within Mexico illegally without passport or visa."

Caught off guard, completely unaware of the claim, bin Alsheiki asked for time;

"Mr. President, I don't know what to say; this is a matter I have no knowledge of. I must ask that you kindly allow me time to consult with my people and gather any information that might be available in Tehran about such a thing, but I can assure you, President Calderon, that I know less about any such thing than obviously you do, sir. I will simply have to have time to find the answer to this charge; I'm sure you understand my situation, Mr. President."

"Let me assure you, sir," Calderon advised him, "that the information I have was taken from reliable sources; I have only deferred to speak of the matter to Iranian representatives of lesser rank, knowing that your presence was at hand, that your schedule was set for arrival in Mexico City. Now that you are here I am ready to hear the explanation. I have instructed Diego Garcia, my Minister of National Defense, to meet with you at the earliest time available for briefing on the matter. I will appreciate your awareness of the sense of urgency we have that there be a resolution of the issue. We cannot tolerate such a situation; these agents are nothing more than illegal invaders of our land. It is our policy that such invaders be shot when captured."

Somewhat overwhelmed, bin Alsheiki was clearly embarrassed at being taken unawares; in his mind the entire assertion must be a mistake.

"Clearly Mr. President, there must be a good explanation for this revelation; true of false, we must get the facts on the table. If you would be so kind, allow me to ask that Minister Garcia call my office early next week after I have had time to organize my staff and to request interpretation of this question from Tehran."

"As you wish, Mr. Ambassador, I will have Garcia contact you Tuesday morning. Thank you for coming and I look forward to your continued presence in our country."

The Mexicans

The last part was a veiled hint intended for bin Alsheiki that his appointment credentials could be withdrawn if he took too long to clear up the matter.

After that, bin Alsheiki began installing his offices and organizing his staff. He would take the day tomorrow to discuss the Calderon complaint with his counterpart in Venezuela. He suspected the invaders might have come from there, knowing some of the recent history of Julio Jimenez's political activity in Mexico. But he was unsure just how the invaders could be Iranians unless Alhaminijah had begun an undercover operation into Mexico from a base in Venezuela. What part would Jimenez be playing in it all, if it truly was as Calderon had suggested, illegal entry? Bin Alsheiki could see this would be an eventful beginning for him. Right now he needed more specific information; it appeared that Calderon knew no more than he did. He was sure it would turn out to be merely a rumor started by an informant wanting a reward. He would delay taking it up with Tehran until Diego Garcia gave him more specific information; that was the correct position to take.

CHAPTER 49
Brave Men and Tunnel Vision

By Friday afternoon, Major Jon Olafsen had prepared the names at the new locations to be surveyed on this last foray across the country. They had eleven cities to visit that hadn't been worked; many of the names on these last lists were for cities already worked. He couldn't assign himself and Misti to go out since he was filling in for Bob Crumpton who was still in Oakland wrapping up reports. Crumpton had kept Burt Walker with him to inventory the munitions at the warehouse. Now, without Walker and Weigand, Jon had just enough teams available to go out. He was holding the new Denver agents in Colorado Springs.

At 3:30 the meeting began with all the agents assembled. Jon asked Preacher Coleman to pray the blessing for the safety of all the agents and the success of their mission. Then he asked them all to keep Bud's memory alive and to remember Burt Walker, who was still grieving.

"OK, then, here we go with the assignments. Randy and Mandy go to Tallahassee and the Pensacola beach. I don't know, maybe I got that in reverse order." (laughter) "Franklin and Dollar go to Boston; Ron and Amy go to Hartford; Pederson and Coleman go to Worcester; Fletcher and Knight go to Providence; Leon and Baskins go to Springfield, Massachusetts; Corbett and Calvetti go to Bridgeport-New Haven; Ferrara and Niel Olafsen go to New York, where the big dogs play; Brownlee and Rodriguez go to Philadelphia; Shep and Solomon go to Newark; Norman and Nielsen go to Jersey City; Reilly and May go to Trenton; Cruz and his team work the new operation at Boulder.

"This time, we're going out on much shorter assignments; mostly one city to a team and you know the reason for that. This is the last foray and we're being tasked to get the coordinated raids off the ground early. General Bragg is working on the umbrella warrant from the federal bench in DC. He's had these last locations for most of the week, so I'm thinking we'll be heading out by the end of next week on the big bust. What I'm saying is, let's get these last cities wrapped up and be back in town ready for the deployment by the middle of the week if that 's possible. In Tallahassee I'm sure that's possible. In New York and Philly, I'm not so sure, but maybe they'll get lucky the first day. Once you get the location pinned down, hop on the plane and fly overnight if you can. And just a reminder to dress low casual and don't be noticed; keep moving even if you have to take pictures of the auto tags and like Bragg said, look stupid if anyone wants to talk. That's it; any questions?"

"Swede, do you think we might have enough time to watch the workplaces for deliveries and follow them back to their distribution point? We're not likely to get those distribution locations any other way and if we miss them they get away free. How about taking an extra day or so even if it takes the whole week?" Shep Turner wanted a greater time frame.

"Good point, Shep. Tell you what; ya'll stay on the site until you get a delivery truck or until I call you in. I'll get with Phil Bragg and see if he'll set a cutoff date. Good thinking. Anyone else?"

"Are those our street maps on the table over there?"

"Those are the maps; we got them in just before the meeting. We get two-day map service through the Air Base here. Be sure to take yours and those are cash envelopes in case you're running short; just sign the register. Same as an ATM allotment, two thousand dollars in each envelope. Maybe it'll save you a stop. And the QRE's are there on the table, too if you don't have your laptop. Make your flight reservations before you leave and try not to pack up when you leave the office; we don't want to look like a company of troops on maneuvers; twos and fours are OK. Anything else? (pause) OK, then, call me if I can help; I'll try to stay close to the office but use my cell to call in if it's not busy. Take care."

For the remainder of the day the agents figured out their best flight schedules, made reservations and headed out on the final foray. Olafsen reported to Crumpton that the teams were on their way and again to General Bragg. Crumpton expected to be back over the weekend;

"It all depends on whether these FBI attorneys can fight off the local lawyers' suits. They think civil liberties are under attack."

By 5:40 the office had cleared; Olafsen thought it all through one more time.

"So far, so good, but Dummy, why the heck did you forget the delivery points?"

He was his own worst critic. The other agents thought differently, like;

"Swede's got the handle on it; he'll make Light Colonel soon." They were more generous critics.

"Jon, are you talking to yourself again? By the way, you didn't include me in your list of unassigned agents; I am an agent now, you know, or have you forgotten since you're in charge now?" Misti seemed a bit peeved.

"Oh, phoo, Misti, they all know you were teamed with me and I'm not going out. Heck, Hon, I'm sorry, really I am; I can see now, I shorted you. You're right as rain and I know it; you are an agent and you deserved recognition. I'll find a way to make it up."

"Promise?"

"Promise."

"How?"

"What, are you studying Indian? You'll just have to help me find a way to make it up to you."

"Hmm. We'll talk about that after dinner, Swede."

"Honey, you know I don't like for you to call me Swede; that's just what the guys got to calling me and I've never been able to shake it. If you want to call me by a nickname, call me Handsome or Sweetie or Big Boy or something; call me Dane, that's a good nickname for a Dane."

The Mexicans

"OK, I'll call you Great Dane; no, I'll call you Dane."

"That's more like it. You sure know how to twist me around your little finger. Dang; when you bat your pretty eyes at me I melt down to the floor."

"That's not the place where I want to melt you down, Jon."

"We're out of here; it's quitting time."

Major Shepherd Turner and Captain David Solomon were scouting new territory; neither had been to Newark before today so they took rooms at a hotel near the airport where they had rented their car.

"We have a couple hours before dinner time, David; what do you want to do, watch the news or find a basketball game on TV, or what?"

"Why don't we look over the map and get these streets pegged, then take a look? They're more than likely in the same area like they were in Houston; those guys seem to congregate. Speaking of congregating, do you want to go to church tomorrow morning?"

"Yeah, if we can find one; there ought to be a list of churches in that directory, restaurants too. I'm fine with that, we can visit around the streets, maybe find a few addresses; that'll get us off to a good start in the morning when the traffic will be bad, no doubt. Saturday ought to be easier driving this city. What're you finding?"

"I found one of them; it's right here where I marked it yellow. These other streets will be nearby. How about I look them up on the street index and you find them on the grid – mark them yellow."

"OK, give me one."

In a few minutes they had them all marked yellow.

"See? All within a few blocks of each other, you can tell by the house numbers. Let's go have a look. This is the same routine Crumpton and I did in Houston and we got home free in a few days. We keep our travel jeans and t-shirts on. Bring your jacket."

It was not a prime area of real estate, naturally. They tried to stay on the perimeter, on the business streets and then when they knew where the target block was, they drove straight through to the next main street a few blocks over. Actually, they were worried for no reason. All the men they saw were sitting on porches or shooting baskets or just standing around talking; no one paid them any attention as they drove straight through.

"There's the block, David; three rooming houses on the list, they all have the house numbers. Let's go to the next street."

After two more streets they had them all spotted on the map.

"Let's head for the barn and get cleaned up. The hotel restaurant looked pretty good and the game starts at 8."

"Plenty of time; we're on a roll, Shep."

That was Saturday; now it was Sunday morning and Solomon had looked up a church for them to attend; both were of the same denomination. After services, they spoke for a few minutes with one of the deacons who targeted them for a kind word, as visitors. Turner told him they were in Newark on business and needed to find the Water Department to check out a property they were interested in. Br. Frank Moscoso gave them directions to the building on the lower side of the downtown district. So that was a start. Then he asked them to join him and his wife for lunch at a nearby family style restaurant; it was hard to refuse Br. Moscoso, so they accepted and followed the couple to the restaurant where they were seated after a few minutes wait and placed their orders. Turner and Solomon took Moscoso's lead and ordered the baked chicken and dumplings with green peas, broccoli and bread pudding.

"My wife's going to wonder where I could've picked up these three or four pounds eating restaurant food, Frank; I may have to call you for verification, what about it David?" Turner kidded with them.

"I can't tell my wife about it when I find this kind of home cooking on the road; she tends to get jealous, so I may have to tell her I found a lump in the dumplings. That wouldn't be a lie if one of you can help me find one."

The Mexicans

Julia Moscoso chided them for making fun of their wives. Solomon apologized.

"Veronica's a good cook but she does get jealous of restaurant cooking when I compliment it; that's just the way she does. I love her and I love her cooking, too."

"Julia has to read a lot of cookbooks these days to keep my waistline where it needs to be since the Department rewrote the rules for cops, especially Inspectors like me who tend to sit and think a lot, right, dear?."

"Or daydream, or nap, or go to a movie in the middle of the day. I always try to keep Frank honest. At least on Sunday," she added.

They had a good lunch and visited the zoo for a couple of hours then returned to church for the evening service, where they met several more of Newark's finest.

"You guys tend to pack up, it looks like. What do we call that, Espirit de Corp in the Spirit?" Solomon liked to joke around.

"Jim Boyle is the guy who packs up enough for all of us; you gotta watch that belly, Jim." Frank Moscoso liked to joke, too.

"Aw, get off me, Frank. Since when did you get the order to keep your eyes on my belly? That's my wife's job, right Christie? Tell him."

"That's a full time job, for me, Frank; but if I don't get him back in shape, he could lose his job or at least a promotion, so with us it's a matter of family survival."

Before leaving the front porch of the church building, they exchanged names and the cops gave them telephone numbers to call.

"Don't feel like you're among strangers here in Newark. Keep the numbers just in case you might need a helping hand while you're here or any other time. Come and see us again."

Back at the motel, they ordered a pot of coffee and talked about the day. They both had a feeling that the encounters they had at church were not so much by chance as by a need they might have had for friendly contacts on this assignment.

"It's a real blessing to visit with believers all the way across the country. God takes care of his own, Shep."

"You got that right, David."

It didn't take them long to find their way back to the streets they had scouted. They were on their way by 6am and by 6:50 they were on their first street; three houses with six addresses, since they were all duplexes. They parked a block up the street and sipped their coffee while they waited for the cars to begin leaving for the workplace, keeping watch with Turner's binoculars.

"The one we follow is the one where three of four guys pack into a car pool; that's been the same everywhere we've been, right, David?"

David had the glasses trained on a house where the front door had just opened.

"Yeah, that's right, and it looks like we got the first car pool coming off the porch right now. Let's hope the car is headed down the street so we don't have to duck if they come up this way."

"I can see them; they're on the other side of the street. Get ready to duck and then I gotta turn around before they get too far gone."

It was a cold morning and the Mexicans had a little trouble starting the car. After a few loud curses made in Spanish, the car responded.

"Guess that car speaks Spanish, too." Solomon quipped.

In a few moments the car drove by their ducked heads, trailing a line of oil smoke, four men slumped in the seats, still waking up, not anxious for another dreary day at the warehouse. Turner pulled away from the curb and backed up into a driveway to make the turn around. By the time they made the top of the hill, they could see the smoke trail and followed it. After a short while and a few turns they found themselves close to the river nearing a railroad yard; soon the car turned off the main street onto an access road leading to a warehouse area by the tracks.

The Mexicans

"This looks like the kind of area we'd expect," Turner was driving. "There they go, into that fenced in yard; it looks like that's the place; they're going to park it right there. We'll keep on like nothing happened and come back by in a few minutes. There's a high point over there on the next street; I think we can keep an eye on the place with the glasses from there. I'm ready for a few more sips of that coffee. Did you get an address or a name on the place?"

"Nothing I could read, but there was a big mailbox at the gate. We might get a number off of it. We'll drive slow and I'll use the glasses next time."

They found a shady knoll a few hundred yards away on the ridge and parked just over the hill where they could keep a watch without being noticed. After twenty minutes they moved back down to the road with the gate and mailbox. Driving a little slower, Solomon was able to pick up the number and they kept on back to the motel. There they had breakfast and looked over the downtown area; it didn't look very appealing and there was no telling what kind of parking they might find.

They decided not to drive, so after breakfast they took a taxi down to the Water Department. With their identification they didn't expect the resistance they got from the staff when they asked for the name of the business operating at the address they had. Even the person in charge for the day refused to open the records to them unless the department head authorized it and she was in the hospital undergoing surgery. It looked like a losing battle with the clerks, but Turner had an ace to play; he called Frank Moscoso's number and got him at the Newark Police Station.

"Frank, this is Shep Turner; I guess you didn't expect to hear from me so soon." He explained the resistance they had run into at the Water Department. "Can you give me a good word here so we can get the name of the owner of this warehouse?"

"Shep, did you show them any identification? That should be enough if it's a photo ID."

"We did, Frank. I didn't mention it yesterday since it didn't seem important, but David and I are Operations Officers with the National Security Agency and this is official business; but that didn't seem to carry enough weight to get a look at the water record. Do you suppose you could call them and get us the go ahead for that information?"

"NSA? Why, heck yes, you can look at those records without a bench warrant. Hold on, Shep, while I get on the house phone and give them a call. Ask the clerk for the number there."

Turner gave Moscoso the number and he made the call. The chief clerk was obviously taken down a peg and apologized as she went to retrieve the record.

"Did that get the help you needed, Shep?"

"It did, and thanks. She's retrieving it right now."

"Now, listen, Shep; you call me for anything at all that I can do while you're here in Newark or anywhere around here. I'll get it done for you with a phone call anywhere around here; they all know me and my team here. Just mention my name anywhere, Captain Frank Moscoso; they all know me, and I'm usually right here at the Station."

"Hey, Frank, Captain, I really appreciate it; David has got the information already. We never know when we might run up on something and this trip could be one of those, so I may be calling again. Now we're going to the Courthouse to get a copy of the property deed. These are bad dudes and we like to get the names on the deed. Maybe you can give them a call before we get there and speed things along for us; would you mind?"

"Why, sure, I'll call them right now. The office is at the Courthouse and the Clerk of Court is Stanley Francis. Just ask for Stanley Francis; he'll be expecting you."

"Thanks again, Frank; we'll catch a cab over there right now. So long and give my regards to Mrs. Moscoso and the others. I won't forget that friendly reception yesterday and your kind hospitality. Thanks again."

"Don't mention it. Come back and visit anytime; you're always welcome here."

The Mexicans

They left the Water Department to the clerks who apologized again and hailed a cab on the street. At the Courthouse, the property records were copied for them in a few minutes, no charge, and they were soon on their way back to the motel.

"A good day, David; it's been a good day."

"How about we watch the news and then head down to the restaurant, Shep? I'm hungry enough to eat the lips off a brontosaurus."

"Be careful if you ever do that; she might think you're wanting to make love."

After dinner Shep Turner called home.

"Bobbie, it's me, Sweetheart; how're you doing?"

"Oh, Shep, are you alright? Are you still in Newark? What did you do today?"

"Yes, Baby, I'm fine. We had a real good day; David found a Southern Baptist church in the directory and we spent the day with some of the people of the church. We had dinner at a real down home family-style restaurant; chicken and dumplings and bread pudding and after dinner we went back for the evening service, too. These people at the church are very friendly; the ones we talked with were mostly cops and their families. Did they get that leak fixed in the bathroom yesterday?"

"Sure did; it's doing just fine, now. Mom and Dad stayed with me for the weekend; I don't know if they'll be here after tomorrow, but I hope so. When do you think you'll be back home?"

"I can't say yet; tomorrow I'll know more after we get started on the work. Give Mom and Dad my love. I'm dog tired now and we have a call at 5:30; we have to get an early start."

"Well, you'd best climb in the bed and dream of me; better be me, you dog."

"It'll be you, Sweetheart; it always is you. I love you."

"I love you, too, Shep. Call me tomorrow. 'Bye."

They were dog tired and went to bed soon after dinner and the call home.

Next morning they were up at 5:30, finished breakfast and by 7 they were headed for the workplace, hoping to catch a delivery truck on its rounds. For the wait, they had newspapers, sports magazines, books on terrorism, the Holy Bible, a sack full of fruit and dark chocolate bars in a cooler chest, and a huge insulated pot of black coffee. After copying down the license tags to check against the cars at the addresses on their list, they settled in for the long watch.

Then, at 8:20 two large vans pulled in through the gates and rolled to a stop alongside the warehouse; the doors of the warehouse swung open. In a few moments a stream of men filed out, each carrying a backpack, and stepped into the vans, six men in each van.

"Shep, those guys look like the workers, the Mexicans; it looks like they're getting ready to go somewhere. See the guys coming out now? They're the ones in charge; khakis and dress shirts with jackets. I think they're getting ready to leave. Do you want me to drive?"

Turner was taping the whole scene on his video camera.

"Yeah, David, come around, I'll scoot over. Let's not lose them; they're up to something."

Solomon pulled away, down the hill, and drove past the warehouse yard with the vans starting to move toward the gate. At the corner, he turned right as he expected the vans would do also; they did. The road went straight alongside the railroad tracks without any main intersections for about two miles. As they approached the intersection, Solomon turned into a driveway where several cars were parked by a small office building; the vans passed by as Solomon backed up, then he pulled back onto the road and saw the vans as they turned onto the approach to Highway 21 a couple of blocks ahead. He sped up and made the turn, keeping the vans in his sight.

Meanwhile, Turner had called Captain Frank Moscoso to alert him to a possible terrorist attack.

The Mexicans

"Frank, this is exactly the way they operated at Berkeley and at Duke; two vans carrying the workers with backpacks full of explosives. They left them at their targets, knowing that the backpacks would not be suspicious on a college campus. I'll bet these guys are headed for a drop, maybe a college campus; you need to get a couple of cars to fall in with us on this tail; this is for real, Frank, I know it from experience. We just turned up onto 21 headed toward 280."

"That don't sound like they're going to a college. Hey, wait a minute, that's in the direction of the Holland Tunnel. Hold on. (pause) Jim, do you know of a college near 280 and the tunnel? (pause) Shep, I've got three cars headed toward you; turn on your emergency blinkers so they'll know you. We need to stop them before they get into the tunnel. If they get in there, they might just blow the vans, people and all, if these guys are like the suicide kind. They already passed up all the colleges. Do you see any of the cars yet?"

"Yes, Frank, there's a flasher coming up behind us about a mile back. We're on the Turnpike now; headed east."

"If they're headed for the tunnel they've got to catch I-78 over to the Skyway and turn back to the north to get in line for the tunnel. We'll pull them over at the Skyway toll station. Maybe you'd better get in front of them at the toll gate and don't let them get through. Our cars will be there by that time."

"The first one is right behind us. He turned off his flasher. We've got a few miles to go to 78, maybe four or five minutes."

"Don't worry, Shep, we'll stop them before they get on the Skyway. But we need to do it real fast before they can set off any of the stuff they might be carrying."

The police car stayed hidden behind Turner and Solomon. He thought he saw another one pull up behind the first one.

"Here we come to the interchange; let's see if he turns toward the Skyway. Yep, there he goes, we're right behind. (pause) OK, I see the toll stiles now. We're going to pull out and around to the front of the vans; here we go, hit it David."

David pulled it off really smooth and they stayed in front of the vans right up to the turnstile. There he set the brake and watched while the police approached the vans. The drivers rolled down their windows and were asked to step out.

"What is wrong, officer?" the leader from the first van spoke first.

"Just step over here and let me see your driver's license."

The officer at the second van did the same. While they looked at the licenses, their partners and the third car officers opened the doors of the vans and looked inside. They ordered the riders to exit and take off their backpacks. Then they ordered them to lie face down on the road. One of the officers called for the paddy wagons.

"But we are just workers, officer; we don't do nothing wrong. We work at the jobs they hire us to do; please, we don't do nothing wrong." There was only one who spoke good English.

"If that's true, you'll be released, but we're taking you to the station and then we'll see what happens to you. Just relax; if you're just hired to work for these people, you don't have to worry. But, don't you know what you're carrying those backpacks? Explosives. You might have been dead by now if we hadn't stopped you in time."

Turner and Solomon showed their Identification to the Lieutenant and began to inspect the backpacks.

"This is it, Lieutenant; just what we expected, timers and all." He was still on the phone to the Captain. "Did you hear that, Frank? There's enough stuff here to blow the tunnel to Hialeah. We need the FBI out here right away; can you make the call? I don't have the number in my phone. And you'd better get a car to the warehouse before anyone there gets nervous and leaves." He gave him the address.

The drivers of the vans were handcuffed and all of the riders as well. Then the wet spots started showing up on the pavement and you could hear some of the men praying softly; some were weeping, unable to hold back their tears. Right now, as far as they could tell their lives were almost without hope. Thoughts of jail played across their minds. What would happen now to their families back home? Maybe they

The Mexicans

would be let go to return home; maybe they would be treated as criminals and locked up. The future looked very bleak; some gave up hope, thinking of a life spent in prison. Soon the place was swarming with FBI and paddy wagons.

Turner and Solomon gave a full account to Sam Cartagena, the FBI agent in charge; describing what the NSA knew of the work being done by the people and the location of their workplace. Moscoso had already detailed a car to the warehouse where they arrested three people in the office, all of Mideast descent, same as the leaders of the vans. In little over an hour the turnstile was cleared and Turner and Solomon were on their way to the Station, along with the FBI agents to file charges and arrest all of the participants.

"If what you say is true, these Mexicans will be sent back to Mexico and not charged with a felony." Cartagena told them. "Right now, they would appear to be innocent of any conspiracy charges. When the bomb squad gets through looking over all this stuff, timers and all, the Mexicans may be thanking God for bringing us down on the operation in time to keep them from being blown to Hialeah."

"Did you say Hialeah? Why Hialeah?"

"I don't know; it just popped into my head. I'm not even sure if there is a Hialeah; I've heard of it someplace, I guess."

"Yeah, I know what you mean."

Turner called Bob Crumpton and gave the report. Crumpton was amazed.

"Already, they've been arrested and booked; the whole bunch, what, nineteen of them? Man, you guys are in high gear."

"We're feeling pretty much like that, Bob; high gear. I'll get a report written before we get back. I'd like to take another look in the morning for a couple hours at least, just in case the delivery truck shows up. He may not know about this."

"Whatever you decide, Shep. Call me when you get ready to leave. I'll call this in to Phil; don't be surprised if you get a call. Phil's going to love this. I suppose you'll have some more statements to make, so I'll let you go. Give my regards to David."

Turner had a great call home before he and David went to dinner. Bobbie had always been so proud of her Captain, now Major, not so much for his work which she truly admired, but she was proud of who he was, the kind of person he was. Ever since their first meeting in Baton Rouge, her love for Shep had grown and grown and she always knew in her heart that this was the perfect man for her; this truly was their match made in Heaven. Stories like this one that showed the faithfulness Shep had toward his duty just charmed her even more, but she worried about him, too, especially after Bud got killed.

"Oh, Shep, I'm so glad it's all over now; but I'm so proud of you for doing things so well. I know it's God who keeps you safe, but it's what's inside of you that makes the difference in how you do what you do. You're so kind; I can tell by your voice that you're hurting for those poor men getting caught up in that stuff. I'll pray for them. I love you. Just keep safe, Darling, and hurry home."

"I'll stay safe, Bobbie, 'cause I love you and I don't ever want anything to interfere with our love; we've got a beautiful life together and nothing's going to change that. I think I'll be home by Thursday; we've got one more look to make at the warehouse. Don't worry now, Hon. I love you"

"I love you, too, Shep. And I've got some good news for you when you get here."

She had planned to tell him of the baby when he got home, but she just couldn't keep it back.

"Oh, Bobbie, I think I know what it is; I think I know but just keep it for me until I get back so I can hold you while you tell me."

"Hurry home, Darling."

The Newark job ended with another win; they tracked a delivery truck back to its warehouse in Allentown, Pennsylvania and phoned the name and address to Jon Olafsen, just in time to catch a ship unloading at Seattle with a manifest that included Industrial Materials

The Mexicans

for delivery to that same address. They figured that delivery point took care of that whole area; New York, New Jersey, Philadelphia and eastern Pennsylvania.

When General Bragg got the whole story he took it in stride.

"Those Louisiana Cajuns are my kind of men."

CHAPTER 50
The Name of the Game

Federico Dominguez was a man of authority in Mexico. As Minister of National Defense he was undeniably the second most powerful man in the country, next to the President. He held absolute authority over all of the provincial police and the dreaded state police, as well. The only problem in Mexico, was that absolute authority at the federal level didn't necessarily mean he had that authority in the states or the communities; it was well known everywhere except perhaps in Mexico City, that federal authority was merely titular authority. Real authority, real ruling power came by way of the Peso, preferably the American Dollar when possible. And Federico Dominguez didn't have a lot of pesos or dollars with which to exercise his authority in all of Mexico. In the rural communities local magistrates held power by taxing and rewarding. In the cities, drug traders ruled by dollars, especially in the border towns. Even the peso politics of South American dictator Julio Jimenez held more ruling power in the cities of Mexico than did Federico Dominguez, Minister of National Defense.

So, when Luis Caldera and Al Maldonado met with Dominguez they were met with feelings of despair from the Minister.

"But how can I call up forty-six teams each with twenty seasoned officers spread across half the country, to put together a coordinated raid on the villages controlled by this Council of Unification? My authority rests in my Presidential appointment; in practical terms that means it is virtually limited to the Federal District surrounding Mexico City. I can issue orders to the state police, but I have no means to back them up without the cooperation of the state and local police officers. Peso power – that's the name of the game."

Major Caldera wasn't too surprised at this confession of impotence.

The Mexicans

"Check my math, Al; fifty teams including 4 captains 4 squad leaders and 16 grunts gives us fifty commanders, one hundred captains, 200 squad leaders and 600 grunts. If the grunts get a thousand each, the squad leaders fifteen hundred, the captains get two thousand and the commanders twenty-five hundred each, that makes one million two hundred and twenty five thousand dollars. Then we add five hundred for each judge or magistrate, one in each village, and that's another twenty-five thousand – gets us to a million, two hundred fifty thousand dollars and Dominguez gets fifty thousand to spread around liberally so everyone knows where the power comes from; one point three million. Did I compute that right, Al?"

"The numbers look to be right, Luis; now what?"

Caldera dialed General Bragg.

"Luis, is that you?"

"How'd you know, General? Do we now have caller ID on the circuit?"

"Yep; they added that just last week. You need to call more often, Luis, you'd keep up better with progress. So what can I do for you? You know you're on TDY from my command."

"I know that, General, that's why I called you direct; temporary duty doesn't have to change my loyalties, does it?"

"No, it doesn't; you're still my responsibility. Now that I know I've just been buttered up, what can I do for you?"

"We're organizing the incursion, but you know how things get done down here; I've got to get some big chips in hand right away. We can't do business with the local police unless we grease the skids, know what I mean?"

"Oh, yeah, I know what you mean; I've heard about all that. What will it take to get the raids on schedule? Don't fudge it; you don't have more than a couple days extra; we're looking at next Wednesday. Can you make it by then?"

"We will, if that's the date. We need one point three million in hundreds by tomorrow. The courier runs down here twice a day from El Paso, but an unmarked helicopter would be more secure. The Presidential Palace - we'll be looking for it in the morning."

"It'll be there before noon; I'll call you when I know. What else? How's Rita Juanita? I love that name."

"I do too. Rita has something to tell me tonight. I'm guessing it'll be a boy; she thinks I don't have a clue, but I've got informers all over the place. How about you; do you like your new digs?"

"It's great in the Virginia mountain country. Congratulations on the good news; let us know about the date. I wouldn't want to miss a chance to see him in the nursery while you're still grinning."

"You got it, General. You'll be the first to know; maybe the second."

"Second's good. I'll let you go now, so I can keep my promise. Take care and watch your back. Those Mexicans are mean as hell."

"Don't think I'm not. I appreciate it. 'Bye." Luis closed his phone.

"OK, Federico, you've got the money and an extra fifty thousand to make it happen by early next Wednesday morning. If not, we keep the money and you get to explain why not."

Dominguez called in his adjutant, a Major General Victor Gonzales. He spoke in Spanish and Caldera heard every word. The General was to gather the entire contingent of military officers in the Federal District; more than three-hundred officers.

"The top fifty will be commanders, each to receive twenty-five hundred American dollars; one hundred will be platoon leaders, each to command two squads, each to receive two thousand American dollars. The next two hundred will lead squads, each to receive fifteen hundred American dollars. Each squad leader will hire three experienced soldiers with weapons from anywhere in the country, each to receive one thousand American dollars; all for a special operation. All are to be quarantined in the military barracks until the operation is completed, that will be in about five days. They will have to arrange troop trucks or aircraft for each Command to reach anywhere in the country overnight from the barracks; that's fifty separate locations.

The Mexicans

"The Commanders will have them in the barracks by the end of the day, Sunday. Itinerary will be announced Monday and transportation must be arranged by Tuesday morning, ready to go Tuesday night. Each platoon will be assigned to a command, but four commands will be unassigned backup, held in abeyance to fill in where needed on a moment's notice. Four men per squad, two squads per platoon, two platoons per command. Each commander will command eighteen subordinates. Here is my command diagram of the operation. The Major General is responsible, so you get either five thousand dollars or you get fired, do we understand?"

"Yes sir. It will be just as you say, General."

Gonzales was out of the door before Dominguez could return his salute.

"You see what I told you about power? This day I have the power of the Presidency, the American Dollar."

"I believed you to begin with," Caldera assured him.

"I can't believe what I just saw and heard in this room", Maldonado was nearly speechless. "Two hours ago we had no way to complete our mission; now it is assured. I am impressed, more than I can say."

"You don't have to say it, Al. When you've been in the service as long as I have, you'll know that it all can be made to happen, but nothing happens unless someone makes it happen. Now I can go home and hear Rita tell me that I'm going to be a father; see, that's what I mean – it wouldn't have happened except that my action caused it to begin to happen, and God caused the life and gave His blessing. The life wouldn't have happened without Him. But we are responsible to do our part, or the thing will never happen."

"I understand what you're saying and that's really great news, Luis. I'll pray that there will be many more for you and Rita; you should have many."

As Luis walked through the door of their home, Rita Juanita warmed up to him with a sly look and smiled sweetly.

"Luis, I have to tell you something today; promise you won't get angry."

"Why should I get angry, Baby? You know I could never get angry with you. Just go ahead and tell me the news; I've been waiting all day, ever since what you said this morning."

He had never called her Baby before tonight. Rita let it pass without comment.

"OK; get ready — we're going to have — the neighbors over for dinner Saturday?"

"No, that's not it; come on now, spit it out, I'm waiting."

"OK, get ready — we're going to have — the kitchen done over?"

"No, that's not it; now cut the crap, Sweetheart, just tell me the news you said you would have."

"OK, then — get ready — we're going to have — a nephew; my sister Anita is pregnant?"

"Now, Baby, that's not it. How about if l tell you, then – we're going to have …"

"Wait! You're going to spoil it; why do you want to spoil my fun?"

"It may be fun for you, but what about me?"

"OK, then, Smarty; we'll say it together. Ready?"

"OK, on the count of three – one, two, three –"

"We're going to have a baby!!"

"I knew it! I knew it! Baby, that's so wonderful; it's going to be a boy – right?"

"What difference does it make?"

"Am I right? It's a boy, right?"

"Too soon to tell, Smarty; how come you can't wait?"

"Baby, we were made for each other; that means we think the same. Like, I think – I love you. Now, see; I know what you're thinking. Am I right?"

"Right again, Smarty. That's just what I was thinking, too – you love me. Now I think I'm going to kiss your two big smart lips. What are you thinking?"

"I read your mind again, Sweetheart – you love me, too. Love - that's the name of the game; just melt right here into my arms, I've got a big kiss I've been holding for you."

CHAPTER 51
The Day of Allah

As the terrorists' Day of Allah approached, the commander sent out the coded message over the internet to the forty-four active cells at their workplaces scattered across the country. It was terse and powerful,

"Prepare for the games to begin in three days. All will play and score at 6 on the Day of Allah."

Each workplace manager began the indoctrination of the workers on the day after receiving the message. The first phase of indoctrination was the distribution of cocaine and a bonus after the lunch break.

"Relax today, men, you have earned an afternoon of rest. This recreational potion will help you to relax. We want you to know that your work is appreciated, so each of you has been given a bonus in the envelope; one hundred dollars for each of you. At the same time, your families are receiving the same amount as bonus. Enjoy the afternoon, but remain in the warehouse; call home if you like."

A few of the men at first rejected the drug, but were encouraged by their co-workers.

"Go ahead, man; it won't hurt you. You'll like it and you'll relax like you never did before."

By mid-afternoon, all but a few were sound asleep. On awakening, many went to the cocaine table for seconds. At quitting time, for many it became a problem to decide who would drive the pool car. In a few instances, the operator of the workplace sent the men home in a van with a driver.

The Mexicans

The second of the three days went one step further in the indoctrination. The men were surprised to find that the workplace had been set up with a display screen and a video projector.

"We have another day of ease today, my friends; the result of your hard work that has gotten us ahead of our schedule. I would like to show you a few films of my family and other relatives preparing for the great Day of Allah back in the homeland. Even the little children are excited about the great events of the day. But first, please have a good breakfast on us; all of this food has been prepared and delivered by the very best caterer in the city and it is here for you as a gift in appreciation of the good work that you men are doing on the job. There is one more surprise today; our Board of Directors has reviewed the financial statements and has found that there is extra money to be distributed to our employees and their families. That is good news for you – another envelope containing another one hundred dollars and another one hundred dollars for your families in Mexico. How do you like that, my friends?"

As expected, the workers at each of the workplaces gave a cheer, high fives all around, and slapped each other on the back.

"Then let us begin with the food. In about an hour we will begin the movies. Have a good day, my friends."

The men had never been treated so well by their employer. Some were suspicious.

"What are they doing this for? He's going to want something for it or maybe they are going to close the place down; be careful, we need to be careful. Don't do no more drugs."

Others were more willing to accept the explanation.

"No sweat, man; this kind of thing goes on in offices all the time when the business makes more money than they expect. Everybody in America gets bonuses and office parties. Just get some food and have a good time. We'll be back to work tomorrow; today we have a day off and a bonus."

The Day of Allah

An hour later, after pigging out on eggs, turkey sausage, home fries, tortillas, refried beans, avocados and key lime pie, the men were treated to a series of films showing activities of the families and relatives the boss had spoken of. What they saw were large crowds of people in some middle-eastern country celebrating with rifles and ammunition belts full of bullets, dancing and shouting and shooting in the air. It was clearly a great celebration. English subtitles explained the reason for the exuberance; a great day in the history of the Moslem world, a day of religious significance. It was all explained in much detail, followed by a history of the Moslem people, heavily weighted by the words of the Quran given by the prophet Mohammed in the seventh century.

By lunch time most of the men had drifted off to sleep, napping quietly while the video player hummed along with the words training their subconscious minds to hate the infidels, the unbelievers, wherever they might be found in the non-Moslem world. After a catered lunch and drinks laced with cocaine, the men's minds were much more open, agreeable to learn the objectives of Jihad and the ultimate sacrifice of the truly faithful in service to Allah. But they all weren't so gullible; some retained their self awareness and rebelled at the idea of self-sacrifice that the videos promised would be so fulfilling.

"That's bullshit, man; ain't nobody stupid enough to believe that stuff; it's bullshit. You ain't telling me that you believe that bullshit, are you? Who's stupid enough to strap a belt full of explosives and ball bearings around his waist and go stepping out into eternity, leaving his wife and kids just because some sixth century Arab wrote a book about what Allah wants people to do in the twenty-first century. I mean, if I was going to kill myself for twenty-five thousand dollars like those stupid Arabs in that movie I'd at least want some time to spend it before I blew myself to Hialeah."

"Where's Hialeah?"

"Hell, I don't know, man, you tell me. You don't like Hialeah, how about Timbuktu or maybe Mukilteo? You like that better? How about Wetumpka? Would you rather blow your ass to Timbuktu

The Mexicans

or Mukilteo? OK, you go ahead, but not me; I'm not crazy, like you. You're crazy."

"Hey, man, chill out; we're all just talking. Take it easy. Relax. Nobody's making you do what those people are doing in the movie. That's just the stuff they want to feed you but that don't mean you have to swallow it, does it? It's called propaganda; that's the game they play to try and get our minds trained right."

"So when they get our minds trained right what comes next, suicide belts?"

These activities had been going on in much the same way and with much the same employee reaction at workplaces all across the Hezbollah terrorist network as they attempted to indoctrinate the immigrant Mexican workers. But, at one workplace there was a distinct deviation from the plan, intended to direct the focus of the nation's defense agencies again on a single terrorist act.

At a few minutes past 2 p.m., Saleem Pushtaki entered the South Boston warehouse, site of the Boston activities of Hezbollah's Mexican operation. Pushtaki was a recent import from Palestine, one of the special immigrants numbered in the recent peace settlement agreement negotiated by the United States between Israel and its difficult neighbor, an agreement hammered out over weeks of laborious negotiations and in the end, hailed as an innovative achievement. Some of the Mexicans liked to call him Pushy because of his sometimes pushy attitude, his manner of motivating the men. Others liked to call him Pussy because of the way he styled his beard. Pushtaki didn't mind the diminutives so long as it helped the men keep their minds off of their work and thereby be easier to control. In the long run, he had only one basic objective and that was to destroy as much of Boston as he could with the limited resources he was given. This afternoon Pushy was in an agreeable mood.

"Have you filled the spaces as I asked?" Pushtaki spoke softly to his Iranian assistant.

"Yes, sir," he answered, knowing that it pleased Pushtaki. "The three all have the same amount of materials and in each car it is covered over with coal from the coal yard. Nothing can be seen beneath the coal."

The Day of Allah

"And the truck; is it loaded and well covered? Is it all tied down tight?"

"Yes Saleem, eight barrels all covered over with bundled lumber and tied down securely. It looks just as it should, a load of lumber."

"Very well, then. We are ready to begin. You will watch to see that no one looks in any trunk and hurry them along if they appear to want to look in. We will proceed as though we are very late and don't want to get stuck in traffic; do you understand?"

"I understand, Mr. Pushtaki. We have no time to waste."

Pushtaki was satisfied with the special preparations; he spoke to the men waiting in the warehouse.

"My good friends, if I may call you my friends; this afternoon we have only one task to accomplish and after that is finished you will be free to leave. We will need your help to load our heavy duty truck that is now ready to go to the airport where a shipment will be waiting. I have fifty dollars for each of you three men that drove your pool car today; it's for the use of your car to carry you and your friends to the airport; you men will be able to leave the airport and go home after we have finished loading the truck. You may fill your cars with gas from our drums in the yard outside before leaving. We must be on our way now, so which ones of you drive the pool cars?"

"I do; it's my car." Three men stepped forward to claim the fifty dollars for each and go fill their tanks with gasoline. Soon they were ready to go.

"Stay behind the truck going through the tunnel; he will pay the toll for all of you. Keep in place behind the truck, so no one gets lost. Vamanos!" Pushy had learned a few Spanish words.

As the cars began their drive and they rolled across the first set of railroad tracks, the three cars banged loudly as the rear passenger frame bumped down onto the chassis.

"Ow! Damn, Manny, what's that all about? Man, your damn shock absorbers are gone - they're gone to hell, Manny."

"Man, I don't know. I guess it's the tank full of gas; it isn't used to all that extra weight. I've never filled it up before; I'm more like five bucks

423

The Mexicans

worth at a time. You can help me change the shocks this weekend. Good thing we got those bonuses, shocks aren't cheap like they used to be."

"Manny, we can't work on the car on Sunday; we'll have to do it on Saturday, right?"

Juanito always tried to be true to the Church's standards. All of the men were Catholic and devout in their religion.

"What do you mean, "we", Manny? My bonus is for me. It's your car isn't it? We pay for the ride don't we?"

Enrique was faithful, too, but he was thinking more about the money.

"Right, Ricky, and you pay your part for the repairs, too, if you want to keep paying for the ride. And don't worry, Juanito, we're not going to work on Sunday. Do we ever work on Sunday? No, we never work on Sunday, Stupid."

"Yeah, Manny, but you got the fifty dollars. After you pay the first fifty, we'll share the rest of the cost of the shocks with you."

Enrique was not convinced about the sharing, yet.

"OK, man, I got a break today," Manuel Escondido was the driver. "Just to show you my generosity, when we get off and back to the street I'll buy us all a beer and burrito."

"Oh, big man! He's going to buy us a beer."

"OK, then, two beers each and a burrito."

"Good. Two beers is good, Manny; that makes you a generous man, like you said to begin with."

In a short while they were turning onto I-93, the chassis still bumping them at each rough spot in the road, headed in the direction of the tunnel and Logan Airport.

"Hey, watch it; that fool is trying to pull over in front of you. We have to stay in line; you'd better move it up a little more."

The Day of Allah

"There's the tunnel up ahead; keep it tight, Manuel. We're OK, now. This line is moving like those lazy Arkansas animals; what do they call them, Mole Asses?"

"Stupid! Molasses is what they put on pancakes in Arkansas; it's not an animal. You're an animal, Enrique."

"Here we go into the tunnel; put on your lights Manny, you can't see anything down in the tunnel."

They were past the toll booth, now.

"Forty minutes and we'll be on our way back."

A great smile of satisfaction passed over Saleem Pushtaki's face as he watched the second hand on the timing clock make its last pass around the face of the clock, headed for the big 12; it would have continued on to make another pass around the face but was interrupted at the big 12 to make no more passes. Saleem Pashtaki's smile was no longer on his face; like the timing clock, he no longer had the face, but he could still see the hooded forms coming to escort him to his new digs.

"Seventy virgins," he thought, "now that's a really great payoff. Allah is great!"

Manuel felt a great surge of energy engulf them.

"What the heck was that", he thought.

Then he looked around and saw that tunnel entrance below him was in chaos; water churning with broken parts of cars and trucks and dead bodies all sweeping away out into the bay.

"Man, what a sight; what happened, I wonder?"

It took Manuel a few moments to realize that he was floating in midair and there were others floating there around him – Enrique, Carlos, Juanito, Roberto, all were nearby and a lot of people he didn't know. They were all looking around, surprised and wondering at their situation. Everybody looked strange, sort of ghostly. About that time Manuel began to drift a little faster and he realized that he was being

425

The Mexicans

pulled away toward the heavens; soon the broken tunnel and all of the mess down there faded from sight and all he knew was that he was really happy to be here and not down there; but he just didn't know yet where 'here' was, but that was alright, too; he still wanted to be here.

CHAPTER 52
It's Time to Go

There he found himself again, the young boy up there on that bicycle in the middle of the busy city street, looking down from outside the twelfth floor of the big Department Store; the one where the display windows were always full of Christmas scenes during the season. There he was, riding the bicycle again, trying to keep that bicycle balanced away up there so it wouldn't fall and at the same time trying to avoid all of those cars down there on the street to keep from having an accident. He couldn't figure it out; how he was able to do it, time after time, and not crash down into the street and all of that traffic. It was scary but he couldn't take time to think about it; he just had to keep going fast enough to keep his balance and make it through all of that traffic, without falling.

It was early, the morning of the 12th; Phil Bragg had woken up and just lay there awhile on his daybed taking time to think back over the last few days to take stock of his situation. It had taken him a few days, but by December 8th he had talked to all of the Police Chiefs both by phone and by confirmation memo and had arranged for the selection of the eight swat-trained men he needed from each of the Chiefs. At that time he had found them all to be ready, just waiting for the call to quarantine. Stanford Turner, his FBI counterpart had his teams of four ready as well. Bragg's own NSA agents were ready four for each of the eighty-eight target sites.

The final plan was to quarantine at a location unknown to the men until time of dispatch on the 10th. The sites for the quarantine had been selected for their proximity to the corresponding targets. Then, with the 10th upon them, Bragg was to give the order to initiate quarantine. During the quarantine the men would be given extensive briefings on the background of the operation. Their instructors had been provided with the same audio-visual material, all prepared by Bragg's team of technicians. That team was to take part in the presentations and even remain quarantined with the men; everyone was on for the long haul. Before issuing the order, Bragg called John Smoltz, Stanford Turner, William George and Reggie Dwyer to give them the heads-up. All were on board, ready for the deployment to quarantine the 1400 men.

Bragg's order had gone out under highest security cryptography to the team leaders who were responsible for the execution of every phase of the operation. "Operation Quarantine" was the name of the first phase of the operation. Everyone knew the meaning of that order; the movement was to begin, the troops were dispatched to their points of shut-in. Not an idle word was spoken during the movement of the men; the route to their individual destinations was purposely designed in round-about fashion, often changing vehicles in garages at remote sites.

By the first light of day on December 11[th,] the men were in their quarantine, rested and ready for their first day of indoctrination and preparation. Bragg got the reports directly from each team leader, verified by each commander. All were in place. By the end of the same day the scouting parties had made their first three trial runs to their targets toward establishing the best routes to be taken on the scheduled morning. Another set of trial runs would occur the following day.

That next day, the day of the 12th, the present day, the trial runs were completed early. The men would get to their bunks by late afternoon. They were all tired and the waiting time would begin to wear on them, so it was important to relax and let sleep come while there were enough hours left to awake refreshed and still have time to get clear heads ready to think through the operation before the Go-hour.

Bob Crumpton's Border District and the Louisiana District had been assigned to West Coast sites; West coast officers had been assigned to Mid-West sites; it was the same across all Districts, officers were assigned to cities outside of their normal operations area to make sure that the element of surprise was guarded, that no officer might be accidentally identified by a known person at any time during the preparations. Every possibility for the potential loss of secrecy that could be anticipated was carefully thought out in the overall plan. Now they were just one long evening and night away from Go.

Crumpton stayed in close contact with his team leaders, keeping up with every move that was made and making certain that all teams were synchronized to Pacific time. The worst part of it was not being able to call home to Rebecca; no one was allowed to have a cell phone in their possession, nor any other electronic device that could give off a signal that might be intercepted. These last three days were pure isolation except for those officers surveying the approach routes. It wasn't all that easy getting to sleep that evening; bed check was at five, alarms were set for three a.m.

Phil Bragg knew it would be a sleepless night spent alone at his office. He sent the staff home by 4:30; he expected to stretch out occasionally on the daybed but knew he couldn't lay there for more than an hour at a time; the details of the operation just kept passing through his mind. He had set the schedule and now he was to follow it. At five a.m. he would begin making calls alerting people to the countdown; first he would call Stanford Turner, then at five-ten he would call John Smoltz, at five-twenty he would call Reginald Dwyer and at five-thirty he would call William George. At six a.m. he would issue the alert to the Operations officers in charge of the site teams under their command. At six-thirty he would begin receiving confirmation replies. At 7:05 a.m. he would issue the command to start the countdown that was to culminate at 7:45 with the coordinated incursion. At that time, the first of the incursion teams, the farthest away from their target would leave for their site and all others would leave at their times in accordance with the 7:45 incursion time.

Before the schedule of alerts, Bragg would spend the intervening hours in thoughtful review of the entire plan and a good bit of the time in soulful prayer for the safety of all of the men under his command this coming day.

"The weight of the world", he thought; that's the name of the game in this job.

The Mexicans

But time wasn't to be on his hands this evening and this night. Exactly at 4:45 p.m. on December 12th, just as he sat down on the daybed Phil Bragg's phone rang with the call from Boston.

"My God, man, the tunnel? They blew up the tunnel?"

"That's right, General; it blew a great big hole at the west entrance below the bay and flooded the whole tunnel in minutes. It was right at the rush hour; hundreds of cars all lined up slowly passing through. All of them are lost under the bay except for the few strong swimmers who made it out helped by the flood current to land on the east end of the tunnel. On the west end it was impossible to get out against the rush of the waters. Mostly all we can do now is count the lost and try to recover the ones we can find. I know there's nothing you can do, but I had to let you know about it since you're in the middle of all that out there."

John Mitchell was the Police Chief; the only man in Boston who was in the know about the incursion operation.

"OK, John, thanks for the heads-up; but we'll have to keep this quiet here in the quarantine. Everyone turned in their phones when they left to go to the sites and we don't have any outside connections in the barracks, no TV or radios. Unless there's something somewhere that got missed, news of the Boston mess won't interfere with the raids. Gotta go now. Take care."

With that, Bragg called his Operations chiefs to see if anything was getting through to them. So far, nothing had disturbed the evening. He alerted the Boston team leader to the tunnel situation. They would continue with the plan and move to the target site to arrest any people that may have been left behind. No one knew who or how many had been involved at the tunnel. From then on Bragg was tied up during the long night with phone calls from Turner, Smoltz, George and Dwyer and others including Harry Foster. Everywhere, the order of the day was to continue the operation, wait for the Go and crack doors at 7:45 am. The time was heavy on their hands, all who were involved and also knew of the tunnel. The importance of this coordinated raid and the need for success was not lost on anyone, especially now. Finally, the time of the countdown was upon General Bragg.

It's Time to Go

He began his heads-up calls at 5 am; first Turner, then Smoltz, then George, then Dwyer and now a new one, at 5:40, Harry Foster, who would report to the President. At six o'clock he issued the joint call to the operations chiefs to prepare for the countdown. At six-thirty he began receiving the confirmations from each of the team leaders and their commanders. At exactly 7:05am he issued the command to begin the countdown and the first of the teams departed for their site. Thereafter, the eighty-eight teams departed according to their countdown delay time.

At 7:45am, plus or minus two minutes or so, all of the teams had entered their corresponding compounds. They battered the ram through the warehouse door and broke down the office door to engulf the occupants with tasers and automatic weapons. Gunfire was prevalent at nearly every site as many of the Hezbollah terrorists refused to surrender, just as they had been instructed to do by their leaders in Detroit. It was short and bloody. The workers typically fell to the floor and tried to avoid any lines of fire; even so, several were killed by the terrorist managers, attempting to avoid the testimony they could give against them and their operations.

Bob Crumpton's men showed the valor under fire they had become noted for. The new men from Denver gave a good account of themselves. Julio Cruz was awarded the bronze star and the purple heart for rushing the defenders and stopping them just as they began to turn their weapons on the Agents, taking several rounds into his body but eliminating all three of the shooters. He would be hospitalized for several weeks, proudly talking of his NSA team and their performance at the Los Angeles workplace. Similar accounts made the newspapers describing the heroic actions of Shep Turner at San Diego, Niel Olafsen at Sacramento and Preacher Coleman at San Francisco. In all, nineteen medals and citations were awarded the Colorado Springs agents. Bob Crumpton was very proud.

Among the Border District officers, Swede Olafsen had earned the greatest number of awards including the Purple Heart and a bronze star for bravery by rescuing Jim Franklin from capture. One of the terrorists who had stayed hidden until everyone thought it was all over appeared out from under a pile of barrels with a long knife and grabbed Franklin, intending to hold him as hostage so that he might escape without arrest. By chance, Swede had just relieved himself in the room behind the pile of barrels and, being unseen, he quietly said to the man, "Hey, look here." And to hear Swede tell it;

"The guy was startled and turned just in time to see my fist flatten his nose. He lost his grip on Franklin enough for me to grab his other arm, the one with the knife and somehow it got turned into his throat. His blood looked just like anyone else's and the guy sort of kneeled down slowly onto the floor and prayed to Allah while he bled to death. His neck artery had been slashed open by his own hand. I tried to help him but he swung the blade at me and I had to give him space."

Jim Franklin got away without injury. Later when it was all over he told of how he had seen the angel again; the one who helped him carry Bill Dollar to safety at the Mississippi River raid.

"He just seemed to look sadly at the man bleeding on the floor and I could see tears flowing from his eyes as he looked at me. I'll never feel contempt for an enemy again; it made me cry, too, and then the angel was gone. I think he wanted to make me a better person by showing compassion for that poor man dying on the floor. That's twice that he's been there when I needed him."

Moses May, Paul Calvetti and "Flaco" Rodriguez took fire and lost a lot of blood but they recovered from their wounds within a few weeks. Moses May had to go through a couple of months in rehabilitation to get his legs back to where he could again dunk a basketball. Glenn Corbett, David Solomon and Simon Pederson all had flesh wounds.

Ray Leon never knew what hit him. As it turned out, it was a steel jacket slug right through his forehead that splattered into twenty-something fragments scattered throughout his head. He was buried at San Antonio, his home town, four days later. Leon had lots of mourners. The funeral was attended by hundreds of family members and friends from all over Texas and Old Mexico. Also attending were the Colorado Springs Agents and many of the others, FBI, NSA and local police, who had participated in the raids. Leon's death cemented a lot of good men together; paying their respects to a fallen comrade in arms. They wore their armbands for thirty days in Ray Leon's honor.

The $2.3 million arrived at the Presidential Palace by unmarked military helicopter just as expected, in time to make the eyes of Minister Federico Dominguez and General Victor Gonzalez open wide. The box was filled with twenty-three-thousand hundred dollar bills and it was addressed to Luis Caldera. It was his to distribute when the agreement was fulfilled; Dominguez and Gonzalez had the authority but he had the power behind the authority. Now, the General could remark about the huge sums of American Dollars already at the Palace and seen personally by the General; it was enough to motivate the officers and the men, realizing that their payday was assured when the job had been accomplished. Caldera turned over the extra fifty thousand dollars to Dominguez to use for influence among the local officials, but mostly he would use it for bonuses to the families of those killed during the operation.

Now was the time for Defense Minister Dominguez to make his report to President Calderon and to receive the President's instructions for the rules of engagement. He knew that the men assembled would prefer to eliminate the invaders and not burden the nation with the eventual pressure from the Europeans; they would insist that Mexico strictly follow the World Court's policy on treatment of prisoners. But he also knew that Calderon would have his job if he did not seek the President's instructions on how to conduct the operation. He visited the President for his final word and approval of procedures, especially pertaining to the treatment of the prisoners. The President was pleased that the operation had been put together so well.

"Federico, my friend, you have done well in all respects and now there is but the final step to be executed; is that correct?"

"Yes, Mr. President, that is correct. And I am here to take instruction from you as to your preference for the final outcome. Where do you wish that the prisoners be taken; there might be as many as a thousand of the invaders to be taken alive, if that is possible. But, of course, we don't know how they will respond; if they have time to make a stand they could choose to fight to the death In which case we may take many casualties but no prisoners. If we are able to take them by surprise as we have planned, we should have no casualties and will have many prisoners"

"Let's not give them any warning. I would prefer that the lives of our sons not be sacrificed for the benefit of illegal invaders of our borders. I don't have any preference for the place that prisoners should be taken, if it turns out that there are prisoners. Our courts will have to deal with them at some time - those that survive. It would be a sorrowful situation if I must go on national television and express my condolences to the good families of the fallen. This is a military matter for military professionals. Thank you for your good work and now proceed with the final solution."

Dominguez returned to speak with General Gonzalez as to the preferred outcome.

"The President does not want to lose our heroic men in this battle. Minimize casualties as best you know how."

"I understand, Minister Dominquez."

It was Al Maldonado's task to call the contact, the one who had made up the list of relatives at each of the villages to find out the house where the Council of Unification were staying in the village. He had completed the calls and was now ready to distribute the addresses to the commanders of the platoons along with the village maps Br. Angel had left with them. It was Tuesday afternoon; the incursions would take place Wednesday morning.

The platoons had been gathered in the barracks since Sunday; the transportation had been arranged by the Commanders who had been informed of the name and location of the village they each would be responsible for. All that remained was to give the go ahead, to dispatch the troops at the time that would put them in the villages at about 5 am the next morning. The event was scheduled to take place just before the time that the raids would be conducted in the United States, to assure that the teams would have the benefit of surprise and the terrorists would not have time to warn their friends in the States.

It's Time to Go

The time had come for dispatch. Maldonado distributed the addresses where the platoons would attack. The commanders took their departure at the time that would put them at the doors of the houses at 5 am, hopefully before the Hezbollah would be up and about. The trucks and aircraft carrying the raiders were now on the way.

The heroic men of Mexico fought valiantly, assisted by the element of surprise, catching the invaders still in their abodes at daybreak. There were few significant casualties; three dead soldiers, twenty-two wounded and there were no prisoners. The people of each village were given a reward to bury the dead Hezbollah. Those villagers whose names were on the lists remained unknown to the Mexican authorities, but they were very sorry to lose their monthly income from the Unification Council, now departed. The families of the three dead men were each given fifteen thousand dollars. When he checked up days later after the operation Minister Gutierrez found he was short five hundred pesos of his own money.

"That's the best deal I've ever made," he thought to himself.

Neither Luis Caldera nor Al Maldonado was present at any of the raids; they knew nothing of the official rules of engagement that had applied.

CHAPTER 53
The Great Weapon Incident

The Iranian Ambassador, Urmia al Puqalla was received by Secretary Morales in her office cordially.

"Ambassador al Puqalla, please come in. It's good to see you."

"Thank you Madam Secretary; I do appreciate your accepting me on such short notice."

"Not at all; you are always welcome; please sit down. What may I do for you today?"

"I am afraid that I bring news of a disconcerting nature; Ayatollah Kalmeshti asked me to personally inform you of an incident he was just made aware of, one which you must deal with quickly."

"Of course. Whatever could it be?"

"Ayatollah Kalmeshti received information from his intelligence minister that a group of dissidents has acquired a great weapon, a nuclear bomb. The weapon has been delivered into your country by ship into the Port of San Francisco. The informer has given credible information; believe me, it has been verified by multiple sources."

"My God, Urmia, what do they propose to do with the thing?"

"We believe they plan to detonate it very soon, but the instigator who we captured was killed by an accomplice who then killed himself without telling who was to give the order for the detonation. You must search for it; that is all we can tell you at the moment but I can assure you we are doing everything possible to learn more."

"Please excuse me."

The Mexicans

Morales called Harry Foster with the news.

"Keep him there, Phyllis. I'll have to move on this very fast. I'll get back to you."

Foster informed the President and William George. George called John Smoltz on his hot wire and Smoltz called Phil Bragg.

"Phil, you need to take charge of the investigation; we're talking about hours, maybe, no more. We have to take this seriously because it's straight from the Ayatollah's mouth; he's as concerned as we are or he wouldn't have brought this to light. They're not ready for a nuclear exchange."

"I'm on my way, John."

General Bragg arranged the jet and boarded a helicopter for Andrews taking his travel bag. Between the helicopter and the jet he called Beatrice.

"Can't talk now, Bea; gotta go for a day or two. I'll tell you about it later. I love you."

And the jet taxied to takeoff for San Francisco as he alerted the NSA District Commander and Stanford Turner, Assistant Director of the FBI.

In San Francisco they lost no time; they dispatched all agents to the streets to gather news of any sort from their informants that might remotely relate to this. The police chief, Teodoro Francisco, took the news personally;

"First the damn Iranians try to use our Mexican immigrants to do their dirty work and now they want to blow the city away. Well, I'm telling you, Hank, someone out there has got to know something and we're gonna wring it out of them. When we get these assholes I'd be surprised if any of our men succeed in taking prisoners; we have a few live explosives on our staff, too. Get every man out on the streets who isn't sucking a tit somewhere. Let's get some results fast but let's keep it quiet; no loose talk or they're likely to blow every one of us to Timbuktu."

"Whatever it takes, Chief, whatever it takes." Colonel Henry Jacobson began pushing buttons for staff to report to him right away. "Timbuktu? Where the hell is that, Chief?"

"How the hell should I know? I've never been to the place. India, I think, Hank, maybe Pakistan."

"Sounds like one of those places you retire to, where you can have a woman to do the cooking and housework and a man to do the maintenance and the heavy lifting while you and the Mrs. play games and stuff, all on a police pension. Anyway, I gotta go; there'll be a room full of guys by the time I get back to my office. I'll keep you informed of everything, Chief."

"Make things happen, Hank. Hey, do you suppose retirement is that good over there?"

"Why not? A buck goes a long way in them African places." He grinned at his intentional show of ignorance and got out real fast.

In ten minutes two dozen cops in street clothes began flooding the turf with a pocketful of twenties and another full of fifties.

"The best news don't come cheap, guys; some news is worth more than some others so don't be cheap. But don't make headlines; this is not about an atom bomb, just about a big deal going down. And we don't want a lot of broken arms."

Jacobsen wanted information from their informants; he didn't want to start a rumor mill.

Meanwhile, Stanford Turner, who was already in San Francisco to testify after the last raid in Oakland, got the order to call out every man he could get on the Coast. In less than an hour he began to get results and by the time Phil Bragg arrived, they had half a dozen reports that suggested something big was going on somewhere in South San Francisco.

"Mr. Turner, what rules apply here?"

Doug Ashcroft, Chief Agent for the San Francisco division, needed to clarify the situation for his men.

The Mexicans

"Because these days we have to cover our ass, you understand. Two of my men had to hire their own defense attorneys to stay out of jail last year. These people around here are like from another country; they hate us like we were the enemy. I'll have a hard time getting my guys to go in on any special situation like this one without a written set of rules of engagement. Some of our guys might've decided to head for Alaska and let the locals handle their nuclear problem, but fortunately, you're here to take the heat. We need the rules of engagement, Mr. Turner."

"You got a recorder on hand, Doug? Turn it on and get it from the horse's mouth; the end that your men will be surprised to hear from, I suspect. Copy this for rules of engagement; this is the final solution facing us right now. We live or we die along with all these assholes out here who think that we're paid to do the job for them by their rules. When faced with a nuclear threat that is more than a rumor but an actual reported incident by a responsible source of information, you shoot to keep the finger off that button. That's it, Doug; that's the rule of engagement. First you find the thing and then you shoot to kill anyone who refuses your order to back off from it."

"That's good enough, Mr. Turner; it's what we need."

Ashcroft hung up the phone, turned on the recorder and played it for his men.

"Now get out to South San Francisco and find the damn thing."

Bragg dispatched some of his agents to the south but most he directed to the streets of San Francisco.

"We got some good leads but no address and you all know how leads can peter out, so pay the money and twist the arms if you have to and try to get corroboration, but let's not lead them. Good information is out there, some better than what we already have, so dig deep and keep in mind that we're all standing on ground zero right now; if that don't motivate you then just do it for me 'cause I hate ground zero. We need a street and house number or a name we can twist to get one. Work fast and work hard, and breath heavy, guys, there's nothing like breathing. I don't expect you're heading into trouble on the street but, in case you do, the rules of engagement are simple; Stay alive."

Later in the day, an NSA officer got a tip from an informant about something a fisherman said about a week ago. It went like this;

"That guy was severely pissed over a guy they delivered something to who beat them out of some of their money. He wasn't drunk enough to tell names or anything very specific; he was just looking for someone to talk to and he was like a lot of them fishermen, throwing stories around to get someone to listen to him talk. But he said it was going to give someone a big blast when they found out about it."

"Who is this guy? Is he a regular around here; where did you run into him, Jimmy?"

Sten Johansen was a trusted guy with his informants and he gave big tip money. He handed him two fifties.

"He works off the wharf on a fishing boat – out for a few weeks and in for a few days."

Sten handed him another fifty.

"What boat, what slip?"

"That dude works for anyone who'll take him on. Mostly he talks about a boat that's a lucky catch. I don't know if that means anything; I guess the boat make good hauls when he hires out on it. When I see him on the Wharf he's usually walking from somewhere back behind Spinoza's, somewhere down that way."

Sten handed him two more fifties.

"What else, Jimmy?"

"Don't know nothing else – oh, wait a minute, I got one more piece; the guy he was pissed at drives a van for some outfit on the Wharf. He said, after they loaded the thing in his wharf buggy – that's a van that picks up and delivers to places on the wharf – that he stiffed them on some of their money. Don't ask me for the license tag or the VIN, 'cause I don't know everything, Sten; you know what I mean?"

The Mexicans

"You did good, Jimmy; now keep floating around that part of the wharf and pick up anything else you can on that fisherman or the van. You know my number; it's always worth a hundred or more." He handed Jimmy two more fifties.

Sten turned and walked leisurely back to where he had parked his car and sat inside to make his call. He wanted to run but contained himself.

"General Bragg, this is Sten Johansen, down on the Wharf. I think I may have a good lead – cost me three hundred – in bits and pieces but this guy is usually reliable. We need to get a rundown on all of the delivery vans working Fishermen's Wharf; the big ticket came off a fishing boat and got loaded into a van, a regular van that works the Wharf. Do you want to call Ted Francisco or do you want me to? You got the clout."

"I'll call him. What else?"

"The guy giving up the information to Jimmy – that's my informant – is a fisherman; works off the Wharf in and out, just like they all do. He just talks when he drinks and likes attention. Jimmy don't know the name of his usual hire but – you know, it sounded kind of funny to me – he most of the time said it was a lucky catch, I guess meaning the boat usually did well, but it could be a name; they all have names like that. Can you run that by someone at the Marine Authority? Maybe there'll be a fishing boat name that will use those words, or something like them. It's worth a try, I believe, General."

"That's two calls. You call the Marine Authority. If this is what it sounds like it is, you can call me Phil. Call me back – and good work, Sten."

Sten had to holler to himself, "Yippee!" Then he called and got the number of the Marine Authority and made the call. He identified himself and asked to speak to the officer in charge; it was Major Charles Dubois.

"Chuck, this is Sten Johansen, NSA; remember me? We made that seminar together last year on homeland security."

"Yeah – Sten Johansen, I remember you; seven-two, 350, right? How've you been?"

"I'm fine, except I just shrunk six inches and lost a hundred pounds. I'm glad to get to talk to you again, Chuck. If you can help me today, when I get off this case, I'm gonna buy you and your wife a KC steak. I need to run down the registration of all the fishing boats that work off the Wharf. I'm looking for words in the name like 'lucky' and 'catch' and I'll hold on if you can check it out while I wait."

"You better let me call you back; I'll get a programmer to run those words against the names and it'll throw out any names that match or sound like them. This guy can find a shrimp turd in a whale's belly; give me a few minutes – get yourself a cup of coffee and a doughnut. I'm on it now."

"I appreciate it, Chuck." He gave him his cell number.

Sten turned the spout on his coffee container open, lit a low tar smoke and sat back thinking it all over, then over again, trying to come up with a way to find the fisherman if the boat name didn't pan out. He figured the best lead was the van but they'd have to have more identification than just a van that works the wharf. There're lots of vans.

"It's got to be the fisherman and the van together for the fisherman to make the identification."

They would have to carry through on both leads. His cell phone rang just as he bitched at himself for lighting up his second cigarette. He snuffed it out in the ashtray as he answered the call.

"Sten, guess what; we found a match on the lucky catch. This has got to be the one – both words, just a different spelling – the Lucky Ketch, K e t c h, a fishing boat and it docks at the Wharf. The guys at the Wharf have the boat docked at slip Q4; that's away down the wharf to the west, but they don't have any idea if the boat is in or out right now. The boat captain is Gunter Thyssen, an import from Iceland. I guess he got fed up with having to unfreeze after each trip out. I really think we got the handle on this one for you, Sten."

The Mexicans

"Oh, man, Chuck, that's awful good news; awful 'cause I owe you and Ginny a steak dinner; good 'cause we may have our claws on the only lead that could have panned out for us. I'm really proud of your guys; in a few days I'll come over and tell them how much. Gotta go, now."

He called General Bragg.

"Phil, I got the names of the fishing boat and the skipper that the talker hires out with. Slip number Q4, down by the west end of the Wharf. I'm headed there now to see if the boat's in or out. If it's out, I'll try to get help from the Coast Guard station. The captain's name is Gunter Thyssen, the boat is the Lucky Ketch – k e t c h. How about getting a warrant to search the boat and hold him and the crew for questioning? They're the only ones that can identify the van and the driver."

"That's a real break, Sten; nice work. We'll have to get a statement from your friend, the informant, Jimmy, is it? And the guys who ran down the boat name at the Marine Authority. We'll get the warrants with the promise of the statements as evidence but you'll have to get their statements, signed, to back us up when we bring these guys in to the Judge. Go ahead and finish your lead there on the wharf and call me back. We'll need to get the Coast Guard to run us out to the boat if it's not in port; I'll get Stan Turner and we'll meet you down there. You'd better get Jimmy if you can find him; we'll need him to identify the guy who told him the story; see if you can have him come to the Wharf; it's worth a hundred or more if we get lucky and find the guy. Anyway you need his statement down on paper."

"I'm on my way now; call you back."

The slip was vacant so Sten called the Coast Guard and asked them to check out the whereabouts of the Lucky Ketch.

"We need to get to them as soon as we can, Bill; I can't tell you how important this is, talking on the phone, but just think about where you might be spending eternity and then hurry on down to take General Bragg and Stanford Turner out to the boat. We'll be looking for you at the main landing here on the Wharf."

"I been hearing of something in the wind."

Bill Donaldson was the Officer of the Day and he didn't need any more information than that.

"Gimme a minute while I find the boat – hold on."

He looked up the boat's number and its last reported location.

"They're about twenty miles up the coast; we can get there within an hour. Say you all will be waiting at the Wharf?"

"I'm calling General Bragg right now. They'll be down here in fifteen minutes or so. I'm at the wharf right now, so just come on when you can; I'll wave you down. Better bring your trusty Trusty."

"Oh, yeah! Don't go anywhere on the water without ol' Trusty. I'll look for you there."

Sten called Phil Bragg.

"We're good to go, Phil. Captain Bill Donaldson is on his way with a cutter to pick us up here at the Wharf – main dock."

"OK, Sten; Turner's coming by to pick me up. We'll be down there in fifteen minutes; see you at the Wharf."

While he waited, Sten ran down Jimmy with a couple of phone calls. He'd be at the Wharf in a half hour.

"Just hang out there until we get back – we have to go out and bring in the boat with the fisherman. I'll call you in an hour; don't go floating anywhere."

The water as they headed from the Bay out to the ocean was choppy but the ocean was fairly calm.

"We'll make good time on this run," Donaldson advised them, "maybe another thirty-five minutes if the surf stays calm. Do you expect these guys to give resistance? I mean, are they the ones doing the damage?"

"No, we think they carried it in to the Wharf from out here somewhere; they're just little fish making a few bucks. They might know what it was

The Mexicans

they transported in; what we really want is the guy they delivered it to, the guy that drove the van on the wharf. Time's real critical, Bill."

It was mid-afternoon when the Coast Guard cutter sighted the Lucky Ketch. Captain Donaldson radioed Gunter Thyssen to be ready for a boarding. As he approached the boat, Thyssen and three fishermen were reeling in their lines making ready to heave to the cutter when it came alongside. With the boat tied off to the cutter's deck, Donaldson and his mate boarded the Lucky Ketch and presented Thyssen with their boarding order.

"Captain Thyssen, General Phil Bragg of the National Security Agency and Stanford Turner, Assistant Director of the FBI are here with me to serve arrest warrants on you and your crew. You will return to port now under arrest. When we reach port you will all remain on the boat until transportation is ready to take you to the police station for booking on suspicion of sedition, transportation of illegal firearms and explosives, conspiracy to engage in acts of terrorism against the United States and other associated charges. Do you understand what I have told you?"

"I don't know what you are talking about; we haven't done anything but try to make a living catching fish. I won't say anything until I talk to my attorney."

"Do you understand what I have told you?"

"Yes, of course I understand. Do you think I'm a fool? I heard what you said."

"Captain Thyssen, you will ply your boat behind my cutter at a distance of one-quarter mile during the return run. You will follow to the pier at the Coast Guard Station at the Embarcadero and tie up where I instruct you to. Do you understand?"

"I understand, yes."

"Very well, then; we will return to our ship and begin the return run."

Sten called Jimmy at the Wharf.

"Jimmy, we're coming in to the Coast Guard station at the Embarcadero. Be there to meet us in about forty minutes."

"I'll catch a trolley and see you there."

CHAPTER 54
The Run Down

Things were getting edgy at the house in South San Francisco. The guy with the phone had just got hung up on by the guy he was talking to in Tehran.

"Jeruselim is dead; Alhaminijah is arrested; Kalmeshti don't say nothing; nobody knows what's going on. We can't do it until we get the order, we just have to wait."

The driver of the van was nervous.

"No, Saleem, we can't just wait; if we wait they will find us here and take us to prison. I would rather go up with this damned city. We can do it by ourselves. Try to call Ahmed again. He can tell us what Alhaminijah wants; he always knows because he is the heir."

"OK, Kalid, OK, OK." He dialed the number and let it ring. After twenty rings a voice came on, "Ahmed is not here; call again in six hours." You could hear the phone drop onto the floor and the speaker cuss. The cussing got louder as he chased it and kicked it by accident beneath a piece of furniture, which he had to move. He called for someone to help. More cussing along with noises of furniture being moved. After a long period of puffing and some shouting the phone was hung up. But not before the NSA's telephone surveillance operation had intercepted the call. It was the twenty rings and the cussing that gave them time to track the call and get the coordinates. General Bragg was informed immediately.

Bragg called Colonel Andy Phelps, the California District Commander.

"Andy, I've got coordinates for a location where the bomb is housed right now; copy these and get the address off the GPS. Then get your team over there fast. I'm passing this to Stan Turner, so they'll be calling you to coordinate the raid."

"OK, hold on a second — got it, Phil. It's in South San Francisco, just like we thought. We're outta here."

Bragg advised Turner. His men were nearby the location.

"We'll go there to wait for Andy's team and keep the place under watch."

About the time Turner's men arrived, the van pulled out of the garage and headed toward the Bayshore Parkway.

"Mr. Turner, they're on their way, out of the garage right now, three guys in the van. They've turned toward the Parkway. This must be it, their making their move."

"Follow that van, Skip; don't let it out of your sight. If it heads over toward 280, stop it. Make sure you stop it before it gets to Millbrae. We can't let them run it into the lake. I'm calling for a skyhook and the troopers; keep on the phone with me."

The van sped up after turning west toward 280.

"We're still with you, Mr. Turner – he's turning west going by San Bruno; I'm gonna stop him, I got my flasher on. He's still moving on; we may need some troops here."

"They're on their way now down 280. See if you can get in front of the van and slow it down."

"It just turned south on 280. We're gonna have to shoot out the tires, Mr. Turner. Go ahead Jose, take a shot now, I can't get much closer."

Jose let go several shots at the tires and hit one of them.

"That's one tire gone, but they're still running. Keep shooting, Jose."

He got another one.

"That's the two rear tires; he's running a lot slower, go for the front tires while I come alongside of them; be careful, better hold a vest

The Run Down

up in your face, Jose; here, take mine. Can you get a shot at the front tires?"

A shotgun sprayed the side of the door, but Jose kept firing.

"That's it, Skip; he's just got one left and that van's swerving a lot. He's gonna have to stop pretty soon or crash."

"Here come the troopers behind us; they maybe can get it stopped. They'll have to run in front of him and force him over to the emergency lane. We're backing off, out of the way, Mr. Turner."

The troopers forced the van to the side of the road amid peppering shotgun spray.

"Here's the skyhook coming in now, Skip; I can see it moving overhead. I hope he can get a hold on the van without any of us having to help him with it down here - - - now, he's dropping his claws down onto the van - - - man, those things are mean; big and sharp and mean. The guys inside aren't moving. One of them's shouting something. The claws hooks poked right through the metal when the chopper tightened it up - - - now they're lifting it off the road. He's moving off to the west; looks like he wants to get it out over the ocean – there he goes, he ain't wasting any time."

"Did you hear that Mr. Turner? The skyhook is carrying the van out toward the ocean; he's got them up pretty high and he's moving real fast - about out of sight now."

"Yeah, Skip; we're going to drop it into the ocean out about a hundred miles or more where there aren't any ships in sight. We're just hoping those guys can't set the thing off before our guys can let it go and get the hell out of there. The Coast Guard is warning all the ships in the area to head north or south of San Francisco as fast as they can. If this thing goes off, we don't know what kind of damage it's capable of doing. You boys ought to head in and get in a fallout shelter or a basement somewhere. The emergency sirens are going off in the city and the radio and TV are telling people to take shelter. Most of these cynics around here will probably give them the finger. You guys did a

The Mexicans

great job; my hat's off to you. The Director will have some words for you, I'm sure. Get back now to a shelter; there might be a lot of fallout if it goes off in the air. Hopefully, the copter will be able to drop it into the ocean; then all we have to worry about is the tidal wave. I'll see you back at the ranch. So long for now."

"So long, Mr. Turner."

About the time the agents were entering the shelter, the 'copter let it go from about ten thousand feet; it hit the water without exploding. The terrorists had worked feverishly inside the van on the ride out over the ocean trying to set off the bomb before they hit the water. Just before the van was released they succeeded in connecting the power loop, expecting at that time to meet Allah and be issued their seventy virgins but they forgot about the forty-second delay. The windows of the van were open and it sank fast. At two hundred feet below the surface it went off sending a giant mushroom cloud of steam and water high over the ocean, blowing the helicopter out of the sky and setting off a tidal wave sixty feet high or more. There was no hope for the pilots, the concussion of the shock wave tore the aircraft apart and everything fell into the sea miles away from the explosion. A Coast Guard spokesman gave the account of the event this way;

"The Air-Sea Rescue Squad had trained every year for just such an occasion; these pilots knew full well that it would probably end up the way it did but that didn't deter them – they volunteered for the assignment to save the lives of thousands of their neighbors."

The Coast Guard sent out emergency warnings to all communities north and south of San Francisco, urging all residents to move inland as quickly as possible; the tidal wave would destroy much of the coastal habitation and vegetation. It would hit land within a few minutes along the northern California coast and within an hour or less at cities as far north as Seattle and Vancouver and as far south as San Diego and Sur de California, Mexico. Vancouver Island would be hit especially hard, the wave washing completely over it, devastating the tourist city of Victoria; there would be very few survivors of that island.

The entire coastline was destined to be a disaster zone with many dead and hundreds of thousands of people displaced and homeless. The inland bay areas at San Francisco and Seattle were fairly well protected from the full rage of the tidal wave, but the water level continued to mount as it began flooding the Bay of San Francisco. Many people quickly took to the hills and the coastal mountain range but the people on the east side of the bay, Oakland and Berkeley and Vallejo, could only rush to the east as fast as possible.

Auto traffic quickly became snarled; people deserted their cars and ran on foot hoping to outrun the rising waters. Those with bicycles and motorcycles fought their way among the people on foot fleeing for every foot of real estate, but only those who managed to leave right away escaped the flood. Rooftops of brick and steel buildings, over forty feet high provided safety; many climbed trees only to ride them down as the roots were washed up from their footings.

Along the Pacific coastline, many people climbed to safety and watched the waves hurl against the cliffs below from where they had climbed, not quite high enough to wash them away but digging huge pieces of the cliffs away and into the sea. The Southern coast had more time to evacuate but it would have taken days to evacuate Los Angeles alone. The palisades provided a restraining barrier in many places but the sixty foot wave broke across the lowlands and swept through the valleys and into the city. The flood extended inland as far as Glendale and Santa Ana with great force. Houses were swept away into heaps.

Long Beach and San Diego were devastated, completely underwater. Those who failed to leave immediately were washed out to sea as the tidal wave withdrew back to sea from the floodplain with as much wrenching force as it had hit with head on. The devastation was immensely cruel, the lives lost were beyond estimate – easily in the tens of thousands in scores of communities along the California coast. Rushing torrents left a wasteland where Los Angeles had been, a city so vibrant, the people so self satisfied; now many faced terrible losses of loved ones and property.

Miles of residential communities were left virtually empty, the ruination swept out to sea as the surge waters receded, sucking everything out, furniture and equipment from the lower floors of the most secure buildings; no fastenings could withstand the rushing torrent. Huge

The Mexicans

piles of debris accumulated, automobiles and trucks and building materials. Thousands of bodies washed out into the ocean, many of them to wash up later along the coastline, many others never to be seen again. The city of Los Angeles and its nearby suburbs was so completely devastated many thought the city could not survive. Later estimates of damage placed the figure in the tens of trillions of dollars.

For weeks in the aftermath of the flood, gangs ravaged throughout, controlling what was left of the cities of Los Angeles and San Diego, dividing up territory and securing it from efforts to reestablish security by shooting anyone attempting to enter their territory. They set up their own survival areas in upper floors of hotels, stockpiling bottled water by the thousands of cases, and thousands of cartons of canned goods, liquor and drugs, the left behind spoils from the food warehouses and drugstores that had been deluged but not washed clean. Chicano gangs from south of the border invaded the city and its environs, establishing and protecting their own Mexican enclaves. President Cooper was called upon by the governors of the Western States to invade that city and others under siege using the National Guard troops, weapons and equipment to take them back from the gangs, and he did, the fourth day after the flood.

The first wave of troops attacked the gangs of Los Angeles from five points, north, east, south and in between. The plan was to secure the perimeter areas first, merging forces at a central point to set up for the next attack. Tanks and armored vehicles were employed leading the attack while troop carriers followed behind, dropping off squads of infantry along the way to maintain control. The gangs in the suburbs regrouped into the hard core of the city and joined forces with other gangs to resist the troops. The final battle was for all the marbles. President Cooper gave the order to shoot to kill anyone who would resist with deadly fire.

"They're not giving up, they're not surrendering, Sir. We will need to use mortars and grenades, if not air support; this is a battle like we those we fought in Iraq and Viet Nam and we're going to lose a lot of good men if we try to take them alive, Mr. President."

General Paul Mc Brayer assessed the situation realistically, not politically, and that was what the president wanted.

"Use the mortars and grenades along with full tank firepower, Paul. I want these killers put out of there by the end of the week, no later."

That gave them five days to mop up the operation and that's what was needed. TV and radio commentators were having a field day second guessing that order. European politicians, University facultics, what was left of the entertainment industry, and left-wing bloggers were sure that this was a political ploy by the president to take control of the nation by military rule. When the last shots were fired, there were very few rioters left standing to surrender.

In the end, the San Francisco event proved the FBI's ability to perform successfully its intelligence gathering role in times of national emergency and to use that intelligence to intercede in terrorist activities. The nation applauded the work of the National Guard and the legitimacy of the FBI in public opinion polls was enhanced as it had never been in thirty years.

The information gathered from the captain and the fishermen of the Lucky Ketch brought sedition charges against the captain of the Pacific Empress and several of the senior management team of the shipping corporation that owned that ship which carried the bomb across the ocean and deposited it for pick-up outside San Francisco. Testimony given by those indicted placed the origin of the bomb to be Kazakhstan. A remnant of the Soviet arsenal, the bomb had been purchased by an agent of Iranian nationality and moved through several countries, eventually loaded onto a ship leaving Lebanon for France and there transferred to a freighter for the Atlantic voyage to Panama where it was transferred to the Pacific Empress, headed for San Francisco. Shipping orders for ports and ships prior to the French connection were non-existent. The property being shipped was labeled as a power turbine but as far as could be determined, it had never been inspected.

Phil Bragg got an unexpected call from Frank Heinkle in Seattle.

"General Bragg, is that offer still open; the one about joining up with your NSA operation?"

"It's still open, Frank."

The Mexicans

"Well, I want to sign up. This last terrorist attack made my mind up for me; I want to be a part of this war, but I want to sign up before they start drafting into the military. Your outfit is where I want to serve, where the action is. What about it? Do I get an application?"

"You do, Frank. I'll deliver it myself if we can take a few days fly fishing up in northern Saskatchewan."

"We can. Why Saskatchewan, General, if you don't mind my asking?"

"We've got an interest up there to pursue. I thought you might have some contacts with charter guides that work the area."

"I go up there several times a year. Yeah, I know lots of them; fishing and hunting both."

"Tell you what, Frank. You make the arrangements for you and me and Nielsen and Bob Crumpton. We'll set out some plans for your operation as an NSA officer at large; unknown to the world, so keep it quiet."

"Sounds good, General. What site do you want to fly into; do you have a preference?"

"Yes, I do. I'll have Crumpton give you a briefing. He knows the spot. Plan on a week, it may take that long to spot what we're after. On second thought, I'll fax the application today so you'll be on the payroll before we go north; this mess here may hold us up a week or two. Fax it back completed."

"That's good. I'll make some contacts after Colonel Crumpton calls with the site location. Thanks, General; I feel good about this."

"I do too, Frank; I do too. I'll talk to Crumpton right away so you'll hear from him soon. Take care, now."

"You, too. So long."

Bragg called Crumpton and gave him the news.

"I'll get with it right away, Phil. I hope we can pick up something on that smuggling operation up there; I'm sure those were illegals 'cause

The Run Down

Carl thought so and he's not even in the business. They killed him just for spotting it; I'd love to get that bunch of murderers."

"Maybe we will, Bob. I know it means a lot to you personally but it may be the way Hezbollah is entering the U.S. six men at a time. And those are probably the management teams, too. Your memo laid the whole thing out pretty clear and I wouldn't be surprised to see it's been going on just like you envisioned."

"It's good news. I'll arrange for Swede to take charge while we're gone. Well, I'll call Frank, now."

"Go ahead, Bob; set it up for when you think it's the best date, say, a couple of weeks, maybe."

"That'll be as soon as we can get away from the California scene, maybe longer, I'm afraid; anyway, it'll be right soon. I'll let you know. So long."

"Let's try to pull out in a couple weeks, Bob; no joke. John and Bill George read your memo; they're aware of the deliveries coming in through Canada, now. We can maybe stop another bad scene, but we can't do much for what's already gone down." So long."

෴

When all the inquiries had been conducted and the editorials and op-eds written, the roles of the NSA, the FBI, the National Guard and the local police forces stood the test. The best that the cynics and the critics could throw at them did them little damage but did provide clearer insight into the political purposes of the naysayers. The damage done by the events in Boston, at the three University campuses and all along the West Coast was viewed in comparison to the saving of the Holland Tunnel, the saving of the cities of the entire San Francisco Bay area from complete and utter nuclear destruction, and the capture of eighty-eight terrorist cells and distribution sites across the country. President Cooper put it in perspective for the world to understand:

"These brave men and women accepted the terrible burden of seeking out and putting down a virtual army of terrorists, ninety cells or more

The Mexicans

of them, all poised to strike at America's people and its infrastructure, using innocent laborers to prepare the means of their planned onslaught. We now know it was the intention of the terrorists to permanently disrupt the economy of the nation and at the same time to destroy the confidence of the American people in their nations' ability to protect them against terrorists among us.

"They were able to inflict substantial damage, we all are keenly aware of that and we grieve for those lives that were lost. But we know also that, except for the selfless efforts of these brave defenders in destroying and bringing to justice those murdering terrorists and the land pirates that followed them, the damage and loss of life that they had in their minds to inflict would have been many hundreds of times greater than the damage the nation experienced.

"They intended to bring this great nation to its knees, but instead they were brought to their own destruction. The nation will recover, and for that, the nation owes a debt of gratitude to these brave defenders who performed so valiantly, some giving their lives to protect us. It's a debt we can never repay, but we can express our deep gratitude and our thanks to them and to a merciful God for giving us these talented, brave men and women. I will do my best as I visit around the nation in the aftermath of this home-front war on terrorism to meet with each one of these men and women, and the graves of the fallen; to visit each one who participated so courageously and to offer my personal thanks for a job well done. In time the full story of events will unfold but for now let us all join as one honoring these brave sons and daughters."

Tears flowed down his cheeks as the President gave his hand salute.

CHAPTER 55
Later Events

Karyl Lynne Foster announced her engagement to her parents. That began the planning for the big wedding that she and Greg Larsen wanted to have as soon as possible. For Lydia and Harry, soon as possible came soon, indeed.

"Now, Karyl, you just busy yourself with the Church and the announcements and the wedding party and your formal outfits for you and the bride's maids. Let me handle the decorations and the reception and the social planning. I know you don't want it to be a political thing, dear, but when your daddy is the President's right hand man, you can't get away so easily. But don't worry; you'll enjoy a little time in the spotlight and I know your dad will love to see you feted by the social people and the paparazzi. Just let me do the social stuff; OK?"

"OK, mother; I knew it would be like this and that's fine. Greg likes to be in the spotlight, so have at it and call me for anything I need to decide."

"I will, dear, you know I will."

And she did. Lydia arranged every detail of the wedding that Karyl would allow her; it was perfect in every way. Karyl was noted as the most beautiful Washington bride of recent times and Greg handled himself just like a diplomat, instead of a lawyer. What a legal future they would have, after this event to get them started.

The reception and the social mix was nothing less than perfectly stunning. Lydia Foster arranged as auspicious an occasion as anyone could recall. Karyl's was not just any wedding; the city would make it a political event and Harry would just have to play it that way; there

The Mexicans

was really no choice. The political and diplomatic invitations went out. The congressmen and senators and the Supreme Court and the ambassadors all showed up and many stayed for an hour or more.

Harry Foster couldn't remember when he had felt so fulfilled at any of the political events of his lifetime and he realized why; for the first time, Lydia was with him, at his side helping with the introductions, and she was stunning.

"Why?" he wondered; "Why have I limited myself to so few social events when I've had such a gracious partner, so personable and ready to share her talents at every occasion?"

"Harry," Lydia asked, "Why haven't we taken more time to participate in those other affairs? I've had such an enjoyable evening. Oh, there's Beatrice Bragg and Phil over there. I'll be back in a bit, Harry; excuse me?"

"Of course, Darling. I'll join you with them in just a minute; don't let them get away."

"Beatrice, how great to see you again! My goodness, is that Phil standing over there with Bob Crumpton? You know I'm always amazed to see how young he looks; you must have a secret potent. Come on, let's go over there and shake things up; they're standing just a little too close to that really young good looker in that fetching gown."

"That's not just a good looking woman, that's Rebecca Crumpton. Did you miss their wedding at Slipsom? It was the most captivating ceremony; the church was so overflowing they decided to hold it outdoors so that everyone could watch the exchange of rings and the kiss. They're a very special pair – Bob is such a cowboy and Rebecca such an intellectual type, but just the most loving couple you could want to meet."

"Honey, I always thought that of you and Phil."

"You're wouldn't be far wrong if you did. These last few days we had in Mexico were like starting it out all over. Don't let me forget to give you the name of the place in Buenaventura; it's to die for. There's no better place in the world for a second honeymoon."

"Did you spend your anniversary in Mexico?"

"Not exactly. We just returned from being the second ones to know of Luis and Rita's new baby boy. We got there before they left the hospital with the brightest baby boy in the whole place, and there were lots of them there; those folks are true believers – no birth control except the headache. They're here too, but not the baby. Luis had a lot to do with destroying the Hezbollah invaders in Mexico. He's Phil's number one officer, right now; just ask him."

"I'm dying to meet them. And I see Miranda nearby with Brother Angel – let's hurry over to them before they get pulled off by someone. This is a really great event; I've got to say so, even if Harry put it all together. Of course, he had a little help – ahem, of course."

"That'd be you, Lydia. I'm right behind you, let's get a glass of champagne and go over there; one glass is safe for you isn't it?"

"Yes, unless I can trap Harry in the bath."

@@

While the country's attention was directed to rebuilding the west coast devastation and the Boston tunnel, President Cooper took a much needed vacation to his retreat at Cape Cod. When Harry Foster suggested he come along and keep Cooper advised on events, he got a big surprise.

"I think I'd like to see how well I can get along for a week on my own, Harry. Why don't you try it too?"

"I think I'd like that, Mr. President. We'll be at Hilton Head; I'll leave my number, see you in a week, Sir."

And that's where this story began; with Harry and Lydia on the beach and getting interrupted after only one day. This time events shied them away from the west coast to the South Carolina beach instead.

Harry Foster enjoyed the beach a lot and so did Lydia. He liked to swim in the ocean, sometimes going out a quarter mile and back while his security team followed in a small boat equipped for sharks. Lydia

The Mexicans

was a pool devotee. An excellent diver from college days, she would often attract a wide audience of spectators as she showed off her form from the high dive. And they loved the scuba diving at Hilton Head, which is why they decided to come here for a week.

"We'll be doing a lot more of this, Lydia. I don't know why I've neglected the personal side of life for so long; the President has no objections to vacations at all."

"You're a work horse, Harry; it's been your life, but you've always been thoughtful and attentive to me and that's why I love you; vacations or not. You know, Harry, I think I'll have one of those icy rum kind of drinks with the long straw. Would you fetch me one, Sweetheart?"

"Has a cat got a climbing gear? Is a pig's butt pork?"

"Oh, Harry, I just love it when you talk romantic. Can we stay another few days?"

"You bet we can, my dear; you know we can. Just relax, Sweetheart; I'll get a cool one for you."

"Oh, Harry, you're so romantic. Did you realize how young you look in that hammock?"

◎◎

Frank Heinkle had made the arrangement for a week charter fishing in northern Canada at the site in Saskatchewan where Carl Burkett spotted the immigrant smuggling activity. He and Bob Crumpton arrived at Seattle's Sea-Tac Airport and were met by a personal taxicab.

"Taxi, mister?" Erik Nielsen smiled out at them form the cab at the loading zone.

"Hello, Erik; yeah I guess we could use a good cab right about now. Where to?"

"Hey, that's my line; but this time we're just going to a hotel nearby at a private airfield in the valley over at Enumclaw; Frank thought you'd enjoy the view of Rainier when we take off in the morning."

"Sound good, Erik; we're ready for that."

Erik had a few items to report, but the one that caught their attention was a story about a pair of Korean physicians.

"These two are having trouble with passports that seem to have been forged; Drs. Lee Cho Kim and Song Te Kim. See, I brought the newspaper account for you to see. They're being detained at the King County Jail while the matter is being litigated by their attorneys."

"Hold it right there. These are the people that we tangled with in Baton Rouge, Bob. Wait a minute while I call John Smoltz. The FBI will want to talk to the two of them; they're North Koreans, posing as South Koreans."

He made the call and they continued on their way.

"We'll find out how that turns out when we get back. All of the stuff we had on them is documented in the final reports; John has it all."

"Well, Phil, if we don't do any good up here at least we'll be having a good time doing it. I'm itching to try those wilderness natural trout."

CHAPTER 56
Epilogue: New Beginnings

The destruction of the West Coast cities captured the attention of the federal government in a big way; the cleanup there would exceed the New Orleans flood cleanup by a thousand-fold. It would provide immediate jobs for thousands of unemployed laborers who would come from the U.S. and Mexico. The NSA Border District was heavily involved investigating reports of terrorists attempting to take advantage of weakened border inspections allowing for the free influx of needed immigrant workers. Bob Crumpton was busy assigning investigating teams of agents to towns and cities on the southern California border.

Meanwhile, Phil Bragg was concerned that all that activity at the southern border was like a magnet, drawing attention from other border locations. He expressed his worries in a meeting with John Smoltz.

"John, my concern is the terrorists will recognize this situation as a very big weakness to our porous borders. As you well know they are always watching for an opportunity to exploit weaknesses. We know they've been bringing in Hezbollah through Canada posing as charter fishermen. They might decide to test the northern border even more for that weakness while all eyes are on the southern border just now."

"You're probably right, Phil, that's a good possibility. What do you have in mind?"

"I'm thinking of the Canadian border provinces, in particular the Atlantic Provinces; Quebec, New Brunswick and Nova Scotia, and the Pacific provinces; British Columbia and Yukon. We've seen what can be done with ocean shipping and local fishing boats these days; there's just no way to guard against the threats that appear to be normal routine activity."

The Mexicans

"OK, I know we've got to do a better job of inspection, but that's in the hands of the Congress to allocate funds. You can imagine how difficult it will be to get even ten percent inspections from the overseas shippers, even those with home offices in the U.S.; they avoid costs, it's business. All that has to be worked out through trade agreements and it'll never be one hundred percent. It's going to be up to us to intercept and inspect in our waters before the ships reach port and right now that's the Coast Guard's responsibility. What we can do is snoop around all places on both sides of the border when we get intelligence that gives us a reason to be there."

"I was hoping you'd say that. You called it right; snooping is the name of the game in this business. Some like to call it investigating; no, investigating is clean work, reporting what you did that you're proud of. Snooping is down and dirty and that's usually what gets the intelligence. Snooping is what I have in mind, too. Let me run this by you and I'll start by giving it a name: Agent at large. I'm thinking of a free-wheeling operations officer, the type of investigator that gets an assignment, works independently and reports back when he needs the troops; all within the rules, nothing under the table.

"The agent at large is the homestead guy; the one that works on the boat, the stevedore; or he's the guy that drives the taxicab; or he's the neighborhood bartender; or maybe he's the owner of a large transcontinental trucking business. He might even be the Mexican farm laborer or the guy at the pawn shop. But whatever he is, he's an unknown to the security business; he's never been there or if he has it was a long ways away and nobody around here knows him. Did you pick up the four Border agents I'm thinking of for the northern border snoops; the independent agents at large?"

"I got Frank Heinkle and Erik Nielsen; they're unknowns, new to the Agency. Who're the other ones?"

"Luis Caldera. Luis is unknown except in Louisiana. What he did in Mexico was undercover, sort of the agent at large; he didn't take part in the incursions. Luis is a guy who knows how to make things happen, really imaginative. I want Caldera on the northwest border where Alaska meets Canada; a fisherman, a stevedore, a dock worker,

Epilogue: New Beginnings

whatever, even a cannery worker. Wherever the leads take him – he's just a guy out to make a living, sending money back to the wife and kid. He'll have to make the trip back to Mexico, now and then, for personal reasons of course, but also for the cover.

"And David Solomon. Solomon is just a Captain, still fairly young and hasn't started a family yet, so he's available to go without any holdbacks and he's always sitting on 'go'. He's been through some of the best training of any of the men. Besides the Mississippi River operation where he was decorated for valor, he was one of the team of three that broke up the leak from our office and he was one of the two who saved the Holland Tunnel by picking up the movement in a heads-up piece of observation and analysis. He's sharp, he's dark skinned, looks Middle-east and he speaks French and German; he'll blend right in to the Atlantic border of Canada. He'll learn to like the weather – maybe, after a few weeks on the docks at Halifax or St. John's.

"Heinkle, I want just like he is, a well known young businessman, and he'll keep digging out information on the shipping containers while he runs his business. But he's a known sportsman in the state and I want him doing a full check on the charter-fishing industry in Canada and Alaska. You know what we found up at that site where Crumpton's friend spotted them; not much, but a lot of trash they picked up showed there were mid-eastern imports coming through that place. There are hundreds of private charters going after trout and salmon and steelhead in very remote places that no one goes to besides them and maybe a few moose. And the same is true with the sports-hunting industry. That's just as lucrative and just as likely to have been infested with terrorists. Heinkle is the well-known unknown, just what we need to plug those holes and he knows how to handle himself – Ranger style.

"Nielsen is a great taxi driver and he stays where he is. Seattle is a sieve, leaking stuff into the country from Alaska, Canada and all the Pacific Islands, not to mention all of Asia and South America, by ship and by air. We need a full-time snoop with eyes and ears who can pick up the rumors and develop informers and snitches. You see what he picked up on the Kim's. This guy is healthy and tough – Ranger style, like Heinkle; he commands respect and he'll be our other man in Seattle –

the unknown. So, how about that, John? I'll need your authorization to deploy the Agents at Large. They'll work alone for the entire time they're working at large, at least until this northern border security is under control and they'll report directly to me."

"Write it up, Phil. I'll sign it and send it to William George in a stack of mundane stuff to be filed in the manual. I like it."

"So will Caldera, Solomon, Heinkle and Nielsen."

The End

2234253

Made in the USA